Praise for Sophie Kinsella and the Shopaholic Trilogy:

"A hilarious tale . . . hijinks worthy of classic *I Love Lucy* episodes . . . too good to pass up."—*USA TODAY*

"[Sophie Kinsella] gives chick-lit lovers a reason to stay home from the mall."
—*ENTERTAINMENT WEEKLY*

"Kinsella's Bloomwood is plucky and funny. . . . You won't have to shop around to find a more winning protagonist." —*PEOPLE*

"Don't wait for a sale to buy this hilarious book."
—*US WEEKLY*

"Perfect for anyone wishing that bank statements came in more colours than just black and red."
—*THE MIRROR* (LONDON)

"If a *crème brûlée* could be transmogrified into a book, it would be *Confessions of a Shopaholic*." —*THE STAR-LEDGER* (NEWARK)

Featured Alternate Selection of Book-of-the-Month Club, Quality Paperback Book Club, Literary Guild, and Doubleday Book Club

Also by Sophie Kinsella

SOPHIE KINSELLA

SHOPAHOLIC

takes

MANHATTAN

A DELL BOOK

SHOPAHOLIC TAKES MANHATTAN
A Dell Book

PUBLISHING HISTORY
Transworld UK edition published 2001
Delta Trade Paperback edition published February 2002
Dell mass market edition / March 2004

Published by Bantam Dell
A Division of Random House, Inc.
New York, New York

Library of Congress Catalog Card Number: 2001047364

ISBN 0-440-24181-2

Manufactured in the United States of America
Published simultaneously in Canada

OPM   10 9 8 7 6 5 4 3 2 1

*For Gemma, who has always known the importance
to a girl of a Denny and George scarf*

Ms. Rebecca Bloomwood
Flat 2
4 Burney Rd.
London SW6 8FD

18 July 2000

Dear Ms. Bloomwood:

Thank you for your letter of 15 July.

It is true that we have known each other a long time, and I am pleased that you consider me "more than just a bank manager." I agree that friendship is important and was glad to hear that you would always lend me money should I need it.

However, I cannot reciprocate, as you suggest, by wiping £1,000 off your overdraft "accidentally on purpose." I can assure you, the money would be missed.

Instead, I am prepared to extend your overdraft limit by another £500, taking it up to £4,000, and suggest that we meet before too long to discuss your ongoing financial needs.

Yours sincerely,

Derek Smeath
Manager

Ms. Rebecca Bloomwood
Flat 2
4 Burney Rd.
London SW6 8FD

23 July 2000

Dear Ms. Bloomwood:

I am glad that my letter of 18 July proved helpful.

I should, however, be grateful if you refrained from referring to me personally on your television show as "Sweetie
Smeathie" and "the best bank manager in the world."

Although naturally I am pleased you feel this way, my su-
periors are a little anxious at the image of Endwich Bank
which is being presented, and have asked that I write to
you on the matter.

With all best wishes,

Derek Smeath
Manager

Ms. Rebecca Bloomwood
Flat 2
4 Burney Rd.
London SW6 8FD

20 August 2000

Dear Ms. Bloomwood:

Thank you for your letter of 18 August.

I was sorry to hear that keeping within your new overdraft limit is proving so difficult. I understand that the
Pied a Terre summer sale is a unique opportunity to save
money in the long run, and I can certainly increase your
limit by £63.50 if, as you say, this would "make all the
difference."

However, I would also recommend that you come into the
branch for a more comprehensive review of your financial
situation. My assistant, Erica Parnell, will be pleased to set
up an appointment.

Yours sincerely,

Derek Smeath
Manager

One

OK, DON'T PANIC. Don't *panic*. It's simply a question of being organized and staying calm and deciding what exactly I need to take. And then fitting it all neatly into my suitcase. I mean, just how hard can that be?

I step back from my cluttered bed and close my eyes, half-hoping that if I wish hard enough, my clothes might magically organize themselves into a series of neatly folded piles. Like in those magazine articles on packing, which tell you how to go on holiday with one cheap sarong and cleverly turn it into six different outfits. (Which I always think is a complete con, because, OK, the sarong costs ten quid, but then they add loads of accessories which cost hundreds, and we're not supposed to notice.)

But when I open my eyes again, the clutter is all still there. In fact, there seems to be even more of it, as if while my eyes were shut, my clothes have been secretly jumping out of the drawers and running around on my bed. Everywhere I look, there are huge great tangled piles of . . . well . . . *stuff*. Shoes, boots, T-shirts, magazines . . . a Body Shop gift basket that was on sale . . . a Linguaphone Italian course which I'm *definitely* going to start soon . . . a facial sauna thingy . . . And, sitting proudly on my dressing table, a fencing mask and sword which I bought yesterday. Only forty quid from a charity shop!

I pick up the sword and experimentally give a little lunge toward my reflection in the mirror. It was a real coincidence, because I've been meaning to take up fencing for ages, ever since I read this article about it in *The Daily World*. Did you know that fencers have better legs than any other athletes? Plus, if you're an expert you can become a stunt double in a film and earn loads of money! So what I'm planning to do is find some fencing lessons nearby, and get really good, which I should think I'll do quite quickly.

And then—this is my secret little plan—when I've got my gold badge, or whatever it is, I'll write to Catherine Zeta-Jones. Because she must need a stunt double, mustn't she? And why shouldn't it be me? In fact she'd probably *prefer* someone British. Maybe she'll phone back and say she always watches my television appearances on cable, and she's always wanted to meet me! We'll probably really hit it off, and turn out to have the same sense of humor and everything. And then I'll fly out to her luxury home, and get to meet Michael Douglas and play with the baby. We'll be all relaxed together like old friends, and some magazine will do a feature on celebrity best friends and have us in it, and maybe they'll even ask me to be . . .

"Hi, Bex!" With a jolt, the happy pictures of me laughing with Michael and Catherine vanish, and my brain snaps into focus. Suze, my flatmate, is wandering into my room, wearing a pair of ancient paisley pajamas, with her blond hair in plaits. "What are you doing?" she asks curiously.

"Nothing!" I say, hastily putting the fencing sword back. "Just . . . you know. Keep fit."

"Oh right," she says vaguely. "So—how's the packing going?" She wanders over to my mantelpiece, picks up a lipstick, and begins to apply it. Suze always does this in my room—just wanders about picking things up and looking at them and putting them down again. She says she loves the way you never know what you might find, like in a junk shop. Which I'm fairly sure she means in a nice way.

"It's going really well," I say. "I'm just deciding which suitcase to take."

"Ooh," says Suze, turning round, her mouth half bright pink. "What about that little cream one? Or your red holdall?"

"I thought maybe this one," I say, hauling my new acid-green shell case out from under the bed. I bought it last weekend, and it's absolutely gorgeous.

"Wow!" says Suze, her eyes widening. "Bex! That's fab! Where did you get it?"

"Fenwicks," I say, grinning broadly. "Isn't it amazing?"

"It's the coolest case I've ever seen!" says Suze, running her fingers admiringly over it. "So . . . how many suitcases have you got now?" She glances up at my wardrobe, on which are teetering a brown leather case, a lacquered trunk, and three vanity cases.

"Oh, you know," I say, shrugging a little defensively. "The normal amount."

I suppose I have been buying quite a bit of luggage recently. But the thing is, for ages I didn't have any, just one battered old canvas bag. Then, a few months ago I had an incredible revelation in the middle of Harrods, a bit like Saint Paul on the road to Mandalay. *Luggage*. And since then, I've been making up for all the lean years.

Besides which, everyone knows good luggage is an investment.

"I'm just making a cup of tea," says Suze. "D'you want one?"

"Ooh, yes please!" I say. "And a KitKat?" Suze grins.

"Definitely a KitKat."

Recently, we had this friend of Suze's to stay on our sofa—and when he left he gave us this huge box full of a hundred KitKats. Which is such a great thank-you present, but it means all we eat, all day long, is KitKats. Still, as Suze pointed out last night, the quicker we eat them, the quicker they'll be gone—so in a way, it's healthier just to stuff in as many as possible right away.

Suze ambles out of the room and I turn to my case. Right. Concentrate. Packing. This really shouldn't take long. All I need is a very basic, pared-down capsule wardrobe for a romantic minibreak in Somerset. I've even written out a list, which should make things nice and simple.

Jeans: two pairs. Easy. Scruffy and not quite so scruffy.

T-shirts:

Actually, make that three pairs of jeans. I've *got* to take my new Diesel ones, they're just so cool, even if they are a bit tight. I'll just wear them for a few hours in the evening or something.

T-shirts:

Oh, and my embroidered cutoffs from Oasis, because I haven't worn them yet. But they don't really count because they're practically shorts. And anyway, jeans hardly take up any room, do they?

OK, that's probably enough jeans. I can always add some more if I need to.

T-shirts: selection. So let's see. Plain white, obviously. Gray, ditto. Black cropped, black vest (Calvin Klein), other black vest (Warehouse, but actually looks nicer), pink sleeveless, pink sparkly, pink—

I stop, halfway through transferring folded-up T-shirts into my case. This is stupid. How am I supposed to predict which T-shirts I'm going to want to wear? The whole point about T-shirts is you choose them in the morning according to your mood, like crystals, or aromatherapy oils. Imagine if I woke up in the mood for my "Elvis Is Groovy" T-shirt and I didn't have it with me?

You know, I think I'll just take them all. I mean, a few T-shirts aren't going to take up much room. I'll hardly even notice them.

I tip them all into my case and add a couple of cropped bra-tops for luck.

Excellent. This capsule approach is working really well. OK, what's next?

Ten minutes later, Suze wanders back into the room, holding two mugs of tea and three KitKats to share. (We've come to agree that four sticks, frankly, doesn't do it.)

"Here you are," she says—then gives me a closer look. "Bex, are you OK?"

"I'm fine," I say, rather pink in the face. "I'm just trying to fold up this insulated vest a bit smaller."

I've already packed a denim jacket and a leather jacket, but you just can't count on September weather, can you? I mean, at the moment it's hot and sunny, but it might well start snowing tomorrow. And what happens if Luke and I go for a really rustic country walk? Besides which, I've had this gorgeous Patagonia vest for ages, and I've only worn it once. I try to fold it again, but it slithers out of my hands and onto the floor. God, this reminds me of camping trips with the Brownies, trying to get my sleeping bag back into its tube.

"How long are you going for, again?" asks Suze.

"Three days." I give up trying to squash the vest into the size of a matchbox, and it springs jauntily back to shape. Discomfited, I sink onto the bed and take a sip of tea. What I don't understand is, how do other people manage to pack so lightly? You see businesspeople all the time, striding onto planes with only a tiny shoe-box suitcase on wheels. How do they do it? Do they have magic shrinking clothes?

"Why don't you take your holdall as well?" suggests Suze.

"D'you think?" I look uncertainly at my overflowing suitcase. Come to think of it, maybe I don't need three pairs of boots. Or a fur stole.

Then suddenly it occurs to me that Suze goes away nearly every weekend, and she only takes a tiny squashy bag. "Suze, how do *you* pack? Do you have a system?"

"I dunno," she says vaguely. "I suppose I still do what they taught us at Miss Burton's. You work out an outfit for each occasion—and stick to that." She begins to tick off on her fingers. "Like . . . driving outfit, dinner, sitting by the pool, game of tennis . . ." She looks up. "Oh yes, and each garment should be used at least three times."

God, Suze is a genius. She knows all this kind of stuff. Her parents sent her to Miss Burton's Academy when she was eighteen, which is some posh place in London where they teach you things like how to talk to a bishop and get out of a sports car in a miniskirt. She knows how to make a rabbit out of chicken wire, too.

Quickly I start to jot some broad headings on a piece

of paper. This is much more like it. Much better than randomly stuffing things into a case. This way, I won't have any superfluous clothes, just the bare minimum.

Outfit 1: Sitting by pool (sunny).
Outfit 2: Sitting by pool (cloudy).
Outfit 3: Sitting by pool (bottom looks huge in morning).
Outfit 4: Sitting by pool (someone else has same swimsuit).
Outfit 5:

The phone rings in the hall, but I barely look up. I can hear Suze talking excitedly—then a moment later, she appears in the doorway, her face all pink and pleased.

"Guess what?" she says. "Guess what?"

"What?"

"Box Beautiful has sold out of my frames! They just phoned up to order some more!"

"Oh, Suze! That's fantastic!" I shriek.

"I know!" She comes running over, and we have a big hug, and sort of dance about, before she realizes she's holding a cigarette and is about to burn my hair.

The amazing thing is, Suze only started making photograph frames a few months ago—but already she's supplying four shops in London, and they're doing really well! She's been in loads of magazines, and everything. Which isn't surprising, because her frames are *so* cool. Her latest range is in purple tweed, and they come in these gorgeous gray sparkly boxes, all wrapped in bright turquoise tissue paper. (I helped choose the exact color, by the way.) She's so successful, she doesn't even make them all herself anymore, but sends off her designs to a little workshop in Kent, and they come back, all made up.

"So, have you finished working your wardrobe out?" she says, taking a drag on her cigarette.

"Yes," I say, brandishing my sheet of paper at her. "I've got it all sorted out. Down to every last pair of socks."

"Well done!"

"And the *only* thing I need to buy," I add casually, "is a pair of lilac sandals."

"Lilac sandals?"

"Mmm?" I look up innocently. "Yes. I need some. You know, just a nice cheap little pair to pull a couple of outfits together . . ."

"Oh right," says Suze, and pauses, frowning slightly. "Bex . . . weren't you talking about a pair of lilac sandals last week? Really expensive, from LK Bennett?"

"Was I?" I feel myself flush a little. "I . . . I don't remember. Maybe. Anyway—"

"Bex." Suze gives me a suddenly suspicious look. "Now tell me the truth. Do you really *need* a pair of lilac sandals? Or do you just want them?"

"No!" I say defensively. "I really need them! Look!"

I take out my clothes plan, unfold it, and show it to Suze. I have to say, I'm quite proud of it. It's quite a complicated flow chart, all boxes and arrows and red asterisks.

"Wow!" says Suze. "Where did you learn how to do that?"

"At university," I say modestly. I got my degree in Business and Accounting—and it's amazing how often it comes in handy.

"What's this box?" she asks, pointing at the page.

"That's . . ." I squint at it, trying to remember. "I think that's if we go out to some really smart restaurant and I've already worn my Whistles dress the night before."

"And this one?"

"That's if we go rock-climbing. And this"—I point to an empty box—"is where I need a pair of lilac sandals. If I don't have them, then this outfit won't work, and neither will this one . . . and the whole thing will disintegrate. I might as well not bother going."

Suze is silent for a while, perusing my clothes plan while I bite my lip anxiously and cross my fingers behind my back.

I know this may seem a little unusual. I know most people don't run every single purchase past their flatmate. But the fact is, a while ago I kind of made Suze a little promise, which was that I'd let her keep tabs on my shopping. You know. Just keep an eye on things.

Don't get the wrong idea here. It's not like I have a problem or anything. It's just that a few months ago, I did get into a . . . Well. A very slight money scrape. It was really just a tiny blip—nothing to worry about. But Suze got really freaked out when she found out how much I owed, and said that for my own good, she'd vet all my spending from now on.

And she's been as good as her word. She's very strict, actually. Sometimes I'm really quite scared she might say no.

"I see what you mean," she says at last. "You haven't really got a choice, have you?"

"Exactly," I say in relief. I take the plan from her, fold it up, and put it into my bag.

"Hey, Bex, is that new?" says Suze suddenly. She pulls

my wardrobe door open and I feel a twinge of nerves. She's frowning at my lovely new honey-colored coat, which I smuggled into the flat the other day when she was in the bath.

I mean, obviously I was planning to tell her about it. I just never got round to it.

Please don't look at the price tag, I think feverishly. Please don't look at the price tag.

"Erm . . . yes," I say. "Yes, it is new. But the thing is . . . I need a good coat, in case I get asked to do an outside broadcast for *Morning Coffee*."

"Is that likely?" asks Suze, puzzledly. "I mean, I thought your job was just sitting in the studio, giving financial advice."

"Well . . . you never know. It's always best to be prepared."

"I suppose so . . ." says Suze doubtfully. "And what about this top?" She pulls at a hanger. "That's new, too!"

"That's to wear on the show," I reply promptly.

"And this skirt?"

"For the show."

"And these new trousers?"

"For the—"

"Bex." Suze looks at me with narrowed eyes. "How many outfits have you got to wear on the show?"

"Well—you know," I say defensively. "I need a few backups. I mean, Suze, this is my career we're talking about. My *career*."

"Yes," says Suze eventually. "Yes, I suppose it is." She reaches for my new red silk jacket. "This is nice."

"I know," I beam. "I bought it to wear on my January special!"

"Have you got a January special?" says Suze. "Ooh, what's it about?"

"It's going to be called *Becky's Fundamental Financial Principles*," I say, reaching for my lip gloss. "It should be really good. Five ten-minute slots, just me!"

"So—what *are* your fundamental financial principles?" asks Suze interestedly.

"Erm . . . well, I haven't really got any yet," I say, carefully painting my lips. "But you know. I'll work them out a bit nearer the time." I snap my lip gloss shut and reach for my jacket. "See you later."

"OK," says Suze. "And remember. Just one pair of shoes!"

"All right! I promise!"

It's really sweet of Suze to be so concerned about me. But she doesn't need to be. To be honest, she doesn't really understand what a changed person I am. OK, I did have a very slight financial crisis earlier this year. In fact, at one point, I was in debt by . . . Well. Really quite a lot.

But then I landed my job on *Morning Coffee,* and everything changed. I turned my life around completely, worked really hard, and paid off all my debts. Yes, I paid them all off! I wrote out check after check—and cleared every single outstanding credit card, every store card, every scribbled IOU to Suze. (She couldn't believe it when I presented her with a check for several hundred pounds. At first she didn't want to take it, but then she changed her mind and went out and bought this most amazing sheepskin coat.)

Honestly, paying off those debts was the most wonderful, exhilarating feeling in the world. It was a few months ago now—but I still feel high as I think about it. There's really nothing to beat being completely and utterly financially solvent, is there?

And just look at me now. I'm a completely different person from the old Becky. I'm a reformed character. I haven't even got an overdraft!

Two

WELL, OK. I have got a bit of an overdraft. But the only reason is, I've been taking the long view recently, and investing quite heavily in my career. Luke, my boyfriend, is an entrepreneur. He's got his own financial PR company and everything. And he said something a few weeks ago which really made sense to me: "People who want to make a million borrow a million first."

Honestly, I must have a naturally entrepreneurial mind or something, because as soon as he said it, I felt this amazing chord of recognition. I even found myself murmuring it aloud. He's so right. How can you expect to make any money if you don't spend it first?

So I've invested in quite a few outfits to wear on television—plus a few good haircuts, and quite a few manicures and facials. And a couple of massages. Because everyone knows you can't perform well if you're all stressed.

I've also invested in a new computer, which cost £2,000—but is an essential item because guess what? I'm writing a self-help book! Just after I'd become a regular on *Morning Coffee,* I met these really nice publishers, who took me out to lunch and said I was an inspiration to financially challenged people every-where. Wasn't that nice? They paid me £1,000 before I'd even written a word—and I get a lot more when it's actually published. The book's going to be called *Becky Bloomwood's Guide to Money*. Or possibly *Manage Money the Becky Bloomwood Way*.

I haven't quite had time to start writing it yet, but I really think the most important thing is to get the title right, and then the rest will just fall into place. And I've already jotted down *loads* of ideas about what to wear in the author photograph.

So basically, it's no surprise that I'm a little overdrawn at the moment. But the point is, all that money is out there, working for me. And luckily my bank manager, Derek Smeath, is very sympathetic to my needs. He's a real sweetie, actually. For a long time we didn't get on at all—which I think was more a communications problem than anything else. But then we met up and had a nice long chat (plus I gave him some advice on what to buy his wife for Christmas) and now I really think he under-stands where I'm coming from. And the truth is, of course, I'm a lot more sensible than I used to be.

For example, I have a completely different attitude toward shopping. My new motto is "Buy Only What You Need." I know, it sounds almost *too* simple—but it really does work. Before each purchase, I ask myself one question: "Do I *need* this?" And only if the answer is yes do I make the purchase. It's all just a matter of self-discipline.

So, for example, when I get to LK Bennett, I'm in-credibly focused and direct. As I walk in, a pair of high-heeled red boots catches my eye—but I quickly look away and head straight for the display of sandals. This is how I shop these days: no pausing, no browsing, no eyeing up other items. Not even that gorgeous new range of sequined pumps over there. I simply go straight to the sandals I want, take them from the rack, and say to the assistant, "I'd like to have these in a six, please."

Direct and to the point. Just buy what you need and nothing else. This is the key to controlled shopping. I'm not even going to *glance* at those cool pink stilettos, even though they'd match my new pink denim skirt perfectly.

Nor those slingbacks with the glittery heels.

They are nice though, aren't they? I wonder what they look like on?

Oh God. This is really hard.

What *is* it about shoes? I mean, I like most kinds of clothes, but a good pair of shoes can just reduce me to jelly. Sometimes, when Suze isn't at home, I open my wardrobe and just *stare* at all my pairs of shoes, like some mad collector. And once I lined them all up on my bed and took a photograph of them. Which might seem a bit weird—but I thought, I've got loads of photos of people I don't really like, so why not take one of something I really love?

"Here you are!"

Thank goodness, the assistant is back, with my lilac sandals in a box—and as I see them, my heart leaps. Oh, these are gorgeous. *Gorgeous*. All delicate and strappy, with a tiny little blackberry by the toe. I fell in love with them as soon as I saw them. They're a bit expensive—but then, everyone knows you should never skimp on shoes, because you'll hurt your feet.

I slip my feet into them with a frisson of delight—and they're just fantastic. My feet suddenly look elegant, and my legs look longer . . . and OK, it's a tiny bit difficult to walk in them, but that's probably because the shop floor is all slippery.

"I'll take them, please," I say, and beam happily at the assistant.

You see, this is the reward for taking such a controlled approach to shopping. When you buy something, you really feel as though you've *earned* it.

We both head toward the checkout, and I keep my eyes carefully away from the rack of accessories. In fact, I barely even notice that purple bag with the jet beading. And I'm just reaching for my wallet, congratulating myself on being so single-minded, when the assistant says conversationally, "You know, we've got these sandals in clementine, as well."

Clementine?

"Oh . . . right," I say after a pause.

I'm not interested. I've got what I came in to buy— and that's the end of the story. Lilac sandals. Not clementine.

"They've just come in," she adds, rooting around on the floor. "I think they're going to be even more popular than the lilac."

"Really?" I say, trying to sound as indifferent as I can. "Well, I'll just take these, I think . . ."

"Here it is!" she exclaims. "I knew there was one around here somewhere . . ."

And I freeze as she puts the most exquisite sandal I've ever seen onto the counter. It's a pale, creamy orange color, with the same strappy shape as the lilac one—but instead of the blackberry, there's a tiny clementine by the toe.

It's instant love. I can't move my eyes away.

"Would you like to try it?" says the girl, and I feel a lurch of desire, right to the pit of my stomach.

Just look at it. It's delicious. It's the most darling shoe I've ever seen. Oh God.

But I don't need a pair of clementine shoes. I don't need them.

Come on, Becky. Just. Say. No.

"Actually . . ." I swallow hard, trying to get control of my voice. "Actually . . ." I can hardly say it. "I'll just take the lilac ones today," I manage eventually. "Thank you."

"OK . . ." The girl punches a code into the till. "That'll be £89, then. How would you like to pay?"

"Er . . . VISA, please," I say. I sign the slip, take my bag, and leave the shop, feeling slightly numb.

I did it! I did it! I completely controlled my desires! I only needed one pair of shoes—and I only bought one. In and out of the shop, completely according to plan. You see, this is what I can do when I really want to. This is the new Becky Bloomwood.

Having been so good, I deserve a little reward, so I go to a coffee shop and sit down outside in the sun with a cappuccino.

I want those clementine shoes, pops into my head as I take the first sip.

Stop. Stop it. Think about . . . something else. Luke. The holiday. Our first ever holiday together. God, I can't wait.

I've been wanting to suggest a holiday ever since Luke and I started going out, but he works so hard, it would be like asking the prime minister to give up running the country for a bit. (Except come to think of it, he does that every summer, doesn't he? So why can't Luke?)

Luke's so busy, he hasn't even met my parents yet, which I'm a bit upset about. They asked him over for Sunday lunch a few weeks ago, and Mum spent ages cooking—or at least, she bought apricot-stuffed loin of pork from Sainsbury's and a really posh chocolate meringue pudding. But at the last minute he had to cancel because there was a crisis with one of his clients in the Sunday papers. So I had to go on my own—and it was all rather miserable, to be honest. You could tell Mum was really disappointed, but she kept saying brightly, "Oh well, it was only a casual arrangement," which it wasn't. He sent her a huge bouquet of flowers the next day to apologize (or at least, Mel, his assistant, did), but it's not the same, is it?

The worst bit was that our next-door neighbors, Janice and Martin, popped in for a glass of sherry "to meet the famous Luke," as they put it, and when they found out he wasn't there, they kept giving me all these pitying looks tinged with smugness, because their son Tom is getting married to his girlfriend Lucy next week. And I have a horrible suspicion that they think I have a crush on him. (Which I don't—in fact, quite the reverse. I actually turned *him* down when we were teenagers. But once people believe something like that, it's completely impossible to convince them otherwise. Hideous.)

When I got upset with Luke, he pointed out that I've never met his parents, either. But I have once—although very briefly. And anyway it's not the same thing, because his family lives miles away, and it's all much more complicated.

To be honest, I find Luke's family setup just a tad weird. He's got a dad and a stepmum in Britain who brought him up with his two half-sisters, and whom he calls Mum and Dad. And then he's got his real mum,

Elinor, who left his dad when he was little, married some rich American, and left Luke behind. Then she left the rich American and married another, even richer American and then . . . was there another one? Anyway, the point is, she lives in New York. So of course I haven't met her. And the rest of his family is in Devon, not exactly handy for a quick Sunday lunch.

I said all this to Luke and I think he got my point. And at least he's making the effort to come on this little holiday. It was Mel, actually, who suggested the weekend idea. She told me Luke hadn't had a proper holiday for three years—and maybe he had to warm up to the idea. So I stopped talking about holidays and started talking about weekends away—and that did the trick! All of a sudden Luke told me to set aside this weekend. He booked the hotel himself and everything. I'm *so* looking forward to it. We'll just do nothing but relax and take it easy—and actually spend some time with each other for a change. Lovely.

I want those clementine shoes.

Stop it.

I take another sip of coffee, lean back, and force myself to survey the bustling street. People are striding along, holding bags and chatting, and there's a girl crossing the road with nice trousers on, which I think come from Nicole Farhi and . . . Oh God.

A middle-aged man in a dark suit is coming along the road toward me, and I recognize him. It's Derek Smeath, my bank manager.

Oh, and I think he's seen me.

OK, don't panic, I instruct myself firmly. There's no need to panic. Maybe once upon a time I would have been thrown by seeing him. I might have tried to hide behind a menu, or perhaps even run away. But that's all in the past. These days, Sweetie Smeathie and I have a very honest and amicable relationship.

Still, I find myself shifting my chair slightly farther away from my LK Bennett bag, as though it hasn't got anything to do with me.

"Hello, Mr. Smeath!" I say brightly as he approaches. "How are you?"

"Very well," says Derek Smeath, smiling. "And you?"

"Oh, I'm fine, thanks. Would you . . . would you like a coffee?" I add politely, gesturing to the empty chair opposite me. And I'm not really expecting him to say yes—but to my astonishment he sits down and picks up a menu.

How civilized is this? I'm having coffee with my bank manager at a pavement cafe! You know, maybe I'll find a way to work this into my *Morning Coffee* slot. "I myself prefer the informal approach to personal finance," I'll say, smiling warmly into the camera. "My own bank manager and I often share a friendly cappuccino as we discuss my current financial strategies . . ."

"As it happens, Rebecca, I've just written a letter to you," says Derek Smeath, as a waitress puts an espresso down in front of him. Suddenly his voice is more serious, and I feel a small lurch of alarm. Oh God, what have I done now? "You and all my customers," he adds. "To tell you that I'm leaving."

"What?" I put my coffee cup down with a little crash. "What do you mean, leaving?"

"I'm leaving Endwich Bank. I've decided to take early retirement."

"But . . ."

I stare at him, appalled. Derek Smeath can't leave Endwich Bank. He can't just leave me in the lurch, just as everything was going so well. I mean, I know we haven't always exactly seen eye to eye—but recently we've developed a really good rapport. He understands me. He understands my overdraft. What am I going to do without him?

"Aren't you too young to retire?" I say, aware of the dismay in my voice. "Won't you get bored?"

He leans back in his chair and takes a sip of espresso. "I'm not planning to give up work altogether. But I think there's a little more to life than looking after people's bank accounts, don't you? Fascinating though some of them have been."

"Well . . . yes. Yes, of course. And I'm glad for you, honestly." I shrug, a little embarrassed. "But I'll . . . miss you."

"Believe it or not," he says, smiling slightly, "I think I'll miss you too, Rebecca. Yours has certainly been one of the most . . . interesting accounts I've dealt with."

He gives me a penetrating look and I feel myself flush slightly. Why does he have to remind me of the past? The point is, that's all over. I'm a different person now. Surely one should be allowed to turn over a new leaf and start again in life.

"Your new career in television seems to be going well," he says, taking a sip of espresso.

"I know! It's so great, isn't it? And it pays really well," I add, a little pointedly.

"Your income has certainly gone up in recent months." He puts down his coffee cup and my heart sinks slightly. "However . . ."

I knew it. *Why* does there always have to be a *however*?

"However," repeats Derek Smeath. "Your outgoings have also risen. Substantially. In fact, your overdraft is now higher than it was at the height of your . . . shall we say, your excesses."

Excesses? That is so mean.

"You really must make more effort to keep within your overdraft limit," he's saying now. "Or, even better, pay it off."

"I know," I say vaguely. "I'm planning to."

I've just spotted a girl on the other side of the road, with an LK Bennett bag. She's holding a great big bag—with *two* shoe boxes in it.

If she's allowed to buy two pairs of shoes, then why aren't I? What's the rule that says you can only buy one pair of shoes at a time? I mean, it's so arbitrary.

"What about your other finances?" Derek Smeath is asking. "Do you have any store card bills, for example?"

"No," I say with a tinge of smugness. "I paid them all off months ago."

"And you haven't spent anything since?"

"Only bits and pieces. Hardly anything."

And what's ninety quid, really? In the greater scheme of things?

"The reason I'm asking these questions," says Derek Smeath, "is that I feel I should warn you. The bank is restructuring somewhat, and my successor, John Gavin, may not have quite the same relaxed approach which I have taken toward your account. I'm not sure you're aware quite how lenient I have been with you."

"Really?" I say, not really listening.

I mean, suppose I took up smoking. I'd easily spend ninety quid on cigarettes without even thinking about it, wouldn't I?

In fact, think of all the money I've saved by *not* smoking. Easily enough to afford one little pair of shoes.

"He's a very capable man," Derek Smeath is saying.

"But also very . . . rigorous. Not particularly known for his flexibility."

"Right," I say, nodding absently.

"I would certainly recommend that you address your overdraft without delay." He takes a sip of coffee. "And tell me, have you done anything about taking out a pension?"

"Erm . . . I went to visit that independent adviser you recommended."

"And did you fill in any of the forms?"

Unwillingly, I drag my attention back to him.

"Well, I'm just considering my options," I say, and put on my wise, financial-expert look. "There's nothing worse than rushing into the wrong investment, you know. Particularly when it comes to something as important as a pension."

"Very true," says Derek Smeath. "But don't spend too long considering, will you? Your money won't save itself."

"I know!" I say and take a sip of cappuccino.

Now I feel a bit uncomfortable. Maybe he's right. Maybe I should put £90 into a pension fund instead of buying another pair of shoes.

But on the other hand—what good is a pension fund of £90? I mean, that's not exactly going to keep me in my old age, is it? Ninety measly quid. And by the time I'm old, the world will probably have blown up, or something.

Whereas a pair of shoes is tangible, it's there in your hand . . .

Oh, sod it. I'm going to get them.

"Mr. Smeath, I have to go," I say abruptly, putting down my cup. "There's something I have to . . . do."

I *have* to get back there as quickly as possible. I pick up my carrier bag and drop a fiver on the table. "Lovely to see you. And good luck in your retirement."

"Best of luck to you too, Rebecca," says Derek Smeath, smiling kindly at me. "But do remember what I've said. John Gavin won't indulge you in the way that I have. So please be careful with your spending."

"I will!" I say brightly.

And without quite running, I'm off down the street, as quick as I can, back to LK Bennett.

Perhaps strictly speaking I didn't exactly need to buy a pair of clementine shoes. But what occurred to me while I was trying them on was, I haven't actually broken my new rule. Because the point is, I *will* need them.

After all, I will need new shoes *at some point,* won't I? Everyone needs shoes. And surely it's far more prudent to stock up now in a style I really like, than to wait until my last pair wears out and then find nothing nice in the shops. It's only sensible. It's like . . . hedging my future position in the shoe market.

As I come out of LK Bennett, gleefully grasping my two shiny new bags, there's a warm, happy glow all around me, and I'm not in the mood to go home. So I decide to pop across the street to Gifts and Goodies. This is one of the shops that carry Suze's frames, and I have a little habit of going in whenever I pass, just to see if anyone's buying one.

I push the door open with a little ping, and smile at the assistant, who looks up. This is such a lovely shop. It's all warm and scented, and full of gorgeous things like chrome wine racks and etched glass coasters. I sidle past a shelf of pale mauve leather notebooks, and look up—

and there they are! Three purple tweed photo frames, made by Suze! I still get a thrill, every time I see them.

And oh my God! I feel a sudden zing of excitement. There's a customer standing there, and she's holding one. She's actually holding one!

To be perfectly honest, I've never actually seen anyone buying one of Suze's frames. I mean, I know people must buy them, because they keep selling out—but I've never actually seen it happen. This is so exciting!

I walk quietly forward just as the customer turns the frame over. She frowns at the price, and my heart gives a little flurry.

"That's a really beautiful photo frame," I say casually. "Really unusual."

"Yes," she says, and puts it back down on the shelf.

No! I think in dismay. Pick it up again!

"It's so difficult to find a nice frame these days," I say conversationally. "Don't you think? When you find one, you should just . . . buy it! Before someone else gets it."

"I suppose so," says the customer, giving me an odd look.

Now she's walking away. What can I do?

"Well, I think I'll get one," I say distinctly, and pick it up. "It'll make a perfect present. For a man, or a woman . . . I mean, everyone needs photograph frames, don't they?"

The customer doesn't seem to be taking any notice. But never mind, when she sees *me* buying it, maybe she'll rethink.

I hurry to the checkout, and the woman behind the till smiles at me. I think she's the shop owner, because I've seen her interviewing staff and talking to suppliers. (Not that I come in here very often, it's just coincidence or something.)

"Hello again," she says. "You really like those frames, don't you?"

"Yes," I say loudly. "And such *fantastic* value!" But the customer's looking at a glass decanter, and not even listening.

"How many of them have you bought, now? It must be about . . . twenty?"

What? My attention snaps back to the shop owner. What's she saying?

"Or even thirty?"

I stare at her in shock. Has she been monitoring me, every time I've been in here? Isn't that against the law?

"Quite a collection!" she adds pleasantly, as she wraps it up in tissue paper.

I've got to say something, or she'll get the idea that it's me buying all Suze's frames instead of the general public. Which is ridiculous. I ask you, thirty! I've only bought about . . . four. Five, maybe.

"I haven't got that many!" I say hurriedly. "I should think you've been mixing me up with . . . other people. And I didn't just come in to buy a frame!" I laugh gaily to show what a ludicrous idea that is. "I actually wanted some of . . . these, too." I grab randomly at some big carved wooden letters in a nearby basket, and hand them to her. She smiles, and starts laying them out on tissue paper one by one.

"P . . . T . . . R . . . R."

She stops, and looks at the letters puzzledly. "Were you trying to make *Peter*?"

Oh for God's sake. Does there always have to be a *reason* to buy things?

"Erm . . . yes," I say. "For my . . . my godson. He's three."

"Lovely! Here we are then. Two E's, and take away one R . . ."

She's looking at me kindly, as if I'm a complete halfwit. Which I suppose is fair enough, since I can't spell *Peter* and it's the name of my own godson.

"That'll be . . . £48," she says, as I reach for my purse. "You know, if you spend £50, you get a free scented candle."

"Really?" I look up with interest. I could do with a nice scented candle. And for the sake of £2 . . .

"I'm sure I could find something . . ." I say, looking vaguely round the shop.

"Spell out the rest of your godson's name in wooden letters!" suggests the shop owner helpfully. "What's his surname?"

"Um, Wilson," I say without thinking.

"Wilson!" And to my horror, she begins to root around in the basket. "W . . . L . . . here's an O . . ."

"Actually," I say quickly, "actually, better not. Because . . . because . . . actually, his parents are divorcing and he might be changing his surname."

"Really?" says the shop owner, and pulls a sympathetic face as she drops the letters back in. "How awful. Is it an acrimonious split, then?"

"Yes," I say, looking around the shop for something else to buy. "Very. His . . . his mother ran off with the gardener."

"Are you serious?" The shop owner's staring at me, and I suddenly notice a couple nearby listening as well. "She ran off with the *gardener*?"

"He was . . . very hunky," I improvise, picking up a jewelry box and seeing that it costs £75. "She couldn't keep her hands off him. The husband found them together in the toolshed. Anyway—"

"Goodness me!" says the shop owner. "That sounds incredible!"

"It's completely true," chimes in a voice from across the shop.

What?

My head whips round—and the woman who was looking at Suze's frames is walking toward me. "I assume you're talking about Jane and Tim?" she says. "Such a terrible scandal, wasn't it? But I thought the little boy was called Toby."

I stare at her, unable to speak.

"Maybe Peter is his baptismal name," suggests the shop owner, and gestures to me. "This is his godmother."

"Oh, you're the godmother!" exclaims the woman. "Yes, I've heard all about you."

This isn't happening.

"Now, perhaps *you* can tell me." The woman comes forward and lowers her voice confidentially. "Did Tim accept Maud's offer?"

I look around the silent shop. Everyone is waiting for my answer.

"Erm . . . yes, he did! Actually, I think I'll pay by cash." I fumble in my purse, and plonk £50 on the counter. "Keep the change."

"What about your scented candle?" says the shop owner. "You can choose from vanilla, sandalwood—"

"Never mind," I say, hurrying toward the door.

"Wait!" calls the woman urgently. "What happened to Ivan?"

"He . . . he emigrated to Australia," I say, and slam the door behind me.

God, that was a bit close. I think I'd better go home.

As I reach the corner of our road, I pause and do a little rearranging of my bags. Which is to say, I put them all in one LK Bennett carrier, and push them down until you can't see them. But it's not that I'm hiding them or anything.

I'm kind of hoping I'll be able to scuttle into my room without Suze seeing me, but as I open the front door, she's sitting on the floor of the hall, parceling something up.

"Hi!" she says. "Did you get the shoes?"

"Yes," I say brightly. "Absolutely. Right size, and everything."

"Let's have a look then!"

"I'll just . . . unpack them," I say casually, and head toward my room, trying to keep relaxed. But I know I look guilty. I'm even *walking* guiltily.

"Bex," she says suddenly. "What else is in that bag? That's not just one pair of shoes."

"Bag?" I turn as though in surprise. "Oh, *this* bag. Erm . . . just a few . . . bits and pieces. You know . . . odds and ends . . ."

I tail away guiltily as Suze folds her arms, looking as stern as she can.

"Show me."

"OK, listen," I say in a rush. "I know I said only one pair. But before you get angry, just look." I reach into my second LK Bennett bag, slip open the box, and slowly pull out one of the clementine sandals. "Just . . . look at that."

"Oh my God," breathes Suze, staring at it. "That's absolutely . . . stunning." She takes it from me and strokes the soft leather gently—then suddenly her stern expression returns. "But did you *need* them?"

"Yes!" I say defensively. "Or at least . . . I was just stocking up for the future. You know, like a kind of . . . investment."

"An investment?"

"Yes. And in a way, it's *saving* money—because now I've got these, I won't need to spend any money on shoes next year. None!"

"Really?" says Suze suspiciously. "None at all?"

"Absolutely! Honestly, Suze, I'm going to live in these shoes. I won't need to buy any more for at least a year. Probably two!"

Suze is silent and I bite my lip, waiting for her to tell me to take them back to the shop. But she's looking down at the sandal again, and touching the little clementine.

"Put them on," she says suddenly. "Let me see!"

With a small thrill I pull out the other sandal and slip them on—and they're just perfect. My perfect clementine slippers, just like Cinderella.

"Oh, Bex," says Suze—and she doesn't have to say anything else. It's all there in her eyes.

Honestly, sometimes I wish I could marry Suze.

After I've paraded back and forth a few times, Suze gives a contented sigh, then reaches inside the big carrier for the Gifts and Goodies bag. "So—what did you get from here?" she says interestedly. The wooden letters spill out, and she begins to arrange them on the carpet.

"P-E-T-E-R. You got a present for Peter!"

"Erm . . . yes," I say vaguely, grabbing for the Gifts and Goodies bag before she can spot her own frame in there. (She once caught me buying one in Fancy Free and got all cross, and said she would always make me one if I wanted it.) "Who's Peter?"

"My machinist!" says Suze. "But you've never met him!"

"Well . . . you know. He sounds nice on the phone . . . anyway, I'd better go and get ready for tomorrow."

"Ooh, that reminds me," says Suze, reaching for a piece of paper. "Luke rang for you!"

"Really?" I say, trying to hide my delight. I always get a little thrill when Luke rings, because, to be honest, he doesn't do it that much. I mean, he phones to arrange times of meeting and that kind of stuff—but he doesn't often phone for a chat. Sometimes he sends me e-mails, but they're not what you'd call chatty, more . . . Well, I don't exactly want to give away our intimate secrets—but put it like this, the first time I got one, I was quite shocked! (But I sort of look forward to them now.)

"He said he'll pick you up from the studio tomorrow at twelve. And the Mercedes has had to go into the garage, so you'll be going down in the MGF."

"Really?" I say. "That's so cool!"

"I know," says Suze, beaming back at me. "Isn't it great? Oh, and he also said can you pack light, because the boot isn't very big."

I stare at her, my smile fading.

"What did you say?"

"Pack light," repeats Suze. "You know: not much luggage, maybe one small bag or holdall . . ."

"I know what 'pack light' means!" I say, my voice shrill with alarm. "But . . . I can't!"

"Of course you can!"

"Suze, have you *seen* how much stuff I've got?" I say, going to my bedroom door and flinging it open. "I mean, just look at that."

Suze follows my gaze uncertainly, and we both stare at my bed. My big acid-green suitcase is full. Another pile of clothes is sitting beside it. And I haven't even *got* to makeup and stuff yet.

"I can't do it, Suze," I wail. "What am I going to do?"

"Phone Luke and tell him?" suggests Suze, "and say he'll have to hire a car with a bigger boot?"

For a moment I'm silent. I try to imagine Luke's face if I tell him he has to hire a bigger car to hold my clothes.

"The thing is," I say at last, "I'm not sure he'd *completely* understand . . ."

The doorbell rings and Suze gets up.

"That'll be Special Express for my parcel," she says. "Listen, Bex, it'll be fine! Just . . . prune away a few things." She goes to answer the door and I'm left staring at my jumbled bed.

Prune away? But prune away what, exactly? I mean, it's not as though I've packed a load of stuff I don't need. If I just start removing things at random my whole system will collapse.

Come on. Think laterally. There *must* be a solution.

Maybe I could . . . secretly fix a trailer onto the car when Luke isn't looking?

Or maybe I could *wear* all my clothes, on top of each other, and say I'm feeling a bit chilly . . .

Oh, this is hopeless. What am I going to do?

Distractedly, I wander out of my room and into the hall, where Suze is handing a padded envelope to a man in uniform.

"That's great," he says. "If you could just sign there . . . Hello!" he adds cheerfully to me, and I nod back, staring blankly at his badge, which reads: *Anything, anywhere, by tomorrow morning.*

"Here's your receipt," says the man to Suze, and

turns to leave. And he's halfway out of the door, when the words suddenly start jumping about in my mind.

Anything.

Anywhere.

By tomorrow—

"Hey, wait!" I call, just as the door's about to slam. "Could you just hold on one sec—"

695 SOHO SQUARE
LONDON W1 5AS

Ms. Rebecca Bloomwood
Flat 2
4 Burney Rd.
London SW6 8FD

4 September 2000

Dear Becky:

You may remember, when we spoke two weeks ago you
assured me the first draft of your book would be with me
within days. I'm sure it's on its way—or has it possibly gotten
lost in the post? Maybe you could send me another copy?

As far as the author photograph goes, just wear whatever you
feel comfortable with. An Agnes B top sounds fine, as do the
earrings you described. And thanks for sending me a Polaroid
of your orange sandals—I'm sure they will look great.

I look forward to seeing the manuscript—and again, let me
say how thrilled and delighted we are that you're writing for
us.

With all best wishes,

Pippa Brady
Editor

PARADIGM BOOKS LTD

Helping you to help yourself
COMING SOON! *Jungle Survival* by Bdgr. Roger Flintwood **(deceased)**

Three

AT FIVE TO TWELVE the next day I'm sitting under the bright lights of the *Morning Coffee* set, wondering how much longer we'll be. Normally my financial advice slot is over by eleven forty, but they got so engrossed with the psychic who reckons she's the reincarnated spirit of Mary Queen of Scots that everything's overrun since then. And Luke will be here any minute, and I've still got to change out of this stuffy suit . . .

"Becky?" says Emma, who's one of the presenters of *Morning Coffee* and is sitting opposite me on a blue sofa. "This sounds like quite a problem."

"Absolutely," I say, dragging my mind back to the present. I glance down at the sheet in front of me, then smile sympathetically at the camera. "So, to recap, Judy, you and your husband Bill have inherited some money. You'd like to invest some of it in the stock market—but he's refusing."

"It's like talking to a brick wall!" comes Judy's indignant voice. "He says I'll lose it all, and it's his money too, and if all I want to do is gamble it away, then I can go to . . ."

"Yes," interrupts Emma smoothly. "Well. This does sound quite a problem, Becky. Two partners disagreeing about what to do with their money."

"I just don't understand him!" exclaims Judy. "This is our one chance to make a serious investment! It's a fantastic opportunity! Why can't he *see* that?"

She breaks off—and there's an expectant silence around the studio. Everyone's waiting for my answer.

"Judy . . ." I pause thoughtfully. "May I ask a question? What outfit is Bill wearing today?"

"A suit," says Judy, sounding taken aback. "A gray suit for work."

"What kind of tie? Plain or patterned?"

"Plain," says Judy at once. "All his ties are plain."

"Would he ever wear, say . . . a polka-dot tie?"

"Never!"

"I see." I raise my eyebrows. "Judy, would it be fair to say Bill is generally quite an unadventurous person? That he doesn't like taking risks?"

"Well . . . yes," says Judy. "Now that you say it, I suppose he is."

"Ah!" says Rory suddenly, on the other side of the sofa. Rory is the other presenter of *Morning Coffee*. He's very chiseled-looking and is great at flirting with film stars, but he's not exactly the Brain of Britain. "I think I see where you're going here, Becky."

"Yes, thanks Rory," says Emma, rolling her eyes at me. "I think we all do. So Becky, if Bill doesn't like risk—are you saying he's right to avoid the stock market?"

"No," I reply. "Actually, I'm not saying that at all. Because maybe what Bill isn't quite seeing is that there's more than one kind of risk. If you invest in the stock market, yes, you risk losing some money in the short term. But if you simply tuck it away in the bank for years and years, an even greater risk is that this inheritance will be eroded over time by inflation."

"Aha," puts in Rory wisely. "Inflation."

"In twenty years' time, it could well be worth very little—compared to what it would probably have achieved on the market. So if Bill is only in his thirties and wants to make a long-term investment—although it seems risky, it's in many ways *safer* to choose a balanced stock market portfolio."

"I see!" says Emma, and gives me an admiring look. "I would never have looked at it like that."

"Successful investment is often simply a question of thinking laterally," I say, smiling modestly.

I *love* it when I get the answer right and everyone looks impressed.

"Does that help you, Judy?" says Emma.

"Yes," says Judy. "Yes, it does! I've videotaped this call, so I'll show it to Bill tonight."

"Oh right!" I say. "Well, check what kind of tie he's wearing first."

Everyone laughs, and I join in after a pause—though I wasn't actually joking.

"Time for one more quick call," says Emma. "And we have Enid from Northampton, who wants to know if she's got enough money to retire on. Enid, is that right?"

"Yes, that's right," comes Enid's voice down the line. "My husband Tony's recently retired, and I was on holiday last week—just at home with him, cooking and so forth. And he . . . we got to thinking . . . how about I retire early, too? But I wasn't sure I had enough saved up, so I thought I'd call in."

"What kind of financial provision have you made for retirement, Enid?" I ask.

"I've a pension which I've contributed to all my life," says Enid hesitantly, "and I've a couple of savings plans . . . and I've a recent inheritance which should see off the mortgage . . ."

"Well!" says Emma brightly. "Even *I* can see that you're pretty well set up, Enid. I'd say, happy retirement!"

"Right," says Enid. "I see. So—there's no reason for me not to retire. It's just as Tony said." There's silence apart from her breathing unsteadily down the line, and Emma gives me a quick glance. I know the producer, Barry, must be yelling into her earpiece to fill the space.

"So good luck, Enid!" she says brightly. "Becky, on the subject of retirement planning—"

"Just . . . hold on a moment," I say, frowning slightly. "Enid, there's no obvious financial reason for you not to retire. But . . . what about the most important reason of all? Do you actually *want* to retire?"

"Well." Enid's voice falters slightly. "I'm in my fifties now. I mean, you have to move on, don't you? And as Tony said, it'll give us a chance to spend more time together."

"Do you enjoy your job?"

There's another silence.

"I do. Yes. It's a good crowd, at work. I'm older than most of them, but somehow that doesn't seem to matter when we're having a laugh . . ."

"Well, I'm afraid that's all we've got time for," cuts in Emma, who has been listening intently to her earpiece. She smiles at the camera. "Good luck in your retirement, Enid . . ."

"Wait!" I say quickly. "Enid, please stay on the line if you'd like to talk about this a bit more. OK?"

"Yes," says Enid after a pause. "Yes, I'd like that."

"We're going to go to weather now," says Rory, who always perks up as the finance slot comes to an end. "But a final word, Becky?"

"Same as always," I say, smiling at the camera. "Look after your money . . ."

". . . and your money will look after you!" chime in Rory and Emma. After a frozen pause, everyone relaxes and Zelda, the assistant producer, strides onto the set.

"Well done!" she says. "Great stuff. Now, Becky, we've still got Enid on line four. But we can get rid of her if you like . . ."

"No!" I say. "I really want to talk to her. You know, I reckon she doesn't want to retire at all!"

"Whatever," says Zelda, ticking something on her clipboard. "Oh, and Luke's waiting for you at reception."

"Already?" I look at my watch. "Oh God . . . OK—can you tell him I won't be long?"

I honestly don't intend to spend that long on the phone. But once I get talking to Enid, it all comes out—about how she's dreading retirement, and how her husband just wants her at home to cook for him. How she really loves her job and she was thinking about taking a computer course but her husband says it's a waste of money . . . By the end I'm completely outraged. I've said exactly what I think, several times over, and am in the middle of asking Enid if she considers herself a feminist, when Zelda taps me on the shoulder and suddenly I remember where I am.

It takes me about another five minutes to apologize to Enid and say I've got to go, then for her to apologize to *me*—and for us both to say good-bye and thank you and don't mention it, about twenty times. Then, as quickly as possible, I head to my dressing room and change out of my *Morning Coffee* outfit into my driving outfit.

I'm quite pleased with my appearance as I look at myself in the mirror. I'm wearing: a Pucci-esque multi-colored top, frayed denim cutoffs, my new sandals, Gucci shades (Harvey Nichols sale—half price!), and my treasured pale blue Denny and George scarf.

Luke's got a real thing about my Denny and George scarf. When people ask us how we met, he always says, "Our eyes met across a Denny and George scarf," which is actually kind of true. He lent me some of the money I needed to buy it, and he still maintains I never paid him back so it's partly his. (Which is *so* not true. I paid him back straight away.)

Anyway, I tend to wear it quite a lot when we go out together. Also when we stay in together. In fact, I'll tell you a small secret—sometimes we even . . .

Actually, no. You don't need to know that. Forget I mentioned it.

As I eventually hurry into reception I glance at my watch—and oh God, I'm forty minutes late. And there's Luke sitting on a squashy chair, wearing the gorgeous polo shirt I bought him in the Ralph Lauren sale. He's talking intently on his mobile phone and sipping a cup of coffee and frowning at something in the paper. But then he looks up and his dark eyes meet mine, and his whole face breaks into a smile. A true, affectionate smile, which makes him seem like a different person.

When I first knew Luke, I only ever saw him busi-nesslike and polite, or scarily angry, or—very occasion-ally—amused. Even after we started seeing each other, it was a long time before he really let his guard down. In fact, the first time he really, really laughed, I was so surprised, I snorted lemonade through my nose.

Even now, whenever I see his face creasing into a real smile, I feel a bit of a lift inside. Because I know he's not like that with everyone. He's smiling like that because it's me. For me.

"I'm really sorry I took so long," I say. "I was just . . ."

"I know," says Luke, closing his paper and standing up. "You were talking to Enid." He gives me a kiss and squeezes my arm. "I saw the last couple of calls. Good for you."

"You just won't believe what her husband's like!" I say as we go through the swing doors and out into the car park. "No wonder she wants to keep working!"

"I can imagine."

"He just thinks she's there to give him an easy life." I shake my head fiercely. "You know, I'm never going to just . . . stay at home and cook your supper. Never in a million years."

There's a short silence, and I look up to see Luke's amused expression.

"Or . . . you know," I add hastily. "Anyone's supper."

"I'm glad to hear it," says Luke mildly. "I'm especially glad if you're never going to cook me Moroccan couscous surprise."

"You know what I mean," I say, flushing slightly. "And you promised you weren't going to talk about that anymore."

My famous Moroccan evening was quite soon after we started going out. I really wanted to show Luke that I could cook—and I'd seen this program about Moroccan cooking which made it look really easy and impressive. Plus there was some gorgeous Moroccan tableware on sale in Debenhams, so it should have all been perfect.

But that soggy couscous. It was the most revolting stuff I've ever seen in my life. Even after I tried Suze's suggestion of stir-frying it with mango chutney. And there was so *much* of it, all swelling up in bowls everywhere . . .

Anyway. Never mind. We had quite a nice pizza in the end.

We're approaching Luke's convertible in the corner of the car park, and he bleeps it open.

"You got my message, did you?" he says. "About luggage?"

"Yes, I did. Here it is."

I hand him the dinkiest little suitcase in the world, which I got from a children's gift shop in Guildford. It's white canvas with red hearts stenciled round it, and I use it as a vanity case.

"Is that it?" says Luke, looking astonished, and I stifle a giggle. Ha! This'll show him who can pack light.

All I've got in this case is my makeup and shampoo—but Luke doesn't need to know that, does he?

"Yes, that's it," I say, raising my eyebrows slightly. "You did say 'pack light.' "

"So I did," says Luke. "But this—" He gestures at the case. "I'm impressed."

As he opens the boot, I get into the driving seat and adjust the seat forward so I can reach the pedals. I've always wanted to drive a convertible!

The boot slams behind me, and Luke comes round, a quizzical look on his face.

"You're driving, are you?"

"Part of the way, I thought," I say carelessly. "Just to

take the pressure off you. You know, it's very dangerous to drive for too long."

"You can drive, can you, in those shoes?" He's looking down at my clementine sandals—and I have to admit, the heel is a bit high for pedaling. But I'm not going to let him know that. "They're new, aren't they?" he adds, looking more closely at them.

And I'm about to say yes, when I remember that the last time I saw him, I had new shoes on—and the time before that, too. Which is really weird and must be one of those random cluster things.

"No!" I reply instead. "Actually, I've had them for ages. Actually . . ." I clear my throat. "They're my driving shoes."

"Your driving shoes," echoes Luke skeptically.

"Yes!" I say, and start the engine before he can say any more. God, this car is amazing! It makes a fantastic roaring sound, and a kind of screech as I move it into gear.

"Becky—"

"I'm fine!" I say, and slowly move off across the car park into the street. Oh, this is such a fantastic moment. I wonder if anybody's watching me. I wonder if Emma and Rory are looking out the window. And that sound guy who thinks he's so cool with his motorbike. He hasn't got a convertible, has he? Accidentally on purpose, I lean on the horn, and as the sound echoes round the car park I see at least three people turning to look. Ha! Look at me! Ha-ha-ha . . .

"My petal," says Luke beside me. "You're causing a traffic jam."

I glance into my rear mirror—and there are three cars creeping along behind me. Which is ridiculous, because I'm not going *that* slowly.

"Try moving it up a notch," suggests Luke. "Ten miles an hour, say?"

"I *am,*" I say crossly. "You can't expect me just to whiz off at a million miles an hour! There is a speed limit, you know."

I reach the exit, smile nonchalantly at the porter at the gate, who gives me a surprised look, and pull out into the road. I signal left and take a last glance back to check if anyone I know has just come out and is watching me admiringly. Then, as a car behind me starts to beep, I carefully pull in at the pavement.

"There we are," I say. "Your turn."

"My turn?" Luke stares at me. "Already?"

"I have to do my nails now," I explain. "And anyway, I know you think I can't drive. I don't want to have you pulling faces at me all the way down to Somerset."

"I do not think you can't drive," protests Luke, half-laughing. "When have I ever said that?"

"You don't need to say it. I can see it coming out of your head in a thought bubble: 'Becky Bloomwood cannot drive.' "

"Well, that's where you're wrong," retorts Luke. "The bubble actually reads: 'Becky Bloomwood cannot drive in her new orange shoes because the heels are too high and pointy.' "

He raises his eyebrows, and I feel myself flush slightly.

"They're my driving shoes," I mutter, shifting over to the passenger seat. "And I've had them for years."

As I reach into my bag for my nail file, Luke gets into the driver's seat, leans over, and gives me a kiss.

"Thank you for doing that stint, anyway," he says. "I'm sure it'll lessen my risk of fatigue on the motorway."

"Well, good!" I say, starting on my nails. "You need to conserve your energy for all those long country walks we're going to go on tomorrow."

There's silence, and after a while I look up.

"Yes," says Luke—and he isn't smiling anymore. "Becky . . . I was going to talk to you about tomorrow." He pauses and I stare at him, feeling my own smile fade slightly.

"What is it?" I say, trying not to sound anxious.

Luke exhales sharply. "Here's the thing. A business opportunity has arisen which I really would like to . . . to take advantage of. And there are some people over from the States who I need to talk to. Urgently."

"Oh," I say, a little uncertainly. "Well—that's OK. If you've got your phone with you . . ."

"Not by phone." He looks straight at me. "I've scheduled a meeting for tomorrow."

"Tomorrow?" I echo, and give a little laugh. "But you can't have a meeting. We'll be at the hotel."

"So will the people I need to talk to," says Luke. "I've invited them down."

I stare at him in shock.

"You've invited businesspeople down on our holiday?"

"Purely for the meeting," says Luke. "The rest of the time it'll just be the two of us."

"And how long will the meeting go on?" I exclaim. "Don't tell me! All day!"

I just can't believe it. After waiting all this time, after getting all excited, after all my packing . . .

"Becky, it won't be as bad as that . . ."

"You *promised* me you'd take time off! You said we'd have a lovely romantic time."

"We will have a lovely romantic time."

"With all your business friends. With all your horrible contacts, networking away like . . . like maggots!"

"They won't be networking with us," says Luke with a grin. "Becky—" He reaches for my hand, but I pull it away.

"To be honest, I don't see any point in my coming if it's just you doing business!" I say miserably. "I might as well just stay at home. In fact—" I open the car door. "In fact, I think I'll go home right now. I'll call a taxi from the studio."

I slam the car door and begin to stride off along the street, my clementine sandals making a click-clack sound against the hot pavement. And I've almost got to the studio gate before I hear his voice, raised so loud that several people turn to look.

"Becky! Wait there!"

I stop and slowly turn on the spot—to see him standing up in the car, dialing a number on his mobile phone.

"What are you doing?" I call suspiciously.

"I'm phoning my horrible business contact," says Luke. "To put him off. To cancel."

I fold my arms and stare at him with narrowed eyes.

"Hello?" he says. "Room 301, please. Michael Ellis. Thanks. I guess I'll just have to fly out and see him in Washington," he adds to me in deadpan tones. "Or wait until the next time he and his associates are all together in Britain. Which could be a while, bearing in mind their completely crazy schedules. Still, it's only business, after all. Only a deal. It's only the deal I've been wanting to make for . . ."

"Oh . . . stop it!" I say furiously. "Stop it. Have your stupid meeting."

"Are you sure?" says Luke, putting a hand over the receiver. "Absolutely sure?"

"Quite sure," I say, giving a morose shrug. "If it's *that* important . . ."

"It's pretty important," says Luke, and meets my eyes, suddenly serious. "Believe me, I wouldn't be doing it otherwise."

I walk slowly back to the car as Luke puts away his mobile phone.

"Thanks, Becky," he says as I get in. "I mean it." He touches my cheek gently, then reaches for the keys and starts up the engine.

As we drive off toward a set of traffic lights, I glance at him, and then at his mobile phone, still sticking out of his pocket.

"Were you *really* phoning your business contact?" I say.

"Were you really going home?" he replies, without moving his head.

This is what's so annoying about going out with Luke. You can't get away with anything.

We drive for about an hour into the countryside, stop for lunch in a little village pub, then drive for another hour and a half down to Somerset. By the time we reach Blakeley Hall, I feel like a different person. It's so good to get out of London—and I'm already incredibly energized and refreshed by all this wonderful country air. As I step out of the car I do a few stretches—and honestly, I already feel fitter and more toned. I reckon if I came to the country every week, I'd lose half a stone, if not more.

"Do you want any more of these?" says Luke, reaching down and picking up the nearly empty packet of Maltesers which I've been snacking on. (I have to eat in the car, otherwise I get carsick.) "And what about these magazines?" He picks up the stack of glossies which have been at my feet, then makes a grab as they all start slithering out of his hands.

"I'm not going to read magazines here!" I say in surprise. "This is the country!"

Honestly. Doesn't Luke know anything about rural life?

As he's getting the bags out of the boot I wander over to a fence and gaze peacefully at a field full of browny-yellow stuff. You know, I reckon I have a real natural affinity for the countryside. It's like I've got this whole nurturing, earth-mother side, which has been gradually creeping up on me. For example, the other day I found myself buying a Fair Isle jersey from French Connection. And I've recently started gardening! Or at least, I've bought some sweet little ceramic flowerpots from The Pier, marked "Basil" and "Coriander"—and I'm definitely going to get some of those little plants from the supermarket and have a whole row of them on the windowsill. (I mean, they're only about 50 pence, so if they die you can just buy another one.)

"Ready?" says Luke.

"Absolutely!" I say, and teeter back toward him, cursing the mud.

We crunch over the gravel to the hotel—and I have to say, I'm impressed. It's a great big old-fashioned country house, with beautiful gardens, and modern sculptures in the gardens and its own cinema, according to the brochure! Luke's been here quite a few times before, and he says it's his favorite hotel. And lots of celebrities come here, too! Like Madonna. (Or was it

Sporty Spice? Someone, anyway.) But apparently they're always very discreet and usually stay in some separate coach-housey bit, and the staff never lets on.

Still, as we go into the reception hall I have a good look around, just in case. There are lots of cool-looking people in trendy spectacles and denim, and there's a blond girl who sort of looks famous-ish, and standing over there . . .

I freeze in excitement. It's him, isn't it? It's Elton John! Elton John himself is standing right there, only a few—

Then he turns round—and it's just a dumpy guy in an anorak and spectacles. Damn. Still, it was *nearly* Elton John.

We've reached the reception desk by now, and a concierge in a trendy Nehru jacket smiles at us. "Good afternoon, Mr. Brandon," he says. "And Miss Bloomwood. Welcome to Blakeley Hall."

He knew our names! We didn't even have to tell him! No wonder celebrities come here.

"I've put you in room 9," he says, as Luke starts to fill in a form. "Overlooking the rose garden."

"Great," says Luke. "Becky, which paper would you like in the morning?"

"The *Financial Times*," I say smoothly.

"Of course," says Luke, writing. "So that's one *FT*—and a *Daily World* for me."

I give him a suspicious look, but his face is completely blank.

"Would you like tea in the morning?" says the concierge, tapping at his computer. "Or coffee?"

"Coffee, please," says Luke. "For both of us, I think." He looks at me questioningly, and I nod.

"You'll find a complimentary bottle of champagne in

your room," says the concierge, "and room service is available twenty-four hours."

I have to say I'm very impressed. This really is a top-class place. They know your face immediately, they give you champagne—and they haven't even mentioned my Special Express parcel yet. Obviously they realize it's a matter of discretion. They realize that a girl doesn't necessarily want her boyfriend knowing about every single package that is delivered to her—and are going to wait until Luke is out of earshot until they tell me about it. *This* is why it's worth coming to a good hotel.

"If there's anything else you require, Miss Bloomwood," says the concierge, looking at me meaningfully, "please don't hesitate to let me know."

You see? Coded messages and everything.

"I will, don't worry," I say, and give him a knowing smile. "In just a moment." I flick my eyes meaningfully toward Luke, and the concierge gives me a blank stare, exactly as though he's got no idea what I'm talking about. God, these people are good!

Eventually, Luke finishes the forms and hands them back. The concierge hands him a big, old-fashioned room key, and summons a porter.

"I don't think we need any help," says Luke, with a smile, and lifts up my dinky suitcase. "I'm not exactly overburdened."

"You go on up," I say. "I just want to . . . check something. For tomorrow." I smile at Luke and after a moment, to my relief, he heads off toward the staircase.

As soon as he's out of earshot, I swivel back to the desk.

"I'll take it now," I murmur to the concierge, who has turned away and is looking in a drawer. He raises his head and looks at me in surprise.

"I'm sorry, Miss Bloomwood?"

"It's OK," I say more meaningfully. "You can give it to me now. While Luke's gone."

A flicker of apprehension passes over the concierge's face.

"What exactly—"

"You can give me my package." I lower my voice. "And thanks for not letting on."

"Your . . . package?"

"My Special Express."

"What Special Express?"

I stare at him, feeling a few misgivings.

"The parcel with all my clothes in it! The one you weren't mentioning! The one . . ."

I tail away at the sight of his face. He doesn't have a clue what I'm talking about, does he? OK. Don't panic. Someone else will know where it is.

"I should have a parcel waiting for me," I explain. "About this big . . . It should have arrived this morning . . ."

The concierge is shaking his head.

"I'm sorry, Miss Bloomwood. There aren't any packages for you."

Suddenly I feel a little hollow.

"But . . . there has to be a package. I sent it by Special Express, yesterday. To Blakeley Hall."

The concierge frowns.

"Charlotte?" he says, calling into a back room. "Has a parcel arrived for Rebecca Bloomwood?"

"No," says Charlotte, coming out. "When was it supposed to arrive?"

"This morning!" I say, trying to hide my agitation. " 'Anything, anywhere, by tomorrow morning'! I mean, this is anywhere, isn't it?"

"I'm sorry," says Charlotte, "but nothing's come. Was it very important?"

"Rebecca?" comes a voice from the stairs, and I turn to see Luke peering down at me. "Is something wrong?"

"No!" I say brightly. "Of course not! What on earth could be wrong?" Quickly I swivel away from the desk and, before Charlotte or the concierge can say anything, hurry toward the stairs.

"Everything all right?" he says as I reach him, and smiles at me.

"Absolutely!" I say, my voice two notches higher than usual. "Everything's absolutely fine!"

I have no clothes. This cannot be happening.

I'm on holiday with Luke, in a smart hotel—and I have no clothes. What am I going to do?

I can't tell him the truth. I just *can't* admit that my dinky suitcase was only the tip of the clothes-berg. Not after having been so smug about it. I'll just have to . . . improvise, I think wildly, as we turn a corner and start walking down another plushy corridor. Wear *his* clothes, like Annie Hall or . . . or rip down the curtains and find some sewing stuff . . . and quickly learn how to sew . . .

Calm down, I tell myself firmly. Just . . . calm down. The parcel is bound to arrive tomorrow morning, so I've only got to last one night. And at least I've got my makeup with me . . .

"Here we are," says Luke, stopping at a door and opening it. "What do you think?"

Oh wow. For a moment all my worries are swept away as I gaze around the enormous airy room. Now I can see why Luke likes this hotel so much. It's gorgeous—exactly like his flat, all huge white bed with an enormous waffle duvet, and a state-of-the-art music system and two suede sofas.

"Take a look at the bathroom," says Luke, and I follow him through—and it's stunning. A great sunken mosaic Jacuzzi, with the hugest shower I've ever seen above, and a whole rack of gorgeous-looking aromatherapy oils.

Maybe I could just spend the whole weekend in the bath.

"So," he says, turning back into the room. "I don't know what you'd like to do . . ." He walks over to his suitcase and clicks it open—and I can see serried rows of shirts, all ironed by his housekeeper. "I suppose we should unpack first . . ."

"Unpack! Absolutely!" I say brightly. I walk over to my own little suitcase and finger the clasp, without opening it. "Or else . . ." I say, as though the idea's just occurring to me, "why don't we go and have a drink—and unpack later!"

Genius. We'll go downstairs and get really pissed, and then tomorrow morning I'll just pretend to be really sleepy and stay in bed until my package comes. Thank God. For a moment there I was starting to—

"Excellent idea," says Luke. "I'll just get changed." And he reaches into his case and pulls out a pair of trousers and a crisp blue shirt.

"Changed?" I say after a pause. "Is there . . . a strict dress code?"

"Oh no, not strict," says Luke. "You just wouldn't go down in . . . say, in what you're wearing at the moment." He gestures to my denim cutoffs with a grin.

"Of course not!" I say, laughing as though the idea's ridiculous. "Right. Well. I'll just . . . choose an outfit, then."

I turn to my case again, snap it open, lift the lid, and look at my makeup bag.

What am I going to do? Luke's unbuttoning his shirt. He's calmly reaching for the blue one. In a minute he's going to look up and say, "Are you ready?"

I need a radical plan of action here.

"Luke—I've changed my mind," I say, and close the lid of my case. "Let's not go down to the bar." Luke looks up in surprise, and I give him the most seductive smile I can muster. "Let's stay up here, and order room service, and . . ." I take a few steps toward him, loosening my wrap top, ". . . and see where the night leads us."

Luke stares at me, his hands still halfway up the buttons of his blue shirt.

"Take that off," I say huskily. "What's the point of dressing up when all we want to do is undress each other?"

A slow smile spreads across Luke's face, and his eyes begin to gleam.

"You're so right," he says, and walks toward me, unbuttoning his shirt and letting it fall to the floor. "I don't know what I was thinking of."

Thank God! I think in relief, as he reaches for my wrap top and gently starts to untie it. This is perfect. This is exactly what I—

Ooh. Mmm.

Actually, this *is* pretty bloody perfect.

Four

By EIGHT THIRTY the next morning, I still haven't got up. I don't want to move an inch. I want to stay in this lovely comfortable bed, wrapped up in this gorgeous white waffle duvet.

"Are you staying there all day?" says Luke, smiling at me. "Not that I don't want to join you." He kisses me on the forehead and I snuggle down in the pillows without replying. I just don't want to get up. I'm so cozy and warm and happy here.

Plus—just a very small point—I still don't have any clothes.

I've already secretly rung down to reception three times about my Special Express. (Once while Luke was in the shower, once while I was in the shower—from the posh bathroom phone—and once very quickly when I sent Luke into the corridor because I said I heard a cat meowing.)

And it hasn't arrived. I have nil clothes. Nada.

Which hasn't mattered up until now, because I've just been lounging around in bed. But I can't possibly eat any more croissants or drink any more coffee, nor can I have another shower, and Luke's half-dressed already.

I'm just going to have to put on yesterday's clothes again. Which is really hideous, but what else can I do? I'll just pretend I'm sentimental about them, or maybe hope I can slip them on and Luke won't even realize. I mean, do men really *notice* what you . . .

Hang on.

Hang on a minute. Where *are* yesterday's clothes? I'm sure I dropped them just there on the floor . . .

"Luke?" I say, as casually as possible. "Have you seen the clothes I was wearing yesterday?"

"Oh yes," he says, glancing up from his suitcase. "I sent them to the laundry this morning, along with my stuff."

I stare at him, unable to breathe.

My only clothes in the whole world have *gone to the laundry*?

"When . . . when will they be back?" I say at last.

"Tomorrow morning." Luke turns to look at me. "Sorry, I should have said. But it's not a problem, is it? I mean, I don't think you have to worry. They do an excellent job."

"Oh no!" I say in a high, brittle voice. "No, I'm not worried!"

"Good," he says, and smiles.

"Good," I say, and smile back.

What am I going to do?

"Oh, and there's plenty of room in the wardrobe," says Luke, "if you want me to hang anything up." He reaches toward my little case and in a panic, I hear myself crying "Nooo!" before I can stop myself. "It's all right," I add, as he looks at me in surprise. "My clothes are mostly . . . knitwear."

Oh God. Oh God. Now he's putting on his shoes. *What am I going to do?*

OK, come on, Becky, I think frantically. Clothes. Something to wear. Doesn't matter what.

One of Luke's suits?

No. He'll just think it's too weird, and anyway, his suits all cost about £1,000 so I won't be able to roll the sleeves up.

My hotel robe? Pretend robes and waffle slippers are the latest fashion? Oh, but I can't walk around in a dressing gown as if I think I'm in a spa. Everyone will laugh at me.

Come on, there *must* be clothes in a hotel. What about . . . the chambermaids' uniforms! Yes, that's more like it! They must keep a rack of them somewhere, mustn't they? Neat little dresses with matching hats. I could tell Luke they're the latest thing from Prada—and just hope no one asks me to clear out their room . . .

"By the way," says Luke, reaching into his case, "you left this behind at my flat."

And as I look up, startled, he chucks something across the room at me. It's soft, it's fabric . . . as I catch it, I want to weep with relief. It's clothes! A single oversized Calvin Klein T-shirt, to be precise. I have never been so glad to see a plain washed-out gray T-shirt in my life.

"Thanks!" I say. And I force myself to count to ten before I add casually, "Actually, maybe I'll wear this today."

"That?" says Luke, giving me a strange look. "I thought it was a nightshirt."

"It is! It's a nightshirt-slash-dress," I say, popping it over my head—and thank God, it comes to halfway down my thighs. It could easily be a dress. And ha! I've got a stretchy black headband in my makeup bag, which just about fits me as a belt.

"Very nice," says Luke quizzically, watching me wriggle into it. "A *little* on the short side . . ."

"It's a minidress," I say firmly, and turn to look at my reflection. And . . . oh God, it is a bit short. But it's too late to do anything about that now. I step into my clementine sandals and shake back my hair, not allowing myself to think about all the great outfits I had planned for this morning.

"Here," says Luke. He reaches for my Denny and George scarf and winds it slowly round my neck. "Denny and George scarf, no knickers. Just the way I like it."

"I'm going to wear knickers!" I say indignantly.

Which is true. I'll wait till Luke's gone, then pinch a pair of his boxer shorts.

"So—what's your deal about?" I ask hurriedly, to change the subject. "Something exciting?"

"It's . . . pretty big," says Luke after a pause. He holds up a pair of silk ties. "Which one will bring me luck?"

"The red one," I say after a little consideration. "It matches your eyes."

"It matches my eyes?" Luke starts to laugh. "Do I look that rough?"

"It *goes* with your eyes. You know what I mean."

"No, you were right first time," says Luke, peering into the mirror. "It matches my eyes perfectly." He glances at me. "You'd almost think I'd had no sleep last night."

"No sleep?" I raise my eyebrows. "Before an important meeting? Surely that's not the way Luke Brandon behaves."

"Very irresponsible," agrees Luke, putting the tie round his neck. "Must be thinking of someone else."

I watch as he knots the tie with brisk, efficient movements. "So come on—tell me about this deal. Is it a big new client?"

But Luke smiles and shakes his head.

"Is it Nat West? I know, Lloyds Bank!"

"Let's just say . . . it's something I want very much," Luke says eventually. "Something I've always wanted. But this is all very boring," he adds in a different tone.

"No, it's not!"

"Very dull indeed. Now—what are you going to do today? Will you be all right?" And now he sounds like *he's* changing the subject.

Actually, I think Luke's a bit sensitive about boring me with his work. Don't get me wrong, I think his business is really fascinating. But there was this one occasion when it was really late at night, and he was telling me about a new range of technical products he was going to represent and I kind of . . . fell asleep.

I think he took it to heart, because recently he's hardly talked about work at all.

"Have you heard the pool is closed this morning?" he says.

"I know," I say, reaching for my blusher. "But that doesn't matter. I'll easily amuse myself."

There's silence and I look up to see Luke surveying me doubtfully.

"Would you like me to order you a taxi to take you to the shops? Bath is quite near here—"

"No," I say indignantly. "I don't want to go shopping!"

Which is true. When Suze found out how much those clementine sandals were, she got all worried that she hadn't been strict enough with me, so I promised not to do any shopping this weekend. She made me cross my heart and swear on—well, on my clementine sandals, actually. And I'm going to make a real effort to keep to it.

I mean, I should be able to last forty-eight hours.

"I'm going to do all lovely rural things," I say, snapping my blusher closed.

"Like . . ."

"Like look at the scenery . . . and maybe go to a farm and watch them milking the cows, or something . . ."

"I see."

"What?" I say suspiciously. "What's that supposed to mean?"

"You're just going to pitch up at a farm, are you, and ask if you can milk the cows?"

"I didn't say *I* was going to milk the cows," I say with dignity. "I said I was going to *watch* the cows. And anyway, I might not go to a farm, I might go and look at some local attractions." I reach for a pile of leaflets on the dressing table. "Like . . . this tractor exhibition. Or . . . St. Winifred's Convent with its famous Bevington Triptych."

"A convent," echoes Luke after a pause.

"Yes, a convent!" I give him an indignant look. "Why shouldn't I visit a convent? I'm actually a very spiritual person."

"I'm sure you are, my darling," says Luke, giving me a quizzical look. "You *might* want to put on more than a T-shirt before you go . . ."

"It's a dress!" I say indignantly, pulling the T-shirt down over my bum. "And anyway, spirituality has nothing to do with clothes. 'Consider the lilies of the field.' " I shoot him a satisfied glance.

"Fair enough." Luke grins. "Well, enjoy yourself." He gives me a kiss. "And Becky, I really am sorry about all this. This wasn't the way I wanted our first weekend away to be."

"Yeah, well," I say, and give him a little poke in the

chest. "You just make sure this mysterious deal is worth it."

And I'm expecting Luke to laugh, or at least smile—but he just gives me a tiny nod, picks up his briefcase, and heads for the door.

I don't actually mind having this morning to myself, because I've always secretly wanted to see what it's like inside a convent. I mean, I know I don't exactly make it to church every week, but I do have a very spiritual side to me. It seems obvious to me that there's a greater force out there at work than us mere mortals—which is why I always read my horoscope in *The Daily World*. Plus I love that plainchant they play in yoga classes, and all the lovely candles and incense. And Audrey Hepburn in *The Nun's Story*.

In fact, to tell you the truth, a part of me has always been attracted to the simplicity of a nun's life. No worries, no decisions, no having to work. Just lovely singing and walking around all day. I mean, wouldn't that be great?

So when I've done my makeup and watched a bit of telly, I go down to reception—and after asking fruitlessly again about my package (honestly, I'm going to sue), I order a taxi to St. Winifred's. As we trundle along the country lanes, I look out at all the lovely scenery, and find myself wondering what Luke's deal can be about. What on earth is this mysterious "something he's always wanted"? I mean, I would have thought he's already got everything he wants. He's the most successful publicist in the financial field, he's got a thriving company, he's won loads of prizes . . . So what could it be?

Big new client? New offices? Expanding the company, maybe?

I screw up my face, trying to remember if I've over-heard anything recently—then, with a jolt, I remember hearing him on the phone a few weeks ago. He was talking about an advertising agency, and even at the time, I wondered why.

Yes. It's obvious, now that I think about it. He's always secretly wanted to be an ad director. That's what this deal is all about. He's going to branch out from PR and start making adverts.

And I could be in them! Yes!

I'm so excited at this thought, I almost swallow my chewing gum. I can be in an ad! Oh, this is going to be *so* cool. Maybe I'll be in one of those Bacardi ads where they're all on a boat, laughing and water-skiing and having a great time. I mean, I know it's usually fashion models, but I could easily be somewhere in the back-ground. Or I could be the one driving the boat. It'll be so fantastic. We'll fly out to Barbados or somewhere, and it'll be all hot and sunny and glamorous, with loads of free Bacardi, and we'll stay in a really amazing ho-tel . . . I'll have to buy a new bikini, of course . . . or maybe two . . . and some new flip-flops . . .

"St. Winifred's," says the taxi driver—and with a start I come to. I'm not in Barbados, am I? I'm in the middle of bloody nowhere, in Somerset.

We've stopped outside an old honey-colored build-ing, and I peer through the window curiously. So this is a convent. It doesn't look that special, actually—just like a school, or a big country house. And I'm wonder-ing whether I should even bother getting out, when I see a nun. Walking past, in black robes, and a wimple, and everything! A real live nun, in her real habitat. And she's completely natural. She hasn't even *looked* at the taxi. This is like being on safari!

I get out and pay the driver—and as I walk toward the heavy front door, I feel prickles of intrigue. There's an elderly woman going in at the same time who seems to know the way, so I follow her along a corridor toward the chapel. And as we walk in, I feel this amazing, holy, almost euphoric sensation coming over me. Maybe it's the lovely smell in the air or the organ music, but I'm definitely getting something.

"Thank you, Sister," says the elderly woman to the nun. And she starts walking off to the front of the chapel—but I stand still, slightly transfixed.

Sister. Wow.

Sister Rebecca.

And one of those lovely flowing black habits, and a fantastic clear nun complexion all the time.

Sister Rebecca of the Holy . . .

"You look a little lost, my dear," a nun says behind me, and I jump. "Were you interested in seeing the Bevington Triptych?"

"Oh," I say. "Erm . . . yes. Absolutely."

"Up there," she points, and I walk tentatively toward the front of the chapel, hoping it will become obvious what the Bevington Triptych is. A statue, maybe? Or a . . . a piece of tapestry?

But as I reach the elderly lady, I see that she's staring up at a whole wall of stained-glass windows. And I have to admit, they're pretty amazing. I mean, look at that huge blue one in the middle. It's fantastic!

"The Bevington Triptych," says the elderly woman. "It simply has no parallel, does it?"

"Wow," I breathe reverentially, staring up with her. "It's beautiful."

And it really is stunning. It just shows, there's no mistaking a real work of art, is there? Real genius just leaps out at you. And I'm not even an expert.

"Wonderful colors," I murmur.

"The detail," says the woman, clasping her hands, "is absolutely incomparable."

"Incomparable," I echo.

And I'm just about to point out the rainbow, which I think is a really nice touch—when I suddenly notice that the elderly woman and I aren't looking at the same window. She's looking at a much smaller, dingier one which I hadn't even noticed.

As inconspicuously as possible, I shift my gaze to the right one—and feel a pang of disappointment. Is *this* the Bevington Triptych? But it isn't even pretty!

"Whereas this Victorian rubbish," the woman suddenly adds savagely, "is absolutely criminal! That rainbow! Doesn't it make you feel sick?" She gestures to my big blue window, and I gulp.

"I know," I say. "It's shocking, isn't it? Absolutely . . . You know, I think I'll just go for a little wander . . ."

Hastily I back away, before she can say any more. And I'm sidling back down the side of the pews, wondering vaguely what to do next, when suddenly I notice a little side chapel in the corner.

Spiritual retreat, reads a notice outside. *A place to sit quietly, pray, and discover more about the Catholic faith.*

Cautiously I poke my head inside the side chapel—and there's an old nun, sitting on a chair, doing embroidery. She smiles at me, and nervously I smile back and walk inside.

I sit down on a dark wooden pew, trying not to make any creaking sounds, and for a while I'm too awestruck to say anything. This is just amazing. The atmosphere is fantastic, all quiet and still—and I feel incredibly cleansed and holy just from being here. I smile again at the nun, shyly, and she puts down her embroidery and looks at me as though waiting for me to speak.

"I really like your candles," I say in a quiet, reverent voice. "Are they from Habitat?"

"No," says the nun, looking a bit startled. "I don't believe so."

"Oh right."

I give a tiny yawn—because I'm still sleepy from all this country air—and as I do so, I notice that one of my nails has chipped. So very quietly, I unzip my bag, get out my nail file, and start to buff it. The nun looks up, and I give her a rueful smile, and point to my nail (silently, because I don't want to ruin the spiritual atmosphere). Then, when I've finished, the edge is looking a bit ragged, so I take out my Maybelline express dry polish and very quickly touch it up.

All the while, the nun is watching me with a perplexed expression, and as I'm finishing, she says, "My dear, are you a Catholic?"

"No, I'm not, actually," I say.

"Was there anything you wanted to talk about?"

"Um . . . not really." I run my hand fondly over the pew I'm sitting on, and give her a friendly smile. "This carving is really nice, isn't it. Is all your furniture as nice as this?"

"This is the chapel," says the nun, giving me a strange look.

"Oh, I know! But you know, loads of people have pews in their houses, too, these days. I saw this article in *Harpers*—"

"My child . . ." The nun lifts a hand to interrupt me. "My child, this is a place of spiritual retreat. Of quietness."

"I know!" I say in surprise. "That's why I came in. For quietness."

"Good," says the nun, and we lapse into silence again.

In the distance, a bell starts tolling, and I notice the nun begins murmuring very quietly under her breath. I wonder what she's saying? My granny used to knit things, and mutter the pattern to herself. Maybe she's lost track of her embroidery.

"Your sewing's going really well," I say encouragingly. "What's it going to be?" She gives a tiny start, and puts down her embroidery.

"My dear," she says, and exhales sharply. Then she gives me a warm smile. "My dear, we have some quite famous lavender fields. Would you like to go and see them?"

"No, it's all right." I beam at her. "I'm just happy, sitting here with you."

The nun's smile wavers slightly. "What about the crypt?" she says. "Would you be interested in that?"

"Not particularly. But honestly, I'm not bored! It's just so lovely here. So . . . tranquil. Just like *The Sound of Music*."

She stares at me as though I'm speaking gibberish, and I realize she's probably been in the convent so long, she doesn't know what *The Sound of Music* is.

"There was this film . . ." I start to explain. Then it occurs to me, maybe she doesn't know what a film is, even. "It's like, moving pictures," I say carefully. "You watch it on a screen. And there was this nun called Maria . . ."

"We have a shop," interrupts the nun urgently. "A shop. What about that?"

A shop! For a moment I feel all excited, and want to ask what they sell. But then I remember the promise I made to Suze.

"I can't," I say regretfully. "I told my flatmate I wouldn't go shopping today."

"Your flatmate?" says the nun. "What does she have to do with it?"

"She just gets really worried about me spending money—"

"Does your flatmate run your life?"

"Well, it's just I made her this quite serious promise a while ago. You know, a bit like a vow, I suppose . . ."

"She'll never know!" says the nun. "Not if you don't tell her."

I stare at her, a bit taken aback.

"But I'd feel really bad, breaking my promise! No, I'll just stay here with you for a bit longer, if that's OK." I pick up a little statue of Mary which has caught my eye. "This is nice. Where did you get it?"

The nun stares at me, her eyes narrowing.

"Don't think of it as shopping," she says at last. "Think of it as making a donation." She leans forward. "You donate the money—and we give you a little something in return. You couldn't really count it as shopping at all. More . . . an act of charity."

I'm silent for a few moments, letting this idea sink in. The truth is, I do always mean to do more for charity, and maybe this is my chance.

"So, it'll be like doing a good deed?" I say, just to be sure.

"Exactly the same. And Jesus and all his angels will bless you for it." She takes hold of my arm. "Now, you go along and have a browse. Come on, I'll show you the way . . ."

As we leave the side chapel, the nun shuts the door and takes down the Spiritual Retreat notice.

"Aren't you coming back?" I say in surprise.

"Not today, no," she says, and gives me an odd look. "I think I'll leave it for today."

You know, it's just like they say—virtue is its own reward. As I arrive back at the hotel later that afternoon, I'm glowing with happiness at all the good I've done. I must have donated at least £50 in that shop, if not more! In fact, not to show off or anything, but I'm obviously naturally very altruistic. Because once I started donating, I couldn't stop! Each time I parted with a bit more money, I felt a real high. And although it's a completely incidental point, I ended up with some really nice stuff in return. Lots of lavender honey, and lavender essential oil, and some lavender tea, which I'm sure will be delicious, and a lavender pillow to help me sleep.

The amazing thing is, I'd never really given lavender much thought before. I just thought of it as a plant in people's gardens. But that young nun behind the table was quite right—it has such vital, life-enhancing properties that it should be part of everyone's life. Plus St. Winifred's lavender is completely organic, she explained, so it's vastly superior to other varieties, but the prices are much lower than many competing mail-order catalogues. She was the one who persuaded me to buy the lavender pillow, actually, and to put my name on the mailing list. She was really quite persistent, for a nun.

When I get back to Blakeley Hall, the minicab driver offers to help me lug it all in, because the box of lavender honey is quite heavy. And I'm standing at the reception desk, giving him a nice hefty tip and thinking I might go and have a nice bath with my new lavender bath essence . . . when the front door into reception swings open. Into the hotel strides a girl with blond hair, a Louis Vuitton bag, and long tanned legs.

I stare at her in disbelief. It's Alicia Billington. Or, as I call her, Alicia Bitch Longlegs. What's *she* doing here?

Alicia is one of the account executives in Brandon Communications—which is Luke's PR company—and we've never exactly got along. In fact, between you and me, she's a bit of a cow and, secretly, I wish Luke would fire her. A few months ago, actually, she nearly did get fired—and it was kind of to do with me. (I was a financial journalist then, and I wrote this piece . . . oh, it's a bit of a long story.) But in the end she just got a stiff warning, and since then, she's really pulled her socks up.

I know all this because I have little chats every now and then with Luke's assistant, Mel, who's a real sweetie and keeps me up on all the gossip. She was telling me only the other day that she reckons Alicia's really changed. She isn't any *nicer,* but she certainly works harder. She badgers journalists until they put her clients into their stories, and often stays really late at the office, tapping at her computer. And only the other day she told Mel she wanted a full list of all the company's clients, with contact names, so she could familiarize herself with them. Plus she wrote some company strategy report which Luke was really impressed by. Mel added gloomily that she reckons Alicia wants a promotion—and I think she could be right.

The trouble with Luke is, he only looks at how hard a person works and what results they get—and not at what a completely horrible cow they are. In fact, just the other day I heard him telling someone how reliable Alicia was in stressful situations and how he's really starting to depend on her. So the chances are, she probably will get a promotion—and become even more unbearable.

As I watch her come in, I'm slightly transfixed. Half of me wants to run away and half of me wants to know what she's doing here. But before I can decide, she spots me, and raises her eyebrows slightly. And oh God, suddenly I realize what I must look like—in a grotty old gray T-shirt that, to be honest, looks nothing like a dress, and my hair a mess, and my face all red from lugging carrier bags full of lavender honey. And she's in an immaculate white suit.

"Rebecca!" she says, and puts her hand over her mouth in mock dismay. "You're not supposed to know I'm here! Just pretend you haven't seen me."

"What . . . what do you mean?" I say, trying not to sound as disconcerted as I feel. "What *are* you doing here?"

"I've just popped in for a quick introductory meeting with the new associates," says Alicia. "You know my parents only live five miles away? So it made sense."

"Oh right," I say. "No, I didn't."

"But Luke's given us all *strict* instructions," says Alicia, "we're not allowed to bother you. After all, this is your holiday!"

And there's something about the way she says it that makes me feel like a child.

"Oh, I don't mind," I say robustly. "When something as . . . as important as this is going on. In fact, Luke and I were talking about it earlier on actually. Over breakfast."

OK, so I only mentioned breakfast to remind her that Luke and I are going out together. Which I *know* is really pathetic. But somehow, whenever I'm talking to

Alicia, I feel we're in some secret little competition, and if I don't fight back, she'll think she's won.

"Really?" says Alicia. "How sweet." Her eyes narrow slightly. "So—what do you think of this whole enterprise? You must have an opinion."

"I think it's great," I say after a pause. "Really great."

"You don't mind?" Her eyes are probing my face.

"Well . . . not really." I shrug. "I mean, it was supposed to be a holiday, but if it's that important—"

"I don't mean the meetings!" says Alicia, laughing a little. "I mean—this whole deal. The whole New York thing."

I open my mouth to reply—then feebly close it again. What New York thing?

And like a buzzard sensing weakness, she leans forward, a tiny, malicious smile at her lips. "You do *know*, don't you, Rebecca, that Luke's going to move to New York?"

I can't move for shock. That's what he's so excited about. Luke's moving to New York. But . . . but why hasn't he told me?

My face feels rather hot and there's a horrible thickening in my chest. He's going to New York and he hasn't even told me.

"Rebecca?"

My head jerks up, and I quickly force a smile onto my face. I can't let Alicia realize this is all news to me. I just *can't*.

"Of course I know about it," I say huskily, and clear my throat. "I know all about it. But I . . . I never discuss business in public. Much better to be discreet, don't you think?"

"Oh, absolutely," she answers—and the way she looks at me makes me think she isn't convinced for a minute. "So . . . will you be going out there too?"

I stare back, my lips trembling, unable to think of an answer, my face growing pinker and pinker—when suddenly, thank God, a voice behind me says, "Rebecca Bloomwood. Parcel for a Miss Rebecca Bloomwood."

My head jerks round in astonishment, and, I don't believe it. A man in uniform is approaching the desk, holding my huge, battered Special Express parcel, which I'd honestly given up for lost. All my things, at last. All my carefully chosen outfits. I can wear anything I like tonight!

But somehow . . . I don't really care anymore. I just want to go off somewhere and be on my own and think for a bit.

"That's me," I say, managing a smile. "I'm Rebecca Bloomwood."

"Oh right!" says the man. "That's nice and easy then. If you could just sign here . . ."

"Well, I mustn't keep you!" exclaims Alicia, eyeing my parcel amusedly. "Enjoy the rest of your stay, won't you?"

"Thanks," I reply. "I will." And, feeling slightly numb, I walk away, clutching my clothes tightly to me.

I go up to our room, dump the parcel on the bed, and sit down next to it, trying to keep perspective on this. OK, let's just go over the facts. Luke's making plans to move to New York. And he hasn't told me.

Yet. He hasn't told me *yet.*

As I think this through, my numbness starts to melt away. Of course. He's probably planning to tell me everything this evening. Waiting for the right moment. That's probably why he brought me here in the first place. He couldn't know that Alicia would stick her oar in, could he?

Feeling better already, I reach for a complimentary packet of biscuits, tear it open, and begin to munch one. It's like they say, don't run before you can walk. Don't cross bridges before you come to them. Don't do . . . that other thing you shouldn't do.

I've just finished my third biscuit and have switched on the television to watch *Ready Steady Cook*, when the door opens and Luke comes in. His eyes are sparkling and he seems full of a suppressed energy. I stare at him, feeling a little weird.

I'm sure he's going to tell me. He wouldn't just move to America without saying anything.

"Did your meetings go well?" I say, my voice feeling false.

"Very well, thanks," says Luke, taking off his tie and throwing it on the bed. "But let's not talk about that." He smiles at me. "Did you have a good day?"

"Fine, thanks!"

"You want to go for a walk? Come on. I haven't seen you all day." He reaches for my hand, pulls me up off the bed, and puts his arms round my waist. "I've missed you," he says against my hair, and his arms tighten around my body.

"Have you?" I give a little laugh. "Well, you know . . . perhaps I should come to your meetings, and hear what they're all about!"

"You wouldn't enjoy them," says Luke, returning my laugh. "Come on, let's go out."

We head down the stairs and out the heavy front door and start walking over the grass toward a group of trees. The sun is still warm, and some people are playing croquet and drinking Pimms. After a while I take off my sandals and walk along barefoot, feeling myself relax.

"Are you hungry?" says Luke casually as we get near a large oak tree. And I'm about to reply, "No, I've just had three biscuits" when I see it, waiting for us in the long grass.

A red-and-white checked picnic blanket. A little wicker hamper. And . . . is that a bottle of champagne? I turn toward Luke in disbelief.

"Is this . . . did you . . ."

"This," says Luke, touching my cheek, "is in some small way to make up. You've been so incredibly understanding, Becky."

"That's all right," I say awkwardly. "If it was for something as important as . . ." I hesitate. "As . . . well, whatever amazing opportunity this might be . . ."

I look at Luke expectantly. This is the perfect moment for him to tell me.

"Even so," says Luke. He moves away and reaches for the champagne bottle and I sit down, trying not to give away my disappointment.

I'm not going to ask him. If he wants to tell me he can. If he doesn't want to . . . then he must have his reasons.

But there's no harm in prompting him, is there?

"I love the countryside!" I exclaim as Luke hands me my champagne. "And I love cities, too." I gesture vaguely in the air. "London . . . Paris . . ."

"Cheers," says Luke, raising his glass.

"Cheers." I take a sip of champagne and think quickly. "So . . . um . . . you've never really told me much about your family."

Luke looks up, a bit surprised.

"Haven't I? Well, there's me and my sister . . . and Mum and Dad . . ."

"And your real mother, of course." Casual, Becky. Casual. "I've always thought she sounds really interesting."

"She's a truly inspiring person," says Luke, his face lighting up. "So elegant . . . you've seen the picture of her?"

"She looks beautiful," I nod encouragingly. "And where is it she lives again?" I wrinkle my brow as though I can't quite remember.

"New York," says Luke, and takes a swig of his drink.

There's a taut silence. Luke stares ahead, frowning slightly, and I watch him, my heart thumping. Then he turns to me, and I feel a spasm of fright. What's he going to say? Is he going to tell me he's moving thousands of miles away?

"Becky?"

"Yes?" I say, my voice half-strangled by nerves.

"I really think you and my mother would love each other. Next time she's in London, I'll be sure to introduce you."

"Oh . . . right," I say. "That would be really great." And morosely, I drain my glass.

Ms. Rebecca Bloomwood
Flat 2
4 Burney Rd.
London SW6 8FD

8 September 2000

Dear Ms. Bloomwood:

Thank you for your letter of 4 September, addressed to
Sweetie Smeathie, in which you ask him to rush through
an extension of your overdraft "before the new guy arrives."

I am the new guy.

I am currently reviewing all customer files and will be in
touch regarding your request.

Yours sincerely,

John Gavin
Overdraft Facilities Director

Five

WE ARRIVE BACK in London the next day—and Luke still hasn't mentioned his deal or New York, or anything. And I know I should just ask him outright. I should casually say, "So what's this I hear about New York, Luke?" and wait and see what he says. But somehow I can't bring myself to do it.

I mean, for a start, he's made it plain enough that he doesn't want to talk about it. If I confront him, he might think I've been trying to find out stuff behind his back. And for another start, Alicia might have got it wrong—or even be making it up. (She's quite capable of it, believe me. When I was a financial journalist she once sent me to the completely wrong room for a press conference—and I'm sure it was deliberate.) So until I'm absolutely certain of my facts, there's no point saying anything.

At least, this is what I tell myself. But I suppose if I'm really honest, the reason is that I just can't bear the idea of Luke turning to me and giving me a kind look and saying, "Rebecca, we've had a lot of fun, but . . ."

So I end up saying nothing and smiling a lot—even though inside, I feel more and more miserable. As we arrive back outside my flat, I want to turn to him and wail, "Are you going to New York? Are you?"

But instead, I give him a kiss, and say lightly, "You will be OK for Saturday, won't you?"

It turns out Luke's got to fly off to Zurich tomorrow and have lots of meetings with finance people. Which of course is very important and I completely understand that. But Saturday is Tom and Lucy's wedding at home, and that's even more important. He just *has* to be there.

"I'll make it," he says. "I promise." He squeezes my hand and I get out of the car and he says he has to shoot off. And then he's gone.

Disconsolately, I open the door to our flat, and a moment later Suze comes out the door of her room, dragging a full black bin liner along the ground.

"Hi!" she says. "You're back!"

"Yes!" I reply, trying to sound cheerful. "I'm back!"

Suze disappears out our door, and I hear her lugging her black bag down the stairs and out of the main front door—then bounding up to our flat again.

"So, how was it?" she says breathlessly, closing the door behind her.

"It was fine," I say, walking into my bedroom. "It was . . . nice."

"Nice?" Suze's eyes narrow and she follows me in. "Only nice?"

"It was . . . good."

"*Good*? Bex, what's wrong? Didn't you have a lovely time?"

I wasn't really planning to say anything to Suze, because after all, I don't know the facts yet. Plus I read in a magazine recently that couples should try to sort their problems out alone, without recourse to others. But as I look at her warm, friendly face, I just can't help it, I hear myself blurting out, "Luke's moving to New York."

"Really?" says Suze, missing the point. "Fantastic! God, I love New York. I went there three years ago, and—"

"Suze, he's moving to New York—but he hasn't told me."

"Oh," says Suze, looking taken aback. "Oh, right."

"And I don't want to bring it up, because I'm not supposed to know, but I keep thinking, why hasn't he told me? Is he just going to . . . *go*?" My voice is rising in distress. "Will I just get a postcard from the Empire State Building saying 'Hi, I live in New York now, love Luke'?"

"No!" says Suze at once. "Of course not! He wouldn't do that!"

"Wouldn't he?"

"No. Definitely not." Suze folds her arms and thinks for a few moments—then looks up. "Are you absolutely sure he hasn't told you? Like, maybe when you were half asleep or daydreaming or something?"

She looks at me expectantly and for a few moments I think hard, wondering if she could be right. Maybe he told me in the car and I just wasn't listening. Or last night, while I was eyeing up that girl's Lulu Guinness handbag in the bar . . . But then I shake my head.

"No. I'm sure I'd remember if he'd mentioned New York." I sink down miserably onto the bed. "He's just not telling me because he's going to chuck me."

"No, he's not!" retorts Suze. "Honestly, Bex, men never mention things. That's just what they're like." She picks her way over a pile of CDs and sits cross-legged on the bed beside me. "My brother never mentioned when he got done for drugs. We had to find it out from the paper! And my father once bought a whole island without telling my mother."

"Really?"

"Oh yes! And then he forgot about it, too. And he only remembered when he got this letter out of the blue inviting him to roll the pig in the barrel."

"To do *what*?"

"Oh, this ancient ceremony thing," says Suze vaguely. "My dad gets to roll the first pig, because he owns the island." Her eyes suddenly brighten. "In fact, he's always looking for people to do it instead of him. I don't suppose you fancy doing it this year, do you? You get to wear this funny hat, and you have to learn a poem in Gaelic, but it's quite easy . . ."

"Suze—"

"Maybe not," says Suze hurriedly. "Sorry." She leans back on my pillow and chews a fingernail thoughtfully. Then suddenly she looks up. "Hang on a minute. Who told you about New York? If it wasn't Luke?"

"Alicia," I say gloomily. "She knew all about it."

"Alicia?" Suze stares at me. "Alicia Bitch Longlegs? Oh, for goodness' sake. She's probably making it up. Honestly, Bex, I'm surprised you even listened!"

And she sounds so sure that I feel my heart giving a joyful leap. Of course. That must be the answer. Didn't I suspect it myself? Didn't I tell you what Alicia was like?

The only thing—tiny niggle—is I'm not sure Suze is completely 100 percent unbiased here. There's a bit of history between Suze and Alicia, which is that they both started working at Brandon Communications at the same time—but Suze got the sack after three weeks

and Alicia went on to have a high-flying career. Not that
Suze really wanted to be a PR girl, but still.

"I don't know," I say doubtfully. "Would Alicia really
do that?"

"Of course she would!" says Suze. "She's just trying
to wind you up. Come on, Bex, who do you trust more?
Alicia or Luke?"

"Luke," I say after a pause. "Luke, of course."

"Well, then!"

"You're right," I say, suddenly feeling more cheerful.
"You're right! I should just trust him, shouldn't I? I
shouldn't listen to gossip and rumors!"

"Exactly. Here are your letters. And your messages."

"Ooh, thanks!" I say, and take the bundle with a little
pang of excited hope. Because you never know, do you,
what might have happened while you're away? Maybe
one of these envelopes is a letter from a long-lost friend,
or an exciting job offer, or news that I've won a holiday!

But of course, they aren't. It's just one boring old bill
after another, which I leaf through dismissively before
dropping the whole lot to the floor without even opening them.

You know, this always happens. Whenever I go away,
I always think I'll come back to mountains of exciting
post, with parcels and telegrams and letters full of scin-
tillating news—and I'm always disappointed. In fact, I
really think someone should set up a company called
holidaypost.com which you would pay to write you
loads of exciting letters, just so you had *something* to
look forward to when you got home.

I turn to my phone messages—and Suze has written
them down really conscientiously:

Your mum—what are you wearing to Tom and
  Lucy's wedding?
Your mum—don't wear violet as it will clash with
  her hat.
Your mum—Luke does know it's morning dress?
Your mum—Luke is definitely coming, isn't he?
David Barrow—please could you ring him.
Your mum—

Hang on. David Barrow. Who's that?

"Hey, Suze!" I yell. "Did David Barrow say who he
was?"

"No," says Suze, appearing in the hall. "He just said
could you ring him."

"Oh right." I look at the message, feeling faintly intrigued. "What did he sound like?" Suze screws up her
nose.

"Oh, you know. Quite posh. Quite . . . smooth."

I'm a little excited as I dial the number. David Barrow. It sounds almost familiar. Maybe he's a film producer or something!

"David Barrow," comes his voice—and Suze is right,
he is quite posh.

"Hello!" I say. "This is Rebecca Bloomwood. I had a
message to call you."

"Ah, Miss Bloomwood! I'm the special customer
manager of La Rosa."

"Oh." I screw up my face puzzledly. La Rosa? What
on earth's—

Oh yes. That trendy boutique in Hampstead. But I've
only been in there about once, and that was ages ago.
So why is he calling me?

"May I say, first, what an honor it is to have a television personality of your caliber as one of our customers."

"Oh! Well—thank you!" I say, beaming at the phone. "It's a pleasure, actually."

This is great. I know exactly why he's calling. They're going to give me some free clothes, aren't they? Or maybe . . . yes! They want me to design a new line for them! God, yes. I'll be a designer. They'll call it the Becky Bloomwood collection. Simple, stylish, wearable garments, with maybe one or two evening dresses . . .

"This is simply a courtesy call," says David Barrow, interrupting my thoughts. "I just want to ensure that you are completely happy with our service and ask if you have any other needs we can help you with."

"Well—thanks!" I say. "I'm very happy, thanks! I mean, I'm not exactly a regular customer but—"

"Also to mention the small matter of your outstanding La Rosa Card account," adds David Barrow as though I haven't spoken. "And to inform you that if payment is not received within seven days, further action will have to be taken."

I stare at the phone, feeling my smile fade. This isn't a courtesy call at all, is it? He doesn't want me to design a collection of clothes. He's phoning about money!

I feel slightly outraged. Surely people aren't just allowed to telephone you in your own home and demand money with no warning? I mean, *obviously* I'm going to pay them. Just because I don't send a check off the moment the bill comes through the letter box . . .

"It has been three months now since your first bill," David Barrow is saying. "And I must inform you that our policy after the three-month period is to hand over all outstanding accounts to—"

"Yes, well," I interrupt coolly. "My . . . accountants are dealing with all my bills at the moment. I'll speak to them."

"I'm so glad to hear it. And of course, we look forward to seeing you again in La Rosa very soon!"

"Yeah, well," I say grumpily. "Maybe."

I put the phone down as Suze comes past the door again, dragging another black bin bag. "Suze, what *are* you doing?" I say, staring at her.

"I'm decluttering!" she says. "It's brilliant. So cleansing! You should try it! So—who was David Barrow?"

"Just some stupid bill I hadn't paid," I say. "Honestly! Phoning me at home!"

"Ooh, that reminds me. Hang on . . ."

She disappears for a moment, then appears again, holding a bundle of envelopes.

"I found these under my bed when I was tidying up, and this other lot were on my dressing table . . . I think you must have left them in my room." She pulls a face. "I think they're all bills, too."

"Oh, thanks," I say, and throw them onto the bed.

"Maybe . . ." says Suze hesitantly, "maybe you should pay some of them off? You know. Just one or two."

"But I have paid them off!" I say in surprise. "I paid them all off in June. Don't you remember?"

"Oh yes!" says Suze. "Yes, of course I do." She bites her lip. "But the thing is, Bex . . ."

"What?"

"Well . . . that was a while ago, wasn't it? And maybe you've built up a few debts since then."

"Since *June*?" I give a little laugh. "But that was only about five minutes ago! Honestly, Suze, you don't need to worry. I mean . . . take this one." I reach randomly for an envelope. "I mean, what have I bought in M&S recently? Nothing!"

"Oh right," says Suze, looking relieved. "So this bill will just be for . . . zero, will it."

"Absolutely," I say, ripping it open. "Zero! Or, you know, ten quid. You know, for the odd pair of knickers—"

I pull out the account and look at it. For a moment I can't speak.

"How much is it?" says Suze in alarm.

"It's . . . it's wrong," I say, trying to stuff it back in the envelope. "It has to be wrong. I'll write them a letter . . ."

"Let me see." Suze grabs the bill and her eyes widen. "Three hundred sixty-five pounds? Bex—"

"It has to be wrong," I say—but my voice is holding less conviction. I'm suddenly remembering those leather trousers I bought in the Marble Arch sale. And that dressing gown. And that phase I went through of eating M&S sushi every day.

Suze stares at me for a few minutes, her face creased anxiously.

"Bex—d'you think all of these other bills are as high as that?"

Silently I reach for the envelope from Selfridges, and tear it open. Even as I do so, I'm remembering that chrome juicer, the one I saw and *had* to have . . . I've never even used it. And that fur-trimmed dress. Where did that go?

"How much is it?"

"It's . . . it's enough," I reply, pushing it quickly back inside, before she can see that it's well over £400.

I turn away, trying to keep calm. But I feel alarmed

and slightly angry. This is all wrong. The whole point is, I paid off my cards. I *paid them off*. I mean, what's the point of paying off all your credit cards if they all just go and sprout huge new debts again? What is the point?

"Look, Bex, don't worry," says Suze. "You'll be OK! I just won't cash your rent check this month."

"No!" I exclaim. "Don't be silly. You've been good enough to me already! I don't want to owe you anything. I'd rather owe M&S." I look round and see her anxious face. "Suze, don't *worry*! I can easily put this lot off for a bit." I hit the letter. "And meanwhile, I'll get a bigger overdraft or something. In fact, I've just asked the bank for an extension—so I can easily ask for a bit more. In fact, I'll phone them right now!"

"What, this minute?"

"Why not?"

I pick up the phone again, reach for an old bank statement, and dial the Endwich number.

"You see, there really isn't a problem," I say reassuringly. "One little phone call is all it'll take."

"Your call is being transferred to the Central Endwich Call Center," comes a tinny voice down the line. "Kindly memorize the following number for future use: 0800 . . ."

"What's going on?" says Suze.

"I'm being transferred to some central system," I say, as Vivaldi's *Four Seasons* starts to play. "They'll probably be really quick and efficient. This is great, isn't it? Doing it all over the phone."

"Welcome to Endwich Bank!" says a new woman's voice in my ear. "Please key in your account number."

What's my account number? Shit! I've got no idea—

Oh yes. On my bank statement.

"Thank you!" says a voice as I finish pressing the

numbers. "Now please key in your personal identification number."

What?

Personal identification number? I didn't know I had a personal identification number. Honestly! They never told me—

Actually . . . maybe that does ring a slight bell.

Oh God. What was it again? Seventy-three-something? Thirty-seven-something?

"Please key in your personal identification number," repeats the voice pleasantly.

"But I don't *know* my bloody personal identification number!" I say. "Quick, Suze, if you were me, what would you choose as a personal identification number?"

"Ooh!" says Suze. "Um . . . I'd choose . . . um . . . 1234?"

"Please key in your personal identification number," says the voice, with a definite edge to it this time.

God, this is really stressful.

"Try my number for my bicycle lock," suggests Suze. "It's 435."

"Suze—I need *my* number. Not yours."

"You might have chosen the same! You never know!"

"Please key in—"

"All right!" I yell, and punch in 435.

"I'm sorry," intones the voice. "This password is invalid."

"I knew it wouldn't work!"

"It might have done!" says Suze defensively.

"It should be four digits, anyway," I say, having a sudden flash of memory. "I had to phone up and register it . . . and I was standing in the kitchen . . . and . . . yes! Yes! I'd just got my new Karen Millen shoes, and I was looking at the price tag . . . and that was the number I used!"

"How much were they?" says Suze in excitement.

"They were . . . £120 reduced to . . . to £84.99!"

"Punch it in! 8499!"

Excitedly I punch in 8499—and to my disbelief, the voice says, "Thank you! You are through to the Endwich Banking Corporation. Endwich—because we care. For debt control, press one. For mortgage arrears, press two. For overdrafts and bank charges, press three. For . . ."

"Right! I'm through." I exhale sharply, feeling a bit like James Bond breaking the code to save the world. "Am I debt control? Or overdrafts and bank charges?"

"Overdrafts and bank charges," says Suze knowledgeably.

"OK." I press three and a moment later a cheerful singsong voice greets me.

"Hello! Welcome to the Endwich Central Call Center. I'm Dawna, how can I help you, Miss Bloomwood?"

"Oh, hi!" I say, taken aback. "Are you real?"

"Yes!" says Dawna, and laughs. "I'm real. Can I help you?"

"Erm . . . yes. I'm phoning because I need an extension to my overdraft. A few hundred pounds if that's all right. Or, you know, more, if you've got it . . ."

"I see," says Dawna pleasantly. "Was there a specific reason? Or just a general need?"

She sounds so nice and friendly, I feel myself start to relax.

"Well, the thing is, I've had to invest quite a bit in my career recently, and a few bills have come in, and kind of . . . taken me by surprise."

"Oh right," says Dawna sympathetically.

"I mean, it's not as if I'm in *trouble*. It's just a temporary thing."

"A temporary thing," she echoes, and I hear her typing in the background.

"I suppose I have been letting things mount up a bit. But the thing was, I paid everything off! I thought I'd be able to relax for a bit!"

"Oh right."

"So you understand?" I give a relieved beam to Suze, who offers me thumbs-up in return. This is more like it. Just one quick and easy call, like in the adverts. No nasty letters, no tricky questions . . .

"I completely understand," Dawna's saying. "It happens to us all, doesn't it?"

"So—can I have the overdraft?" I say joyfully.

"Oh, I'm not authorized to extend your overdraft by more than £50," says Dawna in surprise. "You'll have to get in touch with your branch overdraft facilities director. Who is a . . . let me see . . . Fulham . . . a Mr. John Gavin."

I stare at the phone in dismay.

"But I've already written to him!"

"Well, that's all right, then, isn't it? Now, is there anything else I can help you with?"

"No," I say. "No, I don't think so. Thanks anyway."

I put down the phone disconsolately.

"Stupid bank. Stupid call center."

"So are they going to give you the money?" asks Suze.

"I don't know. It all depends on this John Gavin bloke." I look up and see Suze's anxious face. "But I'm sure he'll say yes," I add hastily. "He's just got to review my file. It'll be fine!"

"I suppose if you just don't spend anything for a

while, you'll easily get back on track, won't you?" she says hopefully. "I mean, you're making loads of money from the telly, aren't you?"

"Yes," I say after a pause, not liking to tell her that after rent, taxi fares, meals out, and outfits for the show, it doesn't actually amount to that much.

"And there's your book, too . . ."

"My book?"

For a moment I stare at her blankly. Then suddenly, with a lift of the heart, I remember. Of course! My self-help book! I've been meaning to do something about that.

Well, thank God. This is the answer. All I have to do is write my book really quickly and get a nice big check—and then I'll pay all these cards off and everything will be happy again. Ha. I don't need any stupid overdraft. I'll start straight away. This evening!

And the truth is, I'm rather looking forward to getting down to my book. I have so many important themes I want to address in it, like poverty and wealth, comparative religion, philosophy maybe. I mean, I know the publishers have just asked for a simple self-help book, but there's no reason why I can't encompass broader questions too, is there?

In fact, if it does really well, I might give lectures. God, that would be great, wouldn't it? I could become a kind of lifestyle guru and tour the world, and people would flock to see me, and ask my advice on all sorts of issues—

"How's it going?" says Suze, appearing at my door in a towel, and I jump guiltily. I've been sitting at my computer for quite a while now but I haven't actually turned it on.

"I'm just thinking," I say, hastily reaching to the back of the computer and flipping the switch. "You know, focusing my thoughts and . . . and letting the creative juices meld into a coherent pattern."

"Wow," says Suze, and looks at me in slight awe. "That's amazing. Is it hard?"

"Not really," I say, after a bit of thought. "It's quite easy, actually."

The computer suddenly bursts into a riot of sound and color, and we both stare at it, mesmerized.

"Wow!" says Suze again. "Did you do that?"

"Erm . . . yes," I say. Which is true. I mean, I did switch it on.

"God, you're so clever, Bex," breathes Suze. "When do you think you'll finish it?"

"Oh, quite soon, I expect," I say breezily. "You know. Once I get going."

"Well, I'll leave you to get on with it, then," says Suze. "I just wanted to borrow a dress for tonight."

"Oh right," I say, with interest. "Where are you going?"

"Venetia's party," says Suze. "D'you want to come too? Oh, go on, come! Everyone's going!"

For a moment I'm tempted. I've met Venetia a few times, and I know she gives amazing parties at her parents' house in Kensington.

"No," I say at last. "I'd better not. I've got work to do."

"Oh well." Suze's face droops briefly. "But I can borrow a dress, can I?"

"Of course!" I screw up my face for a moment, thinking hard. "Why don't you wear my new Tocca dress with your red shoes and my English Eccentrics wrap?"

"Excellent!" says Suze, going to my wardrobe. "Thanks, Bex. And . . . could I borrow some knickers?" she adds casually. "And some tights and makeup?"

I turn in my chair and give her a close look.

"Suze—when you decluttered your room, did you keep *anything*?"

"Of course I did!" she says, a little defensively. "You know. A few things." She meets my gaze. "OK, perhaps I went a bit too far."

"Do you have *any* underwear left?"

"Well . . . no. But you know, I feel so good, and kind of positive about life—it doesn't matter! It's feng shui. You should try it!"

I watch as Suze gathers up the dress and underwear and rifles through my makeup bag. Then she leaves the room and I stretch my arms out in front of me, flexing my fingers. Right. To work.

I open a file, type "Chapter One," and stare at it proudly. Chapter One! This is so cool! Now all I have to do is come up with a really memorable, striking opening sentence.

I sit quite still for a while, concentrating on the empty screen in front of me, then type briskly,

Finance is the

I stop, and take a sip of Diet Coke. Obviously the right sentence takes a bit of honing. You can't just expect it to land straight in your head.

Finance is the most

God, I wish I were writing a book about clothes. Or makeup. *Becky Bloomwood's Guide to Lipstick.*

Anyway, I'm not. So concentrate.

Finance is something which

You know, my chair's quite uncomfortable. I'm sure it can't be healthy, sitting on a squashy chair like this for hours on end. I'll get repetitive strain injury, or something. Really, if I'm going to be a writer, I should invest in one of those ergonomic ones which swivel round and go up and down.

Finance is very

Maybe they sell chairs like that on the Internet. Maybe I should just have a quick little look. Since the computer's on, and everything.

In fact—surely it would be irresponsible of me if I didn't. I mean, you have to look after yourself, don't you? *Mens sana in healthy sana,* or whatever it is.

I reach for my mouse, quickly click onto the Internet icon, and search for "office chairs"—and soon I'm coasting happily through the list. And I've already noted down a few good possibilities—when all of a sudden I land on this incredible Web site which I've never seen before, all full of office supplies. Not just boring white envelopes, but really amazing high-tech stuff. Like smart chrome filing cabinets, and cool pen holders, and really nice personalized nameplates to put on your door.

I scroll through all the photographs, utterly mesmerized. I mean, I know I'm not supposed to be spending money at the moment—but this is different. This is investment in my career. After all—this is my office, isn't it? It should be well equipped. It *needs* to be well equipped. In fact, I can't believe how shortsighted I've been. How on earth was I expecting to write a book without the necessary equipment? It would be like climbing Everest without a tent.

I'm so dazzled by the array of stuff you can get that I almost can't decide what to get. But there are a few essentials which I absolutely must buy.

So I click on an ergonomic swivel chair upholstered in purple to match my iMac, plus a Dictaphone which translates stuff straight into your computer. And then I find myself adding a really cool steel claw which holds up notes while you're typing, a set of laminated presentation folders—which are bound to come in useful—and a mini paper shredder. Which is a complete essential because I don't want the whole world seeing my first drafts, do I? And I'm toying with the idea of some modular reception furniture—except I don't really have a reception area in my bedroom—when Suze comes back into the room.

"Hi! How's it going?"

I jump guiltily, quickly click on "send" without even bothering to check what the final amount was, click off the Internet—and look up just as my Chapter One reappears on the screen.

"You're working really hard!" says Suze, shaking her head. "You should take a break. How much have you done?"

"Oh . . . quite a lot," I say.

"Can I read it?" And to my horror she starts coming toward me.

"No!" I exclaim. "I mean—it's a work in progress.

It's . . . sensitive material." Hastily I close the document and stand up. "You look really great, Suze. Fantastic!"

"Thanks!" She beams at me and twirls around in my dress as the doorbell rings. "Ooh! That'll be Fenny."

Fenella is one of Suze's weird posh cousins from Scotland. Except to be fair, she's not actually that weird anymore. She used to be as peculiar as her brother, Tarquin, and spend the whole time riding horses and shooting fish, or whatever they do. But recently she's moved to London and got a job in an art gallery, and now she just goes to parties instead. As Suze opens the front door I can hear her high-pitched voice—and a whole gaggle of girls' voices following her. Fenny can't move three feet without a huge cloud of shrieking people around her. She's like some socialite version of a rain god.

"Hi!" she says, bursting into my room. She's wearing a really nice pink velvet skirt from Whistles, which I've also got—but she's teamed it with a disastrous brown Lurex polo neck. "Hi, Becky! Are you coming tonight?"

"Not tonight," I say. "I've got to work."

"Oh well." Fenella's face droops just like Suze's did—then brightens. "Then can I borrow your Jimmy Choos? We've got the same size feet, haven't we?"

"OK," I say. "They're in the wardrobe." I hesitate, trying to be tactful. "And do you want to borrow a top? It's just I've actually got the top that goes with your skirt. Pink cashmere with little beads. Really nice."

"Have you?" says Fenny. "Ooh, yes! I shoved on this polo neck without really thinking." As she peels it off, a blond girl in a black shift comes in and beams at me.

"Hi, er . . . Milla," I say, remembering her name just in time. "How are you?"

"I'm fine!" she says, and gives me a hopeful look.

"Fenny said I could borrow your English Eccentrics wrap."

"I'm lending it to Suze," I say, pulling a regretful face. "But what about . . . a purple shawl with sequins?"

"Yes, please! And Binky says, have you still got that black wraparound skirt?"

"I have," I say thoughtfully. "But actually, I've got another skirt I think would look even better on her . . ."

It's about half an hour before everyone has borrowed what they want. Eventually they all pile out of my room, shrieking to me that they'll return it all in the morning, and Suze comes in, looking completely stunning with her hair piled up on her head and hanging down in blond tendrils.

"Bex, are you sure you don't want to come?" she says. "Tarquin's going to be there, and I know he'd like to see you."

"Oh right," I say, trying not to look too appalled at the idea. "Is he in London, then?"

"Just for a few days." Suze looks at me, a little sorrowfully. "You know, Bex, if it weren't for Luke . . . I reckon Tarkie still likes you."

"I'm sure he doesn't," I say quickly. "That was ages ago now. Ages!"

My one and only date with Tarquin is one of those events I am trying very hard never to remember again, ever.

"Oh well," says Suze, shrugging. "See you later. And don't work too hard!"

"I won't," I reply, and give a world-weary sigh. "Or at least, I'll try not to."

I wait until the front door bangs behind her and the taxis waiting outside have roared off. Then I take a sip of tea and turn back to my first chapter.

Chapter One

Finance is very

Actually, I'm not really in the mood for this anymore. Suze is right, I should have a break. I mean, if I sit here hour after hour, I'll get all jaded, and lose the creative flow. And the point is, I've made a good start.

I stand up and stretch, then wander into the sitting room, and pick up a copy of *Tatler*. It's *EastEnders* in a minute, and then it might be *Changing Rooms* or something, or that documentary about the vets. I'll just watch that—and then I'll go back to work. I mean, I've got a whole evening ahead, haven't I? I need to pace myself.

Idly, I flick open the magazine and am scanning the contents page for something interesting when suddenly my eye stops in surprise. It's a little picture of Luke, with the caption *Best of Brandon*, page seventy-four! Why on earth didn't he tell me he was going to be in *Tatler*?

The photograph is his new official one, the one I helped him choose an outfit for (blue shirt, dark blue Fendi tie). He's staring at the camera, looking all serious and businesslike—but if you look closely at his eyes, there's a little friendly spark in there. As I stare at his face I feel a tug of affection and realize Suze is right. I should just trust him, shouldn't I? I mean—what does Alicia Bitchy-pants know about anything?

I turn to page seventy-four, and it's an article on "Britain's Top Movers and Shakers." I scan down the page, and I can't help noticing that some of the movers and shakers are pictured with their partners. Maybe there'll be a picture of me with Luke! After all, somebody might have taken a picture of us together at a party or something, mightn't they? Come to think of it, we were once snapped by the *Evening Standard* at a launch for some new magazine, although it never actually got into the paper.

Ooh! Here he is, number thirty-four! And it's just him, in that same official photo, with not a glimpse of me. Still, I feel a twinge of pride as I see his picture (much bigger than some of the others, ha!) and a caption reading: "Brandon's ruthless pursuit of success has knocked lesser competitors off the starting blocks." Then the piece starts: "Luke Brandon, dynamic owner and founder of Brandon Communications, the blah-di blah-di . . ."

I skim over the text, feeling a pleasant anticipation as I reach the section labeled "Vital Statistics." This is the bit where I'll be mentioned! "Currently dating TV personality Rebecca Bloomwood." Or maybe, "Partner of well-known finance expert Rebecca Bloomwood." Or else—

Luke James Brandon
Age: 34
Education: Cambridge
Current status: Single.

Single?

Luke told them he was *single*?

A hurt anger begins to rise through me as I stare at Luke's confident, arrogant gaze. Suddenly I've had enough of all this. I've had enough of being made to feel insecure and paranoid and wondering what's going on. Hands trembling, I pick up the phone and jab in Luke's number.

"Yes," I say, as soon as the message has finished. "Yes,

well. If you're single, Luke, then I'm single too. OK? And if you're going to New York, then I'm going to . . . to Outer Mongolia. And if you're . . ."

Suddenly my mind goes blank. Shit, and it was going so well.

". . . if you're too cowardly to tell me these things yourself, then maybe it's better for both of us if we simply . . ."

I'm really struggling here. I should have written it all down before I began.

". . . if we just call it a day. Or perhaps that's what you think you've already done," I finish, breathing hard.

"Becky?" Suddenly Luke's deep voice is in my ear, and I jump with fright.

"Yes?" I say, trying to sound dignified.

"What is all this gibberish you're spouting on my machine?" he asks calmly.

"It's not gibberish!" I reply indignantly. "It's the truth!"

" 'If you're single, then I'm single'? What's that supposed to be? Lyrics to a pop song?"

"I was talking about you! And the fact that you've told the whole world you're single."

"I've done what?" says Luke, sounding amused. "When did I do that?"

"It's in *Tatler*!" I say furiously. "This month!" I grab for the magazine and flip it open. "Britain's top movers and shakers. Number thirty-four, Luke Brandon."

"Oh, for God's sake," says Luke. "That thing."

"Yes, that thing!" I exclaim. "That thing! And it says you're single. How do you think it felt for me to see you'd said you were single?"

"It quotes me, does it?"

"Well . . . no," I say after a pause. "It doesn't exactly quote you. But I mean, they must have phoned you up and asked you—"

"They did phone me up and ask me," he says. "And I said no comment."

"Oh." I'm silenced for a moment, trying to think clearly. OK, so maybe he didn't say he was single—but I'm not at all sure I like "no comment." Isn't that what people say when things are going really badly?

"Why did you say no comment?" I say at last. "Why didn't you say you were going out with me?"

"My darling," says Luke, sounding a little weary, "think about it. Do you *want* our private life splashed all over the media?"

"Of course not." I twist my hands into a complicated knot. "Of course not. But you . . ." I stop.

"What?"

"You told the media when you were going out with Sacha," I say in a small voice.

Sacha is Luke's ex-girlfriend.

I can't quite believe I just said that.

Luke sighs.

"Becky, *Sacha* told the media about us. She would have had *People* magazine photographing us in the bath if they'd been interested. That's the kind of girl she was."

"Oh," I say, winding the telephone cord round my finger.

"I'm not interested in that kind of thing. My clients can do what they like, but personally, I can't think of anything worse. Hence the no comment." He pauses. "But you're right. I should have thought. I should have warned you. I'm sorry."

"That's all right," I say awkwardly. "I suppose I shouldn't have jumped to conclusions."

"So are we OK?" says Luke, and there's a warm, teasing note to his voice. "Are we back on course?"

"What about New York?" I say, hating myself. "Is that all a mistake, too?"

There's a long, horrible silence.

"What have you heard about New York?" says Luke at last—and to my horror, he sounds all businesslike and distant.

Oh God. *Why* couldn't I keep my mouth closed?

"Nothing really!" I stammer. "I . . . I don't know. I just . . ."

I tail off feebly, and for what seems like hours, neither of us says anything. My heart is pounding hard, and I'm clutching the receiver so hard, my ear's starting to hurt.

"Becky, I need to talk to you about a few things," says Luke finally. "But now is not the time."

"Right," I say, feeling a pang of fright. "What . . . sort of things?"

"Not now. We'll talk when I get back, OK? Saturday. At the wedding."

"Right," I say again, talking brightly to hide the nerves in my voice. "OK! Well, I'll . . . I'll see you then, then . . ."

But before I can say any more, he's gone.

MANAGING YOUR MONEY
A Comprehensive Guide to Personal Finance

By Rebecca Bloomwood

FIRST EDITION (UK)

(FIRST DRAFT)

PART ONE
Chapter one.

Finance is very

· ENDWICH BANK ·

FULHAM BRANCH
3 Fulham Road
London   SW6   9JH

Ms. Rebecca Bloomwood
Flat 2
4 Burney Rd.
London SW6 8FD

12 September 2000

Dear Ms. Bloomwood:

Further to my letter of 8 September, I have conducted a
thorough examination of your account. Your current overdraft limit vastly exceeds the bank's approved ratios. I cannot see any need for this excessive level of debt, nor that
any genuine attempts have been made to reduce it. The situation is little short of a disgrace.

Whatever special status you have enjoyed in the past will
not be continuing in the future. I will certainly not be in-
creasing your overdraft limit as you request, and would
ask as a matter of urgency that you make an appointment
with me to discuss your position.

Yours sincerely,

John Gavin
Overdraft Facilities Director

Six

I ARRIVE AT MY PARENTS' house at ten o'clock on
Saturday, to find the street full of festivity. There are bal-
loons tied to every tree, our drive is full of cars, and a
billowing marquee is just visible from next door's garden. I get out of my car, reach for my overnight bag,
then just stand still for a few moments, staring at the
Websters' house. God, this is strange. Tom Webster getting married. I can hardly believe it. To be honest—and
this may sound a bit mean—I can hardly believe that
anyone would want to marry Tom Webster. He has
smartened up his act recently, admittedly. He's got a few
new clothes, and a better hairstyle. But his hands are
still all huge and clammy—and frankly, he's not Brad
Pitt.

Still, that's the point of love, I think, closing my car
door with a bang. You love people despite their flaws.
Lucy obviously doesn't mind that Tom's got clammy
hands—and he obviously doesn't mind that her hair's
all flat and boring. It's quite romantic, I suppose.

As I'm standing there, gazing at the house, a girl in
jeans with a circlet of flowers in her hair appears at the
Websters' front door. She gives me an odd, almost ag-

gressive look, then disappears inside the house again. One of Lucy's bridesmaids, obviously. I expect she's a bit nervous, being seen in her jeans.

Lucy's probably in there too, it occurs to me—and instinctively I turn away. I know she's the bride and everything, but to be honest, I'm not desperately looking forward to seeing Lucy again. I've only met her a couple of times and we've never jelled. Probably because she had the idea I was in love with Tom. Still, at least when Luke arrives I'll finally be able to prove them all wrong.

At the thought of Luke, there's a painful stab in my chest, and I take a deep, slow breath to calm myself. I'm determined I'm not going to put the cart before the horse this time. I'm going to keep an open mind, and see what he says today. And if he does tell me he's moving away to New York then I'll just . . . deal with it. Somehow.

Anyway. Don't think about it now. Briskly I head for the front door and let myself in. I head for the kitchen and find my dad drinking coffee in his waistcoat, while Mum, dressed in a nylon cape with her hair in curlers, is buttering a round of sandwiches.

"I just don't think it's right," she's saying as I walk in. "It's not right. They're supposed to be leading our country, and look at them. They're a mess! Dowdy jackets, dreadful ties . . ."

"You really think the ability to govern is affected by what you wear, do you?"

"Hi, Mum," I say, dumping my bag on the floor. "Hi, Dad."

"It's the principle of the thing!" says Mum. "If they're not prepared to make an effort with their dress, then why should they make any effort with the economy?"

"It's hardly the same thing!"

"It's exactly the same thing. Becky, *you* think the chancellor should dress more smartly, don't you? All this lounge suit nonsense."

"I don't know," I say vaguely. "Maybe."

"You see? Becky agrees with me. Now, let me have a look at you, darling." She puts down her knife and surveys me properly, and I feel myself glowing a little, because I know I look good. I'm wearing a shocking pink dress and jacket, a Philip Treacy feathered hat, and the most beautiful black satin shoes, each decorated with a single gossamer butterfly. "Oh, Becky," says Mum at last. "You look lovely. You'll upstage the bride!" She reaches for my hat and looks at it. "This is very unusual! How much did it cost?"

"Erm . . . I can't remember," I say vaguely. "Maybe . . . fifty quid?"

This is not quite true. It was actually more like . . . Well, anyway, quite a lot. Still, it was worth it.

"So, where's Luke?" says Mum, popping my hat back on my head. "Parking the car?"

"Yes, where's Luke?" says my father, looking up, and gives a jocular laugh. "We've been looking forward to meeting this young man of yours at last."

"Luke's coming separately," I say—and flinch slightly as I see their faces fall.

"Separately?" says Mum at last. "Why's that?"

"He's flying back from Zurich this morning," I explain. "He had to go there for business. But he'll be here, I promise."

"He does know the service starts at twelve?" says Mum anxiously. "And you've told him where the church is?"

"Yes!" I say. "Honestly, he'll be here."

I'm aware that I sound slightly snappy, but I can't help it. To be honest, I'm a bit stressed out myself about where Luke's got to. He was supposed to be ringing me when he landed at the airport—and that was supposed to be half an hour ago. But so far I haven't heard anything.

Still. He said he'd be here.

"Can I do anything to help?" I ask, to change the subject.

"Be a darling, and take these upstairs for me," says Mum, cutting the sandwiches briskly into triangles. "I've got to pack away the patio cushions."

"Who's upstairs?" I say, picking up the plate.

"Maureen's come over to blow-dry Janice's hair," says Mum. "They wanted to keep out of Lucy's way. You know, while she's getting ready."

"Have you seen her yet?" I ask interestedly. "Has she got a nice dress?"

"I haven't seen it," says Mum, and lowers her voice. "But apparently it cost £3,000. And that's not including the veil!"

"Wow," I say, impressed. And for a second I feel ever so slightly envious. A £3,000 dress. And a party . . . and loads of presents . . . I mean, people who get married have it all.

As I go up the stairs, there's the sound of blow-drying coming from Mum and Dad's bedroom—and as I go in, I see Janice sitting on the dressing-room stool, wearing a dressing gown, holding a sherry glass, and dabbing at her eyes with a hanky. Maureen, who's been doing Mum's and Janice's hair for years now, is brandishing a hair dryer at her, and a woman I don't recognize with a mahogany tan, dyed blond curly hair, and a lilac silk suit is sitting on the window seat.

"Hello, Janice," I say, going over and giving her a hug. "How are you feeling?"

"I'm fine, dear," she says, and gives a sniff. "A little wobbly. You know. To think of Tom getting married!"

"I know," I say sympathetically. "It doesn't seem like yesterday that we were kids, riding our bikes together!"

"Have another sherry, Janice," says Maureen comfortably, and sloshes a deep brown liquid into her glass. "It'll help you relax."

"Oh, Becky," says Janice, and squeezes my hand. "This must be a hard day for you, too."

I knew it. She does still think I fancy Tom, doesn't she? *Why* do all mothers think their sons are irresistible?

"Not really!" I say, as brightly as I can. "I mean, I'm just pleased for Tom. And Lucy, of course . . ."

"Becky?" The woman on the window seat turns toward me, eyes narrowed suspiciously. "This is Becky?"

And there's not an ounce of friendliness in her face. Oh God, don't say *she* thinks I'm after Tom, too.

"Erm . . . yes." I smile at her. "I'm Rebecca Bloomwood. And you must be Lucy's mother?"

"Yes," says the woman, still staring at me. "I'm Angela Harrison. Mother of the bride," she adds, emphasizing "the bride" as though I don't understand English.

"You must be very excited," I say politely. "Your daughter getting married."

"Yes, well, of course, Tom is devoted to Lucy," she says aggressively. "Utterly devoted. Never *looks* in any other direction." She gives me a sharp glance and I smile feebly back.

Honestly, what am I supposed to do? Throw up all over Tom or something? Tell him he's the ugliest man I've ever known? They'd all still just say I was jealous. They'd say I was in denial.

"Is . . . Luke here, Becky?" says Janice, and gives me a hopeful smile. And suddenly—which is rather bizarre—everyone in the room is completely still, waiting for my answer.

"Not yet, I'm afraid," I say. "I think he must have been held up."

There's silence, and I'm aware of glances flying around the room.

"Held up," echoes Angela, and there's a tone to her voice that I don't much like. "Is that right? Well, there's a surprise."

What's that supposed to mean?

"He's coming back from Zurich," I explain. "I should think the flight's been delayed or something." I look at Janice and, to my surprise, she flushes.

"Zurich," she says, nodding a little too emphatically. "I see. Of course. Zurich." And she shoots me an embarrassed, almost sympathetic look.

What's wrong with her?

"This *is* Luke Brandon we're talking about here," says Angela, taking a puff on her cigarette. "The famous entrepreneur."

"Well—yes," I say, a bit surprised. I mean, I don't *know* any other Lukes.

"And he's your boyfriend."

"Yes!"

There's a slightly awkward silence—and even Maureen seems to be gazing at me curiously. Then, suddenly, I see a copy of this month's *Tatler* lying on the floor by Janice's chair. Oh God.

"That article in *Tatler,* by the way," I say hastily, "is all wrong. He didn't say he was single. He said no comment."

"Article?" says Janice unconvincingly. "I don't know what you're talking about, dear."

"I . . . I don't read magazines," says Maureen, who blushes bright red and looks away.

"We just look forward to meeting him," says Angela, and blows out a cloud of smoke. "Don't we, Janice?"

I stare at her in confusion—then turn to Janice, who will barely meet my eye, and Maureen, who's pretending to root about in a beauty case.

Hang on a minute.

They surely don't think—

"Janice," I say, trying to keep my voice steady. "You know Luke's coming. He even wrote you a reply!"

"Of course he did, Becky!" says Janice, staring at the floor. "Well—as Angela says, we're all looking forward to meeting him."

I feel a swoosh of humiliated color fill my cheeks. What does she think? That I've just *made up* that I'm going out with Luke?

"Well, enjoy your sandwiches, won't you?" I say, trying not to sound as flustered as I feel. "I'll just . . . see if Mum needs me."

When I find Mum, she's on the top-floor landing, packing patio cushions into transparent plastic bags, then suctioning all the air out with the nozzle of her vacuum cleaner.

"I've some of these bags on order for you, by the way," she shouts over the noise of the vacuum. "From Country Ways. Plus some turkey foil, a casserole dish, a microwave egg poacher . . ."

"I don't want any turkey foil!" I yell.

"It's not for you!" says Mum, turning off the vacuum. "They had a special offer—introduce a friend and receive a set of earthenware pots. So I nominated you as the friend. It's a very good catalogue, actually. I'll give it to you to have a browse."

"Mum—"

"Lovely duvet covers. I'm sure you could do with a new—"

"Mum, listen!" I say agitatedly. "Listen. You do believe I'm going out with Luke, don't you?"

There's a slightly too long pause.

"Of course I do," she says eventually.

I stare at her in horror.

"You don't, do you? You all think I've just made it up!"

"No!" says Mum firmly. She puts down her hoover and looks me straight in the eye. "Becky, you've told us you're going out with Luke Brandon, and as far as Dad and I are concerned, that's enough."

"But Janice and Martin. Do they think I've made it up?"

Mum gazes at me—then sighs, and reaches for another patio cushion.

"Oh, Becky. The thing is, love, you have to remember, they once believed you had a stalker. And that turned out to be . . . well. Not quite true. Didn't it?"

A cold dismay creeps over me. OK, maybe I did once kind of pretend I had a stalker. Which I shouldn't have done. But I mean, just because you invent one tiny stalker—that doesn't make you a complete nutcase, does it?

"And the trouble is, we've never actually . . . well, *seen* him with you, have we, love?" Mum's continuing, as she stuffs the cushion into its transparent bag. "Not in the flesh. And then there was that piece in the paper saying he was single . . ."

"He didn't say single!" My voice is shrill with frustration. "He said no comment! Mum, have Janice and Martin told you they don't believe me?"

"No!" Mum lifts her chin defiantly. "They wouldn't dare say a thing like that to me."

"But you know that's what they're saying behind our backs."

We stare at each other, and suddenly I see the strain in Mum's face, hidden behind her bright facade. She must have been *so* hoping we'd pull up together in Luke's flash car, I suddenly realize. She must have been so wanting to prove Janice wrong. And instead, here I am, on my own again . . .

"He'll be here," I say, almost to reassure myself. "He'll be here any minute."

"Of course he will!" exclaims Mum brightly. "And as soon as he turns up—well, then everyone will have to eat their words, won't they?"

The doorbell rings and we both stiffen, staring at each other.

"I'll get that, shall I?" I say, trying to sound casual.

"Why don't you?" agrees Mum, and I can see a tiny shine of hope in her eyes.

Trying not to run, I hurry down the stairs and, with a light heart, fling the front door open. And it's . . . not Luke.

It's a man laden with flowers. Baskets of flowers, a bouquet of flowers, and several flat boxes at his feet.

"Wedding flowers," he says. "Where do you want them?"

"Oh," I say, trying to hide my disappointment. "Actually, you've got the wrong house, I'm afraid. They need to go next door. Number 41."

"Really?" The man frowns. "Let me just look at my list . . . Hold that, would you?"

He thrusts the bridal bouquet at me and starts rooting around his pocket.

"Honestly," I say, "they need to go next door. Look, I'll just get my—"

I turn round, holding Lucy's bouquet with both hands, because it's quite heavy. And to my horror, Angela Harrison is just arriving at the foot of the stairs. She stares at me, and for a moment I almost think she's going to kill me.

"What are you doing?" she snaps. "Give me that!" She wrenches the bouquet out of my hands and brings her face so close to mine I can smell the gin on her breath. "Listen, young lady," she hisses. "I'm not fooled by the smiles. I know what you're up to. And you can just forget it, all right? I'm not having my daughter's wedding wrecked by some deranged little psychopath."

"I'm not deranged!" I exclaim furiously. "And I'm not going to wreck anything! I don't fancy Tom! I've got a boyfriend!"

"Oh yes," she says, folding her arms. "The famous boyfriend. Is he here yet?"

"No, he isn't," I say, and flinch at the expression on her face. "But he . . . he just called."

"He just called," echoes Angela with a little sneer. "To say he can't make it?"

Why won't these people believe that Luke's coming?

"Actually . . . he's half an hour away," I hear myself saying defiantly.

"Good!" says Angela Harrison, and gives me a nasty smile. "Well—we'll see him very soon, then, won't we?"

Oh shit.

By twelve o'clock, Luke still hasn't arrived, and I'm beside myself. This is a complete nightmare. Where *is* he? I loiter outside the church until the very last minute, desperately dialing his number, hoping against hope I'm suddenly going to see him running up the road. But the bridesmaids have arrived, and another Rolls-Royce has just pulled up, and he's still not here. As I see the car door open and a glimpse of wedding dress, I hastily retreat into the church before anyone can think I'm waiting outside to disrupt the bridal procession.

As I creep in, trying not to disturb the organ music, Angela Harrison darts me an evil look, and there's a rippling and whispering from Lucy's side of the church. I sit down near the back, trying to keep composed and tranquil—but I'm well aware that all Lucy's friends are shooting surreptitious glances at me. What the hell has she been telling everyone?

For a second I feel like getting up and walking out. I never wanted to come to this stupid wedding anyway. I only said yes because I didn't want to offend Janice and Martin. But it's too late, the bridal march is starting, and Lucy's walking in. And I have to hand it to her, she's wearing the most drop-dead gorgeous dress I've ever seen. I stare wistfully after it, trying not to imagine what I would look like in a dress like that.

The music stops and the vicar starts talking. I'm aware that people on Lucy's side of the church are still darting me little looks—but I adjust my hat and lift my chin and ignore them.

". . . to join together this man and this woman in holy matrimony," intones the vicar, "which is an honorable estate . . ."

The bridesmaids have got really nice shoes, I notice. I wonder where they're from?

Shame about the dresses, though.

". . . reverently, discreetly, advisedly, soberly, and in the fear of God . . ."

He pauses to look around the congregation, just as I hear a little trilling sound coming from my bag.

Shit. It's my phone.

I pull at the zip—but it's stuck. I don't believe this. You buy an expensive bag, and the bloody zip sticks.

There's another, louder trill. At the front of the church, Angela Harrison turns round in her pew and gives me the evil eye.

"Sorry," I mouth. "I'm just trying to get it . . ."

As it trills for a third time, the vicar stops talking. And oh God, now Tom and Lucy are turning round, too.

"I'm sorry," I gulp, giving another frantic tug at the zip. "I'll just . . . try to . . ."

Face burning, I stand up, squeeze my way past the row of people, and hurry out of the church. As the door clangs shut behind me I wrench so hard at the zip that I pull the stitching undone. I scrabble inside for the phone, and jab at the green button.

"Hello?" I say breathlessly into the mouthpiece. "Luke?"

"Good morning!" says a cheery voice. "Would you be interested in adding a hundred minutes to your monthly plan?"

After carefully turning off my phone I creep back into the church, where the rest of the service goes by in a blur. When it's all over, Lucy and Tom process out, studiously ignoring me as they do so—and everyone gathers around them in the graveyard to throw confetti and take photos. I slip away without anyone noticing, and hurry feverishly up the road to the Websters' house. Because Luke must be there by now. He *must*. He must have arrived late, and decided not to come to the church, but go straight to the reception. It's obvious, when you think about it. It's what any sensible person would do.

I hurry through the Websters' house, which is full of caterers and waitresses—and head straight for the marquee. There's already a joyful smile on my face at the thought of seeing him, and telling him about that awful moment in the church, and seeing his face crease up in laughter—

But the marquee's empty. Completely empty.

I stand there, bewildered, for a few moments—then quickly head out again and hurry toward my parents' house. Because maybe Luke went there, instead, it suddenly occurs to me. Maybe he got the time wrong, or maybe he had to get changed into his wedding outfit. Or maybe—

But he's not there either. Not in the kitchen, not upstairs. And when I dial his mobile number, it clicks straight onto messages.

Slowly, I walk into my bedroom and sink down onto

the bed, trying not to let myself think all the bad thoughts which are creeping into my mind.

He's coming, I tell myself again and again. He's just . . . on his way.

Through the window I can see Tom and Lucy and all the guests starting to arrive in next door's garden. There are lots of hats and morning suits, and waitresses handing round champagne. In fact, it all looks rather jolly. And I know I should be down there with them, but I just can't face it. Not without Luke, not all on my own.

But after sitting there for a while, it occurs to me that by staying up here, I'll just be fueling the intrigue. They'll all think I can't face the happy couple and that I'm off slitting my wrists somewhere. It'll confirm all their suspicions forever. I *have* to go and show my face, even if just for half an hour.

I force myself to stand up, take a deep breath, and put some fresh lipstick on. Then I walk out of the house and round to the Websters'. I slip inconspicuously into the marquee through a side flap and stand watching for a moment. There are people milling about everywhere, and the hubbub is huge, and no one even notices me. Near the entrance, there's a formal lineup with Tom and Lucy and their parents, but no way am I going near that. So instead I sidle off to an empty table and sit down, and after a bit a waitress comes and gives me a glass of champagne.

For a while I just sit there, sipping my drink and watching people and feeling myself start to relax. But then there's a rustling sound in front of me. I look up—and my heart sinks. Lucy is standing right in front of me in her beautiful wedding dress, flanked by a large bridesmaid in a really unflattering shade of green. (Which I think says quite a lot about Lucy.)

"Hello, Rebecca," says Lucy pleasantly—and I can just tell, she's congratulating herself on being so polite to the loony girl who nearly wrecked her wedding.

"Hi," I say. "Listen, I'm really sorry about the service. I honestly didn't mean to . . ."

"That doesn't matter," says Lucy, and gives me a tight smile. "After all, Tom and I are married. That's the main thing." And she gives her wedding-ringed hand a satisfied glance.

"Absolutely!" I say. "Congratulations. Are you going on—"

"We were just wondering," interrupts Lucy pleasantly. "Is Luke here yet?"

My heart sinks.

"Oh," I say, playing for time. "Well . . ."

"It's only that Mummy said you told her he was half an hour away. But no sign of him! Which seems a bit strange, don't you think?" She raises her eyebrows innocently, and her bridesmaid gives a half-snort of laughter. I glance over Lucy's shoulder and see Angela Harrison standing with Tom, a few yards away, watching with gimlet, triumphant eyes. God, they're enjoying this, aren't they?

"After all, that was, oh, a good two hours ago now," Lucy's saying. "At least! So if he *isn't* here, it does seem a teeny bit peculiar." She gives me a mock-concerned look. "Or maybe he's had an accident? Maybe he's got held up in . . . Zurich, was it?"

I stare at her smug, mocking face, and something violent rushes to my head.

"He's here," I say before I can stop myself.

There's a stunned silence. Lucy and her bridesmaid glance at each other, while I take a deep gulp of champagne.

"He's *here*?" says Lucy at last. "You mean, here at the wedding?"

"Absolutely!" I say. "He's . . . he's been here a while, actually."

"But where? Where is he?"

"Well . . . he was here just a few moments ago . . ." I gesture to the chair next to me. "Didn't you see him?"

"No!" says Lucy, with wide eyes. "Where is he now?" And she starts to look around the marquee.

"Just there," I say, pointing vaguely through the crowd. "He's wearing a morning coat . . ."

"And? What else?"

"And he's . . . he's holding a glass of champagne . . ." Thank *God* all men look alike at weddings.

"Which one!" says Lucy impatiently.

"The dark one," I say, and take another gulp of champagne. "Look, he's waving at me." I lift my hand and give a little wave. "Hi, Luke!"

"*Where?*" exclaims Lucy, peering into the crowd. "Kate, can you see him?"

"No!" says the bridesmaid hopelessly. "What does he look like?"

"He's . . . actually, he's just disappeared," I say. "He must be getting me a drink or something."

Lucy turns to me again.

"So—how come he wasn't at the service?"

"He didn't want to interrupt," I say after a pause, and force myself to smile naturally. "Well—I won't keep you. You must want to mingle with your guests!"

"Yes," says Lucy after a pause. "Yes, I will."

Giving me another suspicious look, she rustles off toward her mother, and they all start hobnobbing in a little group, shooting glances at me every so often. Then one of the bridesmaids rushes off to another group of guests, and they all start giving me glances, too. And then one runs off to *another* group. It's like seeing a bushfire begin.

A few moments later, Janice comes up, all flushed and teary-looking, with a flowery hat perched lopsidedly on her head.

"Becky!" she says. "Becky, we've just heard that Luke's here!"

And my heart plummets. Putting down the bride from hell was one thing. But I can't bring myself to lie to Janice. I just can't do it. So I quickly take a gulp of champagne, and wave my glass at her in a vague manner that could mean anything.

"Oh, Becky . . ." Janice clasps her hands. "Becky, I feel absolutely . . . Have your parents met him yet? I know your mother will be over the moon!"

Oh fuck.

Suddenly I feel a bit sick. My parents. I didn't think of that.

"Janice, I've just got to go and . . . and powder my nose," I say, and get hastily to my feet. "See you later."

"And Luke!" she says.

"And Luke, of course!" I say, and give a shrill little laugh.

I hurry to the portaloos without meeting anyone's eye, lock myself in a cubicle, and sit, swigging the last warm dregs of my champagne. OK, let's not panic about this. Let's just . . . think clearly, and go over my options.

Option One: Tell everybody that Luke isn't really here, I made a mistake.

Not unless I want to be stoned to death with champagne glasses and never show my face in Oxshott again.

Option Two: Tell Mum and Dad in private that Luke isn't really here.

But they'll be so disappointed. They'll be mortified, and they won't enjoy the day and it'll be all my fault.

Option Three: Bluff it out—and tell Mum and Dad the truth at the end of the day.

Yes. That could work. It has to work. I can easily convince everyone Luke's here for about an hour or so—and then I'll say he's got a migraine, and has gone off to lie down quietly.

Right, this is what I'm going to do. OK—let's go.

And you know, it's easier than I thought. Before long, everyone seems to be taking it for granted that Luke is around somewhere. Tom's granny even tells me she's already spotted him, and isn't he handsome and will it be my turn next? I've told countless people that he was here just a minute ago, have collected two plates of food from the buffet—one for me, one for Luke (tipped one into the flower bed), and have even borrowed some stranger's morning coat and put it on the chair next to me, as though it's his. The great thing is, no one can prove he's not here! There are so many people milling about, it's impossible to keep track of who's here and who isn't. I should have done this ages ago.

"Group photograph in a minute," says Lucy, bustling up to me. "We all have to line up. Where's Luke?"

"Talking to some guy about property prices," I reply without hesitation. "They were over by the drinks table."

"Well, make sure you introduce me," says Lucy. "I still haven't met him!"

"OK!" I say, and give her a bright smile. "As soon as I track him down!" I take a swig of champagne, look up—and there's Mum in her lime-green wedding outfit, heading toward me.

So far, I've managed to avoid her and Dad completely, basically by running away whenever they've come close. I know it's really bad of me—but I just won't be able to lie to Mum. Quickly I slip out of the marquee into the garden, and head for the shrubbery, dodging the photographer's assistant, who's rounding up all the children. I sit down behind a tree and finish my glass of champagne, staring up blankly at the blue afternoon sky.

I stay there for what seems like hours, until my legs are starting to ache and the breeze is making me shiver. Then at last, I slowly wander back, and slip inconspicuously into the tent. I won't hang around much longer. Just long enough to have a piece of wedding cake, maybe, and some more champagne . . .

"There she is!" comes a voice behind me.

I freeze for an instant—then slowly turn round. To my utter horror, all the guests are standing in neat rows in the center of the marquee, while a photographer adjusts a tripod.

"Becky, where's Luke?" says Lucy sharply. "We're trying to get everybody in."

Shit. *Shit.*

"Erm . . ." I swallow, trying to stay nonchalant. "Maybe he's in the house?"

"No, he's not," says Kate the bridesmaid. "I've just been looking in there."

"Well, he must be . . . in the garden, then."

"But you were in the garden!" says Lucy, narrowing her eyes. "Didn't you see him?"

"Erm . . . I'm not sure." I look round the marquee hurriedly, wondering if I could pretend to spot him in the distance. But it's different when there are no milling crowds. Why did they have to stop milling?

"He must be somewhere!" says a cheerful woman. "Who saw him last?"

There's a deathly silence. Two hundred people are staring at me. I catch Mum's anxious eye, and quickly look away again.

"Actually . . ." I clear my throat. "Now I remember, he was saying he had a bit of a headache! So maybe he went to—"

"Who's seen him *at all*?" cuts in Lucy, ignoring me. She looks around the assembled guests. "Who here can say they've actually seen Luke Brandon in the flesh? Anyone?"

"I've seen him!" comes a wavering voice from the back. "Such a good-looking young man . . ."

"Apart from Tom's gran," says Lucy, rolling her eyes. "Anyone?"

And there's another awful silence.

"I've seen his morning coat," ventures Janice timidly. "But not his actual . . . body," she whispers.

"I knew it. I knew it!" Lucy's voice is loud and triumphant. "He never was here, was he?"

"Of course he was!" I say, trying to sound confident. "I expect he's just in the—"

"You're not going out with Luke Brandon at all, are you?" Her voice lashes across the marquee. "You just made the whole thing up! You're just living in your own sad little fantasy land!"

"I'm not!" To my horror, my voice is thickening, and

I can feel tears pricking at my eyes. "I'm not! Luke and I are a couple!"

But as I look at all the faces gazing at me—some hostile, some astonished, some amused—I don't even feel so sure of that anymore. I mean, if we were a couple, he'd be here, wouldn't he? He'd be here with me.

"I'll just . . ." I say in a trembling voice. "I'll just check if he's . . ."

And without looking anyone in the eye, I back out of the marquee.

"She's a bloody fruit loop!" I hear Lucy saying. "Honestly, Tom, she could be dangerous!"

"*You're* dangerous, young lady!" I hear Mum retorting, her voice shaking a little. "Janice, I don't know how you could let your daughter-in-law be so rude! Becky's been a good friend to you, over the years. And to you, Tom, standing there, pretending this has nothing to do with you. And this is the way you treat her. Come on, Graham. We're going."

And a moment later, I see Mum stalking out of the marquee, Dad in tow, her lime-green hat quivering on her head. They head toward the front drive, and I know they're going back to our house for a nice, calming cup of tea.

But I don't follow them. I can't bring myself to see them—or anyone.

I walk quickly, stumbling slightly, toward the other end of the garden. Then, when I'm far enough away, I sink down onto the grass. I bury my head in my hands—and, for the first time today, feel tears oozing out of my eyes.

This should have been such a good day. It should

have been such a wonderful, happy occasion. Seeing Tom get married, introducing Luke to my parents and all our friends, dancing together into the night . . . And instead, it's been spoiled for everyone. Mum, Dad, Janice, Martin . . . I even feel sorry for Lucy and Tom. I mean, they didn't want all this disruption at their wedding, did they?

For what seems like ages I sit without moving, staring down at the ground. From the marquee I can hear the sounds of a band starting up, and Lucy's voice bossing somebody about. Some children are playing with a bean bag in the garden and occasionally it lands near me. But I don't flicker. I wish I could just sit here forever, without having to see any of them ever again.

And then I hear my name, low across the grass.

At first I think Lucy's right, and I'm hearing imaginary voices. But as I look up, my heart gives an almighty flip and I feel something hard blocking my throat. I don't believe it.

It's him.

It's Luke, walking across the grass, toward me, like a dream. He's wearing morning dress and holding two glasses of champagne, and I've never seen him looking more handsome.

"I'm sorry," he says as he reaches me. "I'm beyond sorry. Four hours late is . . . well, it's unforgivable." He shakes his head.

I stare up at him dazedly. I'd almost started to believe that Lucy was right, and he only existed in my own imagination.

"Were you . . . held up?" I say at last.

"A guy had a heart attack. The plane was diverted . . ." He frowns. "But I left a message on your phone as soon as I could. Didn't you get it?"

I grab for my phone, realizing with a sickening thud that I haven't checked it for a good while. I've been too busy dealing with imaginary Luke to think about the real one. And sure enough, the little message icon is blinking merrily.

"No, I didn't get it," I say, staring at it blankly. "I didn't. I thought . . ."

I break off and shake my head. I don't know what I thought anymore.

"Are you all right?" says Luke, sitting down beside me and handing me a glass of champagne. He runs a finger gently down my face and I flinch.

"No," I say, rubbing my cheek. "Since you ask, I'm not all right. You promised you'd be here. You *promised,* Luke."

"I *am* here."

"You know what I mean." I hunch my arms miserably round my knees. "I wanted you to be there at the service, not arrive when it's all nearly over. I wanted everyone to meet you, and see us together . . ." My voice starts to wobble. "It's just been . . . awful! They all thought I was after the bridegroom—"

"The bridegroom?" says Luke incredulously. "You mean the pale-faced nonentity called Tom?"

"Yes, him." I look up and give a reluctant half-giggle as I see Luke's expression. "Did you meet him, then?"

"I met him just now. And his very unlovely wife. Quite a pair." He takes a sip of champagne and leans back on his elbows. "By the way—she looked rather taken aback to meet me. Almost . . . gobsmacked, one might say. As did most of the guests." He gives me a quizzical look. "Anything I should know?"

"Erm . . ." I clear my throat. "Erm . . . not really. Nothing important."

"I thought as much," says Luke. "So the bridesmaid who cried out, 'Oh my God, he exists!' when I walked in. She's presumably . . ."

"Mad," I say without moving my head.

"Right." He nods. "Just checking."

He reaches out for my hand, and I let him take it. For a while we sit in silence. A bird is wheeling round and round overhead, and in the distance I can hear the band playing "Lady in Red."

"Becky, I'm sorry I was late." His voice is suddenly grave. "There was really nothing I could do. I gave a lot of people a lot of grief, believe me."

"I'm sure you did." I exhale sharply. "You couldn't help it. Just one of those things."

For a while longer we're both silent.

"Good champagne," says Luke eventually, and takes a sip.

"Yes," I say. "It's . . . very nice. Nice and . . . dry . . ." I break off and rub my face, trying to hide how nervous I am.

There's part of me that wants to sit here, making small talk for as long as we can. But another part is thinking, what's the point in putting it off any longer? There's only one thing I want to know. I feel a spasm of nerves in my stomach, but somehow force myself to take a deep breath and turn to him.

"So. How did your meetings in Zurich go? How's the . . . the new deal coming along?"

I'm trying to stay calm and collected—but I can feel my lips starting to tremble, and my hands are twisting themselves into knots.

"Becky . . ." says Luke. He stares into his glass for a moment, then puts it down. "There's something I need to tell you. I'm moving to New York."

I feel cold and heavy. So this is the end to a completely disastrous day. Luke's leaving me. It's the end. It's all over.

"Right," I manage, and give a careless shrug. "I see. Well—OK."

There's silence—and I force myself to look up. The love in Luke's dark eyes hits me like a thunderbolt.

"And I'm really, *really* hoping . . ." He takes both my hands and squeezes them tight. ". . . that you'll come with me."

REGAL AIRLINES

HEAD OFFICE • PRESTON HOUSE • 354 KINGSWAY • LONDON WC2 4TH

Ms. Rebecca Bloomwood
Flat 2
4 Burney Rd.
London SW6 8FD

17 September 2000

Dear Rebecca Bloomwood:

Thank you for your letter of 15 September.

I am glad that you are looking forward to flying with us and have already recommended us highly to all your friends. I agree that word-of-mouth business is invaluable for a company such as ours and may well send our revenues "rocketing."

Unfortunately this does not, as you suggest, qualify you for "a special little thank-you" regarding luggage. Regal Airlines is unable to increase your luggage allowance beyond the standard 20 kg. Any excess weight will be subject to a charge; I enclose an explanatory leaflet.

Please enjoy your flight.

Mary Stevens
Customer Care Manager

PGNI FIRST BANK VISA
7 CAMEL SQUARE
LIVERPOOL LI 5NP

Ms. Rebecca Bloomwood
Flat 2
4 Burney Rd.
London SW6 8FD

19 September 2000

GOOD NEWS!
YOUR NEW CREDIT LIMIT IS £10,000

Dear Ms. Bloomwood:

We are delighted to announce that you have been given an increase to your credit limit. Your new credit limit of £10,000 is available for you to spend immediately and will be shown on your next statement.

You can use your new credit limit to do many things. Pay for a holiday, a car, even transfer balances from other cards!

However, we realize that some customers do not wish to take advantage of increased credit limits. If you would prefer your credit limit to remain at its original level, please call one of our Customer Satisfaction Representatives, or return the form below.

Yours sincerely,

Michael Hunt
Customer Satisfaction Manager

Name: REBECCA BLOOMWOOD   Account Number: 0003 4572 0990 2765
I **would** / **would not** like to take up the offer of my new £10,000 credit limit.
Please delete as appropriate.

Seven

NEW YORK! I'm going to New York! New York!

Everything is transformed. *This* is why Luke has been so secretive. We had a lovely long chat at the wedding, and Luke explained everything to me, and suddenly it all made sense. It turns out he's opening up a new office of Brandon Communications in New York, in partnership with some advertising supremo called Michael Ellis who is based in Washington. And Luke's going to go over there and head it up. He said he's been wanting to ask me all along to come with him—but he knew I wouldn't want to give up my career just to trail along with him. So—this is the best bit—he's been speaking to some contacts in television, and he reckons I'll be able to get a job as a financial expert on an American TV show! In fact, he says I'll get "snapped up" because Americans love British accents. Apparently one producer has already practically offered me a job just from seeing a tape Luke sent him. Isn't that great?

The reason he didn't say anything before was he didn't want to raise my hopes before things started looking definite. But now, apparently, all the investors are on board, and everyone's really positive, and they're hoping to finalize the deal as soon as possible. Michael Ellis's agency advertises for most of the big financial players—and he's already been talking to them all about the new company. So there are loads of potential clients out there for Luke, and that's before he's even started.

And guess what? We're going over there in three days' time! Hooray! Luke's going to have meetings with some of his backers—and I'm going to have some interviews with TV people and explore the city. God, it's exciting. In just seventy-two hours, I'll be there. In the Big Apple. The city that never sleeps. The—

"Becky?"

Oh shit. I snap to attention and hastily smile brightly. I'm sitting on the set of *Morning Coffee,* doing my usual phone-in, and Jane from Lincoln has been explaining over the line that she wants to buy a property but doesn't know which kind of mortgage to take out.

Oh, for goodness' sake. How many times have I explained the difference between repayment plans and endowment policies? You know, sometimes this job can be so interesting, hearing about people and their problems and trying to help them. But other times—to be honest—it's just as boring as *Successful Saving* ever was. I mean, mortgages *again*? I feel like yelling, "Didn't you watch last week's show?"

"Well, Jane!" I say, stifling a yawn. "You're right to be concerned about redemption penalties."

As I speak, my mind begins to drift again toward New York. Just think. We'll have an apartment in Manhattan. In some amazing Upper East Side condo—or maybe somewhere really cool in Greenwich Village. Yes! It's just going to be perfect.

To be honest, I hadn't thought of Luke and me living

together for . . . well, for ages. I reckon if we'd stayed in London, perhaps we wouldn't have. I mean, it's quite a big step, isn't it? But as Luke said, this is the chance of a lifetime for both of us. It's a whole new beginning. It's yellow taxicabs and skyscrapers, and Woody Allen and *Breakfast at Tiffany's*.

The weird thing is that although I've never actually been to New York, I already feel an affinity toward it. Like, for example, I adore sushi—and that was invented in New York, wasn't it? And I always watch *Friends,* unless I'm going out that night. And *Cheers.* (Except now I come to think of it, that's Boston. Still, it's the same thing, really.)

"So really, Jane, whatever you're buying," I say dreamily, "be it a . . . a Fifth Avenue duplex . . . or an East Village walk-up . . . you must maximize the potential of your dollar. Which means . . ."

I stop as I see both Emma and Rory staring at me strangely.

"Becky, Jane is planning to buy a semidetached house in Skegness," says Emma.

"And surely it's pounds?" says Rory, looking around, as though for support. "Isn't it?"

"Yes, well," I say hurriedly. "Obviously, I was just using those as examples. The principles apply wherever you're buying. London, New York, Skegness . . ."

"And on that international note, I'm afraid we'll have to finish," says Emma. "Hope that helped you, Jane, and thanks once again to Becky Bloomwood, our financial expert . . . do you have time for a last word, Becky?"

"The same message as ever," I say, smiling warmly into the camera. "Look after your money . . ."

"And your money will look after you," everyone choruses dutifully.

"And that brings us to the end of the show," says Emma. "Join us tomorrow, when we'll be making over a trio of teachers from Teddington . . ."

". . . talking to the man who became a circus performer at sixty-five . . ." says Rory.

". . . and giving away £5,000 in 'Go On—Have a Guess!' Good-bye!"

There's a frozen pause—then everyone relaxes as the signature music starts blaring out of the loudspeakers.

"So—Becky—are you going to New York or something?" says Rory.

"Yes," I say, beaming back at him. "For two weeks!"

"How nice!" says Emma. "What brought this on?"

"Oh, I don't know . . ." I shrug vaguely. "Just a sudden whim."

I'm not telling anyone at *Morning Coffee* yet about moving to New York. It was Luke's advice, actually. Just in case.

"Becky, I wanted a quick word," says Zelda, one of the assistant producers, bustling onto the set with some papers in her hand. "Your new contract is ready to be signed, but I'll need to go through it with you. There's a new clause about representing the image of the station." She lowers her voice. "After all that business with Professor Jamie."

"Oh right," I say, and pull a sympathetic face. Professor Jamie is the education expert on *Morning Coffee*. Or at least he was, until *The Daily World* ran an exposé on him last month in their series "Are They What They Seem?" revealing that he isn't a real professor at all. In fact, he hasn't even got a degree, except the fake one he bought from the "University of Oxbridge." All the tabloids picked up the story, and kept showing photographs of him in the dunce's hat he wore for last year's telethon. I felt really sorry for him, actually, because he used to give good advice.

And I was a bit surprised at *The Daily World* being so vicious. I've actually written for *The Daily World* myself, once or twice, and I'd always thought they were quite reasonable, for a tabloid.

"It won't take five minutes," says Zelda. "We could go into my office—"

"Well . . ." I say, and hesitate. Because I don't really want to sign anything at the moment. Not if I'm planning to switch jobs. "I'm in a bit of a hurry, actually." Which is true, because I've got to get to Luke's office by twelve, and then start getting my stuff ready for New York. (Ha! Ha-ha!) "Can it wait till I come back?"

"OK," says Zelda. "No problem." She puts the contract back in its brown envelope and grins at me. "Have a great time. Hey, you know, you must do some shopping while you're there."

"Shopping?" I say, as though it hadn't occurred to me. "Yes, I suppose I could."

"Ooh yes!" says Emma. "You can't go to New York without shopping! Although I suppose Becky would tell us we should put our money into a savings plan instead."

She laughs merrily and Zelda joins in. And I smile back, feeling a bit uncomfortable. Somehow, all the people at *Morning Coffee* have got the idea I'm incredibly organized with my money—and, without quite meaning to, I've gone along with it. Still, I don't suppose it really matters.

"A savings plan is a good idea, of course . . ." I hear myself saying. "But as I always say, there's no harm going shopping once in a while as long as you stick to a budget."

"Is that what you're going to do, then?" asks Emma interestedly. "Give yourself a budget?"

"Oh, absolutely," I say wisely. "It's the only way."

Which is completely true. I mean, obviously I'm planning to give myself a New York shopping budget. I'll set realistic limits and I'll stick to them. It's really very simple.

Although what I'll do is make the limits fairly broad and flexible. Because it's always a good idea to allow some extra leeway for emergencies or one-offs.

"You're so virtuous!" says Emma, shaking her head. "Still—that's why you're the financial expert and I'm not . . ." Emma looks up as the sandwich man approaches us with a tray of sandwiches. "Ooh lovely, I'm starving! I'll have . . . bacon and avocado."

"And I'll have tuna and sweet corn," says Zelda. "What do you want, Becky?"

"Pastrami on rye," I say casually. "Hold the mayo."

"I don't think they do that," says Zelda, wrinkling her brow. "They've got ham salad . . ."

"Then a bagel. Cream cheese and lox. And a soda."

"Soda water, do you mean?" says Zelda.

"What's lox?" says Emma puzzledly—and I pretend I haven't heard. I'm not actually sure what lox is—but everyone eats it in New York, so it's got to be delicious.

"Whatever it is," says the sandwich man, "I 'aven't got it. You can 'ave cheese and tomato and a nice packet of Hula Hoops."

"OK," I say reluctantly, and reach for my purse. As I do so, a pile of post that I picked up this morning falls out of my bag, onto the floor. Shit. Hastily, I gather all the letters up, and shove them into my Conran Shop carrier bag, hoping no one spotted them. But bloody Rory was looking straight at me.

"Hey, Becky," he says, giving a guffawing laugh. "Was that a red bill I saw there?"

"No!" I say at once. "Of course not! It's a . . . a birthday card. A joke birthday card. For my accountant. Anyway, I must run. Ciao!"

OK, so that wasn't quite true. It was a red bill. To be honest, there have been quite a few red bills arriving for me over the last few days, which I'm completely intending to get round to paying off when I've got the cash. But I mean, I've got more important things happening in my life than a few crappy final demands. In a few months' time, I'm going to be living on the other side of the Atlantic. I'm going to be an American television star!

Luke says I'll probably earn twice in the States what I do here. If not more! So a few crummy bills won't exactly matter then, will they? A few outstanding pounds won't exactly ruin my sleep when I'm a household name and living in a Park Avenue penthouse.

God, and that'll completely suss that horrible John Gavin. Just imagine his face when I march in and tell him I'm going to be the new anchorwoman on CNN, on a salary six times what he earns. That'll teach him to be so nasty. I finally got round to opening his latest letter this morning, and it actually quite upset me. What does he mean, "excessive level of debt"? What does he mean, "special status"? You know, Derek Smeath would never have been so rude to me, not in a million years.

Luke's in a meeting when I arrive, but that's OK, because I don't mind hanging around. I love visiting the

Brandon Communications offices—in fact, I pop in there quite a lot, just for the atmosphere. It's such a cool place—all blond-wood floors and spotlights and trendy sofas, and people rushing around being really busy and dynamic. Everyone stays really late every night, even though they don't have to—and at about seven o'clock someone always opens a bottle of wine and passes it around.

I've got a present to give his assistant Mel for her birthday, which was yesterday. I'm quite pleased with it actually—it's a gorgeous pair of cushions from the Conran Shop—and as I hand over the carrier bag, I actually hear her gasp, "Oh, Becky! You shouldn't have!"

"I wanted to!" I beam, and perch companionably on her desk as she admires them. "So—what's the latest?"

Ooh, you can't beat a good gossip. Mel puts down the carrier bag and gets out a box of toffees, and we have a lovely old natter. I hear all about her terrible date with an awful guy her mother's been trying to set her up with, and she hears all about Tom's wedding. And then she lowers her voice and starts filling me in on all the office gossip.

She tells me all about the two receptionists who haven't been speaking ever since they came to work in the same Next jacket and both refused to take it off— and the girl in accounts who has just come back from maternity leave and is throwing up every morning but won't admit anything.

"And here's a really juicy one!" she says, handing me the box of toffees. "I reckon Alicia's having an affair in the office."

"No!" I stare at her in amazement. "Really? With who?"

"With Ben Bridges."

I screw up my face, trying to place the name.

"That new guy who used to be at Coupland Foster Bright."

"Him?" I stare at Mel. "Really?"

I have to say I'm surprised. He's very sweet, but quite short and pushy. Not what I would have said was Alicia's type.

"I keep seeing them together, kind of whispering. And the other day Alicia said she was going to the dentist—but I went into Ratchetts and there they were, having a secret lunch—"

She breaks off as Luke appears at the door of his office, ushering out a man in a purple shirt.

"Mel, order a taxi for Mr. Mallory, would you, please?"

"Of course, Luke," says Mel, switching into her efficient secretary voice. She picks up the phone and we grin at each other—then I walk into Luke's office.

His office is so smart. I always forget how grand he is. He's got a sweeping maple desk that was designed by some award-winning Danish designer, and on the shelves in the alcove behind it are all his shiny PR awards.

"Here you are," he says, handing me a sheaf of papers. The top one is a letter from someone called "Howski and Forlano, U.S. Immigration Lawyers," and as I see the words "your proposed relocation to the United States," I feel a tingle of excitement which reaches right to my fingertips.

"This is really happening, isn't it?" I say, walking over to his floor-length window and gazing down at the busy street below. "We're really going to New York."

"The flights are booked," he says, grinning at me.

"You know what I mean."

"I do know just what you mean," he echoes, and wraps me in his arms. "And it's very exciting."

For a while we just stand there, the two of us, looking down at the busy London street below. I can hardly believe I'm planning to leave all this to live in a foreign country. It's exciting and wonderful—but just a little scary, at the same time.

"Do you really think I'll get a job out there?" I say, as I have every time I've seen him in the past week. "Do you honestly think I will?"

"Of course you will." He sounds so assured and confident, I feel myself relax into his arms. "They'll love you. You're talented, and you're charming, and you come with a record of success . . . no question at all." He kisses me and holds me tight for a moment. Then he moves away to his desk, frowns absently, and opens a huge file labeled "New York." No wonder it's so huge. He told me the other day that he's been working toward a New York deal for three years. Three years!

"I can't believe you've been planning this for so long and never told me," I say, watching him scribble something on a Post-it.

"Mmm," says Luke. I clench the papers in my hands slightly harder and take a deep breath. There's something I've been wanting to say for a while—and now is as good a moment as any.

"Luke, what would you have done if I hadn't wanted to go to New York?"

There's silence apart from the hum of the computer.

"I knew you'd want to go," says Luke at last. "It's the next obvious step for you."

"But . . . what if I hadn't?" I bite my lip. "Would you still have gone?" Luke sighs.

"Becky—you do want to go to New York, don't you?"

"Yes! You know I do!"

"So—what's the point in asking what-if questions?

The point is, you want to go, I want to go . . . it's all perfect." He smiles at me and puts down his pen. "How are your parents doing?"

"They're . . . OK," I say hesitantly. "They're kind of getting used to the idea."

Which is sort of true. They were fairly shocked when I told them, I have to admit. In hindsight, perhaps I should have introduced Luke to them *before* making the announcement. Because how it happened was, I hurried into the house—where they were still sitting in their wedding gear, drinking tea in front of *Countdown*—and I switched off the telly and said joyfully, "Mum, Dad, I'm moving to New York with Luke!"

Whereupon Mum just looked at Dad and said, "Oh, Graham. She's gone."

She said afterward she didn't mean it like that—but I'm not so sure.

Then they actually met Luke, and he told them about his plans, and explained about all the opportunities in American TV for me—and I could see Mum's smile fading. Her face seemed to get smaller and smaller, and sort of closed in on itself. She went off to make some tea in the kitchen, and I followed her—and I could see she was upset. But she refused to show it. She just made the tea, with slightly shaking hands, and put out some biscuits—and then she turned to me and smiled brightly, and said, "I've always thought you would suit New York, Becky. It's the perfect place for you."

I stared at her, suddenly realizing what I was talking about. Going and living thousands of miles away from home, and my parents, and . . . my whole life, apart from Luke.

"You'll . . . you'll come and visit lots," I said, my voice trembling slightly.

"Of course we will, darling! All the time!"

She squeezed my hand and looked away—and then we went out into the sitting room, and didn't say much more about it.

But the next morning, when we came down for breakfast, she and Dad were poring over an ad in the *Sunday Times* for holiday properties in Florida, which they claimed they had been thinking about anyway. As we left that afternoon, they were arguing vigorously over whether the Disneyland in Florida was better than the one in California—even though I happen to know neither of them has ever set foot near Disneyland in their lives.

"Becky, I have to get on," says Luke, interrupting my thoughts. "Scottish Prime's new fund launch is tomorrow, and I've got a lot to do." He picks up the phone and dials a number. "I'll see you this evening, OK?"

"OK," I say, still loitering by the window. Then, suddenly remembering, I turn round. "Hey, have you heard about Alicia?"

"What about her?" Luke frowns at the receiver and puts it down.

"Mel reckons she's having an affair! With Ben Bridges! Can you believe it?"

"No, frankly," says Luke, tapping at his keyboard. "I can't."

"So what do you think's going on?" I perch on his desk and look excitedly at him.

"My sweet—" says Luke patiently. "I really do have to get on."

"Aren't you *interested*?"

"No. As long as they're doing their jobs."

"People are more than just their jobs," I say reprovingly. But Luke isn't even listening. He's got that faraway, cutoff look which comes over him when he's concentrating on business.

"Oh well," I say, and roll my eyes. "See you later."

As I come out, Mel is not at her desk—but Alicia is standing there in a smart black suit, staring at some papers. Her face seems more flushed than usual, and I wonder with an inward giggle if she's just been canoodling with Ben.

"Hi, Alicia," I say politely. "How are you?"

Alicia jumps, and she quickly gathers up whatever it is she's reading—then looks at me with a strange expression, as though horns have sprouted from my head.

"Becky," she says slowly. "Well, I never. The financial expert herself. The money guru!"

What *is* it about Alicia? Why does everything she say sound like she's playing some stupid game?

"Yes," I say. "It's me. Where's Mel gone?"

As I approach Mel's desk, I feel sure I left something on it. But I can't quite think what. Did I have an umbrella?

"She's gone to lunch," says Alicia. "She showed me the present you bought her. Very stylish."

"Thanks," I say shortly.

"So." She gives a faint smile. "I gather you're tagging along with Luke to New York. Must be nice to have a rich boyfriend."

God, she's a cow! She'd never say that in front of Luke.

"I'm not 'tagging along,' actually," I retort pleasantly.

"I've got lots of meetings with television executives. It's a completely independent trip."

"But . . ." Alicia frowns thoughtfully. "Your flight's on the company, is it?"

"No! I paid for it myself!"

"Just wondering!" Alicia lifts her hands apologetically. "Well, have a great time, won't you?" She gathers up some folders and pops them into her briefcase, then snaps it shut. "I must run. Ciao."

"See you later," I say, and watch as she walks briskly off to the lifts.

I stand there by Mel's desk for a few seconds longer, still wondering what on earth it was that I put down. Oh, I don't suppose it can be important.

I get home to find Suze in the hall, talking on the phone. Her face is all red and shiny and her voice is trembling, and at once I'm seized by the terror that something awful has happened. Fearfully, I raise my eyebrows at her—and she nods frantically back, in between saying "Yes," and "I see," and "When would that be?"

I sink onto a chair, feeling weak with worry. What's she talking about? A funeral? A brain operation? As soon as I decide to go away—this happens.

"Guess what's happened?" she says shakily as she puts down the phone, and I leap up.

"Suze, I won't go to New York," I say, and impulsively take her hands. "I'll stay here and help you get through whatever it is. Has someone . . . died?"

"No," says Suze dazedly, and I swallow hard.

"Are you ill?"

"No, no, Bex, this is *good* news! I just . . . don't quite believe it."

"Well—what, then? Suze, what is it?"

"I've been offered my own line of home accessories in Hadleys. You know, the department store?" She shakes her head disbelievingly. "They want me to design a whole line! Frames, vases, stationery . . . whatever I want."

"Oh my God!" I clap a hand over my mouth. "That's *fantastic!*"

"This guy just rang up, out of the blue, and said his scouts have been monitoring sales of my frames. Apparently they've never seen anything like it!"

"Oh, Suze!"

"I had no idea things were going so well." Suze still looks shell-shocked. "This guy said it was a phenomenon! Everyone in the industry is talking about it. Apparently the only shop that hasn't done so well is that one which is miles away. Finchley or somewhere."

"Oh, right," I say vaguely. "I don't think I've ever even been to that one."

"But he said that had to be a blip—because all the other ones, in Fulham and Notting Hill and Chelsea, have all soared." She gives an embarrassed smile. "Apparently in Gifts and Goodies, around the corner, I'm the number-one best-seller!"

"Well, I'm not surprised!" I exclaim. "Your frames are easily the best thing in that shop. *Easily* the best." I throw my arms around her. "I'm so proud of you, Suze. I always knew you were going to be a star."

"Well, I never would have done it if it weren't for you! I mean, it was you who got me started making frames in the first place . . ." Suddenly Suze looks almost tearful. "Oh, Bex—I'm really going to miss you."

"I know," I say, biting my lip. "Me too."

For a while, we're both silent, and I honestly think I

might start crying any second. But instead, I take a deep breath and look up. "Well, you'll just have to launch a New York branch."

"Yes!" says Suze, brightening. "Yes, I could do that, couldn't I?"

"Of course you could. You'll be all over the world soon." I give her a hug. "Hey, let's go out tonight and celebrate."

"Oh, Bex, I'd love to," says Suze, "but I can't. I'm going up to Scotland. In fact—" She looks at her watch, and pulls a face. "Oh, I didn't realize how late it was. Tarquin'll be here any moment."

"Tarquin's coming here?" I say in shock. "Now?"

Tarquin is Suze's cousin and is one of the richest people in Britain. (He's also one of the worst-dressed.) He's very sweet, and I never used to take much notice of him—until, a few months ago, we spent a truly toe-curling evening together. Even the memory of it makes me feel uncomfortable. Basically, the date was going fine (at least, fine given that I didn't find him attractive or have anything in common with him)—until Tarquin caught me flicking through his checkbook. Or at least, I think he did. I'm still not quite sure what he saw—and to be honest, I'm not keen to find out.

"I'm driving him up to my aunt's house for this dreary family party thing," says Suze. "We're going to be the only ones there under ninety."

As she hurries off to her room, the doorbell rings and she calls over her shoulder, "Could you get that, Bex? It's probably him."

Oh God. Oh God. I *really* don't feel prepared for this.

Trying to assume an air of confident detachment, I swing open the front door and say brightly, "Tarquin!"

"Becky," he says, staring at me as though I'm the lost treasure of Tutankhamen.

And he's looking as bony and strange as ever, with an odd green hand-knitted jersey stuffed under a tweed waistcoat, and a huge old fob watch dangling from his pocket. I'm sorry, but surely the fifteenth-richest man in England, or whatever he is, should be able to buy a nice new Timex?

"Well—come on in," I say overheartily, throwing my hand out like an Italian restaurant owner.

"Great," says Tarquin, and follows me into the sitting room. There's an awkward pause while I wait for him to sit down; in fact, I start to feel quite impatient as he hovers uncertainly in the middle of the room. Then suddenly I realize he's waiting for *me* to sit down, and hastily sink down onto the sofa.

"Would you like a titchy?" I ask politely.

"Bit early," says Tarquin, with a nervous laugh.

("Titchy" is Tarquin-speak for drink, by the way. And trousers are "tregs" and . . . you get the picture.)

We lapse into another dreadful silence. I just can't stop remembering awful details from our date—like when he tried to kiss me and I pretended to be absorbed in a nearby picture. Oh God. Forget. Forget.

"I . . . I heard you were moving to New York," Tarquin says suddenly, staring at the floor. "Is that true?"

"Yes," I say, unable to stop myself smiling. "Yes, that's the plan."

"I went to New York once myself," Tarquin says. "Didn't really get on with it."

"No," I say consideringly. "No, I can believe that. It's a bit different from Scotland, isn't it? Much more . . . frantic."

"Absolutely!" he exclaims, as if I've said something very insightful. "That was just it. Too frantic. And the people are absolutely extraordinary. Quite mad, in my opinion."

Compared to what? I want to retort. At least they don't call water "Ho" and sing Wagner in public.

But that wouldn't be kind. So I say nothing, and he says nothing—and when the door opens, we both look up gratefully.

"Hi!" says Suze, appearing at the door. "Tarkie, you're here! Listen, I've just got to get the car, because I had to park a few streets away the other night. I'll beep when I get back, and we can whiz off. OK?"

"OK," says Tarquin, nodding. "I'll just wait here with Becky."

"Lovely!" I say, trying to smile brightly.

Suze disappears, I shift awkwardly in my seat, and Tarquin stretches his feet out and stares at them. Oh, this is excruciating. The very sight of him is niggling at me more and more—and suddenly I realize I *have* to say something now, otherwise I'll disappear off to New York and the chance will be lost.

"Tarquin," I say, and exhale sharply. "There's something I . . . I really want to say to you. I've been wanting to say it for a while, actually."

"Yes?" he says, his head jerking up. "What . . . what is it?" He meets my eyes anxiously, and I feel a slight pang of nerves. But now I've started, I've got to carry on. I've got to tell him the truth. I push my hair back, and take a deep breath.

"That jumper," I say. "It *really* doesn't go with that waistcoat."

"Oh," says Tarquin, looking taken aback. "Really?"

"Yes!" I say, feeling a huge relief at having got it off my chest. "In fact . . . it's frightful."

"Should I take it off?"

"Yes. In fact, take the waistcoat off, too."

Obediently he peels off the jumper and the waistcoat—and it's amazing how much better he looks when he's just in a plain blue shirt. Almost . . . normal! Then I have a sudden inspiration.

"Wait here!"

I hurry to my room and seize one of the carrier bags sitting on my chair. There's a jumper inside which I bought a few days ago for Luke's birthday, but I've discovered he's already got exactly the same one, so I was planning to take it back.

"Here!" I say, arriving back in the sitting room. "Put this on. It's Paul Smith."

Tarquin slips the plain black jumper over his head and pulls it down—and what a difference! He's actually starting to look quite distinguished.

"Your hair," I say, staring critically at him. "We need to do something with that."

Ten minutes later I've wetted it, blow-dried it, and smoothed it back with a bit of mousse. And . . . I can't tell you. It's a transformation.

"Tarquin, you look wonderful!" I say—and I really mean it. He's still got that thin, bony look, but suddenly he doesn't look geeky anymore, he looks kind of . . . interesting.

"Really?" says Tarquin, staring down at himself. He looks a little shell-shocked, but the point is, he'll thank me in the long run.

A car horn sounds from outside, and we both jump.

"Well—have a good time," I say, suddenly feeling

like his mother. "Tomorrow morning, just wet your hair again and push your fingers through it, and it should look OK."

"Right," says Tarquin, looking as though I've just given him a long mathematical formula to memorize. "I'll try to remember. And the jersey? Shall I return it by post?"

"Don't return it!" I say in horror. "It's yours to keep, and *wear*. A gift."

"Thank you," says Tarquin. "I'm . . . very grateful, Becky." He comes forward and pecks me on the cheek, and I pat him awkwardly on the hand. And as he disappears out the door, I find myself hoping that he'll get lucky at this party, and find someone. He really does deserve it.

As I hear Suze's car drive away, I wander into the kitchen and make a cup of tea, wondering what to do for the rest of the afternoon. I was half-planning to do some more work on my self-help book. But my other alternative is to watch *Manhattan,* which Suze taped last night, and would be really useful research for my trip. Because, after all, I need to be well prepared.

I can always work on the book when I get back from New York. Exactly.

I'm just happily putting the video into the machine when the phone rings.

"Oh, hello," says a girl's voice. "Sorry to disturb you. Is that Becky Bloomwood, by any chance?"

"Yes," I say, reaching for the remote control.

"This is Sally," says the girl. "I'm the new secretary at *Morning Coffee.* We met the other day."

"Oh. Erm . . . yes!" I wrinkle my brow, trying to re-member.

"We just wanted to check on which hotel you're stay-ing at in New York, in case we need to contact you ur-gently."

"I'll be at the Four Seasons."

"Four . . . Seasons," says Sally carefully. "Excellent."

"Do you think they might want me to do a report from New York or something?" I ask excitedly. That would be so cool! A special report from New York!

"Maybe," says Sally. "And that's with a Mr. . . . Luke Brandon?"

"That's right."

"For how many nights?"

"Erm . . . thirteen? Fourteen? I'm not sure." I'm squinting at the telly, wondering if I've gone too far back. Surely they don't show that Walker's crisps ad anymore?

"And are you staying in a room or a suite?"

"I think it's a suite. I could find out . . ."

"No, don't worry," says Sally pleasantly. "Well, I won't trouble you anymore. Enjoy your trip."

"Thanks!" I say, just as I find the start of the film. "I'm sure we will!"

The phone goes dead, and I walk over to the sofa, frowning slightly. Why did Sally need to know whether I was in a suite? Unless—maybe she was just curious.

But then I forget all about it, as Gershwin's *Rhapsody in Blue* suddenly crashes through the air, and the screen is filled with pictures of Manhattan. I stare at the televi-sion, utterly gripped. This is where we're going! In three days' time we'll be there! I just cannot, cannot wait!

21 September 2000

Dear Rebecca:

Thank you for your letter and good wishes. I am
thoroughly enjoying my retirement, thank you.

I am sorry to hear that you are having such difficulties
dealing with John Gavin. May I assure you that he is not
a heartless android programmed to make your life
miserable. If you ever were cast out on the street with
nothing but a pair of shoes, I'm sure he would be
concerned, rather than "laugh evilly and walk away."

If you persevere with your good intentions, I'm certain
your relationship with him will improve. You have every
ability to keep your accounts in check, as long as your re-
solve remains steady.

I look forward to hearing how you get along.

With very best wishes,
Derek Smeath

REGAL AIRLINES

HEAD OFFICE • PRESTON HOUSE • 354 KINGSWAY • LONDON WC2 4TH

Ms. Rebecca Bloomwood
Flat 2
4 Burney Rd.
London SW6 8FD

23 September 2000

Dear Rebecca Bloomwood:

Thank you for your letter of 18 September, and I was
sorry to hear that our luggage policy has been giving
you anxiety attacks and frown lines.

I accept that you may well weigh considerably less
than, as you put it, "a fat businessman from Antwerp,
stuffing his face full of doughnuts." Unfortunately
Regal Airlines is still unable to increase your luggage
allowance beyond the standard 20 kg.

You are welcome to start a petition and to write to
Cherie Blair. However, our policy will remain the
same.

Please enjoy your flight.

Mary Stevens
Customer Care Manager

Eight

I was *made* to live in America.

We've only been here one night, but already I'm completely in love with the place. For a start, our hotel is fantastic—all limestone and marble and amazing high ceilings. We're staying in an enormous suite overlooking Central Park, with a paneled dressing room and the most incredible bath that fills up in about five seconds. Everything is so grand, and luxurious, and kind of . . . *more*. Like last night, after we arrived, Luke suggested a quick nightcap downstairs—and honestly, the martini they brought me was the hugest drink I've ever seen. In fact, I nearly couldn't finish it. (But I managed it in the end. And then I had another one, just because it would have been churlish to refuse.)

Plus, everyone is so nice all the time. The hotel staff smile whenever they see you—and when you say "thank you," they reply "you're welcome," which they would *never* do in Britain, just kind of grunt. To my amazement, I've already been sent a lovely bouquet of flowers and an invitation to lunch from Luke's mother, Elinor, and another bouquet from the TV people I'm meeting on Wednesday, and a basket of fruit from someone I've never heard of but who is apparently "desperate" to meet me!

I mean, when did Zelda from *Morning Coffee* last send me a basket of fruit?

I take a sip of coffee, and smile blissfully at Luke. We're sitting in the restaurant finishing breakfast before he whizzes off for a meeting, and I'm just deciding what to do with my time. I haven't got any interviews for a couple of days—so it's completely up to me whether I take in a few museums, or stroll in Central Park . . . or . . . pop into a shop or two . . .

"Would you like a refill?" comes a voice at my ear, and I look up to see a smiling waiter offering me a coffeepot. You see what I mean? They've been offering us endless coffee since we sat down, and when I asked for an orange juice they brought me a huge glass, all garnished with frosted orange peel. And as for those scrummy pancakes I've just polished off . . . I mean, pancakes for breakfast. It's pure genius, isn't it?

"So—I guess you'll be going to the gym?" says Luke, as he folds up his copy of the *Daily Telegraph*. He reads all the papers every day, American and British. Which is quite good, because it means I can still read my *Daily World* horoscope.

"The gym?" I say puzzledly.

"I thought that was going to be your routine," he says, reaching for the *FT*. "A workout every morning."

And I'm about to say, "Don't be ridiculous!"—when it occurs to me that I might have rashly announced something along those lines last night. After that second martini.

Still—that's OK. I can go to the gym. In fact, it would

be *good* to go to the gym. And then I could . . . well, I could always take in a few sights, I suppose. Maybe look at a few famous buildings.

You know, I'm sure I read somewhere that Bloomingdale's is quite an admired piece of architecture.

"And then what will you do?"

"I don't know," I say vaguely, watching as a waiter puts a plate of French toast down on the table next to ours. God, that looks delicious. Why don't we have stuff like this in Europe? "Go and explore New York, I guess."

"I was asking at reception—and there's a guided walking tour which leaves from the hotel at eleven. The concierge highly recommended it."

"Oh right," I say, taking a sip of coffee. "Well, I suppose I could do that . . ."

"Unless you wanted to get any shopping out of the way?" Luke adds, reaching for the *Times,* and I stare at him slightly incredulously. You don't "get shopping out of the way." You get *other things* out of the way.

Which, in fact, makes me think. Maybe I should do this tour—and then I've got sightseeing ticked off.

"The guided tour sounds good," I say. "In fact, it'll be a great way to get to know my new home city. The Statue of Liberty, Central Park . . ."

"Don't go to Central Park," puts in Luke.

"Why not? Is it dangerous?"

"It can be, but that's not why." Luke looks up with that serious, affectionate expression of his. "The truth is, I'd love to introduce it to you myself. It's one of my favorite places in the world."

"OK." I smile at him, feeling touched. "I won't go to Central Park."

As he shakes open the *Times* I look at him more carefully. His jaw is set and he doesn't quite have his usual confident demeanor. In fact he looks . . . nervous, I realize in surprise.

"Feeling all right?" I say encouragingly. "All set for your meeting? Who's it with, anyway?"

"Mason Forbes Stockbrokers," says Luke. "One of the companies I'm very much hoping to sign up as a client."

"Excellent! Well, I'm sure it'll go brilliantly."

"I hope so." He's silent for a moment. "It's all been talk up to now. Talk and plans and promises. But now I need to start getting a few results. A few signatures on the line."

"You'll get your signatures!" Confidently, I pick up *The Daily World.* "Just listen to your horoscope: 'A day for doing deals and winning hearts. If you have faith in yourself, others will too. You are beginning a streak of success.' " I look up. "You see? It's in your stars!"

"Let me see that," says Luke, and plucks the paper from my hand before I can stop him.

Damn.

"You do *slightly* have to read between the lines . . ." I add quickly.

"I see," he says, gazing down at the horoscope page with a smile. "Yes, that would explain it. So, do you want to hear yours?"

"I've already—"

" 'Spend today exploring new surroundings,' " says Luke, as though reading. " 'Remember to hold your bag tightly to you and that over here it's called a purse. Have a nice day—but don't feel obliged to tell complete strangers to have one.' "

He smiles at me and I laugh. As he puts away the paper I take a sip of coffee and glance around the dining room at all the smart businessmen and groomed women sitting on luxurious striped chairs. Piano music is tinkling discreetly and I feel like I'm at the hub of some cosmopolitan, civilized world. At a nearby table a woman in black is talking about the First Lady's wardrobe, and I listen eagerly until she gives me a look.

The First Lady. I mean, it sounds so much more impressive than "prime minister's wife."

"God, just think, Luke," I say dreamily. "In a few weeks' time, this will be our home city. We'll be real New Yorkers!"

I'll have to buy a few more black things before then, I find myself thinking. Everyone here seems to wear black . . .

"Becky—" says Luke. He puts down his paper—and suddenly he looks rather grave. "There's something I've been meaning to say to you. Everything's been such a rush, I haven't had a chance—but it's something I really think you need to hear."

"OK," I say apprehensively. "What is it?"

"It's a big step, moving to a new city, especially a city as extreme as New York. It's not the same as London . . ."

"I know," I nod. "You have to have your nails done."

Luke gives a puzzled frown before carrying on: "I've been here many times—and even I find it overwhelming at times. The sheer pressure and pace of life here is, frankly, on another level from London."

"Right. So—what are you saying?"

"I'm saying I think you should take it slow. Don't expect to fit in straight away. You may well find it a bit of a shock to begin with."

I stare at him, discomfited.

"Don't you think I'll be able to stand the pace?"

"I'm not saying that," says Luke. "I'm just saying—get to know the city gradually. Get the feel of it; see if you can really see yourself living here. You may hate it! You may decide you can't possibly move here. Of course, I very much hope you don't—but it's worth keeping an open mind."

"Right," I say slowly. "I see."

"So just see how today goes—and we'll talk some more this evening. OK?"

"OK," I say, and drain my coffee thoughtfully.

I'll show Luke I can fit into this city. I'll show him I can be a true New Yorker. I'll go to the gym, and then I'll eat a bagel, and then I'll . . . shoot someone, maybe?

Or maybe just the gym will be enough.

I'm actually quite looking forward to doing a workout, because I bought this fab DKNY exercise outfit in the sales last year, and this is the first time I've had the chance to wear it! I did mean to join a gym, in fact I even went and got a registration pack from Holmes Place in Fulham. But then I read this really interesting article which said you could lose loads of weight just by fidgeting. Just by twitching your fingers and stuff! So I thought I'd go for that method instead, and spend the money I saved on a new dress.

But it's not that I don't like exercise or anything. And if I'm going to live in New York, I'll have to go to the gym every day. I mean, it's the law or something. So this is a good way to acclimatize.

As I reach the entrance to the fitness center I glance at my reflection—and I'm secretly quite impressed. They say people in New York are all pencil thin and fit, don't they? But I reckon I look much fitter than some of these characters. I mean, look at that balding guy over there in the gray T-shirt. He looks like he's never been near a gym in his life!

"Hi there," says a voice. I look up and see a muscular guy in trendy black Lycra coming toward me. "I'm Tony. How are you today?"

"I'm fine, thanks," I say, and casually do a little hamstring stretch. (At least, I think it's my hamstring. The one in your leg.) "Just here for a workout."

Nonchalantly I swap legs, clasp my hands, and stretch my arms out in front of me. I can see my reflection on the other side of the room—and though I say it myself, I look pretty bloody cool.

"Do you exercise regularly?" asks Tony.

"Not in a gym," I say, reaching down to touch my toes—then changing my mind halfway down and resting my hands on my knees. "But I walk a lot."

"Great!" says Tony. "On a treadmill? Or cross-country?"

"Round the shops, mostly."

"OK . . ." he says doubtfully.

"But I'm often holding quite heavy things," I explain. "You know, carrier bags and stuff."

"Right . . ." says Tony, not looking that convinced. "Well . . . would you like me to show you how the machines work?"

"It's all right," I say confidently. "I'll be fine."

Honestly, I can't be bothered listening to him explain every single machine and how many settings it has. I mean, I'm not a moron, am I? I take a towel from the pile, drape it around my neck, and head off toward a running machine, which should be fairly simple. I step up onto the treadmill and survey the buttons in front of me. A panel is flashing the word "time" and after some thought I enter "40 minutes," which sounds about right. I mean, that's how long you'd go on a walk for, isn't it? It flashes "program" and after scrolling down the choices I select "Everest," which sounds much more interesting than "hill walk." Then it flashes "level." Hmm. Level. I look around for some advice—but Tony is nowhere to be seen.

The balding guy is getting onto the treadmill next to mine, and I lean over.

"Excuse me," I say politely. "Which level do you think I should choose?"

"That depends," says the guy. "How fit are you?"

"Well," I say, smiling modestly. "You know . . ."

"I'm going for level 5, if it's any help," says the guy, briskly punching at his machine.

"OK," I say. "Thanks!"

Well, if he's level 5, I must be at least level 7. I mean, frankly, look at him—and look at me.

I reach up to the machine and punch in "7"—then press "start." The treadmill starts moving, and I start walking. And this is really pleasant! I really should go to the gym more often. Or, in fact, join a gym.

But it just shows, even if you don't work out, you can still have a level of natural baseline fitness. Because this is causing me absolutely no problems at all. In fact, it's far too easy. I should have chosen level—

Hang on. The machine's tilting upward. And it's speeding up. I'm running to catch up with it.

Which is OK. I mean, this is the point, isn't it? Having a nice healthy jog. Running along, panting a little, but that just means my heart is working. Which is perfect. Just as long as it doesn't get any—

It's tilting again. And it's getting faster. And faster.

I can't do this. My face is red. My chest is hurting. I'm

panting frenziedly, and clutching the sides of the machine. I can't run this fast. I have to slow down a bit.

Feverishly I jab at the panel—but the treadmill keeps whirring round—and suddenly cranks up even higher. Oh no. Please, no.

"Time left: 38.00" flashes brightly on a panel in front of me. *Thirty-eight more minutes?*

I glance to my right—and the balding guy is sprinting easily along as though he's running through a field of daisies. I want to ask him for help, but I can't open my mouth. I can't do anything except keep my legs moving as best I can.

But all of a sudden he glances in my direction—and his expression changes.

"Miss? Are you all right?"

He hastily punches at his machine, which grinds to a halt, then leaps down and jabs at mine.

The treadmill slows down, then comes to a rather abrupt standstill—and I collapse against one of the side bars, gasping for breath.

"Have some water," says the man, handing me a cup.

"Th-thanks," I say, and stagger down off the treadmill, still gasping. My lungs feel as if they're about to burst, and when I glimpse my reflection opposite, my face is beet red.

"Maybe you should leave it for today," says the man, gazing at me anxiously.

"Yes," I say. "Yes, maybe I will." I take a swig of water, trying to get my breath back. "I think actually the trouble is, I'm not used to American machines."

"Could be," says the man, nodding. "They can be tricky. Of course, this one," he adds, slapping it cheerfully, "was made in Germany."

"Right," I say after a pause. "Yes. Well, anyway. Thanks for your help."

"Any time," says the man—and as he gets back onto his treadmill I can see him smiling.

Oh God, that was really embarrassing. As I make my way, showered and changed, to the foyer of the hotel for the walking tour, I feel a little deflated. Maybe Luke's right. Maybe I won't cope with the pace of New York. Maybe it's a stupid idea, my moving here with him. I mean, if I can't keep up with a treadmill, how am I going to keep up with a whole city?

A group of sightseers has already assembled—mostly much older than me and attired in a variety of sensible windbreakers and sneakers. They're all listening to a young, enthusiastic man who's saying something about the Statue of Liberty.

"Hi there!" he says, breaking off as I approach. "Are you here for the tour?"

"Yes, please," I say.

"And your name?"

"Rebecca Bloomwood," I say, flushing a little as all the others turn to look at me. "I paid at the desk, earlier."

"Well, hi, Rebecca!" says the man, ticking something off on his list. "I'm Christoph. Welcome to our group. Got your walking shoes on?" He looks down at my boots (bright purple, kitten heel, last year's Bertie sale) and his cheery smile falters. "You realize this is a three-hour tour? All on foot?"

"Absolutely," I say in surprise. "That's why I put these boots on."

"Right," says Christoph after a pause. "Well—OK." He looks around. "I think that's it, so let's start our tour!"

He leads the way out of the hotel, onto Fifty-seventh Street. It's a wide and busy street, with canopied entrances and trees planted at intervals and limousines pulling up in front of expensive-looking shops. As everyone else follows Christoph briskly along the pavement, I find myself walking slowly, staring upward. It's an amazingly clear, fresh day—with almost blinding sunlight bouncing off the pavements and buildings—and as I look around I'm completely filled with awe. God, this city is an incredible place. I mean, obviously I knew that New York would be full of tall skyscrapers. But it's only when you're actually standing in the street, staring up at them, that you realize how . . . well, how *huge* they are. I gaze up at the tops of the buildings against the sky, until my neck is aching and I'm starting to feel dizzy. Then slowly my eyes wander down, floor by floor to shop-window level. And I find myself staring at two words. *Prada* and *Shoes*.

Ooh.

Prada Shoes. Right in front of me.

I'll just have a really quick look.

As the others all march on, I hurry up to the window and stare at a pair of deep brown pumps with cream stitching. God, those are divine. I wonder how much they are? You know, Prada is probably really cheap over here. Maybe I should just pop in and—

"Rebecca?"

With a start I come to and look round to see the tour group twenty yards down the street, all staring at me.

"Sorry," I say, and reluctantly pull myself away from the window. "I'm coming."

"There'll be time for shopping later," says Christoph cheerfully.

"I know," I say, and give a relaxed laugh. "Sorry about that."

"Don't worry about it!"

Of course, he's quite right. There'll be plenty of time to go shopping. Plenty of time.

Right. I'm really going to concentrate on the tour.

"So, Rebecca," says Christoph brightly, as I rejoin the group. "I was just telling the others that we're heading down East Fifty-seventh Street to Fifth Avenue, the most famous avenue of New York City."

"Great!" I say. "That sounds really good!"

"Fifth Avenue serves as a dividing line between the 'East Side' and the 'West Side,'" continues Christoph. "Anyone interested in history will like to know that . . ."

I'm nodding intelligently as he speaks, and trying to look interested. But as we walk down the street, my head keeps swiveling from left to right, like someone watching a tennis game. Christian Dior, Hermès, Chanel . . . This street is just incredible. If only we could just slow down a bit, and have a proper look— but Christoph is marching on ahead like a hike leader, and everybody else in the group is following him happily, not even glancing at the amazing sights around them. Do they not have eyes in their heads?

". . . where we're going to take in two well-known landmarks: Rockefeller Center, which many of you will associate with ice-skating . . ."

We swing round a corner—and my heart gives a swoop of excitement. Tiffany's. It's Tiffany's, right in front of me! I *must* just have a quick peek. I mean, this is what New York is all about. Little blue boxes, and

white ribbon, and those gorgeous silver beans . . . I sidle up to the window and stare longingly at the beautiful display inside. Wow. That necklace is absolutely
stunning. Oh God, and look at that watch, with all
those little diamonds round the edge. I wonder how
much something like that would—

"Hey, everybody, wait up!" rings out Christoph's
voice. I look up—and they're all bloody miles ahead
again. How come they walk so fast, anyway? "Are you
OK there, Rebecca?" he calls, with a slightly forced
cheeriness. "You're going to have to try to keep up! We
have a lot of ground to cover!"

"Sorry," I say, and scuttle toward the group. "Just
having a quick little look at Tiffany's." I grin at a woman
next to me, expecting her to smile back. But she looks
at me blankly and pulls the hood of her baggy gray
sweatshirt more tightly over her head.

"As I was saying," Christoph says as we stride off
again, "above Fourteenth Street, Manhattan was designed as a grid, so that . . ."

And for a while I really try to concentrate. But it's no
good. I can't listen. I mean, come on. This is Fifth Avenue! There are women striding along in immaculate
coats and sunglasses, yellow taxicabs honking at each
other, two men are standing on a street corner, arguing
in Italian . . . And everywhere I look, there are fabulous
shops. There's Gucci—and that's the hugest Gap I've
ever seen in my life . . . and oh God, look at that window display over there! And we're just walking straight
past Armani Exchange and no one's even pausing . . .

What is *wrong* with these people? Are they complete
philistines?

We walk on a bit farther, and I'm trying my best to
catch a glimpse inside a window full of amazing-

looking hats when . . . oh my God. Just . . . just look there. It's Saks Fifth Avenue. Right there, across the street. One of the most famous department stores in the world. Floors and floors of clothes and shoes and bags . . . And thank God, at *last*, Christoph is coming to his senses and stopping.

"This is one of New York's most famous landmarks," he's saying, with a gesture. "Many New Yorkers regularly visit this magnificent place of worship—once a week or even more often. Some even make it here daily! We don't have time to do more than have a quick look inside—but those that are interested can always make a return trip."

"Is it very old?" asks a man with a Scandinavian accent.

"The building dates from 1879," says Christoph, "and was designed by James Renwick."

Come on, I think impatiently, as someone else asks a question about the architecture. Who cares who designed it? Who cares about the stonework? It's what's inside that matters.

"Shall we go in?" says Christoph at last.

"Absolutely!" I say joyfully, and hurry across the street toward the entrance.

It's only as my hand is actually on the door that I realize no one else is with me. Where've they all gone? Puzzled, I look back—and the rest of the group is processing into a big stone church, outside which there's a board reading "St. Patrick's Cathedral."

Oh.

Oh, I see. When he said "magnificent place of worship" he meant . . .

Right. Of course.

I hesitate, hand on the door, feeling torn. I should go

into the cathedral. I should take in some culture and come back to Saks later.

But then—how is that going to help me get to know whether I want to live in New York or not? Looking around some old cathedral?

Put it like this—how many millions of cathedrals do we have in England? And how many branches of Saks Fifth Avenue?

"Are you going in?" says an impatient voice behind me.

"Yes!" I say, coming to a decision. "Absolutely. I'm going in."

I push my way through the heavy wooden doors and into the store, feeling almost sick with anticipation. I haven't felt this excited since Octagon relaunched their designer floor and I was invited to the cardholders' champagne reception.

I mean, visiting any shop for the first time is exciting. There's always that electric buzz as you push open the door; that hope, that *belief*, that this is going to be the shop of all shops, which will bring you everything you ever wanted, at magically low prices. But this is a thousand times better. A million times. Because this isn't just any old shop, is it? This is a world-famous shop. I'm actually here. I'm in Saks on Fifth Avenue in New York. As I walk slowly into the store—forcing myself not to rush—I feel as though I'm setting off for a date with a Hollywood movie star.

I wander through the perfumery, gazing around at the elegant Art Deco paneling; the high, airy ceilings; the foliage everywhere. God, this has to be one of the most beautiful shops I've ever been in. At the back are old-fashioned lifts which make you feel you're in a film with Cary Grant, and on a little table is a pile of store directories. I pick one up, just to get my bearings . . . and I don't quite believe it. There are ten floors to this store.

Ten.

I stare at the list, transfixed. I feel like a child trying to choose a sweetie in a chocolate factory. Where am I going to start? How should I do this? Start at the top? Start at the bottom? All these names, jumping out at me, calling to me. Anna Sui. Calvin Klein. Kate Spade. Kiehl's. I am going to hyperventilate.

"Excuse me?" A voice interrupts my thoughts and I turn to see a girl with a Saks name badge smiling at me. "Can I help you?"

"Um . . . yes," I say, still staring at the directory. "I'm just trying to work out where to start, really."

"Were you interested in clothes? Or accessories? Or shoes?"

"Yes," I say dazedly. "Both. All. Everything. Erm . . . a bag," I say randomly. "I need a new bag!"

Which is true. I mean, I've brought bags with me—but you can always do with a new bag. Plus, I've been noticing that all the women in Manhattan seem to have very smart designer bags—so this is a very good way of acclimatizing myself to the city.

The girl gives me a friendly smile.

"Bags and accessories are through there," she says, pointing. "You might want to start there and work your way up."

"Yes," I say. "That's what I'll do. Thanks!"

God, I adore shopping abroad. I mean, shopping anywhere is always great—but the advantages of doing it abroad are:

1. You can buy things you can't get in Britain.
2. You can name-drop when you get back home. ("Actually, I picked this up in New York.")
3. Foreign money doesn't count, so you can spend as much as you like.

OK, I know that last one isn't entirely true. Somewhere in my head I know that dollars are proper money, with a real value. But I mean, *look* at them. I just can't take them seriously. I've got a whole wodge of them in my purse, and I feel as though I'm carrying around the bank from a Monopoly set. Yesterday I went and bought some magazines from a newsstand, and as I handed over a twenty-dollar bill, it was just like playing shop. It's like some weird form of jet lag—you move into another currency and suddenly feel as though you're spending nothing.

So as I walk around the bag department, trying out gorgeous bag after gorgeous bag, I'm not taking too much notice of the prices. Occasionally I lift a price tag and make a feeble attempt to work out how much that is in real money—but I have to confess, I can't remember the exact exchange rate.

But the point is, it doesn't matter. Because this is America, and everyone knows that prices in America are really low. It's common knowledge. So basically, I'm working on the principle that everything's a bargain. I mean, look at all these gorgeous designer handbags. They're probably half what they'd cost in England, if not less!

As I'm hovering over the DKNY display, an elderly woman wearing a gold-colored suit and carrying a Gucci tote comes up to me.

"Which one matches?" she says. "This . . . " She holds out a tan satin bag. ". . . or this . . . " She holds out a paler one. "It's for evening," she adds.

"Erm . . ." I look at her suit and at the bags again—and wonder how to tell her they don't match at all. "The thing is, they're both a kind of brownish color . . . and your suit's more of a golden, yellowish . . ."

"Not the suit!" she exclaims. "The dog!"

I look at her perplexedly—then spot a tiny face poking out of the Gucci tote. Oh my God! Is that a real live *dog*?

"Don't hide, Muffy!" says the woman, reaching into the bag and hauling it out. And honestly, it's more like a rat than a dog—except a rat with a Gucci collar and a diamante name tag.

"You want your bag to match your . . . dog?" I say, just to be sure.

"If I can't find anything, I'll just have to have her hair tinted again." The woman sighs. "But it's so time-consuming . . ."

"No, don't do that!" I say hastily. "I think the paler bag goes perfectly."

"I think you're right." She gives it a critical look, then nods. "Thank you for your help. Do you have a dog?"

"Erm . . . not on me."

The woman stares at me suspiciously—then stuffs the dog back in the Gucci tote. She walks off, and I resume my search, wondering if I need to buy a dog in order to be a real New Yorker. Except I only like big ones. And you couldn't exactly lug a Labrador around in a Fendi clutch, could you?

Eventually I choose a beautiful Kate Spade bag in tan leather, and take it up to the counter. It costs five hundred dollars, which sounds quite a lot—but then, "a million lira" sounds like a lot too, doesn't it? And that's only about fifty pence. So this is *sure* to be a bargain.

As the assistant hands me my receipt, she even says something about it being "a gift"—and I beam in agreement.

"A complete gift! I mean, in London, it would probably cost—"

"Gina, are you going upstairs?" interrupts the woman, turning to a colleague. "Gina will show you to the seventh floor," she says, and smiles at me.

"Right," I say, in slight confusion. "Well . . . OK."

Gina beckons me briskly and, after a moment's hesitation, I follow her, wondering what's on the seventh floor. Maybe some complimentary lounge for Kate Spade customers, with free champagne or something!

It's only as we're approaching a department entitled "Gift Wrapping" that I suddenly realize what's going on. When I said *gift*, she must have thought I meant it was an actual—

"Here we are," says Gina brightly. "The Saks signature box is complimentary—or choose from a range of quality wrap."

"Right!" I say. "Well . . . thanks very much! Although actually, I wasn't really planning to—"

But Gina has already gone—and the two ladies behind the gift wrap counter are smiling encouragingly at me.

This is a bit embarrassing.

"Have you decided which paper you'd like?" says the elder of the two ladies, beaming at me. "We also have a choice of ribbons and adornments."

Oh, sod it. I'll get it wrapped. I mean, it only costs $7.50—and it'll be nice to have something to open when I get back to the hotel room.

"Yes!" I say, and beam back. "I'd like that silver paper, please, and some purple ribbon . . . and one of those clusters of silver berries."

The lady reaches for the paper and deftly begins to wrap up my bag—more neatly than I've ever wrapped anything in my life. And you know, this is quite fun! Maybe I should always get my shopping gift wrapped.

"Who's it to?" says the lady, opening a card and taking out a silver pen.

"Um . . . to Becky," I say vaguely. Three girls, all wearing jeans and high-heeled boots, have come into the gift wrap room—and I'm slightly intrigued by their conversation.

". . . below wholesale . . ."

". . . sample sale . . ."

". . . Earl jeans . . ."

"And who is it from?" says the gift wrap lady pleasantly.

"Um . . . from Becky," I say without thinking. The gift wrap lady gives me a rather strange look and I suddenly realize what I've said. "A . . . a different Becky," I add awkwardly.

". . . sample sale . . ."

". . . Alexander McQueen, pale blue, 80 percent off . . ."

". . . sample sale . . ."

". . . sample sale . . ."

I cannot bear this any longer.

"Excuse me," I say, turning round. "I didn't mean to eavesdrop on your conversation—but I just have to know one thing. What is a sample sale?"

The whole gift wrap area goes quiet. Everyone is staring at me, even the lady with the silver pen.

"You don't know what a sample sale is?" says a girl in a

leather jacket eventually, as though I've said I don't know my alphabet.

"Erm . . . no," I say, feeling myself flush red. "No, I . . . I don't." The girl raises her eyebrows, reaches in her bag, rummages around, and eventually pulls out a card. "Honey, *this* is a sample sale."

I take the card from her—and as I read, my skin starts to prickle with excitement.

SAMPLE SALE
Designer clothes, 50–70% off.
Ralph Lauren, Comme des Garçons, Gucci.
Bags, shoes, hosiery, 40–60% off.
Prada, Fendi, Lagerfeld.

"Is this for real?" I breathe at last, looking up. "I mean, could . . . could *I* go to it?"

"Oh yeah," says the girl. "It's for real. But it'll only last a day."

"A day?" My heart starts to thump in panic. "Just one day?"

"One day," affirms the girl solemnly. I glance at the other girls—and they're nodding in agreement.

"Sample sales come without much warning," explains one.

"They can be anywhere. They just appear overnight."

"Then they're gone. Vanished."

"And you just have to wait for the next one."

I look from face to face, utterly mesmerized. I feel like an explorer learning about some mysterious nomadic tribe.

"So you wanna catch this one today," says the girl in blue, tapping the card and bringing me back to life, "you'd better hurry."

I have never moved as fast as I do out of that shop. Clutching my Saks Fifth Avenue carrier, I hail a taxi, breathlessly read out the address on the card, and sink back into my seat.

I have no idea where we're heading or what famous landmarks we're passing—but I don't care. As long as there are designer clothes on sale, then that's all I need to know.

We come to a stop, and I pay the driver, making sure I tip him about 50 percent so he doesn't think I'm some stingy English tourist—and, heart thumping, I get out. And I have to admit, on first impression, things are not promising. I'm in a street full of rather uninspiring-looking shop fronts and office blocks. On the card it said the sample sale was at 405, but when I follow the numbers along the road, 405 turns out to be just another office building. Am I in the wrong place altogether? I walk along the pavement for a little bit, peering up at the buildings—but there are no clues. I don't even know which district I'm in.

Suddenly I feel deflated and rather stupid. I was supposed to be going on a nice organized walking tour today—and what have I done instead? I've gone rushing off to some strange part of the city, where I'll probably get mugged any minute. In fact, the whole thing was probably a scam, I think morosely. I mean, honestly. Designer clothes at 70 percent discount? I should have realized it was far too good to be—

Hang on. Just . . . hang on a minute.

Another taxi is pulling up, and a girl in a Miu Miu dress is getting out. She consults a piece of paper, walks briskly along the pavement, and disappears inside the door of 405. A moment later, two more girls appear along the street—and as I watch, they go inside, too.

Maybe this is the right place.

I push open the glass doors, walk into a shabby foyer, and nod nervously at the concierge sitting at the desk.

"Erm . . . excuse me," I say politely. "I was looking for the—"

"Twelfth floor," he says in a bored voice. "Elevators are in the rear."

I hurry toward the back of the foyer, summon one of the rather elderly lifts, and press twelve. Slowly and creakily the lift rises—and I begin to hear a kind of faint hubbub, rising in volume as I get nearer. The lift suddenly pings and the doors open and . . . Oh my God. Is this the *queue*?

A line of girls is snaking back from a door at the end of the corridor. Girls in cashmere coats, girls in black suits, girls tossing their springy ponytails around, and chattering excitedly into their mobile phones. There's not a single one who isn't wearing full makeup and smart shoes and carrying some sort of designer bag, even if it's the teeniest little Louis Vuitton coin purse— and the babble of conversation is peppered with names of fashion houses. They're all pressing forward, firmly moving their stilettos inch by inch along the floor, and all have the same urgent look in their eyes. Every so often somebody pushes their way out of the door, holding an enormous, nameless carrier bag—and about three girls push their way in. Then, just as I join the end of the line, there's a rattling sound, and a woman opens up a door, a few yards behind me.

"Another entrance this way," she calls. "Come this way!"

In front of me, a whole line of heads whips round. There's a collective intake of breath—and then it's like a tidal wave of girls, all heading toward me. I find myself running toward the door, just to avoid being knocked down—and suddenly I'm in the middle of the room, slightly shaken, as everybody else peels off and heads for the racks.

I look around, trying to get my bearings. There are racks and racks of clothes, tables covered in bags and shoes and scarves. I can already spot Ralph Lauren knitwear . . . a rack full of fabulous coats . . . there's a stack of Prada bags . . . I mean, this is like a dream come true! Everywhere I look, girls are feverishly sorting through garments, looking for labels, trying out bags. Their manicured nails are descending on the stuff like the claws of birds of prey and I can't believe quite how fast they're working. As I see the girl who was standing in front of me in the line, I feel a surge of panic. She's got a whole armful of stuff, and I haven't even started. If I don't get in there, everything will be gone. I have to grab something now!

I fight my way through to one of the racks and start leafing through chiffon pleated dresses. Three hundred dollars, reduced to seventy dollars! I mean, even if you only wore it once . . . And oh God, here are some fantastic print trousers, some label I've never heard of, but they're reduced by 90 percent! And a leather coat . . . and those Prada bags. I *have* to get one of the Prada bags!

As I breathlessly reach for one, my hand collides with another girl's.

"Hey!" she says at once, and snatches the bag up. "I was there first!"

"Oh," I say. "Erm . . . sorry!" I quickly grab another one which, to be honest, looks exactly the same. As the girl starts examining the interior of her bag, I can't help staring at her nails. They're filed into square shapes and carefully decorated in two different shades of pink. How long did that take to do? As she looks up, I see her hair is two-tone as well—brown with aubergine tips—while her mouth is carefully lined with purple and filled in with pale mauve.

"Got a problem?" she says, suddenly looking at me, and I jump.

"No! I was just wondering—where's the changing room?"

"Changing room?" She chuckles. "Are you kidding? No such thing."

"Oh." I look around again, and notice a spectacular black girl, about nine feet tall, stripping off to her bra and knickers. "I see. So we . . . change right here? Great!" I swallow. "No problem at all."

Hesitantly I start unbuttoning my coat, telling myself that I've got no alternative—and no one's watching anyway. But Two-Tone Girl's expression is changing as she gazes at me.

"Are you British?"

"Yes! Did you recognize my accent?"

"I love the British!" Her eyes light up. "That film, *Notting Hill*? I loved that!"

"Oh right! So did I, actually."

"That Welsh guy. He was hilarious!" She suddenly frowns as I step out of my shoes. "Hey, but wait. You shouldn't have to get changed out here."

"Why not?"

"Because you're British! Everyone knows the Brits are reserved. It's like . . . your national disease or something."

"Honestly, it's fine . . ."

"Don't worry about it. I'll take care of it." To my horror the girl strides over and pokes the woman in black standing by the door. "Excuse me? This girl is British. She needs privacy to try on her things. OK?"

The woman turns to stare at me as though I'm a Martian and I smile nervously back.

"Really, don't worry. I don't mind . . ."

"She needs privacy!" insists the girl. "They're different than us. It's a whole other culture. Can she go behind those racks there?"

"Please. I don't want to—"

"Whatever," says the woman, rolling her eyes. "Just don't mess up the displays."

"Thanks," I say to the girl, a little awkwardly. "I'm Becky, by the way."

"Jodie." She gives me a wide grin. "Love your boots!"

I disappear behind the rack and begin trying on all the clothes I've gathered. With each one I feel a little frisson of delight—and when I get to the Prada bag, it's a surge of pure joy. Prada at 50 percent off! I mean, this would make the whole trip worthwhile, just on its own.

When I've eventually finished, I come out from behind the rack to see Jodie wriggling into a stretchy white dress.

"This sample sale is so great!" she exclaims. "I'm just like . . . where do I stop?"

"I know what you mean." I give her a blissful smile. "That dress looks great, by the way."

"Are you going to buy all that?" she says, giving my armload an impressed look.

"Not all of it." I reach into the pile. "Not . . . these trousers. But everything else."

"Cool! Go, girl."

As I happily head toward the paying table, the room is reverberating with high-pitched female voices and I can hear snippets of conversation floating around.

"I have to have it," a girl is saying, holding up a coat against herself. "I just *have* to have it."

"OK, what I'm going to do is, I'm just going to put the $450 I spent today onto my mortgage," another girl is saying to her friend as they walk out, laden with bags. "I mean, what's $450 over thirty years?"

"One hundred percent cashmere!" someone else is exclaiming. "Did you see this? It's only fifty dollars! I'm going to take three."

I dump my stuff on the table and look around the bright, buzzing room at the girls milling about, grabbing at merchandise, trying on scarves, piling their arms full of glossy new gorgeous things. And I feel a sudden warmth, an overwhelming realization. These are my people. I've found my homeland.

Several hours later, I arrive back at the Four Seasons, still on a complete high. After the sample sale, I ended up going out for a "welcome to New York" coffee with Jodie. We sat at a marble table, sipping our decaf Frappuccinos and nibbling at nonfat cranberry muffins, and both worked out exactly how much money we'd saved on our bargains ($1,230 in my case!). We agreed to meet up again during my visit—and then Jodie told me all about this amazing Web site that sends you information on these kinds of events every day. Every day! I mean, the possibilities are limitless. You could spend your *whole life* going to sample sales!

You know. In theory.

I go up to our room—and as I open the door I see Luke sitting at the desk, reading through some papers.

"Hi!" I say breathlessly, dumping my bags on the enormous bed. "Listen, I need to use the laptop."

"Oh right," says Luke. "Sure." He picks up the laptop from the desk and hands it to me, and I go and sit on the bed. I open the laptop, consult the piece of paper Jodie gave me, and type in the address.

"So, how was your day?" asks Luke.

"It was great!" I say, tapping the keys impatiently. "I made a new friend, and I saw lots of the city . . . Ooh, and look in that blue bag! I got you some really nice shirts!"

"Did you start to get a feel for the place?"

"Oh, I think so. I mean, obviously it's early . . ." I frown at the screen. "Come *on*, already."

"But you weren't too overwhelmed?"

"Mmm . . . not really," I say absently. Aha! Suddenly the screen is filling up with images. A row of little sweeties at the top—and logos saying, *It's fun. It's fashion. In New York City.* The Daily Candy home page!

I click on "Subscribe" and briskly start to type in my e-mail details, as Luke gets up and comes toward me, a concerned look on his face.

"So tell me, Becky," he says. "I know it must all seem very strange and daunting to you. I know you couldn't possibly find your feet in just one day. But on first impressions—do you think you could get used to New York? Do you think you could ever see yourself living here?"

I type the last letter with a flourish, press "Send," and look at him thoughtfully.

"You know what? I think I probably could."

HOWSKI AND FORLANO

US IMMIGRATION LAWYERS

568 E. 56TH STREET

NEW YORK, NY 10016

Ms. Rebecca Bloomwood
Flat 2
4 Burney Rd.
London SW6 8FD
UNITED KINGDOM

September 28, 2000

Dear Ms. Bloomwood:

Thank you for your completed U.S. immigration forms. As you know, the authorities will wish to evaluate the assets and unique talents which you can bring to this country.

Under section B69 referring to special abilities, you write, "I'm really good at chemistry, ask anyone at Oxford." We did in fact contact the vice-chancellor of Oxford University, who failed to display any familiarity with your work.

As did the British Olympic long-jump coach.

We enclose fresh forms and request that you fill them out again.

With kind regards,

Edgar Forlano

Nine

Two days later, I'm feeling quite dazzled by all the sights and sounds of New York. I've walked so many blocks my feet ache, and I've really seen some awe-inspiring things. Like, in Bloomingdale's, they have a chocolate factory! And there's a whole district full of nothing but shoe shops!

I keep trying to get Luke along to look at all these amazing sights—but he just has meeting after meeting. He's seeing about twenty people a day—wooing potential clients and networking with media people, and even looking round office spaces in the financial district. As he said yesterday at breakfast, he needs to hit the ground running when he arrives. I was about to make a little joke about "Break a leg!" . . . but then I decided against it. Luke's taking everything a bit seriously at the moment.

As well as setting up the new company, he's had briefings from Alicia in London every morning—and she keeps sending through faxes for him to approve, and needlessly long e-mails. I just know she's only doing it all to show off to Luke—and the really annoying thing is, it's working. Like, a couple of clients rang up to complain about things, but when he called Alicia she had already leapt into action and sorted it out. So then I had to hear for fifteen minutes about how marvelous she is, and what a great job she's doing—and keep nodding my head as though I completely agreed. But I still can't stand her. She rang up the other morning when Luke was out, and when I picked up, she said "*So* sorry to disturb your beauty sleep!" in this really patronizing way, and rang off before I could think of a good reply.

Still, never mind. On the positive side, Luke and I did manage to get our walk in Central Park—even if it was only for five minutes. And one afternoon, Luke took me on the Staten Island Ferry, which was fantastic—except for the moment when I lost my new baseball cap overboard.

Obviously, I didn't *mean* to shriek so loudly. Nor did I mean for that old woman to mishear and think I'd lost my "cat"—and I certainly didn't want her to insist the boat should be stopped. It caused a bit of a kerfuffle, actually, which was rather embarrassing. Still, never mind—as Luke said, at least all those tourists with their video cameras had something to film.

But now it's Wednesday morning. The holiday is over—and I've got a slight dentisty feeling of dread. It's my first appointment today with a pair of important TV people from HLBC. I'm actually quite scared.

Luke's left early for a breakfast meeting with Michael and some top PR headhunter who's going to supply him with staff, so I'm left alone in bed, sipping coffee and nibbling at a croissant, and telling myself not to get nervous. The key is not to panic, but to stay calm and cool. As Luke kept reassuring me, this meeting is not an interview as such, it's simply a first-stage introduction. A "getting-to-know-you" lunch, he called it.

But in a way, lunch is even more scary than an interview. What if I knock something over? What if I don't tip all the right people? What if I can't think of anything to say and we sit there in an embarrassing silence?

I spend all morning in our room, trying to read the *Wall Street Journal* and watching CNN—but that only freaks me out even more. I mean, these American television presenters are so slick and immaculate. They never fluff their words, and they never make jokes, and they know everything. Like who's the trade secretary of Iraq, and the implications of global warming for Peru. And here I am, thinking I can do what they do.

My other problem is, I haven't done a proper interview for years. *Morning Coffee* never bothered to interview me, I just kind of fell into it. And for my old job on *Successful Saving,* I just had a cozy chat with Philip, the editor, who already knew me from press conferences. So the idea of having to impress a pair of complete strangers from scratch is completely terrifying.

"Just be yourself," Luke kept saying. But frankly, that's a ridiculous idea. Everyone knows, the point of an interview is not to demonstrate who you are, but to pretend to be whatever sort of person they want for the job. That's why they call it "interview technique."

My interview outfit consists of a beautiful black suit I got at Whistles, with quite a short skirt and discreet red stitching. I've teamed it with high-heeled court shoes and some very sheer, very expensive tights. (Or "hose" as I must now start calling them. But honestly. It sounds like Shakespeare or something.) As I arrive at the restaurant where we're meeting, I see my reflection in a glass door—and I'm quite impressed. But at the same time, half of me wants to run away, give up on the idea, and buy myself a nice pair of shoes to commiserate.

I can't, though. I have to go through with this. The reason my stomach feels so hollow and my hands feel so damp is that this really matters to me. I can't tell myself I don't care and it's not important, like I do about most things. Because this really does matter. If I don't manage to get a job in New York, then I won't be able to live here. If I screw this interview up, and word gets around that I'm hopeless—then it's all over. Oh God. Oh God . . .

OK, calm down, I tell myself firmly. I can do this. I can do it. And afterward, I'm going to reward myself with a little treat. The Daily Candy Web site e-mailed me this morning, and apparently this huge makeup emporium in SoHo called Sephora is running a special promotion today, until four. Every customer gets a goody bag—and if you spend fifty dollars, you get a free special engraved beauty box! I mean, how cool would that be?

About two seconds after the e-mail arrived, I got one from Jodie, the girl I met at the sample sale. I'd been telling her I was a bit nervous about meeting Luke's mother—and she said I should get a makeover for the occasion and Sephora was definitely the place, did I want to meet up? So that will be fun, at least . . .

There, you see, I feel better already, just thinking about it. OK, go girl. Go get 'em.

I force myself to push open the door, and suddenly I'm in a very smart restaurant, all black lacquer and white linen and colored fish swimming in tanks.

"Good afternoon," says a maître d' dressed entirely in black.

"Hello," I say. "I'm here to meet—"

Shit, I've completely forgotten the names of the people I'm meeting.

Oh, great start, Becky. This is really professional.

"Could you just . . . hang on?" I say, and turn away,

flushing red. I scrabble in my bag for the piece of paper—and here we are. Judd Westbrook and Kent Garland.

Kent? Is that really a name?

"It's Rebecca Bloomwood," I say to the maître d', hastily shoving the paper back in my bag, "meeting Judd Westbrook and Kent Garland of HLBC."

He scans the list, then gives a frosty smile. "Ah yes. They're already here."

Taking a deep breath, I follow him to the table—and there they are. A blond woman in a beige trouser suit and a chiseled-looking man in an equally immaculate black suit and sage-green tie. I fight the urge to run away, and advance with a confident smile, holding out my hand. They both look up at me, and for a moment neither says anything—and I feel a horrible conviction that I've already broken some vital rule of etiquette. I mean, you do shake hands in America, don't you? Are you supposed to kiss? Or bow?

But thankfully the blond woman is getting up and clasping my hand warmly.

"Becky!" she says. "*So* thrilled to meet you. I'm Kent Garland."

"Judd Westbrook," says the man, gazing at me with deep-set eyes. "We're very excited to meet you."

"Me too!" I say. "And thank you so much for your lovely flowers!"

"Not at all," says Judd, and ushers me into a chair. "It's a delight."

"An enormous pleasure," says Kent.

There's an expectant silence.

"Well, it's a . . . a fantastic pleasure for me, too," I say hastily. "Absolutely . . . phenomenal."

So far so good. If we just keep telling each other

what a pleasure this is, I should do OK. Carefully I place my bag on the floor, along with my copies of the *FT* and the *Wall Street Journal*. I thought about the *South China Morning Post*, too, but decided that might be a bit much.

"Would you like a drink?" says a waiter, appearing at my side.

"Oh yes!" I say, and glance nervously around at the table to see what everyone else is having. Kent and Judd have both got tumblers full of what looks like G&T, so I'd better follow suit. "A gin and tonic, please."

To be honest, I think I need it, just to relax. As I open my menu, both Judd and Kent are gazing at me with an alert interest, as though they think I might suddenly burst into blossom or something.

"We've seen your tapes," says Kent, leaning forward. "And we're very impressed."

"Really?" I say—and then realize I shouldn't sound quite so astonished. "Really," I repeat, trying to sound nonchalant. "Yes, well, I'm proud of the show, obviously . . ."

"As you know, Rebecca, we produce a show called *Consumer Today*," says Kent. "We don't have a personal finance segment at present, but we'd love to bring in the kind of advisory slot you're doing in Britain." She glances at Judd, who nods in agreement.

"It's obvious you have a passion for personal finance," he says.

"Oh," I say, taken aback. "Well—"

"It shines through your work," he asserts firmly. "As does the pincerlike grip you have on your subject."

Pincerlike grip?

"You know, you're pretty unique, Rebecca," Kent is saying. "A young, approachable, charming girl, with such a high level of expertise and conviction in what you're saying . . ."

"You're an inspiration for the financially challenged everywhere," agrees Judd.

"What we admire the most is the patience you show these people."

"The empathy you have with them . . ."

". . . that faux-simplistic style of yours!" says Kent, and looks at me intently. "How do you keep that up?"

"Erm . . . you know! It just . . . comes, I suppose . . ." The waiter puts a drink in front of me and I grab it thankfully. "Well, cheers, everyone!" I say, lifting my glass.

"Cheers!" says Kent. "Are you ready to order, Rebecca?"

"Absolutely!" I reply, quickly scanning the menu. "The ahm . . . sea bass, please, and a green salad." I look at the others. "And shall we share some garlic bread?"

"I'm wheat-free," says Judd politely.

"Oh, right," I say. "Well . . . Kent?"

"I don't eat carbohydrates," she says pleasantly. "But you go ahead. I'm sure it's delicious!"

"No, it's OK," I say hastily. "I'll just have the sea bass."

God, how could I be so stupid? Of course Manhattanites don't eat garlic bread.

"And to drink?" says the waiter.

"Erm . . ." I look around the table. "I don't know. A sauvignon blanc, maybe? What does everyone else want?"

"Sounds good," says Kent with a friendly smile, and I breathe a sigh of relief. "Just some more Pellegrino for me," she adds, and gestures to her tumbler.

"And me," says Judd.

Pellegrino? They're on *Pellegrino*?

"I'll just have water too!" I say quickly. "I don't need wine! It was just an idea. You know—"

"No!" says Kent. "You must have whatever you like!" She smiles at the waiter. "A bottle of the sauvignon blanc, please, for our guest."

"Honestly—" I say, flushing red.

"Rebecca," says Kent, lifting a hand with a smile. "Whatever makes you comfortable."

Oh great. Now she thinks I'm a complete alcoholic. She thinks I can't survive one getting-to-know-you lunch without hitting the booze.

Well, never mind. It's done now. And it'll be OK. I'll just drink one glass. One glass, and that's it.

And that is honestly what I mean to do. Drink one glass and leave it at that.

But the trouble is, every time I finish my glass, a waiter comes along and fills it up again, and somehow I find myself drinking it. Besides which, it would look rather ungrateful to order a whole bottle of wine and leave it undrunk.

So the upshot is, by the time we've finished our food, I'm feeling quite . . . Well. I suppose one word might be *drunk*. Another might be *pissed*. But it's not a problem, because we're having a really good time, and I'm actually being really witty. Probably because I've relaxed a little. I've told them lots of funny stories about behind the scenes at *Morning Coffee,* and they've listened carefully and said it all sounds "quite fascinating."

"Of course, you British are very different from us," says Kent thoughtfully, as I finish telling her about the time Dave the cameraman arrived so pissed he keeled over in the middle of a shot, and got Emma picking her nose. God, that was funny. In fact, I can't stop giggling, just remembering it.

"We just love your British sense of humor," says Judd, and stares intently at me as though expecting a joke.

OK, quick. Think of something funny. British sense of humor. Erm . . . *Fawlty Towers? Ab Fab?*

"Don't mention the war!" I hear myself exclaiming. "Sweetie darling." I give a snort of laughter, and Judd and Kent exchange puzzled looks.

Just then, the coffee arrives. At least, I'm having coffee, Kent's having English breakfast tea, and Judd's having some weird herbal thing which he gave to the waiter to make.

"I adore tea," says Kent, giving me a smile. "So calming. Now, Rebecca. In England, the custom is that you turn the pot three times clockwise to keep away the devil. Is that right? Or is it counterclockwise?"

Turn the pot? I've never heard of turning the bloody pot.

"Erm . . . let me remember."

I screw my face up thoughtfully, trying to remember the last time I drank tea from a teapot. But the only image that comes to me is of Suze dunking a teabag in a mug while she tears a KitKat open with her teeth.

"I think it's counterclockwise," I say at last. "Because of the old saying, 'The devil he creeps around the clock . . . but never backward he will go.' "

What the hell am I talking about? Why have I suddenly put on a Scottish accent?

"Fascinating!" says Kent, taking a sip of tea. "I adore all these quaint old British customs. Do you know any others?"

"Absolutely!" I say brightly. "I know loads!"

Stop it, Becky. Just stop now.

"Like, we have a very old custom of . . . of . . . 'turning the tea cake.' "

"Really?" says Kent. "I've never heard of that one."

"Oh yes," I say confidently. "What happens is, you take your tea cake . . ." I grab a bread roll from a passing waiter. "And you . . . rotate it above your head like so . . . and you . . . you say a little rhyme . . ."

Crumbs are starting to fall on my head, and I can't think of anything to rhyme with *tea cake,* so I put my bread roll down and take a sip of coffee. "They do it in Cornwall," I add.

"Really?" says Judd with interest. "My grandmother comes from Cornwall. I'll have to ask her about it!"

"Only in some bits of Cornwall," I explain. "Just in the pointy bits."

Judd and Kent give each other puzzled looks—then both burst into laughter.

"Your British sense of humor!" says Kent. "It's so refreshing."

For a moment I'm not quite sure how to react—then I start laughing too. God, this is great. We're getting on like a house on fire! Then Kent's face lights up.

"Now, Rebecca, I was meaning to say. I have rather an exciting opportunity for you. I don't know what your plans were for this afternoon. But I have a rather unique ticket . . . to . . ."

She pauses for effect, smiling widely, and I stare at her in sudden excitement. A Gucci invitation sample sale! It has to be!

". . . the Association of Financiers Annual Conference!" she finishes proudly.

For a few moments I can't speak.

"Really?" I say at last, my voice slightly more high-pitched than usual. "You're . . . you're joking!"

How on earth am I going to get out of this one?

"I know!" says Kent delightedly. "I thought you'd be pleased. So if you're not doing anything else this afternoon . . ."

I *am* doing something! I want to wail. I'm going to Sephora to get made over!

"There are some very high-profile speakers," puts in Judd. "Bert Frankel, for one."

"Really?" I say. "Bert Frankel!"

I've never heard of bloody Bert Frankel.

"So . . . I have the pass right here . . ." says Kent, reaching for her bag.

Quick. I have to say something or I'll find myself spending a precious afternoon in New York sitting in some dreary conference hall.

"What a shame!" I hear myself exclaiming. "Because actually . . ."

I *can't* tell them I have to go and try on lipstick.

"Actually . . . I was planning to visit the Guggenheim this afternoon."

Phew. No one can argue with culture.

"Really?" says Kent, looking disappointed. "Couldn't it wait until another day?"

"I'm afraid not," I say. "There's a particular exhibit I've been absolutely longing to see since . . . since I was a child of six."

"Really?" says Kent, eyes wide.

"Yes." I lean forward earnestly. "Ever since I saw a photograph of it in my granny's art book, it's been my ambition since childhood to come to New York City and see this piece of art. And now that I'm here . . . I just can't wait any longer. I hope you understand . . ."

"Of course!" says Kent. "Of course we do! What an inspiring story!" She exchanges impressed looks with Judd, and I smile modestly back. "So—which piece of art is it?"

I stare at her, still smiling. OK, quick, think. The Guggenheim. Modern paintings? Sculpture?

I'm fifty-fifty on modern paintings. If only I could phone a friend.

"Actually . . . I'd rather not say," I say at last. "I consider artistic preference a very . . . private matter."

"Oh," says Kent, looking a little taken aback. "Well, of course, I didn't mean to intrude in any way—"

"Kent," says Judd, glancing at his watch again. "We really have to—"

"You're right," says Kent. She takes another sip of tea, and stands up. "I'm sorry, Rebecca, we have a meeting at two thirty. But it's been such a pleasure."

"Of course!" I say. "No problem!"

I struggle to my feet and follow them out of the restaurant. As I pass the wine bucket I realize with a slight lurch that I've more or less drunk the whole bottle. How embarrassing. But I don't think anybody noticed.

We arrive outside the restaurant, and Judd has already hailed a taxi for me.

"Great to meet you, Rebecca," he says. "We'll report back to our vice-president of production, and we'll . . . be in touch! Enjoy the Guggenheim."

"Absolutely!" I say, shaking hands with each of them. "I will. And thank you so much!"

I get into the taxi and slam the door behind me.

"Hi," I say to the taxi driver, watching as Judd and Kent walk away. "I'd like to go to—"

"The Guggenheim," chips in the driver. "I heard."

"No, actually, I'd like to go to SoHo. Sephora on Broadway."

The driver swivels in his seat to look at me. He's huge and swarthy, and his face is creased in a frown.

"What about the Guggenheim?"

"Erm . . . I'll go later on."

"Later on?" says the driver. "You can't rush the Guggenheim. The Guggenheim is a very fine museum. Picasso. Kandinsky. You don't want to miss it."

"I won't miss it! Honestly, I promise. If we could just go to Sephora now? Please?"

There's a disapproving silence from the front.

"All right," he says at last, and starts the engine.

As we drive off, I sink happily into my seat. I think lunch went really well, actually. Except maybe when I told them the anecdote about Rory and the guide dog. And when I tripped over on my way to the loos. But then, that could happen to anybody. The truth is, I really am settling into New York. It's only been three days, but I'm getting the language and everything. Like, yesterday, I said "Go figure" without even thinking. And I called a skirt *cute*!

We pull up at a pedestrian crossing and I'm peering interestedly out, wondering which street we're at— when suddenly I freeze in horror.

There are Judd and Kent. Right there, in front of us. They're crossing the road, and Kent is saying something animatedly, and Judd is nodding. Oh God. I can't let them see me heading in the wrong direction. Quick, hide.

My heart thumping, I sink down off my seat and kind of crouch on the floor, trying to hide behind my *Wall Street Journal*. God, why isn't there more *space* in these taxis?

"You OK back there?" says the taxi driver.

"Fine," I gulp. I raise my head cautiously—and thank goodness Judd and Kent have disappeared. As I scramble back up onto the seat, I bump my head on the window.

"Hey there!" says a disembodied voice, making me jump with fright. "You be careful! Safety counts, OK? So buckle up!"

"OK," I say humbly. "Sorry about that. I'm really sorry. I won't do it again."

I fasten my seat belt with clumsy fingers, and catch the eye of the driver in the mirror.

"It's a recorded announcement," he says scornfully. "You're talking to a tape machine."

I knew that.

We arrive at Sephora on Broadway, and I thrust wodges of dollars at the driver. As I get out of the cab, he looks closely at me.

"Have you been drinking, lady?"

"No," I say indignantly. "I mean . . . yes. But it was just a bit of wine at lunch . . ."

The taxi driver shakes his head and drives off, and I head unsteadily into Sephora. To be honest, I am feeling a little giddy. I push open the door and . . . wow. Spotlights are dancing about the bright interior, landing on shiny black counters; on the deep-red carpet underfoot; on the glass packaging of a thousand nail polishes. There's music pounding, and girls milling everywhere, and trendy guys in black polo necks and headsets handing out goody bags. As I turn dazedly around, I've never seen so much makeup in my life. Rows and rows of lipsticks. Rows and rows of eye shadows. In all the colors of the rainbow. And oh look, there are little chairs where you can sit and try it all on, with personal mirrors. This place is . . . I mean, it's heaven.

"Hi, Becky, you made it!" I look up to see Jodie waving across a display of hairbrushes. She's wearing a stripy red-and-white jersey dress today, and as she gets nearer I see that her nails have been revarnished stripy red-and-white to match. "Ready for your makeover?"

She ushers me to one of the little chairs and I get into it, feeling a pleasant anticipation. A girl in black comes over with a friendly smile and introduces herself as Mona, my makeup specialist for today.

"Had you thought what look you were after?" she says as she switches on a spotlight and guides it toward my face.

"Well, it's for lunch with my boyfriend's mother," I explain. "I want to look kind of . . . groomed."

"Polished but subtle?"

"Exactly!"

"I have you," says Mona, nodding. "Taupes and beiges. The hardest look to pull off."

"Taupe?" says Jodie, wrinkling her brow. "Did anyone ever look good in taupe?"

"And maybe a soft color on the lips," says Mona, ignoring Jodie. "Let me start with a light base . . ."

She reaches for a cosmetic sponge and smooths color gently over my face. As she starts shading my eyes I see Jodie standing back, a critical look on her face.

"For this elegant look, less is more," says Mona.

"Right," I say, nodding knowledgeably. "Absolutely."

"I'll just fetch a mascara . . ."

She disappears toward the front of the shop and I close my eyes. If I'm honest, my head's still spinning from all that wine, and I'm finding it quite hard to balance on this tiny chair.

Suddenly I feel a coldness on my cheek, and look up. Jodie is standing in front of me, dipping her fingers into a small pot.

"What are you doing?" I say feebly.

"Jazzing you up a bit!" she says, and dabs my other cheek. "All this neutral crap! Like that's what you wanted from a makeover."

"Well—"

"I know you're too polite to complain. You Brits really need to get some attitude." She stands back and gives a satisfied nod. "Now, did you ever wear false eyelashes? Because they have a great range here."

"Jodie, I'm not sure . . ."

"Hey!" We both look up to see Mona approaching, an affronted expression on her face. "What the hell is going on? What's happened to her face?"

"She looked boring," says Jodie defiantly.

"She looked classic!" Mona sticks her hands on her hips. "Well, you've ruined it now."

"What have I got on my face?" I demand, and pull the mirror toward me. My own face stares back. Smooth and beige, with softly shadowed eyes, discreetly colored lips . . . and silver sparkles on my cheeks.

"Looks great, doesn't it?" says Jodie unapologetically. "Much better with the glitter."

I glance at Mona's annoyed face and suddenly feel a bit guilty.

"Actually, Mona," I say quickly, "I'd really like to buy

some of the products you used. In fact . . . all of them. Would that be possible?"

"Oh," says Mona, unbending a little. "Well—yes, of course. They are from a rather expensive line . . ."

"That doesn't matter!" I turn hastily to Jodie. "And . . . I'll buy the glitter too. I'll buy it all!"

Ten minutes later I find myself outside Sephora, clutching two carrier bags full of makeup, a whole set of new cosmetic brushes, a silver shower cap, and something called "buffing paste," which I threw in at the last moment. I'm not sure quite what it is—but the jar is absolutely gorgeous!

"OK," I say, looking dazedly around the busy street in front of me. "Where next?"

"Babe, I have to go," says Jodie, looking up from her pager. "I've already had a five-hour lunch break. But if you want the true SoHo experience, there's Dean and Deluca right in front of you . . ." She swivels me by the shoulders until I'm facing across the street. ". . . and just along is Scoop, which is *the* place to pick up the most expensive T-shirt in the universe . . ."

"What about that?" I say, pointing to a gorgeous, glowing shop window that has caught my eye.

"Kate's Paperie. To die for."

"What does it sell?" I say puzzledly. "Just paper?"

"Just paper!" She gives a raucous chuckle. "You go take a look. And listen, you want to get together again sometime?"

"I'd love to!" I say in delight. "I'll be here for at least another week. Thanks, Jodie."

"No problem."

I watch as Jodie hurries off toward the subway and

suddenly notice that the spiky heels of her shoes are painted in red-and-white stripes, too. That's so cool! Where did she get them?

"Jodie!" I cry, but she can't hear me. Never mind, I'll ask her next time.

As she disappears down into the subway station I walk slowly toward Kate's Paperie. I'm not really interested in paper, to be honest. In fact, I probably won't bother going in. But it can't hurt to have a little—

I stop in my tracks as I reach the window, and stare at the display, astounded. When Jodie said *paper,* I imagined piles of photocopying sheets. I had no idea she meant . . . I mean, just look at that display of marbled wrapping paper. And that decoupage box. And that amazing beaded ribbon! I've never seen anything like it!

I push the door open and walk around, marveling at the arrangements of beautiful wrapping paper adorned with dried flowers, raffia, and bows, the photograph albums, the boxes of exquisite writing paper . . . And oh God, just look at the greeting cards!

You see, this is it. This is why New York is so great. They don't just have boring old cards saying Happy Birthday. They have handmade creations with twinkly flowers and witty collages, saying things like "Congratulations on adopting twins!" and "So sad to hear you broke up!"

I walk up and down, utterly dazzled by the array. I just *have* to have some of these cards. Like this fantastic pop-up castle, with the flag reading "I love your remodeled home!" I mean, I don't actually know anyone who's remodeling their home, but I can always keep it until Mum decides to repaper the hall. And this one covered in fake grass, saying "To a smashing tennis coach with thanks." Because I'm planning to have some tennis lessons next summer, and I'll want to thank my coach, won't I?

I scoop up a few more, and then move on to the invitation rack. And they're even better! Instead of just saying "Party" they say things like "We're Meeting at the Club for Brunch!" and "Come Join Us for an Informal Pizza!"

You know, I think I should buy some of those. It would be shortsighted not to. Suze and I might easily hold a pizza party, mightn't we? And we'll never find invitations like this in Britain. And they're so sweet, with glittery little pizza slices all the way down the sides! I carefully put five boxes of invitations in my basket, along with all my lovely cards, and a few sheets of candy-striped wrapping paper, which I just can't resist, then head to the checkout. As the assistant scans everything through, I look around the shop again, wondering if I've missed anything—and it's only when she announces the total that I look up in slight shock. That much? Just for a few cards?

For a moment I wonder whether I really do need them all. Like the card saying "Happy Hanukkah, Boss!"

But then—they're bound to come in useful one day, aren't they? And if I'm going to live in New York, I'm going to have to get used to sending expensive cards all the time, so really, this is a form of acclimatization.

As I head toward the door, I'm dimly aware of a ringing, burbling sort of sound—and all of a sudden I realize it's my own mobile phone.

"Hi!" I say, clutching it to my ear. "Who's this?"

"Hi. It's me," says Luke. "I heard your lunch went well."

"Really?" I say, feeling a jolt of surprise. "Where did you hear that?"

"I've just been speaking to some people at HLBC. Apparently you were quite a hit. Very entertaining, they said."

"Wow! Really? Are you sure?"

"Quite sure. They were saying how charming you were, and how cultured . . . I even hear they put you in a taxi to the Guggenheim afterward."

"That's right," I say, reaching to look at a paper knife. "They did."

"Yes, I was quite intrigued to hear all about your burning childhood dream," says Luke. "Kent was very impressed."

"Really?" I say vaguely. "Well, that's good."

"Absolutely." Luke pauses. "Slightly strange that you didn't mention the Guggenheim this morning, though, isn't it? Or indeed . . . ever. Bearing in mind you've been longing to go there since you were a child of six."

Suddenly I hear the amusement in his voice, and snap to attention. He's bloody well rung up to tease me, hasn't he?

"Have I never mentioned the Guggenheim?" I say innocently, and put the paper knife back. "How very odd."

"Isn't it?" says Luke. "Most peculiar. So, are you there now?"

Bugger.

For a moment, I'm silenced. I simply can't admit to Luke that I've gone shopping again. Not after all that teasing he gave me about my so-called guided tour. I mean, OK, I know ten minutes out of a three-hour city tour isn't that much—but I got as far as Saks, didn't I?

"Yes," I say defiantly. "Yes, I am, actually."

Which is kind of almost true. I mean, I can easily go there after I've finished here.

"Great!" says Luke. "What particular exhibit are you looking at?"

Oh, shut up.

"What's that?" I say, suddenly raising my voice. "Sorry, I didn't realize! Luke, I have to turn my mobile off. The . . . um . . . curator is complaining. But I'll see you later."

"Six at the Royalton Bar," he says. "You can meet my new associate, Michael. And I'll look forward to hearing all about your afternoon."

Now I feel a bit guilty. I shouldn't have told Luke I was at the Guggenheim. I should have told the truth.

But it doesn't matter . . . because what I'll do is I'll go there right now. Right this minute! After all, I can always come back to SoHo another day, can't I?

I walk slowly along the crowded street, telling myself that what I'll do is hail a cab and go straight up there. Without delay. Straight to the Guggenheim and immerse myself in some wonderful culture. Excellent. I can't wait, actually.

I arrive at a street corner and come to a standstill. A lit-up taxi crawls past—but for some strange reason my arm doesn't rise. Across the street is a stall selling fake designer sunglasses, and I feel a sudden pang of longing to go and rifle through them. And look there, that shop's doing a discount on Calvin Klein jeans. And I do actually *need* some new jeans . . . And I haven't even been into Dean and Deluca . . .

Oh, why couldn't the Guggenheim be in SoHo?

Hang on a minute.

People are pushing past me but I don't move. My eye is riveted by something fixed to the facade above an entrance. I don't quite believe what I'm seeing.

The word GUGGENHEIM stares back at me, as large as life. It's like God heard my prayers.

But what's going on? Has the Guggenheim suddenly *moved*? Are there two Guggenheims?

As I hurry toward the doors, I realize this place looks quite small for a museum—so maybe it's not the main Guggenheim. Maybe it's some trendy SoHo offshoot! Yes! I mean, if London can have the Tate Gallery and Tate Modern, why can't New York have the Guggenheim and Guggenheim SoHo? That sounds so cool!

I cautiously push the door open—and sure enough, it's all white and spacious, with modern art on pedestals and people wandering around quietly, whispering to one another.

You know, this is what all museums should be like. Nice and small, for a start, so you don't feel exhausted as soon as you walk in. I mean, you could probably do this lot in about half an hour. Plus, all the things look really interesting. Like, look at those amazing red cubes in that glass cabinet! And this fantastic abstract print, hanging on the wall.

As I'm gazing admiringly at the print, a couple come over and look at it too, and start murmuring to each other about how nice it is. Then the girl says casually, "How much is it?"

And I'm about to turn to her with a friendly smile and say "That's what I always want to know, too!"—when to my astonishment the man reaches for it and turns it over. And there's a price label fixed onto the back!

A price label in a museum! I don't believe it! This place is perfect! *Finally,* some forward-thinking person has agreed with me—that people don't want to just look at art, they want to know how much it is. I'm going to write to the people at the Victoria and Albert about this.

And you know, now that I look around properly, *all* the exhibits seem to have a price on them. Those red cubes in the cabinet have got a price label, and so has that chair, and so has that . . . that box of pencils.

How weird, having a box of pencils in a museum. Still, maybe it's installation art. I walk over to have a closer look—and there's something printed on each pencil. Probably some really meaningful message about art, or life . . . I lean close, interested, and find myself reading the words "Guggenheim Museum Store."

What?

Is this a—

I lift my head and look around bewilderedly.

Am I in a *shop*?

Suddenly I start noticing things I hadn't seen before. Like a pair of cash registers on the other side of the room. And there's somebody walking out with a couple of carrier bags.

How could I have not recognized a *shop*? But . . . this makes less and less sense. Is it just a shop on its own?

"Excuse me," I say to a fair-haired boy wearing a name badge. "Can I just check—this *is* a shop?"

"Yes, ma'am," says the boy politely. "This is the Guggenheim Museum Store."

"And where's the actual Guggenheim Museum? With all the Picassos and things?"

"To see the Picassos you have to go to the main museum, on Fifth Avenue at Eighty-ninth Street," says the boy.

"Right." I look at him confusedly. "So let me just get this straight. You can come here and buy loads of stuff—and no one minds whether you've been to the museum or not? I mean, you don't have to show your ticket or anything?"

"No, ma'am."

"So you . . . you can just shop?" My voice rises in delight. "It's perfect!" Suddenly I see the boy's shocked expression and quickly add, "I mean, obviously I *do* want to look at the art. Very much so. I was just . . . you know. Checking."

"If you're interested in visiting the museum," says the boy, "I can give you a location map. Did you want to pay a visit?"

"Erm . . ."

Now, let's not make any hasty decisions.

"Erm . . . I'm not sure," I say carefully. "Could you just give me a minute?"

"Sure," says the boy, giving me a slightly odd look, and I sit down on a white seat, thinking hard.

OK, here's the thing. I mean, obviously I could get in a cab, and whiz up to wherever it is, and spend all afternoon looking at the Picassos.

Or else . . . I could just buy a book *about* the Picassos. Because the thing is, do you actually need to see a piece of art in the flesh to appreciate it? Of course you don't. And in a way, flicking through a book would be *better* than trekking round lots of galleries—because I'm bound to cover more ground more quickly and actually learn far more.

Besides, what they have in this shop is art, isn't it? I mean, I've already taken in some pretty good culture. Exactly.

Several hours later, I arrive at the Royalton with a huge, exhilarated grin on my face. I haven't had such a successful afternoon shopping since . . . well, since yesterday.

I check all my carrier bags in at the cloakroom, then head for the small circular bar where Luke has told me to meet him and his new associate, Michael Ellis.

I've heard quite a lot about this Michael Ellis during the last few days. Apparently he owns a huge advertising agency in Washington and is best friends with the president. Or is it the vice-president? Something like that, anyway. Basically, he's a big shot, and crucial to Luke's new deal. So I'd better make sure I impress him.

God, this place is trendy, I think as I walk in. All leather and chrome and people in severe black outfits with haircuts to match. I walk into the dim circular bar, and there's Luke, sitting at a table. To my surprise, he's on his own.

"Hi!" I say, and kiss him. "So—where's your friend?"

"Making a call," says Luke. He gestures to a waiter. "Another gimlet here, please." He gives me a quizzical look as I sit down. "So, my darling. How was the Guggenheim?"

"It was good," I say with a triumphant beam. Ha, ha-di-ha. I've been doing my homework in the cab. "I particularly enjoyed a fascinating series of acrylic forms based on simple Euclidean shapes."

"Really?" says Luke, looking a bit surprised.

"Absolutely. The way they absorb and reflect pure light . . . Riveting. Oh and by the way, I bought you a present." I plonk a book on his lap entitled *Abstract Art and Artists,* and take a sip of the drink that has been placed in front of me, trying not to look too smug.

"You really went to the Guggenheim!" says Luke, leafing through the book incredulously.

"Erm . . . yes," I say. "Of course I did!"

OK, I know you shouldn't lie to your boyfriend. But it's kind of true, isn't it? I *did* go to the Guggenheim. In the broadest sense of the word.

"This is really interesting," Luke's saying. "Did you see that famous sculpture by Brancusi?"

"Erm . . . well . . ." I squint over his shoulder, trying to see what he's talking about. "Well, I was more concentrating on the . . . um . . ."

"What's that on your cheek?" says Luke, suddenly staring at me. I put a hand up in surprise and feel a trace of silver glitter. I'd forgotten all about that.

"It was . . . a piece of installation art," I hear myself saying. "Entitled *Constellations*. They had all this, um . . . glitter, and they smeared it on you . . ."

"Here comes Michael now," interrupts Luke. He closes the book and I quickly put it back in its carrier bag. Thank God for that. I look up interestedly to see what this famous Michael looks like—and nearly choke on my drink.

I don't believe it. It's him. Michael Ellis is the balding guy from the gym. Last time he saw me, I was dying at his feet.

"Hi!" says Luke, standing up. "Becky, meet Michael Ellis, my new associate."

"Hi again," I say, trying to smile composedly. "How are you?"

Oh, this shouldn't be allowed. There should be a rule which says that people you've met in the gym should *never* meet you in real life.

"We've already had the pleasure of meeting," says Michael Ellis, shaking my hand with a twinkle and sitting down opposite. "Becky and I worked out together at the hotel gym. Didn't catch you there this morning, though."

"This morning?" says Luke, giving me a puzzled look as he sits down again. "I thought you said the gym was closed, Becky."

Shit.

"Oh. Um, well . . ." I take a deep gulp of my drink and clear my throat. "When I said it was *closed,* what I really meant was . . . was . . ." I tail away feebly into silence.

And I so wanted to make a good impression.

"What am I thinking of?" exclaims Michael suddenly. "I must be going crazy! It wasn't this morning. The gym *was* closed this morning. Due to vital repair work, I believe." He grins broadly and I feel myself blushing.

"So, anyway," I say, hurriedly changing the subject. "You're . . . you're doing a deal with Luke. That's great! How's it all going?"

I only really ask to be polite, and steer attention away from my gym activities. I'm expecting them both to start explaining it to me at great length, and I can nod my head at intervals and enjoy my drink. But to my surprise, there's an awkward pause.

"Good question," says Luke at last, and looks at Michael. "What did Clark say?"

"We had a long conversation," says Michael. "Not entirely satisfactory."

I look from face to face, feeling disconcerted.

"Is something going wrong?"

"That all depends," says Michael.

He starts to tell Luke about his phone call with whoever Clark is, and I try to listen intelligently to their conversation. But the trouble is, I'm starting to feel quite giddy. How much have I drunk today? I don't even want to think about it, to be honest. I loll against the leather backrest, my eyes closed, listening to their voices chatting what seems far above my head.

". . . some sort of paranoia . . ."

". . . think they can change the goalposts . . ."

". . . overheads . . . cost reduction . . . with Alicia Billington heading up the London office . . ."

"Alicia?" I struggle to an upright position. "Alicia's going to run the London office?"

"Almost definitely," says Luke, stopping midsentence. "Why?"

"But—"

"But what?" says Michael, looking at me with interest. "Why shouldn't she run the London office? She's bright, ambitious . . ."

"Oh. Well . . . no reason," I say feebly.

I can't very well say, "Because she's a complete cow."

"You've heard she's just got engaged, by the way?" says Luke. "To Ed Collins at Hill Hanson."

"Really?" I say in surprise. "I thought she was having an affair with . . . whassisname."

"With who?" says Michael.

"Erm . . . thingy." I take a sip of gimlet to clear my head. "She was having secret lunches with him, and everything!"

What's his name again? I really am pissed.

"Becky likes to keep abreast of the office gossip," says Luke with an easy laugh. "Unfortunately one can't always vouch for its accuracy."

I stare at him crossly. What's he trying to say? That I'm some kind of rumormonger?

"Nothing wrong with a bit of office gossip," says Michael with a warm smile. "Keeps the wheels turning."

"Absolutely!" I say emphatically. "I couldn't agree more. I always say to Luke, you should be *interested* in the people who work for you. It's like when I give financial advice on my TV show. You can't just look at the numbers, you have to *talk* to them. Like . . . like Enid from Northampton!" I look at Michael expectantly, before remembering that he doesn't know who Enid is. "On paper she was ready to retire," I explain. "Pension and everything. But in real life . . ."

"She . . . wasn't ready?" suggests Michael.

"Exactly! She was really enjoying work and it was only her stupid husband who wanted her to give up. She was only fifty-five!" I gesture randomly with my glass. "I mean, don't they say life begins at fifty-five?"

"I'm not sure they do," says Michael, smiling. "But maybe they should." He gives me an interested look. "I'd like to catch your show one day. Is it shown in the States?"

"No, it isn't," I say regretfully. "But I'll be doing the same thing on American TV soon, so you'll be able to watch it then!"

"I look forward to that." Michael looks at his watch and drains his glass. "I have to go, I'm afraid. We'll speak later, Luke. And very nice to meet you, Becky. If I ever need financial advice, I'll know where to come."

As he leaves the bar, I lean back against my squashy seat and turn to look at Luke. His easy demeanor has vanished, and he's staring tensely into space while his fingers methodically tear a matchbook into small pieces.

"Michael seems really nice!" I say. "Really friendly."

"Yes," says Luke distantly. "Yes, he is."

I take a sip of gimlet and look at Luke more carefully. He's got exactly the same expression he had last month, when one of his staff cocked up a press release and some confidential figures were made public by mistake.

My mind spools back over the conversation I was half-listening to—and as I watch his face I start to feel a bit worried.

"Luke," I say at last. "What's going on? Is there some kind of hitch with your deal?"

"No," says Luke without moving.

"So what did Michael mean when he said, 'That all depends'? And all that stuff about them changing the goalposts?"

I lean forward and try to take his hand, but Luke doesn't respond. As I gaze at him in anxious silence, I gradually become aware of the background chatter and music all around us in the dim bar. At the next table a woman's opening a little box from Tiffany's and gasping—something which would normally have me throwing my napkin onto the floor and sidling over to see what she's got. But this time I'm too concerned.

"Luke?" I lean forward. "Come on, tell me. Is there a problem?"

"No," says Luke shortly, and tips his glass back into his mouth. "There's no problem. Things are fine. Come on, let's go."

Ten

I WAKE up the next morning with a pounding headache. We went on from the Royalton to someplace for dinner, and I drank even more there—and I can't even remember getting back to the hotel. Thank God I don't have an interview today. To be honest, I could quite happily spend the whole day in bed with Luke.

Except that Luke is already up, sitting by the window, talking grimly into the phone.

"OK, Michael. I'll talk to Greg today. God knows. I have no idea." He listens for a bit. "That may be the case. But I'm not having a second deal collapse on us." There's a pause. "Yes, but that would put us back—what, six months? OK. I hear what you're saying. Yes, I will. Cheers."

He puts down the receiver and stares tensely out the window, and I rub my sleepy face, trying to remember if I packed any aspirin.

"Luke, what's wrong?"

"You're awake," says Luke, turning round, and gives me a quick smile. "Did you sleep well?"

"What's wrong?" I repeat, ignoring him. "What's wrong with the deal?"

"Everything's fine," says Luke shortly, and turns back to the window.

"Everything isn't fine!" I retort. "Luke, I'm not blind. I'm not deaf. I can tell something's up."

"A minor blip," says Luke after a pause. "You don't need to worry about it." He reaches for the phone again. "Shall I order you some breakfast? What would you like?"

"Stop it!" I cry frustratedly. "Luke, I'm not some . . . some stranger! We're going to live together, for God's sake! I'm on your side. Just tell me what's really going on. Is your deal in trouble?"

There's silence—and for an awful moment I think Luke's going to tell me to mind my own business. But then he pushes his hands through his hair, exhales sharply, and looks up.

"You're right. The truth is, one of our backers is getting nervous."

"Oh," I say, and pull a face. "Why?"

"Because some *fucking* rumor's going around that we're about to lose Bank of London."

"Really?" I stare at him, feeling a cold dismay creep down my back. Even I know how important Bank of London is to Brandon Communications. They were one of Luke's first clients—and they still bring in about a quarter of the money the company makes every year. "Why would people be saying that?"

"Fuck knows." He pushes his hair back with his hands. "Bank of London denies it completely, of course. But then, they would. And of course it doesn't help that I'm here, not there . . ."

"So are you going to fly back to London?"

"No." He looks up. "That would give out completely the wrong signals. Things are shaky enough here already. If I suddenly disappear . . ." He shakes his head and I stare at him apprehensively.

"So—what happens if your backer pulls out?"

"We find someone else."

"But what if you can't? Will you have to give up on coming to New York?"

Luke turns to look at me—and he's suddenly got that blank, scary expression that used to make me want to run away from him at press conferences.

"Not an option."

"But I mean, you've got a really successful business in London," I persist. "I mean, you don't *have* to set up one in New York, do you? You could just . . ."

I tail away at the look on his face.

"Right," I say nervously. "Well—I'm sure it'll all be OK. In the end."

For a while we're both silent—then Luke seems to come to, and looks up.

"I'm afraid I'm going to have to hold a few hands today," he says abruptly. "So I won't be able to make this charity lunch with you and my mother."

Oh shit. Luke's mother. Of course, that's today.

"Can't she rearrange?" I suggest. "So we can both go?"

"Unfortunately not," says Luke. He gives a quick smile, but I can see true disappointment on his face, and I feel a flash of indignation toward his mother.

"Surely she could find time—"

"She's got a very busy schedule. And as she pointed out, I didn't give her very much warning." He frowns. "You know, my mother's not just some . . . society lady of leisure. She has a lot of important commitments. She can't just drop everything, much as she would like to."

"Of course not," I say hurriedly. "Anyway, it'll be fine.

I'll just go along to this lunch with her on my own, shall I?" I add, trying to sound as though I'm not at all intimidated by this prospect.

"She has to go to the spa first," says Luke, "and she suggested you accompany her."

"Oh right!" I say cautiously. "Well, that could be fun . . ."

"And then there's the charity lunch she's going to take you to. It'll be a chance for you two to get to know one another. I really hope you hit it off."

"Of course we will," I say firmly. "It'll be really nice." I get out of bed and go and put my arms around Luke's neck. His face still looks strained, and I put up my hand to smooth away the creases in his brow. "Don't worry, Luke. People will be queuing up to back you. Round the block."

Luke gives a half-smile and kisses my hand.

"Let's hope so."

As I sit in reception, waiting for Luke's mother to arrive, I feel a combination of nerves and intrigue. I mean, for a start, what are we going to talk about? If I were meeting his stepmum, she could tell me all about Luke when he was a little boy, and bring out all the embarrassing photographs. But Luke's real mum barely saw him when he was a little boy. Apparently she just used to send him huge presents at school, and visit about every three years.

You'd think that would have made him a bit resentful—but he adores her. In fact, he simply can't find one bad thing to say about her. I once asked him whether he minded that she left him—and he got all defensive and said she had no choice. And he's got this enormous glamorous photograph of her in his study at home—much bigger than the one of his dad and stepmum on their wedding day. I do sometimes wonder what they think about that. But it's not something I really feel I can bring up.

"Rebecca?" A voice interrupts my thoughts and I look up, startled. A tall, elegant woman in a pale suit, with very long legs and crocodile shoes, is staring down at me. It's the glamorous photograph in the flesh! And she looks just the same as she does in the picture, with high cheekbones and dark, Jackie Kennedy–style hair—except her skin is kind of tighter, and her eyes are unnaturally wide. In fact, it looks as though she might have some difficulty closing them.

"Hello!" I say, getting awkwardly to my feet and holding out my hand. "How do you do?"

"Elinor Sherman," she says in a strange half-English, half-American drawl. Her hand is cold and bony, and she's wearing two enormous diamond rings that press into my flesh. "So pleased to meet you."

"Luke was very sorry he couldn't make it," I say, and hand her the present he gave me to give. As she undoes the wrapping, I can't help goggling. An Hermès scarf!

"Nice," she says dismissively, and puts it back into the box. "My car is waiting."

"Luke was really hoping we might get to know each other a bit," I say, with a friendly smile.

"I have until two fifteen," says Elinor crisply.

"Oh," I say. "Well, never m—"

"So that should be ample time. Shall we go?"

Blimey. A car with a chauffeur. And a crocodile Kelly bag—and are those earrings *real* emeralds?

As we drive away, I can't help surreptitiously staring at Elinor. Now I'm close up I realize she's older than I first thought, probably in her fifties. And although she looks wonderful, it's a bit as though that glamorous photo has been left out in the sun and lost its color— and then been painted over with makeup. Her lashes are heavy with mascara and her hair is shiny with lacquer and her nails are so heavily varnished, they could be red porcelain. She's so completely . . . done. Groomed in a way I know I could never be, however many people went to work on me.

I mean, I'm looking quite nice today, I think. In fact, I'm looking really sharp. There was a spread in American *Vogue* on how black and white is *the* look at the moment, so I've teamed a black pencil skirt with a white shirt I found in the sample sale the other day, and black shoes with fantastic high heels. And I've shaded my eyes just like Mona showed me. I was really pleased with myself this morning. But now, as Elinor surveys me, I'm suddenly aware that one of my nails is very slightly chipped, and my shoe has got a tiny smear on the side—and oh God, is that a thread hanging down from my skirt? Should I quickly try to pull it off?

Casually, I put my hand down on my lap to cover up the loose thread. Maybe she didn't see. It's not that obvious, is it?

But Elinor is silently reaching into her bag, and a moment later she hands me a pair of small silver tortoiseshell-handled scissors.

"Oh . . . er, thanks," I say awkwardly. I snip the offending thread, and hand back the scissors, feeling like a schoolchild. "That always happens," I add, and give a nervous little giggle. "I look in the mirror in the morning and I think I look fine, but then the minute I get out of the house . . ."

Great, now I'm gabbling. Slow down, Becky.

"The English are incapable of good grooming," says Elinor. "Unless it's a horse."

The corners of her lips move a couple of millimeters up into a smile—although the rest of her face is static—and I burst into sycophantic laughter.

"That's really good! My flatmate loves horses. But I mean, you're English, aren't you? And you look absolutely . . . immaculate!"

I'm really pleased I've managed to throw in a little compliment, but Elinor's smile abruptly disappears. She gives me a blank stare and suddenly I can see where Luke gets that impassive scary expression from.

"I'm a naturalized American citizen."

"Oh right," I say. "Well, I suppose you've been here for a while. But I mean, in your heart, aren't you still . . . wouldn't you say you're a . . . I mean, Luke's very English . . ."

"I have lived in New York for the majority of my adult life," says Elinor coldly. "Any attachment of mine to Britain has long disappeared. The place is twenty years out of date."

"Right." I nod fervently, trying to look as though I understand completely. God, this is hard work. I feel like I'm being observed under a microscope. Why couldn't Luke have come? Or why couldn't she have rescheduled? I mean, doesn't she *want* to see him?

"Rebecca, who colors your hair?" says Elinor abruptly.

"It's . . . it's my own," I say, nervously touching a strand.

"Meione," she echoes suspiciously. "I don't know the name. At which salon does she work?"

For a moment I'm completely silenced.

"Erm . . . well," I flounder at last. "Actually . . . I . . . I'm not sure you'll have heard of it. It's very . . . tiny."

"Well, I think you should change colorist," says Elinor. "It's a very unsubtle shade."

"Right!" I say hurriedly. "Absolutely."

"Guinevere von Landlenburg swears by Julien on Bond Street. Do you know Guinevere von Landlenburg?"

I hesitate thoughtfully, as though going through a mental address book. As though checking all the many, many Guineveres I know.

"Um . . . no," I say at last. "I don't think I do."

"They have a house in South Hampton." She takes out a compact and checks her reflection. "We spent some time there last year with the de Bonnevilles."

I stiffen. The de Bonnevilles. As in Sacha de Bonneville. As in Luke's old girlfriend.

Luke never told me they were friends of the family.

OK, I'm not going to stress. Just because Elinor is tactless enough to mention Sacha's family. It's not as though she's actually mentioned *her*—

"Sacha is such an accomplished girl," says Elinor, snapping her compact shut. "Have you ever seen her water-ski?"

"No."

"Or play polo?"

"No," I say morosely. "I haven't."

Suddenly Elinor is rapping imperiously on the glass panel behind the driver.

"You took that corner too fast!" she says. "I won't tell

you again, I don't wish to be rocked in my seat. So, Rebecca," she says, sitting back in her seat and giving me a dissatisfied glance. "What are your own hobbies?"

"Uhm . . ." I open my mouth and close it again. My mind's gone completely blank. Come on, I must have some hobbies. What do I do at the weekends? What do I do to relax?

"Well, I . . ."

This is completely ridiculous. There *must* be things in my life other than shopping.

"Well, obviously, I enjoy . . . socializing with friends," I begin hesitantly. "And also the . . . the study of fashion through the um . . . medium of magazines . . ."

"Are you a sportswoman?" says Elinor, eyeing me coldly. "Do you hunt?"

"Erm . . . no. But . . . I've recently taken up fencing!" I add in sudden inspiration. I've got the outfit, haven't I? "And I've played the piano since I was six."

Completely true. No need to mention that I gave up when I was nine.

"Indeed," says Elinor, and gives a wintry smile. "Sacha is also very musical. She gave a recital of Beethoven piano sonatas in London last year. Did you go to it?"

Bloody Sacha. With her bloody water-skiing and bloody sonatas.

"No," I say defiantly. "But I . . . I gave one myself, as it happens. Of . . . of Wagner sonatas."

"Wagner sonatas?" echoes Elinor suspiciously.

"Erm . . . yes." I clear my throat, trying to think how to get off the subject of accomplishments. "So! You must be very proud of Luke!"

I'm hoping this comment will trigger a happy speech from her lasting ten minutes. But Elinor simply looks at me silently, as though I'm speaking nonsense.

"With his . . . his company and everything," I press on doggedly. "He's such a success. And he seems very determined to make it in New York. In America." Elinor gives me a patronizing smile.

"No one is anything till they make it in America." She looks out the window. "We're here."

Thank God for that.

To give Elinor her due, the beauty spa is absolutely amazing. The reception area is exactly like a Greek grotto, with pillars and soft music and a lovely scent of essential oils in the air. We go up to the reception desk, where a smart woman in black linen calls Elinor "Mrs. Sherman" very deferentially. They talk for a while in lowered voices, and the woman occasionally gives me a glance and nods her head, and I try to pretend not to be listening, looking at the price list for bath oils. Then abruptly Elinor turns away and ushers me to a seating area where there's a jug of mint tea and a sign asking patrons to respect the tranquility of the spa and keep their voices down.

We sit in silence for a while—then a girl in a white uniform comes to collect me and takes me to a treatment room, where a robe and slippers are waiting, all wrapped in embossed cellophane. As I get changed, she's busying herself at her counter of goodies, and I wonder pleasurably what I've got in store. Elinor insisted on paying for all my treatments herself, however much I tried to chip in—and apparently she selected the "top-to-toe grooming" treatment, whatever that is. I'm hoping it'll include a nice relaxing aromatherapy massage—but as I sit down on the couch, I see a pot full of wax heating up.

I feel an unpleasant lurch in my tummy. I've never been that great at having my legs waxed. Which is not because I'm afraid of pain, but because—

Well, OK. It's because I'm afraid of pain.

"So—does my treatment include waxing?" I say, trying to sound lighthearted.

"You're booked in for a full waxing program," says the beautician, looking up in surprise. "The 'top-to-toe.' Legs, arms, eyebrows, and Brazilian."

Arms? Eyebrows? I can feel my throat tightening in fear. I haven't been this scared since I had my jabs for Thailand.

"Brazilian?" I say in a scratchy voice. "What . . . what's that?"

"It's a form of bikini wax. A total wax."

I stare at her, my mind working overtime. She can't possibly mean—

"So if you'd like to lie down on the couch—"

"Wait!" I say, trying to keep my voice calm. "When you say 'total,' do you mean . . ."

"Uh-huh." The beautician smiles. "Then, if you wish, I can apply a small crystal tattoo to the . . . area. A love heart is quite popular. Or perhaps the initials of someone special?"

No. This can't be real.

"So, if you could just lie back on the couch and relax—"

Relax? *Relax?*

She turns back to her pot of molten wax—and I feel a surge of pure terror.

"I'm not doing it," I hear myself saying, and slither off the couch. "I'm not having it."

"The tattoo?"

"Any of it."

"*Any* of it?"

The beautician comes toward me, the wax pot in hand—and in panic I dodge behind the couch, clasping my robe defensively around me.

"But Mrs. Sherman has already prepaid for the entire treatment—"

"I don't care what she's paid for," I say, backing away. "You can wax my legs. But not my arms. And definitely not . . . that other one. The crystal love heart one."

The beautician looks worried.

"Mrs. Sherman is one of our most regular customers. She specifically requested the 'top-to-toe wax' for you."

"She'll never know!" I say desperately. "She'll never know! I mean, she's not exactly going to *look,* is she? She's not going to ask her son if his initials are tattooed on his girlfriend's . . ." I can't bring myself to say *area.* "I mean, come on. Is she?"

I break off, and there's a tense silence, broken only by the sound of tootling panpipes.

Then suddenly the beautician gives a snort of laughter. I catch her eye—and find myself starting to laugh, too, albeit slightly hysterically.

"You're right," says the beautician, sitting down and wiping her eyes. "You're right. She'll never know."

"How about a compromise?" I say. "You do my legs and eyebrows and we keep quiet about the rest."

"I could give you a massage instead," says the beautician. "Use up the time."

"There we are, then!" I say in relief. "Perfect!"

Feeling slightly drained, I lie down on the couch, and the beautician covers me up expertly with a towel.

"So, does Mrs. Sherman have a son, then?" she says, smoothing back my hair.

"Yes." I look up, taken aback. "Has she never even mentioned him?"

"Not that I recall. And she's been coming here for years . . ." The beautician shrugs. "I guess I always assumed she didn't have any children."

"Oh right," I say, and lie back down, trying not to give away my surprise.

When I emerge an hour and a half later, I feel fantastic. I've got brand-new eyebrows, smooth legs, and a glow all over from the most wonderful aromatherapy massage.

Elinor is waiting for me in reception, and as I come toward her, she runs her eyes appraisingly up and down my body. For a horrible moment I think she's going to ask me to roll up my sleeves to check the smoothness of my arms—but all she says is, "Your eyebrows look a lot better." Then she turns and walks out, and I hurry after her.

As we get back into the car, I ask, "Where are we having lunch?"

"Nina Heywood is holding a small informal charity lunch for Ugandan famine relief," she replies, examining one of her immaculate nails. "She holds events like this nearly every month. Do you know the Heywoods? Or the van Gelders?"

Of course I don't bloody know them.

"No," I hear myself saying. "But I know the Websters."

"The Websters?" She raises her arched eyebrows. "The Newport Websters?"

"The Oxshott Websters. Janice and Martin." I give her an innocent look. "Do you know them?"

"No," says Elinor, giving me a frosty look. "I don't believe I do."

For the rest of the journey we travel in silence. Then suddenly the car is stopping and we're getting out, and walking into the grandest, most enormous lobby I've ever seen, with a doorman in uniform and mirrors everywhere. We go up what seems like a zillion floors in a gilded lift with a man in a peaked cap, and into an apartment. And I have *never* seen anything like it.

The place is absolutely enormous, with a marble floor and a double staircase and a grand piano on a platform. The pale silk walls are decorated with enormous gold-framed paintings, and on pedestals around the room there are cascading flower arrangements like I've never seen before. Pin-thin women in expensive clothes are talking animatedly to one another, a smaller number of well-dressed men are listening politely, there are waitresses handing out champagne, and a girl in a flowing dress is playing the harp.

And this is a *small* charity lunch?

Our hostess Mrs. Heywood is a tiny woman in pink, who is about to shake hands with me when she's distracted by the arrival of a woman in a bejeweled turban. Elinor introduces me to a Mrs. Parker, a Mr. Wunsch, and a Miss Kutomi, then drifts away, and I make conversation as best I can, even though everyone seems to assume I must be a close friend of Prince William.

"Tell me," says Mrs. Parker urgently. "How is that poor young man bearing up after his . . . great loss?" she whispers.

"That boy has a natural nobility," says Mr. Wunsch fiercely. "Young people today could learn a lot from him. Tell me, is it the army he's headed for?"

"He . . . he hasn't mentioned it," I say helplessly. "Would you excuse me."

I escape to the bathroom—and that's just as huge and sumptuous as the rest of the apartment, with racks of luxury soaps and bottles of free perfume, and a comfy chair to sit in. I kind of wish I could stay there all day, actually. But I don't dare linger too long in case Elinor comes looking for me. So with a final squirt of Eternity, I force myself to get up and go back into the throng, where waiters are moving quietly around, murmuring, "Lunch will be served now."

As everyone moves toward a set of grand double doors I look around for Elinor but I can't see her. There's an old lady in black lace sitting on a chair near to me, and she begins to stand up with the aid of a walking stick.

"Let me help," I say, hurrying forward as her grip falters. "Shall I hold your champagne glass?"

"Thank you, my dear!" The lady smiles at me as I take her arm, and we walk slowly together into the palatial dining room. People are pulling out chairs and sitting down at circular tables, and waiters are hurrying round with bread rolls.

"Margaret," says Mrs. Heywood, coming forward and holding out her hands to the old lady. "There you are. Now let me find your seat . . ."

"This young lady was assisting me," says the old lady as she lowers herself onto a chair, and I smile modestly at Mrs. Heywood.

"Thank you, dear," she says absently. "Now, could

you take my glass too, please . . . and bring some water to our table?"

"Of course!" I say with a friendly smile. "No problem."

"And I'll have a gin and tonic," adds an elderly man nearby, swiveling in his chair.

"Coming right up!"

It just shows, what Mum says is right. The way to make a friend is to give a helping hand. I feel quite special, helping out the hostess. It's almost like I'm throwing the party with her!

I'm not sure where the kitchen is, but the waiters are all heading toward one end of the room. I follow them through a set of double doors, and find myself in the kind of kitchen Mum would absolutely die for. Granite and marble everywhere, and a fridge which looks like a space rocket, and a pizza oven set into the wall! There are waiters in white shirts hurrying in and out with trays, and two chefs standing at a central island hob, holding sizzling pans, and someone's yelling, "Where the *fuck* are the napkins?"

I find a bottle of water and a glass, and put them on a tray, then start looking around to see where the gin might be. As I bend down to open a cupboard door, a man with cropped bleached hair taps me on the shoulder.

"Hey. What are you doing?"

"Oh hi!" I say, standing up. "I'm just looking for the gin, actually. Somebody wanted a gin and tonic."

"We haven't got time for that!" he barks. "Do you realize how short-staffed we are? We need food on tables!"

Short-staffed? I stare at him blankly for a moment. Then, as my eye falls on my black skirt and the realization hits me, I give a shocked laugh.

"No! I'm not a . . . I mean, I'm actually one of the . . ."

How do I say this without offending him? I'm sure being a waiter is actually very fulfilling. Anyway, he's probably an actor in his spare time.

But while I'm dithering, he dumps a silver platter full of smoked fish in my arms.

"Get! Now!"

"But I'm not—"

"Now! *Food on tables!*"

With a pang of fright I quickly hurry away. OK. What I'll do is I'll just get away from him, and put this platter down somewhere, and find my place.

Cautiously I walk back into the dining room, and wander about between the tables, looking for a handy surface to leave the platter. But there don't seem to be any side tables or even spare chairs. I can't really leave it on the floor, and it would be a bit too awkward to reach between the guests and dump it on a table.

This is really annoying, actually. The platter's quite heavy, and my arms are starting to ache. I pass by Mr. Wunsch's chair and give him a little smile, but he doesn't even notice me. It's as though I'm suddenly invisible.

This is ridiculous. There *must* be somewhere I can put it down.

"Will-you-serve-the-food!" hisses a furious voice behind me, and I feel myself jump.

"OK!" I retort, feeling slightly rattled. "OK, I will!"

Oh, for goodness' sake. It's probably easier just to serve it. Then at least it'll be gone, and I can sit down. Hesitantly I approach the nearest table.

"Erm . . . would anyone like some smoked fish? I think this is salmon . . . and this is trout . . ."

"Rebecca?"

The elegantly coiffured head in front of me swivels round and I give a startled leap. Elinor is staring up at me, her eyes like daggers.

"Hi," I say nervously. "Would you like some fish?"

"*What* do you think you're doing?" she says in a low, furious voice.

"Oh!" I swallow. "Well, I was just, you know, helping out . . ."

"I'll have some smoked salmon, thanks," says a woman in a gold jacket. "Do you have any nonfat French dressing?"

"Erm . . . well, the thing is, I'm not actually . . ."

"Rebecca!" Elinor's voice comes shooting out of her barely opened mouth. "Put it down. Just . . . sit down."

"Right. Of course." I glance uncertainly at the platter. "Or should I serve it, since I'm here anyway . . ."

"Put it down. Now!"

"Right." I look helplessly about for a moment, then see a waiter coming toward me with an empty tray. Before he can protest I deposit the smoked fish platter on his tray, then hurry round with trembling legs to my empty chair, smoothing down my hair.

As I sit down, and spread my thick napkin over my knees, there's silence around the table. I try a friendly little smile, but nobody responds. Then an old lady wearing about six rows of huge pearls and a hearing aid leans toward Elinor and whispers, so audibly we can all hear, "Your son is dating . . . a *waitress*?"

BECKY BLOOMWOOD'S
NEW YORK BUDGET

DAILY BUDGET (PROPOSED)

Food	$50
Shopping	~~$50~~ $100
Expenses	~~$50~~ ~~$60~~ $100
TOTAL	$250

DAILY BUDGET (REVISED)

DAY THREE

Food	$50
Shopping	$100
Expenses	$365
Other expenses	$229
Unique sample sale opportunity	$567
Further unique sample sale opportunity	$128
Unavoidable contingency expense	$49
Essential business-linked expense (shoes)	

Eleven

"SHE DID?" There's a long pause. Luke frowns and glances at me. "Well, I'm sure she didn't . . ." He breaks off into silence and I feel a flutter of apprehension.

It's a couple of days later, and on the other end of the phone, speaking to Luke, is Elinor. God only knows what she's saying about me. I wish we had a speaker phone.

On second thought, no, I don't.

"Really?" Luke looks surprised. "I see. Interesting." He clears his throat. "And on that matter—what about the two of us trying to meet up?"

Thank goodness. They've stopped talking about me.

"Oh, I see." The deflation in Luke's voice is unmistakable. "No, of course I understand. Yes, I will. Bye, then." He puts down the phone and gazes down at it for a few seconds.

"So!" I say, trying to sound relaxed. "What did your mother think of me?"

"Oh! Well . . ." Luke screws up his face puzzledly. "She said you were . . . overzealous. What did she mean by that?"

"I've no idea!" I give a shrill laugh. "Probably just . . .

you know . . . hardworking! So, erm . . . did she mention your gift?" I add, changing the subject.

"No," says Luke after a pause. "As a matter of fact, she didn't."

"Oh," I say, feeling a pang of indignation toward Elinor. "Well, you know, she did absolutely love it."

"Do you think?"

"Absolutely!" I say emphatically. "She . . . she almost cried, she was so pleased. And she said you were the best son in the whole world."

"Really?" Luke's face glows with pleasure. "She said that?"

I smile vaguely and reach down for my shoes. Maybe that wasn't quite true. But I mean, I can't tell him she just shoved it back into the box as though it were a pair of socks from Woolworth's, can I?

"See you later." Luke picks up his briefcase and gives me a kiss. "And good luck this morning."

"Thanks!" I beam back, and feel a small trickle of excitement.

All of a sudden, things have started to happen over here. I keep getting phone calls from people who want to meet me, which Luke says is the "snowball effect" and he expected it all along. Yesterday I had three meetings with different sets of TV executives—today I've got a breakfast meeting with a Greg Walters from Blue River Productions. He's the one who sent me the basket of fruit and was "desperate" to see me. I've never had anyone desperate to see me before in my entire life!

An hour later, I'm sitting in the Four Seasons restaurant, feeling like a movie star. Greg Walters is tall and tanned and has already dropped the name of every TV network I've ever heard of.

"You're hot," he now keeps saying, in between bites of croissant. "You realize that?"

"Erm . . . well . . ."

"No." He lifts a hand. "Don't be coy. You're all over town. Folks are fighting over you." He takes a sip of coffee and looks me in the eye. "I'll be frank—I want to give you your own show."

I stare at him, almost unable to breathe for excitement.

"Really? My own show? Doing what?"

"Whatever. We'll find you a winning format." He takes a gulp of coffee. "You're a political commentator, right?"

"Um . . . not really," I say awkwardly. "I do personal finance. You know, mortgages and stuff?"

"Right." Greg nods. "Finance. So I'm thinking . . . off the top of my head . . . Wall Street. Wall Street meets *Ab Fab* meets Oprah. You could do that, right?"

"Erm . . . absolutely!"

I beam confidently at him and take a bite of croissant.

"I have to go," he says as he finishes his coffee. "But I'm going to call you tomorrow and set up a meeting with our head of development. Is that OK?"

"Fine!" I say, trying to look as nonchalant as possible. "That would be good."

As he walks off, a huge grin of delight spreads across my face. My own show! Things are just going better and better. Everyone I speak to seems to want to offer me a job, and they all keep buying me nice meals, and yesterday, someone said I could have a career in Hollywood, no question. Hollywood!

I mean, just imagine if I get my own show in Hollywood! I'll be able to live in some amazing house in Beverly Hills, and go to parties with all the film stars. Maybe Luke will start a Los Angeles branch of his company. I mean, people out there need PR—and he could easily switch from finance to movies. And . . . yes! We could set up a film production company together!

"What a pleasant surprise," says a cheerful voice, and I look up dazedly to see Michael Ellis pulling out a chair at another table.

"Oh," I say, wrenching my mind away from the Oscars. "Oh, hello. Do join me!" And I gesture politely to the chair opposite.

"I'm not disturbing you?" he says, sitting down.

"No. I was having a meeting but it's over." I look around vaguely. "Is Luke with you?"

Michael shakes his head.

"He's talking to some people at JD Slade this morning. The big guns."

A waiter comes and clears away Greg's plate, and Michael orders a cappuccino.

"So—how are things going?" I ask, lowering my voice slightly. "Luke told me about one of the backers getting nervous."

"Right." Michael nods gravely. "I don't know what the hell's going on there."

"But why do you *need* backers?" I ask. "I mean, Luke's got loads of money . . ."

"Never invest your own money," says Michael. "First rule of business. Besides which, Luke has very grand plans, and grand plans tend to need a lot of capital." He looks up. "You know, he's very driven, that man of yours. *Very* determined to succeed over here."

"I know," I say, rolling my eyes. "All he ever does is work."

"Work is good," says Michael, frowning into his coffee. "Obsession is . . . not so good." He's silent for a moment, then looks up with a smile. "But I gather things are going well for you?"

"They are, actually," I say, unable to maintain my calm. "In fact, they're going brilliantly! I've had all these fantastic meetings, and everybody says they want to give me a job! I just had a meeting with Greg Walters from Blue River Productions—and he said he was going to give me my own show. And yesterday, someone was talking about Hollywood!"

"That's great," says Michael. "Really great." He takes a sip of coffee and looks at me thoughtfully. "If I could just say a word?"

"What?"

"These TV people. You don't necessarily want to believe every single word they say."

I look at him, a little discomfited.

"What do you mean?"

"These guys like talking big," says Michael, slowly stirring his coffee. "It makes them feel good. And they believe everything they say at the time when they're saying it. But when it comes to the cold hard dollar . . ." He stops, and looks up at me. "I just don't want you to be disappointed."

"I won't be disappointed!" I retort indignantly. "Greg Walters said the whole town was fighting over me!"

"I'm sure he did," says Michael. "And I very much hope they are. All I'm saying is—"

He stops as a uniformed concierge stops by our table.

"Miss Bloomwood," he says. "I have a message for you."

"Thanks!" I say in surprise.

I open the envelope he gives me, and pull out the sheets of paper—and it's a message from Kent Garland at HLBC.

"Well!" I say, unable to stop a smile of triumph. "It looks like HLBC wasn't just talking big. It looks like they mean business." I give the piece of paper to Michael Ellis, wanting to add, "So there!"

" 'Please call Kent's assistant to arrange a screen test,' " reads Michael aloud. "Well, looks like I'm wrong," he says, smiling. "And I'm very glad about it." He lifts his coffee cup toward me. "So here's to a successful screen test."

OK. What am I going to wear tomorrow? *What am I going to wear?* I mean, this is the most important moment of my life, a screen test for American television. My outfit has to be sharp, flattering, photogenic, immaculate . . . I mean, I've got nothing. Nothing.

I leaf through all my clothes for the millionth time, and flop back down on the bed, exhausted. I can't believe I've come all this way without one single screen-test outfit.

Well, there's nothing for it. I've got no choice.

I pick up my bag and check that I've got my wallet—and I'm just reaching for my coat when the phone rings.

"Hello?" I say into the receiver, hoping it might be Luke.

"Bex!" comes Suze's voice, all tinny and distant.

"Suze!" I say in delight. "Hi!"

"How's it going?"

"It's going really well!" I say. "I've had loads of meetings, and everyone's being really positive! It's just brilliant!"

"Bex! That's great."

"How about you?" I frown slightly at her voice. "Is everything OK?"

"Oh yes!" says Suze. "Everything's fine. Except . . ." She hesitates. "I just thought you should know, a man phoned up this morning about some money you owe a shop. La Rosa, in Hampstead."

"Really?" I pull a face. "Them again?"

"Yes. He asked me when you were going to be out of the artificial limb unit."

"Oh," I say after a pause. "Right. So—what did you say?"

"Bex, why did he think you were in the artificial limb unit?"

"I don't know," I say evasively. "Maybe he heard something. Or . . . or I may possibly have written him the odd little letter . . ."

"Bex," interrupts Suze, and her voice is quivering slightly. "You told me you'd taken care of all those bills. You promised!"

"I have taken care of them!" I reach for my hairbrush and begin to brush my hair.

"By telling them your *parachute* didn't open in time?" cries Suze. "I mean, honestly, Bex—"

"Look, don't stress. I'll sort it all out as soon as I come home."

"He said he was going to have to take extreme action! He said he was very sorry, but enough allowances had been made, and—"

"They always say that," I say soothingly. "Suze, you really don't have to worry. I'm going to earn loads over here. I'll be loaded! And I'll be able to pay everything off, and everything will be fine."

There's silence, and I imagine Suze sitting on the floor of the sitting room, winding her hair tightly round her fingers.

"Really?" she says at last. "Is it all going well, then?"

"Yes! I've got a screen test tomorrow, and this guy wants to give me my own show, and they're even talking about Hollywood!"

"Hollywood?" breathes Suze. "That's amazing."

"I know!" I beam at my own reflection. "Isn't it great? I'm hot! That's what the guy from Blue River Productions said."

"So—what are you going to wear for your screen test?"

"I'm just off to Barneys," I say happily. "Choose a new outfit!"

"*Barneys?*" exclaims Suze in horror. "Bex, you *promised* me you weren't going to go overboard! You completely promised me you were going to stick to a budget."

"I have! I've completely stuck to it! It's all written out and everything! And anyway, this is a business expense. I'm investing in my career."

"But—"

"Suze, you can't make money unless you spend it first. Everyone knows that! I mean, you have to spend money on your materials, don't you?"

There's a pause.

"I suppose so," says Suze doubtfully.

"And anyway, what are credit cards for?"

"Oh Bex . . ." Suze sighs. "Actually, that's funny— that's just what the council tax girl said yesterday."

"What council tax girl?" I frown at my reflection and reach for an eyeliner.

"The girl who came round this morning," says Suze vaguely. "She had a clipboard. And she asked loads of questions about me, and the flat, and how much rent you paid me . . . we had a really nice chat. And I was telling her all about you being in America, and Luke . . . and your TV job . . ."

"Great," I say, not really listening. "That sounds really good. Listen, Suze, I've got to run. But honestly, don't worry. If anyone else phones for me, just don't take the call. OK?"

"Well . . . OK," says Suze. "And good luck tomorrow!"

"Thanks!" I say, and put down the phone. Ha-ha-ha! Off to Barneys!

Barneys. I've kind of been saving it for last, like an extra-special chocolate. Now, as I push through the distinctive black revolving doors and walk slowly across the pale mosaic floor, looking at all the beautiful people peering into cabinets full of contemporary jewelry . . . I feel like Goldilocks picking the right chair. The music is buzzy and the atmosphere is great, and everyone looks like they're having a great time . . .

For a while I linger at a cabinet with a stunning aquamarine crystal necklace in it. I'd look just like a mermaid in that. I wonder how much it is? I'm just peering to see the price tag when an assistant approaches—and I come to with a jolt. I'm not here to buy a necklace. I'm going to buy what I *need*.

Feeling virtuous, I force myself to move away from the cabinet. Down to business. I study the store guide, then I take the escalator up to the top floor of the store, glimpsing tanks of fish, cages of brightly colored birds . . . and everywhere I look, gorgeous clothes.

Oh God, the *clothes*. They are just the most beautiful things I've ever seen! Everywhere I look, I see shapes and colors and designs I just want to grab and touch and stroke. But I can't just spend all day marveling at candy-colored knitwear and beaded mules. I have to be focused. An outfit for tomorrow, nothing else.

Right. So what exactly do I want? Maybe a jacket, so I look authoritative—but it has to be the right jacket. Not too boxy, not too stiff . . . just nice clean lines. And maybe a skirt. Or just look at those trousers. They would look fantastic, if I had the right shoes . . .

I wander slowly round each floor, making mental notes. Then at last, when I'm sure I haven't left anything out, I start collecting all my possibilities. A Calvin Klein jacket . . . and a skirt . . .

"Excuse me?"

A voice interrupts me just as I'm reaching for a sleeveless top, and I turn in surprise. A woman in a black trouser suit is smiling at me.

"Would you like any help with your shopping to-day?"

"Erm . . . oh, thanks!" I say. "If you could hold these . . ." I hand her the garments I've already picked out and her smile flickers slightly.

"When I said help . . . we're running a unique pro-motion of our personal shopping department today. We'd like to introduce the concept to a wider audience. So if you'd like to take up the offer of an introductory session, there are some slots still available."

"Oh right," I say interestedly. "What exactly would that—"

"Our trained, experienced personal shoppers can help you find exactly what you're searching for," says the woman pleasantly. "They can help you find your own style, focus on designs that suit you, and guide you through the daunting fashion maze." She gives a tight little laugh, and I get the feeling she's said this little spiel quite a few times today.

"I see," I say thoughtfully. "The thing is . . . I'm not sure I really need guiding. So thanks very much, but—"

"The service is complimentary," says the woman. "Today we're also offering tea, coffee, or a glass of champagne."

Champagne? Free champagne?

"Ooh!" I say. "Well, actually—that sounds really good. Yes, please!"

And actually, I think as I follow her to the third floor, these trained shoppers must really know their stuff—and they'll probably have a completely different eye. They'll probably show me a whole side of myself that I've never even seen before!

We arrive at a suite of large dressing rooms, and the woman shows me in with a smile.

"Your personal shopper today will be Erin," she says. "Erin has only recently joined us, so she will be receiving some occasional guidance from a senior Barneys shopper. Will that be all right?"

"Absolutely!" I say, taking off my coat.

"Would you prefer tea, coffee, or champagne?"

"Champagne," I say quickly. "Thanks."

"Very well," she says with a smile. "Ah, and here's Erin."

I look up with interest, to see a tall thin girl coming into the dressing room. She's got straight blond hair and a small, kind of squashed-looking mouth. In fact her whole face looks as though she were once squeezed between a pair of lift doors and never quite recovered.

"Hello," she says, and I watch her mouth in fascination as she smiles. "I'm Erin—and I'll be helping you find the outfit to best suit your needs."

"Great!" I say. "Can't wait!"

I wonder how this Erin got her job. Not by her taste in shoes, certainly.

"So . . ." Erin looks at me thoughtfully. "What were you looking for today?"

"I have a screen test tomorrow," I explain. "I want to look kind of . . . smart and sassy, but approachable, too. Maybe with a little witty twist somewhere."

"A witty twist," echoes Erin, scribbling on her pad. "Right. And were you thinking . . . a suit? A jacket?"

"Well," I say, and launch into an exact explanation of what I'm looking for. Erin listens carefully, and I notice a dark-haired woman in tortoiseshell glasses occasionally coming to the door of our dressing room and listening too.

"Right," says Erin, when I've finished. "Well, you certainly have some ideas there . . ." She taps her teeth for a moment. "I'm thinking . . . we have a very nice fitted jacket by Moschino, with roses on the collar . . ."

"Oh, I know the one!" I say in delight. "I was thinking of that, too!"

"Along with . . . there's a new skirt in the Barneys collection . . ."

"The black one?" I say. "With the buttons just here? Yes, I thought of that, but it's a bit short. I was thinking of the knee-length one. You know, with the ribbon round the hem . . ."

"We'll see," says Erin, with a pleasant smile. "Let me line up some pieces for you, and we can have a look."

As she goes off to gather up clothes, I sit down and sip my champagne. This isn't bad, actually. I mean, it's much less effort than trawling round the shop myself. I can half-hear a murmured conversation going on in the dressing room next door—and suddenly a woman's voice rises in distress, saying, "I just want to show that bastard. I just want to *show* him!"

"And we will show him, Marcia," replies a calm, soothing voice, which I think belongs to the woman in tortoiseshell glasses. "We will. But not in a cherry-red pantsuit."

"Okaaay!" Erin is back in the dressing room, wheeling in a rack of clothes. I run my eye quickly over them, and notice quite a few of the things I'd already picked out for myself. But what about the knee-length skirt? And what about that amazing aubergine trouser suit with the leather collar?

"So, here's the jacket for you to try . . . and the skirt . . ."

I take the clothes from her, and look doubtfully at the skirt. I just know it's going to be too short. But then, she's the expert, I suppose . . . Quickly I change into the skirt and jacket—then come and stand in front of the mirror, next to Erin.

"The jacket's fabulous!" I say. "And it fits me perfectly. I *love* the cut."

I don't really want to say anything about the skirt. I mean, I don't want to hurt her feelings—but it looks all wrong.

"Now, let's see," says Erin. She stands with her head on one side and squints at my reflection. "I'm thinking a skirt to the knee might look better, after all."

"Like the one I told you about!" I say in relief. "It's on the seventh floor, right next to the—"

"Possibly," she says, and smiles. "But I have a few other skirts in mind . . ."

"Or the Dolce & Gabbana one on the third floor," I add. "I was looking at it earlier. Or the DKNY."

"DKNY?" says Erin, wrinkling her brow. "I don't believe . . ."

"The assistant there told me they're new in. *So* nice. You should have a look at them!" I turn round and look carefully at her outfit. "You know what? The mauve DKNY would look really good with that turtleneck you're wearing. And you could team it with a pair of those new Stephane Kelian boots with the spiky heels. You know the ones?"

"I know the ones," says Erin tightly. "The crocodile and suede ones." I look at her in surprise.

"No, not those ones. The *new* range. With the stitching up the back. They're so gorgeous! In fact they'd go well with the knee-length skirt . . ."

"Thank you!" interrupts Erin sharply. "I'll bear that in mind."

Honestly. I'm only giving her a few hints. You'd think she'd be pleased I was so interested in her shop!

Although, I have to say, she doesn't seem to know it very well.

"Hello there!" comes a voice from the door—and the woman in tortoiseshell glasses is leaning against the door frame, looking at me interestedly. "Everything all right?"

"Great, thanks!" I say, beaming at her.

"So," says the woman, looking at Erin. "You're going to try the knee-length skirt for our customer. Is that right?"

"Yes," says Erin, and gives a rather forced smile. "I'll just go get it."

As she disappears, I can't resist sidling over to the rack of clothes, just to see what else she brought. The woman in glasses watches me for a moment, then comes in and holds out her hand.

"Christina Rowan," she said. "I head up the personal shopping department."

"Well, hello!" I say, looking at a pale blue Jill Stuart shirt. "I'm Becky Bloomwood."

"And you're from England, I guess, by your accent?"

"London, but I'm going to move to New York!"

"Are you, indeed." Christina Rowan gives me a friendly smile. "Tell me, what do you do, Becky? Do you work in fashion?"

"Oh no. I'm in finance."

"Finance! Really." She raises her eyebrows.

"I give financial advice on the telly. You know, pensions and stuff . . ." I reach for a pair of soft cashmere trousers. "Aren't these beautiful? Much better than the Ralph Lauren ones. *And* they're cheaper."

"They're great, aren't they?" She gives me a quizzical look. "Well, it's nice to have such an enthusiastic customer." She reaches into the pocket of her jacket and pulls out a business card. "Do come back and visit us when you're here again."

"I will!" I beam at her. "And thanks very much!"

It's four o'clock by the time I finally leave Barneys. I hail a cab and travel back to the Four Seasons. As I push open the door to our room and look at my reflection in the silent dressing table mirror, I'm still on a kind of glittery high, almost a hysterical excitement at what I've just done. What I've just bought.

I know I went out just planning to buy a single outfit

for my screen test. But I ended up . . . Well, I suppose I just got a bit . . . a bit carried away. So my final list of purchases goes like this:

1. Moschino jacket
2. Knee-length Barneys skirt
3. Calvin Klein underwear
4. Pair of new tights and . . .
5. Vera Wang cocktail dress.

Just . . . before you say anything, I *know* I wasn't supposed to be buying a cocktail dress. I *know* that when Erin said, "Are you interested in evening wear?" I should simply have said no.

But oh God. Oh *God*. That Vera Wang dress. Inky purple, with a low back and glittering straps. It just looked so completely movie-star perfect. Everyone crowded round to see me in it—and when I drew back the curtain, they all gasped.

And I just stared at myself, mesmerized. Entranced by what I could look like, by the person I could be. There was no question. I had to have it. I *had* to. As I signed the credit card slip . . . I wasn't me anymore. I was Grace Kelly. I was Gwyneth Paltrow. I was a glittering somebody else, who can casually sign a credit card slip for thousands of dollars while smiling and laughing at the assistant, as though this were a nothing purchase.

Thousands of dollars.

Although, for a designer like Vera Wang, that price is actually quite . . .

Well, it's really very . . .

I feel slightly sick. I don't even want to think about how much it cost. The point is, I'll be able to wear it for years. Yes! Years and years. And I *need* designer clothes if I'm going to be a famous television star. I mean, I'll have important events to go to—and I can't just turn up in M&S, can I? Exactly.

And I've got a £10,000 credit card limit. That's the real point. I mean, they wouldn't give it to me if they didn't think I could afford it.

Suddenly I hear a sound at the door, and quickly rise to my feet. Heart thumping, I go to the wardrobe I've been stashing all my shopping in, open the door, and quickly shove my Barneys bags inside—then close the door and turn round with a smile, just as Luke enters the room, talking on his mobile.

"Of course I'm in fucking control," he's spitting furiously into the phone. "What the fuck do they think they're—" He breaks off and is silent for a few moments. "I don't need to fly back to London! Alicia has it all in hand. She says there's absolutely no problem with Provident Assurance, she spoke to them today and they're very happy. Someone's just shit-stirring, God knows who. Yes, I know," he says in a calmer voice. "Yes. OK, will do. I'll see you tomorrow, Michael. Thanks."

He switches off his mobile, puts it away, and looks at me as though he's almost forgotten who I am. But then his brow softens and he smiles.

"Hi!" he says, and drops his briefcase onto a chair.

"Hi!" I say brightly, moving away from the wardrobe door. "Stranger."

"I know," says Luke, rubbing his face wearily. "I'm sorry. Things have been . . . a bit of a nightmare, to be frank. I heard about your screen test, though. Fantastic news."

He goes to the minibar, pours himself a scotch, and

downs it. Then he pours himself another one and takes a slug while I watch anxiously. His face is pale and tense, I notice, and there are shadows under his eyes.

"Is it all . . . going OK?" I ask gingerly.

"It's going," he replies. "That's about as much as I can say." He walks over to the window and stares out over the glittering Manhattan skyline, and I bite my lip nervously.

"Luke—couldn't someone else go to all these meetings? Couldn't someone else fly out and take some of the load? Like . . . Alicia?"

It nearly kills me even to mention her name—but I honestly am getting a bit worried. Slightly to my relief, though, Luke shakes his head.

"I can't bring in somebody new at this stage. I've been managing it all until now; I'll just have to see it through. I just had no idea they'd be so pedantic. I had no idea they'd be so . . ." He sits down in an armchair and takes a slug of his drink. "I mean, Jesus, they ask a lot of questions. I know Americans are thorough but—" He shakes his head disbelievingly. "They have to know *everything*. About every single client, every single potential client, everybody who's ever worked for the company, every single bloody memo I've ever sent . . . Is there any possibility of litigation here? Who was your receptionist in 1993? What car do you drive? What fucking . . . toothpaste do you use? And now, with these rumors . . . they're picking everything apart all over again."

He breaks off and drains his glass, and I stare at him in dismay.

"They sound awful!" I say, and the flicker of a smile passes across Luke's face.

"They're not awful. They're just very conservative,

old-school investors—and something's rattling them. I don't know what." He exhales sharply. "I just need to keep them steady."

His voice is trembling slightly—and as I glance at his hand I see that it's clenched tightly around his glass. I've never seen Luke like this, to be honest. He usually looks so utterly in control, so completely smooth . . .

"Luke, I think you should have an evening off. You haven't got a meeting tonight, have you?"

"No," says Luke, looking up. "But I need to go through some of these forecasts again. Big meeting tomorrow, with all the investors. I need to be prepared."

"You are prepared!" I reply. "What you need is to be *relaxed*. If you work all night, you'll just be tired and tense and ratty." I go over to him, take his glass out of his hand, and start to massage his shoulders. "Come on, Luke. You really need a night off. I bet Michael would agree. Wouldn't he?"

"He's been telling me to lighten up," admits Luke after a long pause.

"Well, then, lighten up! Come on, a few hours of fun never did anybody any harm. Let's both dress up and go somewhere really nice, and dance, and drink cocktails . . ." I kiss him gently on the back of his neck. "I mean, why on earth come to New York and not enjoy it?"

There's silence—and for an awful moment I think Luke's going to say he hasn't got time. But then suddenly he turns round—and thank God, I can see the faint glimmer of a smile.

"You're right," he says. "Come on. Let's do it."

It turns into the most magical, glamorous, glossy evening of my life. I put on my Vera Wang dress and

Luke puts on his smartest suit, and we go to a fabulous restaurant all done like an Art Deco cruise ship, where beautiful people are eating lobster and there's an old-fashioned jazz band, just like in the movies. Luke orders Bellinis, and we toast each other, and as he relaxes, he tells me more about his deal. In fact, he confides in me more than he ever has before.

"This city," he says, shaking his head. "It's a demanding place. Like . . . skiing down the edge of a precipice. If you make one mistake—that's it. You fall."

"But if you don't make any mistakes?"

"You win," says Luke. "You win it all."

"You're going to win," I say confidently. "You're going to wow them all tomorrow."

"And you're going to wow them at your screen test," says Luke, as a waiter appears at our table with our first course—the most amazing sculptures made out of seafood, presented on hexagonal plates. He pours our wine, and Luke lifts his glass in a toast.

"To you, Becky. You're going to be a huge success."

"No, *you're* going to be a huge success," I reply, feeling a glow of pleasure all around me. "We're both going to be huge successes!"

Maybe it's the Bellini, going to my head—but suddenly I feel again exactly as I did in Barneys. I'm not the old Becky—I'm someone new and sparkling. Surreptitiously I glance at myself in a nearby mirror, and feel a twinge of delight. I mean, just look at me! All poised and groomed, in a New York restaurant, wearing a thousands-of-dollars dress, with my wonderful, successful boyfriend—and a screen test tomorrow for American television!

I feel completely intoxicated with happiness. This expensive, glossy world is where I've been heading all

along. Limos and flowers; waxed eyebrows and designer clothes from Barneys; a purse stuffed with business cards of TV executives. These are my people; this
is where I'm meant to be. My old life seems a million,
zillion miles away, like a tiny dot on the horizon. Mum
and Dad and Suze . . . my untidy room in Fulham . . .
EastEnders with a pizza . . . I mean, let's face it. That
was never really me, was it?

We end up staying out for hours. We dance to the
jazz band, eat passion fruit sorbet, and talk about
everything in the world but work. Luke asks the band
to play "These Foolish Things," which is a song I completely love—and then sings along as we dance (very
out of tune, but I don't say anything). When we get
back to the hotel we're both laughing, and tripping
slightly as we walk, and Luke's hand is making its way
deftly inside my dress.

"Miss Bloomwood?" says the concierge as we pass
the desk. "There's a message for you to call a Susan
Cleath-Stuart, in London. Whatever time you get in.
Apparently it's urgent."

"Oh God," I say, rolling my eyes. "She'll just be calling to lecture me about how much I spent on my new
dress. 'How much? Oh Bex, you *shouldn't* have . . .' "

"It's a fantastic dress," says Luke, running his hands
appreciatively up and down it. "Although there's far too
much of it. You could lose this bit here . . . and this
bit . . ."

"Would you like the number?" says the concierge,
holding out a piece of paper.

"No, thanks," I say, waving my hand. "I'll call her tomorrow."

"And please," adds Luke, "hold all calls to our room, until further notice."

"Very well," says the concierge with a twinkle. "Good night, sir. Good night, ma'am."

We travel up in the lift, grinning stupidly at each other in the mirrors—and as we arrive at our room, I realize that I'm really feeling quite drunk. My only consolation is, Luke looks completely plastered, too.

"That," I say, as the door closes behind us, "was the best night of my life. The very best."

"It isn't over yet," says Luke, coming toward me with a meaningful gleam in his eye. "I feel I need to reward you for your most insightful comments, Miss Bloomwood. You *were* right. All work and no play . . ." He starts to pull my Vera Wang straps gently down off my shoulders. "Makes Jack . . ." he murmurs against my skin. "A very . . ."

And suddenly we're tumbling down onto the bed together, and his mouth is on mine, and my mind is wheeling with alcohol and delight. As he's pulling off his shirt, I catch a glimpse of myself in the mirror. I stare at my intoxicated, happy self for an instant, and hear a voice inside saying: remember this moment forever. Remember this moment, Becky, because right now, life is perfect.

The rest is a haze of drunken, blurry pleasure, drifting into oblivion. The last thing I remember is Luke kissing me on the eyelids and telling me to sleep well and that he loves me. That's the last thing.

And then, like a car crash, it happens.

Are They What They Seem?

FINANCE GURU IS MONEY MESS!

NEW YORK—She sits on the *Morning Coffee* sofa, advising millions of viewers on financial issues. But *The Daily World* can exclusively reveal that hypocritical Becky Bloomwood is herself on the brink of financial disaster. Becky, whose catchphrase is "Look after your money—and it will look after you," is being pursued for debts totaling thousands, and her own bank manager has labeled her a "disgrace."

Summons

La Rosa clothes boutique has issued a summons against bankrupt Becky, while flatmate Susan Cleath-Stuart (right) admits Becky is often behind in her rent. Meanwhile feckless Becky is unashamedly jet-setting in New York with entrepreneur boyfriend Luke Brandon (below, right). "Becky quite blatantly uses Luke for his money," said one inside source at Brandon Communications. Miss Cleath-Stuart meanwhile admits she would like to see Becky gone. "I could do with more space for my work," she says. "Maybe I'll have to hire an office."

Spendaholic

Staying in the swanky Four Seasons Hotel, the wayward 26-year-old revealed she had no idea how much her accommodation cost. Our reporter watched as she splurged over £100 on greeting cards alone, then went on a further spree, buying luxury clothes and gifts totaling £1,000, in just a few hours.

Shocked

Viewers of *Morning Coffee* were outraged to discover the truth about the self-styled money expert. "I'm quite appalled," commented Irene Watson of Sevenoaks. "I phoned Becky a few weeks ago to ask advice on my banking arrangements. Now I wish I'd never listened to a word, and will certainly be taking further advice." Mother-of-two Irene added, "I'm shocked and disgusted that the producers of *Morning Coffee* **turn to page 4**

Twelve

At first, I don't realize anything is wrong. I wake up feeling extremely bleary—to see Luke handing me a cup of tea.

"Why don't you check the messages?" he says, giving me a kiss, and heads toward the shower. After a few sips of tea, I lift the telephone receiver and press the star button.

"You have twenty-three messages," says the telephone voice—and I gape at it in astonishment. Twenty-three?

Perhaps they're all job offers! is my first thought. Perhaps it's people calling from Hollywood! In great excitement I press the button to hear the first one. But it's not a job offer—it's Suze—and she's sounding really hassled.

"Bex, please ring me. As soon as you get this. It's . . . it's really urgent. Bye."

The voice asks me if I'd like to hear my remaining messages—and for a moment I hesitate. But Suze did sound pretty desperate—and I remember with a twinge of guilt that she called last night, too. I dial the number—and to my surprise, it clicks onto her answer machine.

"Hi! It's me!" I say as soon as Suze's voice has finished

speaking. "Well, you're not in, so I hope whatever it is has sorted itself—"

"Bex!" Suze's voice practically bursts my eardrum. "Oh my God, Bex, where have you been?"

"Out," I say puzzledly. "And then asleep. Suze, is everything—"

"Bex, I never said those things!" she interrupts, sounding distressed. "You have to believe me. I'd never say *anything* like that. They just . . . twisted everything round. I told your mum, I didn't have any idea—"

"My mum?" I say in puzzlement. "Suze, slow down. What are you talking about?"

There's silence.

"Oh God," says Suze. "Bex, haven't you seen it?"

"Seen what?" I say.

"*The Daily World,*" says Suze. "I . . . I thought you got all the British papers."

"We do," I say, rubbing my dry face. "But they'll still be outside the door. Is there . . . is there something about me?"

"No," says Suze a little too quickly. "No. I mean . . . there is this one very tiny thing. But it's not worth looking at. I really wouldn't bother. In fact—throw *The Daily World* away, I would. Just . . . put it in the bin, without even opening it."

"There's something nasty, isn't there?" I say apprehensively. "Do my legs look really fat?"

"It's really nothing!" says Suze. "Nothing! So anyway . . . have you been to Rockefeller Center yet? It's supposed to be great! Or FAO Schwarz? Or . . ."

"Suze, stop," I interrupt. "I'm going to go and get it. I'll call you back."

"OK, look, Bex, just remember," says Suze in a rush.

"Hardly *anyone* reads *The Daily World*. You know, like about three people. And it's tomorrow's fish-and-chips. And everyone knows the newspapers make up complete lies . . ."

"Right," I say, trying to sound relaxed. "I'll remember that. And don't worry, Suze! These stupid little things don't faze me!"

But as I put the phone down, my hand is trembling slightly. What on earth can they have said about me? I hurry to the door, grab the pile of papers, and cart them all back to the bed. I seize hold of *The Daily World* and feverishly start to leaf through it. Page after page . . . but there's nothing there. I go back to the beginning and leaf through more carefully, looking at all the tiny box items—and there really is no mention of me at all. I lean back on my pillows, bemused. What on earth is Suze going on about? Why on earth is she so—

And then I spot the center double-page spread. A single folded sheet, lying on the bed, which must have fallen out as I grabbed hold of the paper. Very slowly I reach for it. I open it. And it's as though someone's punched me in the stomach.

There's a picture of me. It's a photo I don't recognize—not very flattering. I'm walking along, in some street . . . A New York street, I realize with a lurch. And I'm holding lots of shopping bags. And there's a picture of Luke, in a circle. And a little picture of Suze. And the headline reads . . .

I can't even tell you what it says. I can't even say it. It's . . . it's too awful.

It's a huge article, spanning the whole center spread. As I read it, my heart is thudding; my head feels hot and cold. It's so nasty. It's so . . . personal. Halfway through I can't stand it anymore. I close the paper, and stare ahead, breathing hard, feeling as though I might throw up.

Then almost immediately, with trembling hands, I open it again. I have to see exactly what they've said. I have to read every horrible, humiliating line.

When I've finally finished, I sit, breathing hard, trying to keep control. I can't quite believe this is really happening. This paper has already been printed millions of times. It's too late to stop it. In Britain, I suddenly realize, this has been out for hours. My parents will have seen it. Everyone I know will have seen it. I'm powerless.

As I'm sitting there, the telephone gives a shrill ring, and I jump with fright. After a moment it rings again, and I stare at it in terror. I can't answer. I can't talk to anybody, not even Suze.

The phone rings for the fourth time, and Luke strides out of the bathroom, a towel round his waist and his hair slicked back.

"Aren't you going to get that?" he says shortly, and grabs for the receiver. "Hello? Yes, Luke Brandon here."

I feel a swoop of fear, and wrap the duvet more tightly around me.

"Right," Luke is saying. "Fine. I'll see you then." He puts the phone down and scribbles something on a pad of paper.

"Who was that?" I say, trying to keep my voice steady.

"A secretary from JD Slade," he says, putting his pen down. "Change of venue."

He starts to get dressed, and I say nothing. My hand tightens around the *Daily World* page. I want to show him . . . but I don't want to show him. I don't want him to read those horrible things about me. But I can't let him see it from someone else.

I can't sit here forever, saying nothing. I close my eyes—then take a deep breath and say, "Luke, there's a thing about me in the paper."

"Good," says Luke absently, doing up his tie. "I thought you might get a bit of publicity. Which paper?"

"It's . . . it's not good," I say, and lick my dry lips. "It's really awful."

Luke looks at me properly and sees my expression.

"Oh, Becky," he says, "it can't be that bad. Come on, show me. What does it say?" He holds out his hand, but I don't move.

"It's just . . . really horrible. And there's a great big picture—"

"Did you have a bad hair day?" says Luke teasingly, and reaches for his jacket. "Becky, no piece of publicity is ever 100 percent perfect. You're always going to find *something* to fret about, whether it's your hair, or something you said . . ."

"Luke!" I say despairingly. "It's nothing like that. Just . . . have a look."

Slowly I unfold the paper and give it to Luke. He takes it cheerfully—but as he gazes at it, his smile slowly disappears.

"What the fuck— Is that *me*?" He glances at me briefly, and I swallow, not daring to say anything. Then he scans the page while I watch nervously.

"Is this true?" he says at last. "Any of it?"

"N-no!" I stammer. "At least . . . not . . . not all of it. Some of it is . . ."

"Are you in debt?"

I meet his gaze, feeling my face turn crimson.

"A . . . a little bit. But I mean, not like they say . . . I mean, I don't know anything about a summons . . ."

"Tuesday afternoon!" He hits the paper. "For Christ's

sake. You were at the Guggenheim. Find your ticket, we'll prove you were there, get a retraction—"

"I . . . Actually . . . Luke . . ." He looks up and I feel a lurch of pure fear. "I didn't go to the Guggenheim. I . . . I went . . . shopping."

"You went . . ." He stares at me—then silently starts to read again.

When he's finished he stares ahead expressionlessly.

"I don't believe this," he says, so quietly I can barely hear him.

He looks as grim as I feel—and for the first time this morning I feel tears pricking at my eyes.

"I know," I say shakily. "It's awful. They must have been following me. They must have been there all along, watching me, *spying* on me . . ." I look at him for a response, but he's just staring straight ahead. "Luke, don't you have anything to say? Do you realize—"

"Becky, do *you* realize?" he interrupts. He turns toward me—and at his expression I feel the blood draining from my face. "Do you realize quite how bad this is for *me*?"

"I'm really sorry," I gulp. "I know you hate being in the paper . . ."

"It's not a bloody question of—" He stops himself, and says more calmly, "Becky, do you realize how this is going to make me look? Today of all fucking days?"

"I . . . I didn't . . ." I whisper.

"I have to go into a meeting in an hour's time and convince a stuffy, conservative New York investment bank that I'm fully in control of every aspect of my business and personal life. They'll all have seen this. I'll be a joke!"

"But of course you're in control!" I say in alarm. "Luke, surely they'll realize . . . surely they won't—"

"Listen," says Luke, turning round. "Do you know what the perception of me is in this city? The general perception here—for some inexplicable reason—is that I'm losing my touch."

"Losing your touch?" I echo in horror.

"That's what I've heard." Luke takes a deep, controlled breath. "What I've been doing over the last few days is working my fucking *arse* off to convince these people that their perception is wrong. That I'm on top of it. That I have the media taped. And now . . ." He hits the paper sharply and I wince.

"Maybe . . . maybe they won't have seen it."

"Becky, they see everything," says Luke. "That's their job. That's—"

He breaks off as the phone rings. After a pause, he picks it up.

"Hi, Michael. Ah. You've seen it. Yes, I know. Unfortunate timing. All right. See you in a sec." He puts down the phone and reaches for his briefcase, without looking at me.

I feel cold and shivery. What have I done? I've wrecked everything. Phrases from the article keep popping into my mind, making me feel sick. *Feckless Becky . . . hypocritical Becky . . .* And they're right. They're all right.

When I look up, Luke's closing his briefcase with a snap.

"I have to go," he says. "I'll see you later." At the door he hesitates, and turns round, looking suddenly confused. "But I don't understand. If you weren't at the Guggenheim—where did you get the book you gave me?"

"At the museum shop," I whisper. "On Broadway."

"But the sparkle stuff on your face. You said it was—"

"I . . . I had a makeover. Luke, I'm so sorry . . . I . . ."

I tail away into a hideous silence. I can feel my heart thumping, the blood pulsing in my ears. I don't know what to say, how to redeem myself.

Luke stares at me blankly, then gives a brief nod, turns, and reaches for the door handle.

When the door has closed behind him, I sit quite still for a while, staring straight ahead. I can't quite believe all this is really happening. Just a few hours ago we were toasting each other with Bellinis. I was wearing my Vera Wang dress and we were dancing to Cole Porter and I was giddy with happiness. And now . . .

The phone starts to ring, but I don't move. Only on the eighth ring do I stir myself and pick it up.

"Hello?"

"Hello!" says a bright voice. "Is that Becky Bloomwood?"

"Yes," I say cautiously.

"Becky, it's Fiona Taggart from the *Daily Herald*. I'm so glad I've tracked you down! Becky, we'd be really interested in running a two-part feature on you and your . . . little problem, shall we call it?"

"I don't want to talk about it," I mutter.

"Do you deny it, then?"

"No comment," I say, and thrust the phone down with a trembling hand. Immediately it rings again, and I pick it up.

"No comment, all right?" I exclaim. "No comment! No—"

"Becky? Darling?"

"Mum!" At the sound of her voice I feel myself dissolving into tears. "Oh, Mum, I'm so sorry," I gulp. "It's so awful. I've messed everything up. I just didn't know . . . I didn't realize . . ."

"Becky!" comes her voice down the line, familiar and reassuring. "Love! You don't have to be sorry! It's those scumbag reporters who should be sorry. Making up all those stories. Putting words in people's mouths. Poor Suzie phoned us up, very upset. You know, she gave that girl three bourbon biscuits and a KitKat, and this is the thanks she gets. A load of outlandish lies! I mean, pretending to be from the council tax. They should be prosecuted!"

"Mum . . ." I close my eyes, almost unable to say it. "It's not all lies. They . . . they didn't make everything up." There's a short silence, and I can hear Mum breathing anxiously down the line. "I am kind of in a . . . a bit of debt."

"Well," says Mum after a pause—and I can hear her gearing herself up to be positive. "Well. So what? Even if you are, is it any of their business?" She pauses, and I hear a voice in the background. "Exactly! Dad says, 'if the American economy can be in debt by billions and still survive, then so can you.' "

God, I love my parents. If I told them I'd committed murder they'd soon find some reason why the victim had it coming to him.

"I suppose so," I gulp. "But it's Luke's big meeting today, and all his investors will have seen it . . ."

"So what? There's no such thing as bad publicity. Now you keep your chin up, Becky! Best foot forward. Suzie told us you've got a screen test today. Is that right?"

"Yes. I just don't know what time. The producer's supposed to call me."

"Well, then. You put a nice brave face on. Run

yourself a bath and have a nice cup of tea and put three sugars in it. And a brandy, Dad says. And if any reporters ring up, just tell them to get lost."

"Have you had any reporters bothering you?" I say in alarm.

"A chap came round asking questions this morning," says Mum breezily. "But Dad went for him with the hedge trimmer."

In spite of myself I giggle.

"I'd better go, Mum. But I'll call you later. And . . . thanks."

As I put down the phone, I feel a million times better. Mum's right. I've just got to be positive and go to my screen test and do as well as I possibly can. And Luke probably did overreact a little bit. He'll probably come back in a much better mood.

I ring up the hotel reception and tell them to hold all calls except from HLBC. Then I run my bath, empty a whole bottle of Uplift bath oil from Sephora into it, and wallow for half an hour in rose geranium. As I dry myself I put on MTV and dance around the room to Janet Jackson—and by the time I'm dressed in my knock-'em-dead outfit from Barneys I'm feeling pretty positive, if a little wobbly around the knees. I can do this. I *can*.

They haven't called yet, so I pick up the phone and ring down to reception.

"Hi," I say. "Just checking if HLBC have called for me this morning."

"I don't believe so," says the girl pleasantly.

"Are you sure? They didn't leave a message?"

"No, ma'am."

"OK. Thanks."

I put the phone down and think for a few moments.

Well—that's all right, I'll just call them. I mean, I need to know what time the test is, don't I? And Kent told me to call her anytime, whatever I needed. She said, don't even hesitate.

I take her business card out of my bag and carefully punch in the number.

"Hello!" says a bright voice. "Kent Garland's office, this is her assistant, Megan. How can I help you?"

"Hello!" I say. "It's Rebecca Bloomwood here. Could I speak to Kent, please?"

"Kent's in a meeting right now," says Megan pleasantly. "Could I take a message?"

"Well, I'm just phoning to see what time my screen test is today," I say. And just saying it gives me a surge of confidence. Who cares about the crappy *Daily World*, anyway? I'm going to be on American television. I'm going to be a huge celebrity.

"I see," says Megan. "Rebecca, if you could just hold on a moment . . ."

She puts me on hold, and I find myself listening to a tinny version of "Heard It through the Grapevine." It comes to an end, and a voice tells me how important my call is to the HLBC Corporation . . . and then it starts again . . . when suddenly Megan is back.

"Hi, Rebecca? I'm afraid Kent's going to have to postpone the screen test. She'll give you a call if she wants to rearrange."

"What?" I say, staring blankly at my made-up face in the mirror. "Postpone? But . . . why? Do you know when it'll be rescheduled?"

"I'm not sure," says Megan pleasantly. "Kent's very busy right now with the new series of *Consumer Today*."

"But . . . but that's what the screen test is for! The

new series of *Consumer Today*!" I take a deep breath, try-ing not to sound too anxious. "Do you know when she'll rearrange it for?"

"I really couldn't say. Her diary's very full at the mo-ment . . . and then she has a two-week vacation . . ."

"Listen," I say, trying to stay calm. "I'd really like to talk to Kent, please. It's quite important. Couldn't you get her for me? Just for a second."

There's a pause—then Megan sighs.

"I'll see if I can fetch her."

The tinny song begins again—then suddenly Kent is on the line.

"Hi, Becky. How are you?"

"Hi!" I say, trying to sound relaxed. "I'm fine. I just thought I'd see what was happening today. About the screen test?"

"Right," says Kent thoughtfully. "Tell the truth, Becky, a couple of issues have come up, which we need to think about. OK? So we'll be passing on the screen test until we're a little more decided about things."

Suddenly I feel paralyzed by fear. Oh, please, no.

She's seen *The Daily World*, hasn't she? That's what she's talking about. I clutch the receiver tightly, my heart thudding, desperately wanting to explain it all; wanting to tell her that it all sounds far worse than it really is. That half of it isn't even true; that it doesn't mean I'm not good at what I do . . .

But I just can't bring myself to. I can't bring myself even to mention it.

"So we'll be in touch," Kent says. "Apologies for put-ting you out today—I was going to have Megan call you later . . ."

"That's all right!" I say, trying to sound bright and easy. "So . . . when do you think we might reschedule?"

"I'm really not sure . . . Sorry, Becky. I'm going to have to run. There's a problem on the set. But thanks for calling. And enjoy the rest of your trip!"

The phone goes silent and I slowly put it down.

I'm not having my screen test. They don't want me, after all.

And I bought a new outfit and everything.

I can feel my breath coming quicker and quicker— and for an awful moment I think I might cry.

But then I think of Mum—and force myself to lift my chin. I'm not going to let myself collapse. I'm going to be strong and positive. HLBC aren't the only fish in the sea. There are plenty of other people who want to snap me up. Plenty! I mean, look at . . . look at Greg Walters. He said he wanted me to meet his head of development, didn't he? Well, maybe we can fix something up for today. Yes! Perhaps by the end of today, I'll have my own show!

Quickly I find the number and dial it with trembling hands—and to my joy, I get straight through. This is more like it. Straight to the top.

"Hi, Greg? It's Becky Bloomwood here."

"Becky! Great to hear from you!" says Greg, sounding a little distracted. "How're you doing?"

"Erm . . . fine! It was really nice to meet you yesterday," I say, aware that my voice is shrill with nerves. "And I was very interested in all your ideas."

"Well, that's great! So—are you enjoying your trip?"

"Yes! Yes, I am." I take a deep breath. "Greg, you were saying yesterday that I should meet up with your head of development—"

"Absolutely!" says Greg. "I know Dave would adore to meet you. We both think you have huge potential. Huge."

Relief floods over me. Thank God. Thank—

"So next time you're in town," Greg is saying, "you give me a call, and we'll set something up."

I stare at the phone, prickly with shock. Next time I'm in town? But that could be months. It could be never. Doesn't he want to—

"Promise you'll do that?"

"Erm . . . OK," I say, trying to keep the thickening dismay out of my voice. "That would be great!"

"And maybe we'll meet up when I next come over to London."

"OK!" I say brightly. "I hope so. Well . . . see you soon. And good to meet you!"

"Great to meet you too, Becky!"

I'm still smiling my bright fake smile as the phone goes dead. And this time I just can't stop the tears from gathering in my eyes and dripping slowly down my face, taking my makeup with them.

I sit alone in the hotel room for hours. Lunchtime comes and goes, but I can't face any food. The only positive thing I do is listen to the messages on the phone and delete them all except one from Mum, which I listen to over and over again. It's the one she must have left as soon as she got *The Daily World.*

"Now," she's saying. "There's a bit of fuss here over a silly article in the paper. Don't take any notice of it, Becky. Just remember, that picture will be going in a million dog baskets tomorrow."

For some reason that makes me laugh each time I hear it. So I sit there, half-crying, half-laughing, letting a pool of wet tears gather on my skirt and not even bothering to wipe it away.

I want to go home. For what seems like an eternity I sit on the floor, rocking backward and forward, letting my thoughts circle round and round. Going over the same ground over and over again. How could I have been so stupid? What am I going to do now? How can I face anyone, ever again?

I feel as though I've been on a crazy roller coaster ever since I got to New York. Like some sort of magical Disney ride—except instead of whizzing through space, I've been whizzing through shops and hotels and interviews and lunches, surrounded by light and glitter and voices telling me I'm the next big thing.

And I believed every moment of it. I had no idea it wasn't real.

When, at long last, I hear the door opening, I feel almost sick with relief. I have a desperate urge to go and throw myself into Luke's arms, burst into tears, and listen to him tell me it's all right. But as he comes in, I feel my whole body contract in fear. His expression is taut and set; he looks as though his face is carved out of stone.

"Hi," I say at last. "I . . . I wondered where you were."

"I had lunch with Michael," says Luke shortly. "After the meeting." He takes off his coat and puts it carefully onto a hanger while I watch fearfully.

"So . . ." I hardly dare ask the question. "Did it go well?"

"Not particularly well, no."

My stomach gives a nervous flip. What does that mean? Surely . . . surely it can't be . . .

"Is it . . . off?" I manage at last.

"Good question," says Luke. "The people from JD Slade say they need more time."

"Why do they need time?" I say, licking my dry lips.

"They have a few reservations," says Luke evenly. "They didn't specify exactly what those reservations were."

He pulls off his tie roughly and starts to unbutton his shirt. He's not even looking at me. It's as though he can't bring himself to see my face.

"Do you . . ." I swallow. "Do you think they'd seen the piece?"

"Oh, I think so," says Luke. There's an edge to his voice which makes me flinch. "Yes, I'm pretty sure they'd seen it."

He's fumbling over the last shirt button. Suddenly, in irritation, he rips it off.

"Luke," I say helplessly. "I'm . . . I'm so sorry. I . . . I don't know what I can do." I take a deep breath. "I'll do anything I can."

"There's nothing," says Luke flatly.

He heads into the bathroom and after a few moments I hear the sound of the shower. I don't move. I can't even think. I feel paralyzed, as though I'm crouching on a ledge, trying not to slip.

Eventually Luke comes out and, without even acknowledging me, pulls on a pair of black jeans and a black turtleneck. He pours himself a drink and there's silence. Outside the window I can see right across Manhattan. The air is turning dusky and lights are coming on in windows everywhere, right into the distance. But I feel as though the world has shrunk to this room, these four walls. I haven't been out all day, I abruptly realize.

"I didn't have my screen test, either," I say at last.

"Really." Luke's voice is flat and uninterested, and in spite of myself, I feel a faint spark of resentment.

"Don't you even want to know why?" I say, tugging at the fringe of a cushion.

There's a pause—then Luke says, as though with tremendous effort, "Why?"

"Because no one's interested in me anymore." I push my hair back off my head. "You're not the only one who's had a bad day, Luke. I've wrecked all my chances. No one wants to know me anymore."

Humiliation creeps over me as I remember all the telephone messages I had to listen to this morning, politely canceling meetings and calling off lunches.

"And I know it's all my own fault," I continue. "I *know* that. But even so . . ." My voice starts to wobble treacherously, and I take a deep breath. "Things really aren't great for me either." I look up—but Luke hasn't moved an inch. "You could . . . you could show a little sympathy."

"Show a little sympathy," echoes Luke evenly.

"I know I brought it on myself . . ."

"That's right! You did!" Luke's voice explodes in pent-up frustration, and at last he turns to face me. "Becky, no one forced you to go and spend that money! I mean, I know you like shopping. But for Christ's sake. To spend like this . . . It's bloody irresponsible. Couldn't you have stopped yourself?"

"I don't know!" I retort shakily. "Probably. But I didn't know it was going to become such a . . . a bloody life-and-death issue, did I? I didn't *know* I was being followed, Luke. I didn't do this on purpose." To my horror, I feel a tear making its way down my cheek. "You know, I didn't hurt anybody. I didn't kill anybody. Maybe I was a bit naive . . ."

"A bit naive. That's the understatement of the year."

"OK, so I was naive! But I didn't commit any crime—"

"You don't think throwing away opportunity is a

crime?" says Luke furiously. "Because as far as I'm concerned . . ." He shakes his head. "Jesus, Becky! We both
had it all. We *had* New York." His hand clenches into a
fist. "And now, look at us both. All because you're so
bloody *obsessed* by shopping—"

"Obsessed?" I cry. Suddenly I can't stand his accusing
gaze anymore. "*I'm* obsessed? What about you?"

"What do you mean?" he says dismissively.

"You're obsessed by work! By making it in New York!
The first thing you thought of when you saw that piece
wasn't me or . . . or how I was feeling, was it? It was
how it affected you and your deal." My voice rises
tremulously. "All you care about is your own success,
and I always come second. I mean, you didn't even
bother to *tell* me about New York until it was all decided! You just expected me to . . . to fall in line and do
exactly what you wanted. No wonder Alicia said I was
tagging along!"

"You're not tagging along," he says impatiently.

"Yes, I am! That's the way you see me, isn't it? As
some little nobody, who has to be . . . to be slotted into
your grand magnificent plan. And I was so stupid, I just
went along with it . . ."

"I haven't got time for this," says Luke, standing up.

"You've never got time!" I say tearfully. "Suze has got
more time for me than you have! You didn't have time
to come to Tom's wedding; our holiday turned into a
meeting; you didn't have time to visit my parents . . ."

"So I don't have a lot of time!" yells Luke suddenly,
shocking me into silence. "So I can't sit around making
mindless tittle-tattle with you and Suze." He shakes his
head in frustration. "Do you realize how fucking *hard* I
work? Do you have any idea how important this deal is?"

"*Why* is it important?" I hear myself shrieking. "Why

is it so bloody important to make it in America? So you can impress your complete cow of a mother? Because if you're trying to impress her, Luke, then I'd give up now! She'll never be impressed. Never! I mean, she hasn't even bothered to *see* you! God, you buy her an Hermès scarf—and she can't even rearrange her schedule to find five minutes for you!"

I break off, panting, into complete silence.

Oh fuck. I shouldn't have said that.

I dart a look at Luke, and he's staring at me, his face ashen with anger.

"What did you call my mother?" he says slowly.

"Look, I . . . I didn't mean it." I swallow, trying to keep control of my voice. "I just think . . . there's got to be a sense of proportion in all this. All I did was a bit of shopping . . ."

"A bit of shopping," echoes Luke scathingly. "A *bit* of shopping." He gives me a long look—then, to my horror, heads to the huge cedarwood wardrobe where I've been stashing all my stuff. He opens it silently and we both stare at the bags crammed to the ceiling.

And as I see it all, I feel a slight nausea overcoming me. All those things which seemed so vital when I bought them, all those things which I got so excited about . . . now just look like a great big pile of rubbish bags. I could barely even tell you what's in any of the packages. It's just . . . stuff. Piles and piles of stuff.

Without saying anything, Luke closes the door again, and I feel shame drenching over me like hot water.

"I know," I say, in a voice barely above a whisper. "I know. But I'm paying for it. I really am."

I turn away, unable to meet his eye, and suddenly I just have to get out of this room. I have to get away from Luke, from myself in the mirror, from the whole horrendous day.

"I'll . . . I'll see you later," I mutter and without looking back, head for the door.

The bar downstairs is dimly lit, soothing, and anonymous. I sink into a sumptuous leather chair, feeling weak and achy, as though I've got the flu. When a waiter comes up, I order an orange juice, then, as he's walking away, change my order to a brandy. It arrives in a huge glass, warm and reviving, and I take a few sips—then look up as a shadow appears on the table in front of me. It's Michael Ellis. I feel my heart sink. I really don't feel up to talking.

"Hello," he says. "May I?" He gestures to the chair opposite and I nod weakly. He sits down and gives me a kind look as I drain my glass. For a while, we're both silent.

"I could be polite, and not mention it," he says at last. "Or I could tell you the truth—which is that I was very sorry for you this morning. Your British papers are vicious. No one deserves that kind of treatment."

"Thank you," I mumble.

A waiter appears, and Michael orders two more brandies without even asking.

"All I can tell you is, people aren't dumb," he says as the waiter walks off. "No one's going to hold it against you."

"They already have," I say, staring at the table. "My screen test for HLBC was called off."

"Ah," says Michael after a pause. "I'm sorry to hear that."

"No one wants to know me anymore. They're all saying they've 'decided to go another way' or they 'feel I don't really suit the American market' and . . . you know. Basically just, 'Go away.' "

As I talk, I can feel my eyes filling up with hot tears. I so wanted to tell all this to Luke. I wanted to pour out all my woes—and for him to give me a huge, uncritical hug. Tell me it was their loss, not mine, like my parents would, or Suze would. But instead, he made me feel even worse about myself. He's right—I've thrown everything away, haven't I? I had opportunities people would kill for, and I wasted them.

Michael is nodding gravely.

"That happens," he says. "I'm afraid these idiots are like a pack of sheep. One gets spooked, they all get spooked."

"I just feel like I've wrecked everything," I say, feeling my throat tightening. "I was going to get this amazing job, and Luke was going to be this huge success. It was all going to be perfect. And I've just chucked it all in the bin. It's all my fault."

To my horror, tears are spilling out of my eyes. I can't stop them. And suddenly I give a huge sob. Oh, this is so embarrassing.

"I'm sorry," I whisper. "I'm just a complete disaster."

I bury my hot face in my hands and hope that Michael Ellis will tactfully slip away and leave me alone. Instead, I feel a hand on mine, and a handkerchief being slipped into my fingers. I wipe my face gratefully with the cool cotton and eventually raise my head.

"Thanks," I gulp. "Sorry about that."

"That's quite all right," says Michael calmly. "I'd be the same."

"Yeah, right," I mutter.

"You should see me when I lose a contract. I bawl my

eyes out. My secretary has to run out for Kleenex every half hour." He sounds so completely deadpan, I can't help giving a little smile. "Now, drink your brandy," he says, "and let's get a few things straight. Did you invite *The Daily World* to take pictures of you with a long-range lens?"

"No."

"Did you call them, offering an exclusive on your personal habits and suggesting a choice of offensive headlines?"

"No." I can't help giving a half-giggle.

"So." He gives me a quizzical look. "This would be all your fault because . . ."

"I was naive. I should have realized. I should have . . . seen it coming. I was stupid."

"You were unlucky." He shrugs. "Maybe a little foolish. But you can't heap all the blame on yourself."

An electronic burble sounds from his pocket, and he reaches for his mobile.

"Excuse me a moment," he says, and turns away. "Hi there."

As he talks quietly into the phone I fold a paper coaster over and over. I want to ask him something—but I'm not sure I want to hear the answer.

"Sorry about that," says Michael. As he puts his phone away he gives me a rueful smile and shakes his head. "Never do business with friends."

"Really? Was that a friend?"

Michael nods. "An old friend of the family. I did a campaign for him on credit as a favor. He promised when business picked up, he'd write a check. Well, as far as I'm concerned, business has picked up."

"And he hasn't paid you?" I take a sip of my drink, grateful to have something to distract me.

"He's bought himself a nice new Mercedes."

"That's terrible!" I exclaim.

"That's what friends are for. To exploit the shit out of you. I should have learned that by now." He rolls his eyes humorously, but I'm still frowning.

"Do you know his family?"

"Sure. We used to spend Thanksgiving together."

"Right." I think for a moment. "So—have you mentioned this to his wife?"

"His wife?" Michael looks surprised, and I raise my eyebrows knowingly at him.

"I bet you if you told his wife, you'd get the money back."

Michael stares at me for a second—then bursts into laughter.

"You know, I think you have something there. I'll try it!" He drains his glass, then glances down at the mangled coaster in my fingers. "So. Are you feeling better?"

"Yes. Thanks. But there's something I wanted to—" I take a deep breath. "Michael, was it my fault that Luke's deal fell through? I mean, did the *Daily World* thing come into it?"

He gives me a sharp look. "We're being frank here, right?"

"Yes," I say, feeling a shaft of apprehension. "We're being frank."

"Then, to be honest, I can't say it helped proceedings," says Michael. "There were various . . . remarks made this morning. Some oh-so-funny jokes. I have to hand it to Luke, he took it all pretty well."

I stare at him, feeling cold.

"Luke didn't tell me that."

Michael shrugs. "I wouldn't have thought he particularly wanted to repeat any of the comments."

"So it *was* my fault."

"Uh-uh." Michael shakes his head. "That's not what I said." He leans back in his chair. "Becky, if this deal had been really strong, it would have survived a bit of adverse publicity. My guess is JD Slade used your little . . . embarrassment as an excuse. There's some bigger reason, which they're keeping to themselves . . ."

"What?"

"Who knows? The rumor about Bank of London? A difference in business ethos? For some reason, they seem to have suffered a general loss of confidence in the whole idea."

I stare at him, remembering what Luke said.

"Do people really think Luke's losing his touch?"

"Luke is a very talented individual," says Michael carefully. "But something's gotten into him over this deal. He's almost *too* driven. I told him this morning, he needs to prioritize. There's obviously a situation with Bank of London. He should be talking to them. Reassuring them. Frankly, if he loses them, he's in big trouble. And it's not just them. Some problem or other seems to have cropped up with Provident Assurance— another huge client." He leans forward. "If you ask me, he should be on a plane back to London this afternoon."

"And what does he want to do?"

"He's already setting up meetings with every New York investment bank I've ever heard of." He shakes his head. "That boy seems fixated by making it in America."

"I think he wants to prove something," I mutter. *To his mother,* I nearly add.

"So Becky . . ." Michael gives me a kind look. "What are you going to do? Try to set up some more meetings?"

"No," I say after a pause. "To be honest, I don't think there's any point."

"So will you stay out here with Luke?"

An image of Luke's frozen face flashes through my mind, and I feel a stab of pain.

"I don't think there's much point doing that, either." I take a deep swig of wine and try to smile. "You know what? I think I'm just going to go home."

Thirteen

I GET OUT OF THE TAXI, hoist my suitcase onto the pavement, and look miserably up at the gray English sky. It's really all over.

Until the very last minute, I had a secret, desperate hope that someone might change their mind and offer me a job. Or that Luke might beg me to stay. Every time the phone rang I felt jittery, hoping that somehow a miracle was about to happen. But nothing happened. Of course it didn't.

When I said good-bye to Luke it was as though I were acting a part. I wanted to throw myself on him in tears, slap his face, *something*. But I just couldn't. I had to salvage some kind of dignity, somewhere. So it was almost businesslike, the way I phoned the airline, packed up my stuff, and ordered a cab. I couldn't bring myself to kiss him on the mouth when I left, so I gave him two brisk pecks on each cheek and then turned away before either of us could say anything.

Now, twelve hours later, I feel completely exhausted. I sat awake all through the overnight flight, stiff with misery and disappointment. Only a few days ago I was flying out, thinking I was about to start a fantastic new life in

America, and instead, I'm back here with less than I even started with. And everyone, but *everyone,* knows it. A couple of girls at the airport obviously recognized me, and started whispering and giggling as I was waiting for my bags.

And oh God, I know I'd have been just the same if I'd been them. But right then, I felt so raw with humiliation, I nearly burst into tears.

I lug my bags dejectedly up the steps and let myself into the flat. And for a few moments I just stand there, looking around at the coats and old letters and keys in the bowl. Same old hall. Same old life. Back to square one. I catch sight of my haggard reflection in the mirror and quickly look away.

"Hi!" I call. "Anyone in? I'm back."

There's a pause—then Suze appears at her door in a dressing gown. "Bex?" she exclaims. "I didn't expect you back so early! Are you all right?" She comes nearer, pulling her dressing gown around her, and peers worriedly at my face. "Oh, Bex." She bites her lip. "I don't know what to say."

"It's fine," I say. "I'm fine. Honestly."

"Bex—"

"Really. I'm fine." I turn away before the sight of Suze's anxious face reduces me to tears, and scrabble in my bag. "So anyway . . . I got you that Clinique stuff you asked for . . . and the special face stuff for your mum . . ." I hand the bottles to her and begin to root roughly around again. "There's some more stuff for you in here somewhere . . ."

"Bex—don't worry about it. Just come and sit down, or something." Suze clutches the Clinique bottles to her and peers at me uncertainly. "Would you like a drink or something?"

"No!" I make myself smile. "I'm all right, Suze! I've decided the best thing is just to get on, and not think about what's happened. In fact—I'd rather we didn't talk about it at all."

"Really?" says Suze. "Well . . . OK. If you're sure that's what you want."

"That's what I want." I take a deep breath. "Really. I'm fine. So, how are *you*?"

"I'm OK," says Suze, and gives me another anxious look. "Bex, you look really pale. Have you eaten anything?"

"Airplane food. You know." I take off my coat with trembling fingers and hang it on a peg.

"Was the . . . the flight OK?" says Suze.

"It was great!" I say with a forced brightness. "They were showing the new Billy Crystal film."

"Billy Crystal!" says Suze. She gives me a hesitant glance, as though I'm some psychotic patient who has to be handled carefully. "Was it a . . . a good film? I love Billy Crystal."

"Yes, it was. It was a good film. I was really enjoying it, actually." I swallow hard. "Until my earphones stopped working in the middle."

"Oh dear!" says Suze.

"It was a really crucial bit. Everyone else on the plane was laughing away—and I couldn't hear anything." My voice starts to wobble treacherously. "So I . . . I asked this stewardess if I could have some new earphones. But she didn't understand what I meant, and she got really ratty with me because she was trying to serve drinks . . . And then I didn't want to ask her again. So I don't quite know how the film finished. But apart from that, it was really good . . ." Suddenly I give a huge sob.

"And you know, I can always rent it on video or some-thing . . ."

"Bex!" Suze's face crumples in dismay and she drops the Clinique bottles on the floor. "Oh God, Bex. Come here." She envelops me in a hug, and I bury my head in her shoulder.

"Oh, it's all awful," I weep. "It was just so humiliat-ing, Suze. Luke was so cross . . . and they canceled my screen test . . . and suddenly it was like . . . like I had some infectious disease or something. And now no-body wants to know me, and I'm not going to move to New York after all . . ."

I look up, wiping my eyes—and Suze's face is all pink and distressed.

"Bex, I feel so bad," she exclaims.

"*You* feel bad? Why should you feel bad?"

"It's all my fault. I was such a moron! I let that girl from the paper in here, and she probably poked about when I was making her cup of stupid coffee. I mean, why did I have to offer her coffee? It's all my stupid fault."

"Of course it's not!"

"Will you ever forgive me?"

"Will I ever forgive *you*?" I stare at her, my face quiver-ing. "Suze . . . I should be asking you to forgive *me*! You tried to keep tabs on me. You tried to warn me, but I didn't even bother to call you back . . . I was just so . . . stupid, so *thoughtless* . . ."

"No, you weren't!"

"I was." I give another huge sob. "I just don't know what happened to me in New York. I went mad. Just . . . the shops . . . all these meetings . . . I was going to be this huge star and earn loads of money . . . And then it all just disappeared."

"Oh, Bex!" Suze is practically crying herself. "I feel so terrible!"

"It's not your fault!" I reach for a tissue and blow my nose. "If it's anyone's fault, it's *The Daily World*'s."

"I *hate* them!" says Suze savagely. "They should be strung up and flogged. That's what Tarkie said."

"Oh right," I say after a pause. "So . . . he . . . he saw it, did he?"

"To be honest, Bex—I think most people saw it," says Suze reluctantly.

I feel a painful lurch as I think about Janice and Martin reading it. About Tom and Lucy reading it. All my old school friends and teachers reading it. All the people I've ever known, reading my most humiliating secrets.

"Look, come on," says Suze. "Leave all your stuff. Let's have a nice cup of tea."

"OK," I say after a pause. "That would be really nice." I follow her into the kitchen and sit down, leaning against the warm radiator for comfort.

"So—how are things going with Luke now?" says Suze cautiously as she puts on the kettle.

"Not great." I fold my arms tightly round myself. "In fact . . . it's not going at all."

"Really?" Suze gazes at me in dismay. "God, Bex, what happened?"

"Well, we had this big row . . ."

"About the article?"

"Kind of." I reach for a tissue and blow my nose. "He said it messed up his deal, and I was obsessed by shopping. And I said he was obsessed with work . . . and I . . . I said his mother was a . . . a complete cow . . ."

"You called his mother a *cow*?" Suze looks so taken aback, I give a shaky giggle.

"Well, she is! She's awful. And she doesn't even love

Luke. But he can't see it . . . all he wants is to land the biggest deal in the world and impress her. He can't think about anything else but that."

"So what happened then?" says Suze, handing me a mug of tea.

I bite my lip, remembering that last painful conversation we had, while I was waiting for my taxi to take me to the airport. The polite stilted voices, the way we didn't look each other in the eye.

"Before I left, I said I didn't think he had time for a proper relationship at the moment."

"Really?" Suze's eyes widen. "You called it off?"

"I didn't mean to." My voice is barely above a whisper. "I wanted him to say he *did* have time. But he didn't say anything. It was . . . awful."

"Oh, Bex." Suze stares at me over her mug. "Oh, Bex."

"Still, never mind," I say, trying to sound upbeat. "It's probably all for the best." I take a sip of tea and close my eyes. "Oh God, that's good. That's so good." For a while I'm silent, letting the steam warm my face, feeling myself relax. I take a few more sips, then open my eyes. "They just cannot make tea in America. I went to one place, and they gave me this . . . cup full of hot water, and a tea bag in a packet. And the cup was *see-through*."

"Ooh." Suze pulls a face. "Yuck." She reaches for the tin of biscuits and takes out a couple of Hobnobs. "Who needs America, anyway?" she says robustly. "I mean, everyone knows American TV is rubbish. You're better off here."

"Maybe I am." I stare into my mug for a while, then take a deep breath and look up. "You know, I thought a lot on the plane. I decided I'm going to make this a real turning point in my life. I'm going to concentrate on my career, and finish my book, and be really focused—and just . . ."

"Show them," finishes Suze.

"Exactly. Just show them."

It's amazing what a bit of home comfort does for the spirit. Half an hour and three cups of tea later, I'm feeling a million times better. I'm even quite enjoying telling Suze about New York, and all the things I did. When I tell her about going to the spa, and where exactly they wanted to put a crystal tattoo, she starts laughing so hard she almost chokes.

"Hey," I say, a sudden thought striking me. "Have you finished the KitKats?"

"No, I haven't," says Suze, wiping her eyes. "They seem to go more slowly when you're not around. So, what did Luke's mum say? Did she want to see the results?" And she starts gurgling with laughter again.

"Hang on, I'll just get a couple," I say, and start to head toward Suze's room, where they're kept.

"Actually—" says Suze, and her laughter abruptly stops. "No, don't go in there."

"Why?" I say, stopping in surprise. "What's in your . . ." I tail off as Suze's cheeks slowly turn pink. "Suze!" I say, backing quietly away from the door. "No. Is there someone in there?"

I stare at her, and she pulls her dressing gown around her defensively, without saying anything.

"I don't believe it!" My voice squeaks incredulously. "I go away for five minutes and you start having a torrid affair!"

This is cheering me up more than anything else. There's nothing like hearing a juicy piece of gossip to raise your spirits.

"It's not a torrid affair!" says Suze at last. "It's not an affair at all."

"So, who is it? Do I know him?"

Suze gives me an agonized look.

"OK, just . . . I just have to explain. Before you . . . you jump to the wrong conclusion, or . . ." She closes her eyes. "God, this is hard."

"Suze, what's wrong?"

Suddenly there's the sound of stirring from inside Suze's bedroom, and we stare at each other.

"OK, listen. It was just a one-off," she says quickly. "Just a . . . a really impetuous, stupid . . . I mean . . ."

"What's wrong, Suze?" I pull a face. "Oh God, it's not Nick, is it?"

Nick is Suze's last boyfriend—the one who was constantly depressed and getting drunk and blaming Suze. A complete nightmare, to be honest. But I mean, that was over months ago.

"No, it's not Nick. It's . . . Oh God."

"Suze—"

"OK! But you have to promise to—"

"To what?"

"To not . . . react."

"Why should I react?" I say, laughing a little. "I mean, I'm not a prude! All we're talking about is . . ."

I tail off as Suze's door opens—and it's only Tarquin, looking not at all bad, in chinos and the jumper I gave him.

"Oh," I say in surprise. "I thought you were going to be Suze's new—"

I break off and look at Suze with a grin.

But she doesn't grin back. She's chewing her nails, avoiding my eyes—and her cheeks growing redder and redder.

I glance at Tarquin—and *he* looks away, too.

No. *No.*

She can't mean—

No.

But . . .

No.

My brain can't cope with this. Something's about to short-circuit.

"Erm, Tarquin," says Suze, in a high-pitched voice. "Could you go and buy some croissants?"

"Oh, ahm . . . OK," says Tarquin, a little stiltedly. "Morning, Becky."

"Morning!" I say. "Nice to . . . to see you. Nice . . . jumper."

There's a frozen silence in the kitchen as he walks out, which remains until we hear the front door slam. Then, very slowly, I turn to face Suze.

"Suze . . ."

I don't even know how to begin.

"Suze . . . that was Tarquin."

"Yes, I know," she says, studying the kitchen counter intently.

"Suze . . . are you and Tarquin—"

"No!" she exclaims, as though she's been scalded. "No, of course not! It's just . . . we just . . ." She stops.

"You just . . ." I say encouragingly.

"Once or twice . . ."

There's a long pause.

"With Tarquin," I say, just to make sure.

"Yes," she says.

"Right," I say, nodding my head as though this is a completely reasonable scenario. But my mouth is twitching and I can feel a strange pressure rising inside me—half shock, half hysterical laughter. I mean, Tarquin. *Tarquin!*

A sudden giggle escapes from me and I clamp my hand over my mouth.

"Don't laugh!" wails Suze. "I knew you'd laugh!"

"I'm not laughing!" I protest. "I think it's great!" I give another snort of laughter, and try to pretend I'm coughing. "Sorry! Sorry. So—how did it happen?"

"It was at that party in Scotland!" she wails. "There was no one else there except loads of ancient aunts. Tarquin was the only other person under ninety. And somehow . . . he looked all different! He had on this really nice Paul Smith jersey, and his hair looked kind of cool—and it was like, is that really Tarquin? And I got quite pissed—and you know what that does to me. And there he was . . . ." She shakes her head helplessly. "I don't know. He was just . . . transformed. God knows how it happened!"

There's silence. I can feel my cheeks growing redder and redder.

"You know what, Suze," I admit sheepishly at last. "I think it kind of might have been . . . my fault."

"*Your* fault?" She raises her head and stares at me. "How come?"

"I gave him the jumper. And the hairstyle." I flinch at her expression. "But I mean, I had no idea it would lead to . . . to this! All I did was give him a look!"

"Well, you've got a lot to answer for!" cries Suze. "I've been so stressed. I just keep thinking, I must be a complete pervert."

"Why?" I say, my eyes brightening. "What does he get you to do?"

"No, silly! Because we're cousins. Well, distant cousins, but still . . ."

"Ooh." I pull a face—then realize that isn't exactly tactful. "But I mean, it's not against the law or anything, is it?"

"Oh God, Bex!" wails Suze. "That really makes me feel better."

She picks up her mug and mine, takes them over to the sink, and starts to run the tap.

"I just can't believe you're having a relationship with Tarquin!" I say.

"We're not having a relationship!" squeals Suze, as though I've scalded her. "That's the point. Last night was the very last time. We're both completely agreed. It'll never happen again. *Never.* And you mustn't tell anyone."

"I won't."

"No, I'm serious, Bex. You mustn't tell anyone. No one!"

"I won't! I promise! In fact—" I say, having a sudden idea. "I've got something for you."

I hurry into the hall, open one of my suitcases, and scrabble for the Kate's Paperie carrier bag. I pluck a card from the pile, scribble "To Suze, love Bex" inside, and return to the kitchen, sealing the envelope.

"Is this for me?" says Suze in surprise. "What is it?"

"Open it!"

She tears it open, looks at the picture of a zipped-up pair of lips, and reads aloud the printed message:

Roomie—your secret's safe with me.

"Wow!" she says, wide-eyed. "That's so cool! Did you buy it especially? But I mean . . ." She frowns. "How did you know I'd have a secret?"

"Er . . . just a hunch," I say. "You know. Sixth sense."

"You know, Bex, that reminds me," says Suze, flipping the envelope back and forth in her fingers. "You got quite a lot of post while you were away."

"Oh right."

In the astonishment of hearing about Suze and Tarquin, I'd kind of forgotten about everything else. But now the hysteria which has been lifting my spirits starts to evaporate. As Suze brings over a pile of unfriendly-looking envelopes, my stomach gives a nasty flip, and I suddenly wish I'd never come home. At least while I was away, I didn't have to know about any of this.

"Right," I say, trying to sound nonchalant and on top of things. I leaf through the letters without really looking at them—then put them down. "I'll look at them later. When I can give them my full attention."

"Bex . . ." Suze pulls a face. "I think you'd better open this one now." She reaches for the pile and pulls out a brown envelope with the word SUMMONS on the front.

I stare at it, feeling mortified. A summons. It was true. I've been summonsed. I take the envelope from Suze, unable to meet her eye, and rip it open with trembling fingers. I scan the letter without saying anything, feeling a growing coldness at the base of my spine. I can't quite believe people would actually take me to court. I mean, court is for criminals. Like drug dealers and murderers. Not for people who just miss a couple of bills.

I stuff the letter back into its envelope and put it on the counter, breathing hard.

"Bex . . . what are you going to do?" says Suze, biting her lip. "You can't just ignore that one."

"I won't. I'll pay them."

"But can you afford to pay them?"

"I'll have to."

There's silence, apart from the drip-drip of the cold-water tap into the sink. I look up, to see Suze's face contorted with worry.

"Bex—let me give you some money. Or Tarkie will. He can easily afford it."

"No!" I say, more sharply than I'd intended. "No, I don't want any help. I'll just . . ." I rub my face. "I'll go and see the guy at the bank. Today. Right now."

With a sudden surge of determination I scoop up the pile of letters and head to my room. I'm not going to let all this defeat me. I'm going to wash my face, and put on some makeup, and get my life back in order.

"What will you say?" says Suze, following me down the corridor.

"I'll explain the situation to him honestly, and ask him for a bigger overdraft . . . and take it from there. I'm going to be independent and strong, and stand on my own two feet."

"Good for you, Bex!" says Suze. "That's really fantastic. Independent and strong. That's really great!" She watches as I try to open my suitcase with shaking fingers. As I struggle with the clasp for the third time, she comes over and puts a hand on my arm. "Bex—would you like me to come too?"

"Yes, please," I say in a small voice.

Suze won't let me go anywhere until I've sat down and had a couple of brandies for Dutch courage. Then she tells me how she read an article the other day that said your best negotiating weapon is your appearance—so I must choose my outfit for seeing John Gavin very carefully. We go right through my wardrobe and end up with a plain black skirt and gray cardigan which I reckon shouts "frugal, sober, and steady." Then she has to choose her own "sensible, supportive friend" outfit (navy trousers and a white shirt). And we're almost ready to go when Suze decides that if nothing else works, we might have to flirt outrageously with him, so we both change into sexy underwear. Then I look at myself in the mirror and suddenly decide I look too drab. So I quickly change into a pale pink cardigan, which means changing my lipstick.

At last we get out of the house and arrive at the Fulham branch of Endwich Bank. As we go in, Derek Smeath's old assistant, Erica Parnell, is showing out a middle-aged couple. Between you and me, she and I have never exactly got on. I don't think she can be quite human—she's been wearing exactly the same navy blue shoes every time I've seen her.

"Oh, hello," she says, shooting me a look of dislike. "What do you want?"

"I'd like to see John Gavin, please," I say, trying to sound matter-of-fact. "Is he available?"

"I shouldn't think so," she says coldly. "Not without notice."

"Well . . . could you possibly just check?"

Erica Parnell rolls her eyes.

"Wait there," she says and disappears behind a door marked "Private."

"God, they're horrible here!" says Suze, lolling against a glass partition. "When I go to see my bank manager he gives me a glass of sherry and asks me about all the family! You know, Bex, I really think you should move to Coutts."

"Yes, well," I say. "Maybe."

I'm feeling slightly jittery as I leaf through a pile of

insurance brochures. I'm remembering what Derek Smeath said about John Gavin being rigorous and in-flexible. Oh God, I miss old Smeathie.

Oh God, I miss Luke.

The feeling hits me like a hammer blow. Since I got back from New York I've been trying not to think about him at all. But as I stand here, all I wish is that I could talk to him. I wish I could see him looking at me like he used to before everything went wrong. With that quizzical little smile on his face, and his arms wrapped tightly around me.

I wonder what he's doing now. I wonder how his meetings are going.

"Come this way," comes Erica Parnell's voice, and my head jerks up. Feeling slightly sick, I follow her down a blue-carpeted corridor, into a chilly little room fur-nished with a table and plastic chairs. As the door closes behind her, Suze and I look at each other.

"Shall we run away?" I say, only half-joking.

"It's going to be fine!" says Suze. "He'll probably turn out to be really nice! You know, my parents once had this gardener, and he seemed really grumpy—but then we found out he had a pet rabbit! And it was like, he was a completely different—"

She breaks off as the door swings open and in strides a guy of about thirty. He's got thinning dark hair, is wearing a rather nasty suit, and is holding a plastic cup of coffee.

He doesn't look as though he's got a friendly bone in his body. Suddenly I wish we hadn't come.

"Right," he says with a frown. "I haven't got all day. Which of you is Rebecca Bloomwood?"

The way he says it, it's like he's asking which one of us threw up on the carpet.

"Erm . . . I am," I say nervously.

"And who's this?"

"Suze is my—"

"People," says Suze confidently. "I'm her people." She looks around the room. "Do you have any sherry?"

"No," says John Gavin, looking at her as though she's subnormal. "I don't have any sherry. Now what's this about?"

"OK, first of all," I say nervously, "I've brought you something." I reach into my bag and hand him another Kate's Paperie envelope.

It was my own idea to bring him a little something to break the ice. After all, it's only good manners. And in Japan, this is how business is done all the time.

"Is this a check?" says John Gavin.

"Erm . . . no," I say, coloring slightly. "It's a . . . a handmade card."

John Gavin gives me a look, then rips the envelope open and pulls out a card printed in silver, with pink feathers glued to the corners.

Now that I look at it, maybe I should have chosen a less girly one.

Or not brought one at all. But it seemed so perfect for the occasion.

Friend—I know I've made mistakes, but can we start over?

John Gavin reads incredulously. He turns it over, as though suspecting a joke. "Did you *buy* this?"

"It's nice, isn't it!" says Suze. "You get them in New York."

"I see. I'll bear that in mind." He puts it up on the table and we all look at it. "Miss Bloomwood, why exactly are you here?"

"Right!" I say. "Well. As my greeting card states, I'm aware that I have . . ." I swallow. "Perhaps not been the perfect . . . ideal customer. However, I'm confident that we can work together as a team, and achieve harmony."

So far so good. I learned that bit off by heart.

"Which means?" says John Gavin.

I clear my throat. "Um . . . due to circumstances beyond my control, I have recently found myself in a slight financial . . . situation. So I was wondering whether you could perhaps temporarily . . ."

"Very kindly . . ." puts in Suze.

"Very kindly . . . perhaps extend my overdraft a little further, on a . . . a short-term . . ."

"Goodwill . . ." interjects Suze.

"Goodwill . . . temporary . . . short-term basis. Obviously to be paid back as soon as is feasibly and humanly possible." I stop, and draw breath.

"Have you finished?" says John Gavin, folding his arms.

"Erm . . . yes." I look to Suze for confirmation. "Yes, we have."

There's silence while John Gavin drums his Biro on the table. Then he looks up and says, "No."

"No?" I look at him puzzledly. "Is that just . . . no?"

"Just no." He pushes back his chair. "So if you'll excuse me—"

"What do you mean, no?" says Suze. "You can't just say no! You have to weigh up the pros and cons!"

"I have weighed up the pros and the cons," says John Gavin. "There are no pros."

"But this is one of your most valued customers!" Suze's voice rises in dismay. "This is Becky Bloomwood of TV fame, who has a huge, glittering career in front of her!"

"This is Becky Bloomwood who has had her over-draft limit extended six times in the last year," says John Gavin in a rather nasty voice. "And who each time has failed to keep within those limits. This is Becky Bloom-wood who has consistently lied, who has consistently avoided meetings, who has treated bank staff with little or no respect, and who seems to think we're all here solely to fund her appetite for shoes. I've looked at your file, Miss Bloomwood. I know the picture."

There's a subdued little silence. I can feel my cheeks getting hotter and hotter and I've got a horrible feeling I might cry.

"I don't think you should be so mean!" says Suze in a burst. "Becky's just had a really awful time! Would *you* like to be in the tabloids? Would *you* like to have some-one stalking you?"

"Oh, I see!" His voice glints with sarcasm. "You ex-pect me to feel sorry for you!"

"Yes!" I say. "No. Not exactly. But I think you should give me a chance."

"You think I should give you another chance. And what have you done to *merit* another chance?" He shakes his head, and there's silence.

"I just . . . I thought if I explained it all to you . . ." I tail off feebly and shoot Suze a hopeless look to say, "Let's just forget it."

"Hey, is it hot in here?" says Suze in a sudden husky voice. She takes off her jacket, shakes back her hair, and runs one hand down her cheek. "I'm feeling really . . . hot. Are you feeling hot, John?"

John Gavin shoots her an irritated look.

"What precisely did you want to explain to me, Miss Bloomwood?"

"Well. Just that I really want to sort things out," I say,

my voice trembling. "You know, I really want to turn things around. I want to stand on my own two feet, and—"

"Stand on your own two feet?" interrupts John Gavin scathingly. "You call taking handouts from a bank 'standing on your own two feet'? If you were really standing on your own two feet, you'd have no overdraft. You'd have a few *assets* by now! You, of all people, shouldn't need telling that."

"I . . . I know," I say, my voice barely above a whisper. "But the fact is, I have got an overdraft. And I just thought—"

"You thought what? That you're special? That you're an exception because you're on the television? That the normal rules don't apply to you? That this bank *owes* you money?"

His voice is like a drill in my head and suddenly I feel myself snap.

"No!" I cry. "I don't think that. I don't think any of that. I know I've been stupid, and I know I've done wrong. But I think that everyone does wrong occasionally." I take a deep breath. "You know, if you look at your files, you'll see I *did* pay off my overdraft. And I *did* pay off my store cards. And OK, I'm in debt again. But I'm trying to sort it out—and all you can do is . . . is sneer. Well, fine. I'll sort myself out without your help. Come on, Suze."

Shaking slightly, I get to my feet. My eyes are hot, but I'm *not* going to cry in front of him. There's a shaft of determination inside me, which strengthens as I turn to face him.

"Endwich—because we care," I say.

There's a long, tense silence. Then, without saying anything else, I open the door and walk out.

As we walk home, I feel almost high with determination. I'll show him. I'll show that John Gavin. And all of them. The whole world.

I'm going to pay off my debts. I don't know how—but I'm going to do it. I'll take an extra job waitressing, maybe. Or I'll get down to it, and finish my self-help book. I'll just make as much money as I can, as quickly as I can. And then I'll go into that bank with a huge check, and plonk it down in front of him, and in a dignified but pointed voice, I'll say—

"Bex?" Suze grabs my arm—and I realize I'm walking straight past our house.

"Are you OK?" says Suze as she lets us in. "Honestly, what a bastard."

"I'm fine," I say, lifting my chin. "I'm going to show him. I'm going to pay off my overdraft. Just wait. I'm going to show them all."

"Excellent!" says Suze. She bends down and picks up a letter from the doormat.

"It's for you," she says. "From *Morning Coffee!*"

"Oh right!" As I'm opening the envelope, I feel a huge leap of hope. Maybe they're offering me a new job! Something with a huge salary, enough to pay off my debts straight away. Maybe they've sacked Emma and I'm going to take her place as the main presenter! Or maybe . . .

Oh my God. Oh my God, no.

Morning Coffee

East-West Television
Corner House
London NW8 4DW

Ms. Rebecca Bloomwood
Flat 2
4 Burney Rd.
London SW6 8FD

2 October 2000

Dear Becky:

First of all, bad luck on your recent unfortunate bout of
publicity! I really felt for you, and I know I also speak for
Rory, Emma, and all the rest of the team.

As you know, the Morning Coffee family is a fiercely loyal and
supportive one, and it is our policy never to allow adverse
publicity to stand in the way of talent. However, completely
coincidentally, we have recently been reviewing all our regular contributors. Following some discussion, we have decided to rest you from your slot for a while.

I must emphasize that this is just a temporary measure.
However, we would appreciate it if you would return your
East-West TV pass in the envelope provided and also sign
the enclosed release document.

The work you've done for us has been fabulous (obviously!). We just know that your talents will flourish else-
where and that this will not prove a setback to someone as
dynamic as yourself!

With very best wishes,

Zelda Washington

Assistant Producer

695 SOHO SQUARE
LONDON W1 5AS

Ms. Rebecca Bloomwood
Flat 2
4 Burney Rd.
London SW6 8FD

4 October 2000

Dear Becky:

Thank you very much for your first draft of *Manage Money the Bloomwood Way*. We appreciated the care that had gone into your work. Your writing is well paced and fluent, and you certainly made some interesting points.

Unfortunately, 500 words—however excellent they are—is not quite enough for a self-help book. Your suggestion that we could "pad out the rest with photographs" is unfortunately not really workable.

Sadly, we have therefore decided that this is not a viable project and, as a result, would request that you return our advance forthwith.

With all best wishes,

Pippa Brady
Editor

Helping you to help yourself
OUT NOW! *Jungle Survival* by Bdgr. Roger Flintwood **(deceased)**

Fourteen

FOR THE NEXT FEW DAYS, I don't leave the house. I don't answer the phone and I don't talk to anyone. I feel physically raw, as though people's gazes, or their questions, or even the sunlight, might hurt me. I need to be in a dark place, on my own. Suze has gone to Milton Keynes for a big sales and marketing conference with Hadleys, so I'm all alone in the flat. I order takeout, drink two bottles of white wine, and don't once get out of my pajamas.

When Suze returns, I'm sitting on the floor in the sitting room where she left me, staring blankly at the television, stuffing KitKats into my mouth.

"Oh God," she says, dropping her bag on the floor. "Bex, are you OK? I shouldn't have left you on your own."

"I'm fine!" I say, looking up and forcing my stiff face to twist into a smile. "How was the sales conference?"

"Well . . . it was really good, actually," says Suze, looking abashed. "People kept congratulating me on the way my frames have been selling. They'd all heard of me! And they did a presentation of my new designs, and everybody loved them . . ."

"That's really great, Suze," I say, and reach up to squeeze her hand. "You deserve it."

"Well. You know." She bites her lip—then picks up an empty wine bottle from the floor and puts it on the table.

"So, did . . . Luke call?" she says hesitantly.

"No," I say, after a long silence. "No, he didn't." I look at Suze, then look away again.

"What are you watching?" she says, as an ad for Diet Coke comes on.

"I'm watching *Morning Coffee*," I say. "It's the financial advice slot coming up next."

"What?" Suze's face creases in dismay. "Bex, let's switch channels." She reaches for the remote control, but I grab it.

"No!" I say, staring rigidly at the screen. "I want to see it."

The familiar *Morning Coffee* music blasts out of the screen as the signature graphic of a cup of coffee appears and then melts away to a studio shot.

"Hello!" says Emma cheerily to camera. "Welcome back. And it's time for us to introduce our new money expert, Clare Edwards!"

I stare at Clare's familiar face, feeling a fresh humiliation seep over me. When they promoted her appearance earlier on I was so shocked I spilled my coffee on my hand. It still hurts.

"Who's Clare Edwards?" says Suze, staring at the screen in distaste.

"I used to work with her on *Successful Saving*," I say without moving my head. "She used to sit next to me."

The camera pans away to show Clare sitting on the sofa opposite Emma, staring grimly back.

"She doesn't look like much fun," says Suze.

"She isn't."

"So, Clare," says Emma brightly. "What's your basic philosophy of money?"

"Do you have a catchphrase?" interjects Rory cheerfully.

"I don't believe in catchphrases," says Clare, giving Rory a disapproving look. "Personal finance isn't a trivial matter."

"Right!" says Rory. "Of course not. Erm . . . so—do you have any top tips for savers, Clare?"

"I don't believe in futile and misleading generalizations," says Clare. "All savers should choose a spread of investments suitable to their individual requirements and tax status."

"Absolutely!" says Emma after a pause. "Right. Well—let's go to the phones, shall we? And it's Mandy from Norwich."

As the first caller is put through, the phone in our sitting room rings.

"Hello?" says Suze, picking it up and zapping the sound on the television, "Ooh, hello, Mrs. Bloomwood. Do you want to speak to Becky?"

She raises her eyebrows at me and I wince back. I've only spoken to Mum and Dad briefly since my return. They know I'm not going to move to New York—but that's all I've said to them so far. I just can't face telling them how badly everything else has turned out too.

"Becky, love, I was just watching *Morning Coffee!*" exclaims Mum. "What's that girl doing, giving out financial advice?"

"It's . . . it's OK, Mum, don't worry!" I say, feeling my nails dig into my palm. "They just . . . they got her to cover while I was away."

"Well. They could have chosen someone better! She's

got a miserable face on her, hasn't she?" Her voice goes muffled. "What's that, Graham? Dad says, at least she shows how good *you* are! But surely, now that you're back, they can let her go?"

"I don't think it's as simple as that," I say after a pause. "Contracts and . . . things."

"So, when will you be back on? Because I know Janice will be asking."

"I don't know, Mum," I say desperately. "Listen, I've got to go, OK? There's someone at the door. But I'll talk to you soon!"

I put down the phone and bury my head in my hands.

"What am I going to do?" I say hopelessly. "What am I going to do, Suze? I can't tell them I've been fired. I just can't." To my dismay, tears squeeze out of the sides of my eyes. "They're so proud of me. And I just keep letting them down."

"You don't let them down!" retorts Suze hotly. "It wasn't your fault that stupid *Morning Coffee* completely overreacted. And I bet they're regretting it now. I mean, *look* at her!"

She turns up the sound, and Clare's voice drones sternly through the room. "Those who fail to provide for their own retirement are the equivalent of leeches on the rest of us."

"I say," says Rory. "Isn't that a bit harsh?"

"I mean, listen to her!" says Suze. "She's awful!"

"Maybe she is," I say after a pause. "But even if they get rid of her too they'll never ask me back. It would be like saying they made a mistake."

"They *have* made a mistake!"

The phone rings again and she looks at me. "Are you in or out?"

"Out. And you don't know when I'll be back."

"OK . . ." She picks up the phone. "Hello? Sorry, Becky's out at the moment."

"Wendy, you've made every mistake possible," Clare Edwards is saying on the screen. "Have you never heard of a deposit account? And as for remortgaging your house to buy a boat . . ."

"No, I don't know when she'll be back," says Suze. "Would you like me to take a message?" She picks up a pen and starts writing. "OK . . . fine . . . yes. Yes, I'll tell her. Thanks."

"So," I say as she puts the phone down. "Who was that?"

And I know it's stupid—but as I look up at her, I can't help feeling a hot flicker of hope. Maybe it was a producer from another show. Maybe it was someone wanting to offer me my own column. Maybe it was John Gavin, ringing to apologize and offer me free, unlimited overdraft facilities. Maybe it was the one phone call that will make everything all right.

"It was Mel. Luke's assistant."

"Oh." I stare at her in apprehension. "What did she want?"

"Apparently some parcel has arrived at the office, addressed to you. From the States. From Barnes & Noble."

I stare at her blankly—then, with a pang, suddenly remember that trip to Barnes & Noble I made with Luke. I bought a whole pile of coffee-table books, and Luke suggested I send them back on the company courier bill instead of lugging them around. It seems like a million years ago now.

"Oh yes, I know what that is." I hesitate. "Did she . . . mention Luke?"

"No," says Suze apologetically. "She just said pop in anytime you want. And she said she was really sorry about what happened . . . and if you ever want a chat, just call."

"Right." I hunch my shoulders up, hug my knees, and turn up the television volume.

For the next few days, I tell myself I won't bother going. I don't really want those books anymore. And I can't quite cope with the thought of having to go in there—having to face all the curious looks from Luke's staff, and hold my head up and pretend to be OK.

But then, gradually, I start to think I'd like to see Mel. She's the only one I can talk to who really knows Luke, and it would be nice to have a heart-to-heart with her. Plus, she might have heard something of what's going on in the States. I know Luke and I are effectively over, I know it's really nothing to do with me anymore. But I still can't help caring about whether he's got his deal or not.

So four days later, at about six o'clock in the evening, I walk slowly toward the doors of Brandon Communications, my heart thumping. Luckily it's the friendly doorman on duty. He's seen me visit enough times to just wave me in, so I don't have to have any big announcements of my arrival.

I walk out of the lift at the fifth floor, and to my surprise, there's no one on reception. How weird. I wait for a few seconds—then wander past the desk and down the main corridor. Gradually my steps slow down—and a puzzled frown comes to my face. There's something wrong here. Something different.

It's too quiet. The whole place is practically dead. When I look across the open-plan space, most of the chairs are empty. There aren't any phones ringing; there aren't any people striding about; there aren't brainstorming sessions going on.

What's going on? What's happened to the buzzy Brandon C atmosphere? What's *happened* to Luke's company?

As I pass the coffee machine, two guys I half-recognize are standing, talking by it. One's got a disgruntled expression and the other is agreeing—but I can't quite hear what they're talking about. As I come near, they stop abruptly. They shoot me curious looks, then glance at each other and walk off, before starting to talk again, but in lowered voices.

I can't quite believe this is Brandon Communications. There's a completely different feel about the place. This is like some deadbeat company where no one cares about what they're doing. I walk to Mel's desk—and, along with everyone else, she's already left for the night. Mel, who normally stays till at least seven, then takes a glass of wine and gets changed in the loos for whatever great night out she's got planned.

I root around behind her chair until I find the parcel addressed to me, and scribble a note to her on a Post-it. Then I stand up, hugging the heavy package to me, and tell myself that I've got what I came for. Now I should leave. There's nothing to keep me.

But instead of walking away, I stand motionless. Staring at Luke's closed office door.

Luke's office. There are probably faxes from him in there. Messages about how things are going in New York. Maybe even messages about me. As I gaze at the smooth blank wood, I feel almost overwhelmed by an urge to go in and find out what I can.

But then—what exactly would I do? Look through

his files? Listen to his voice mail? I mean, what if someone caught me?

I'm standing there, torn—knowing I'm not *really* going to go and rifle through his stuff, yet unable just to
walk away—when suddenly I stiffen in shock. The handle of his office door is starting to move.

Oh shit. *Shit.* There's someone in there! They're coming out!

In a moment of pure panic, I find myself ducking
down out of sight, behind Mel's chair. As I curl up into
a tiny ball I feel a thrill of terror, like a child playing
hide-and-seek. I hear some voices murmuring—and
then the door swings open and someone comes out.
From my vantage point, all I can see is that it's a female,
and she's wearing those new Chanel shoes which cost
an absolute bomb. She's followed by two pairs of male
legs, and the three begin to walk down the corridor. I
can't resist peeping out from behind the chair—and of
course. It's Alicia Bitch Longlegs, with Ben Bridges and
a man who looks familiar but whom I can't quite place.

Well, I suppose that's fair enough. She's in charge
while Luke is away. But does she have to take over
Luke's office? I mean, why can't she just use a meeting
room?

"Sorry we had to meet here," I can just hear her saying. "Obviously, next time, it'll be at 17 King Street."

They continue talking until they reach the lifts, and I
pray desperately that they'll all get inside one and disappear. But as the lift doors ping open, only the
familiar-looking man gets in—and a moment later, Alicia and Ben are heading back toward Luke's office.

"I'll just get those files," says Alicia, and goes back
into Luke's office, leaving the door open. Meanwhile,
Ben is lolling against the water dispenser, pressing the

buttons on his watch and staring intently at the tiny screen.

This is horrendous! I'm trapped until they leave. My knees are starting to hurt and I've got an awful feeling that if I move an inch, one of them will crack. What if Ben and Alicia stay here all night? What if they come over to Mel's desk? What if they decide to *make love* on Mel's desk?

"OK," says Alicia, suddenly appearing at the door. "I think that's it. Good meeting, I thought."

"I suppose." Ben looks up from his watch. "Do you think Frank's right? Do you think he might sue?"

Frank! Of course. That other man was Frank Harper. The publicity guy from Bank of London. I used to see him at press conferences.

"He won't sue," says Alicia calmly. "He's got too much face to lose."

"He's lost a fair amount already," says Ben, raising his eyebrows. "He'll be the invisible man before too long."

"True," says Alicia, and smirks back at him. She looks at the pile of folders in her arms. "Have I got everything? I think so. Right, I'm off. Ed will be waiting for me. See you tomorrow."

They both disappear down the corridor and this time, thank God, they get into a lift. When I'm quite sure they've gone, I sit back on my heels with a puzzled frown. What's going on? Why were they talking about suing? Suing who? And how come Bank of London was here?

Is Bank of London going to sue Luke? It sounds like everything's a complete mess! I thought Alicia was supposed to have everything under control.

For a while I just sit still, trying to work it all out. But I'm not really getting anywhere—and suddenly it occurs to me that I ought to get out while the going's good. I get up, wincing at the cramp in my foot, and shake out my legs as the circulation returns to them. Then I pick up my parcel, shake back my head, and as nonchalantly as possible, walk down the corridor toward the lifts. Just as I'm pressing the "Summon" button, my mobile phone rings inside my bag, and I give a startled jump. Shit, my phone! Thank *God* that didn't happen while I was hiding behind Mel's desk!

"Hello?" I say, as I get into the lift.

"Bex! It's Suze."

"Suze!" I say, and give a shaky giggle. "You have no idea how you nearly just got me in trouble! If you'd rung like, five minutes ago, you would have completely . . ."

"Bex, listen," says Suze urgently. "You've just had a call."

"Oh right?" I press the ground-floor button. "From who?"

"From Zelda at *Morning Coffee*! She wants to talk to you! She said, do you want to meet for a quick lunch tomorrow?"

That night, I barely get an hour's sleep. Suze and I stay up till late, deciding on what I should wear—and when I've gone to bed, I lie awake, staring at the ceiling, feeling my mind flip around like a fish. Will they offer my old job back after all? Will they offer me a different job? Maybe they'll upgrade me! Maybe they'll give me my own show!

But by the early hours of the morning, all my wild fantasies have faded away, leaving the simple truth. The truth is, all I really want is my old job back. I want to be able to tell Mum to start watching again, and to start paying off my overdraft . . . and to start my life all over again. Another chance. That's all I want.

"You see?" says Suze the next morning as I'm getting ready. "You see? I *knew* they'd want you back. That Clare Edwards is crap! Completely and utterly—"

"Suze," I interrupt. "How do I look?"

"Very good," says Suze, looking me up and down approvingly. I'm wearing my black Banana Republic trousers and a pale fitted jacket over a white shirt, and a dark green scarf round my neck.

I would have worn my Denny and George scarf—in fact, I even picked it up from the dressing table. But then, almost immediately, I put it down again. I don't quite know why.

"Very kick-ass," adds Suze. "Where are you having lunch?"

"Lorenzo's."

"*San Lorenzo?*" Her eyes widen impressively.

"No, I don't think so. Just . . . Lorenzo's. I've never been there before."

"Well, you make sure you order champagne," says Suze. "And tell them you're fighting off loads of other offers, so if they want you to come back, they're going to have to pay big bucks. That's the deal, take it or leave it."

"Right," I say, unscrewing my mascara.

"If their margins suffer, then so be it," says Suze emphatically. "For a quality product you have to pay quality prices. You want to close the deal at *your* price, on *your* terms."

"Suze . . ." I stop, mascara wand on my lashes. "Where are you getting all this stuff?"

"What stuff?"

"All this . . . margins and close the deal stuff."

"Oh, that! From the Hadleys conference. We had a seminar from one of the top salespeople in the U.S.! It was great! You know, a product is only as good as the person selling it."

"If you say so." I pick up my bag and check that I've got everything—then look up and take a deep breath. "Right, I'm going."

"Good luck!" says Suze. "Except you know, there is no luck in business. There's only drive, determination, and more drive."

"OK," I say dubiously. "I'll try to remember that."

The address I've been given for Lorenzo's is a street in Soho—and as I turn into it, I can't see anything that looks obviously like a restaurant. It's mostly just office blocks, with a few little newsagenty-type shops, and a coffee shop, and a . . .

Hang on. I stop still and stare at the sign above the coffee shop. "Lorenzo's coffee shop and sandwich bar."

But surely . . . this can't be where we're meeting?

"Becky!" My head jerks up, and I see Zelda walking along the street toward me, in jeans and a Puffa. "You found it all right!"

"Yes," I say, trying not to look discomfited. "Yes, I found it."

"You don't mind just a quick sandwich, do you?" she says, sweeping me inside. "It's just that this place is quite convenient for me."

"No! I mean . . . a sandwich would be great!"

"Good! I recommend the Italian chicken!" She eyes me up and down. "You look very smart. Off somewhere nice?"

I stare at her, feeling a pang of mortification. I can't admit I dressed up specially to see her.

"Erm . . . yes." I clear my throat. "A . . . a meeting I've got later."

"Oh well, I won't keep you long. Just a little proposition we wanted to put to you." She shoots me a quick smile. "We thought it would be nicer to do it face-to-face."

This isn't exactly what I imagined for our power lunch. But as I watch the sandwich guy smoothing Italian chicken onto our bread, adding salad, and slicing each sandwich into four quarters, I start to feel more positive. OK, maybe this isn't a grand place with tablecloths and champagne. Maybe they aren't pushing the boat out. But then, that's probably good! It shows they still think of me as part of the team, doesn't it? Someone to have a relaxed sandwich with, and thrash out ideas for the forthcoming season.

Maybe they want to take me on board as a features consultant. Or train me to become a producer!

"We all felt for you dreadfully, Becky," says Zelda as we make our way to a tiny wooden table, balancing our trays of sandwiches and drinks. "How are things going? Have you got a job lined up in New York?"

"Um . . . not exactly," I say, and take a sip of my mineral water. "That's all kind of . . . on hold." I see her eyes watching me appraisingly, and quickly add, "But I've been considering lots of offers. You know—various projects, and . . . and ideas in development . . ."

"Oh good! I'm so glad. We all felt very bad that you had to go. And I want you to know, it wasn't my decision." She puts her hand on mine briefly, then removes it to take a bite of her sandwich. "So now—to business." She takes a sip of tea, and I feel my stomach flutter with nerves. "You remember our producer, Barry?"

"Of course I do!" I say, slightly taken aback. Are they

expecting me to have forgotten the name of the producer already?

"Well, he's come up with quite an interesting idea." Zelda beams at me, and I beam back. "He thinks the *Morning Coffee* viewers would be really interested to hear about your . . . little problem."

"Right," I say, feeling my smile freeze on my face. "Well, it's . . . it's not really a—"

"And he thought perhaps you would be ideal to take part in a discussion and/or phone-in on the subject." She takes a sip of tea. "What do you think?"

I stare at her in confusion.

"Are you talking about going back to my regular slot?"

"Oh no! I mean, we could hardly have you giving financial advice, could we?" She gives a little laugh. "No, this would be more of a one-off, topical piece. 'How shopping wrecked my life.' That kind of thing." She takes a bite of sandwich. "And ideally, it would be quite a . . . how can I put this? An *emotional* piece. Maybe you could bare your soul a little. Talk about your parents, how this has ruined their lives too . . . problems in your childhood . . . relationship trouble . . . these are just ideas, obviously!" She looks up. "And you know, if you were able to cry . . ."

"To . . . to cry?" I echo disbelievingly.

"It's not compulsory. By *any* means." Zelda leans earnestly forward. "We want this to be a good experience for you too, Becky. We want to help. So we'd have Clare Edwards in the studio too, to offer you advice . . ."

"Clare Edwards!"

"Yes! You used to work with her, didn't you? That was why we thought of approaching her. And you know, she's quite a hit! She really tells the callers off! So we've decided to rename her Scary Clare and give her a whip to crack!"

She beams at me but I can't smile back. My whole face is prickling with shock and humiliation. I've never felt so belittled in my life.

"So what do you think?" she says, slurping at her smoothie.

I put down my sandwich, unable to take another bite.

"I'm afraid my answer's no."

"Oh! There'd be a fee, of course!" she says. "I should have mentioned that at the beginning."

"Even so. I'm not interested."

"Don't answer yet. Think about it!" Zelda flashes me a cheery smile, then glances at her watch. "I must dash, I'm afraid. But it's lovely to see you, Becky. And I'm *so* glad things are going well for you."

After she's gone I sit still for a while, sipping at my mineral water. I'm outwardly calm—but inside I'm burning with mortified rage. They want me to go on and cry. That's all they want. One article in one crappy tabloid—and suddenly I'm not Becky Bloomwood, financial expert. I'm Becky Bloomwood, failure and flake. I'm Becky Bloomwood, watch her cry and pass the hankies.

Well, they can just bloody well stuff their bloody hankies. They can just take their stupid, bloody . . . stupid . . . stupid . . . bloody . . .

"Are you all right?" says the man at the next table—and to my horror I realize I'm muttering aloud.

"I'm fine," I say. "Thanks." I put down my glass and walk out of Lorenzo's, my head high and my chin stiff.

I walk down the road and turn a corner without even noticing where I'm going. I don't know the area and I don't have anyplace I need to get to—so I just walk, almost hypnotizing myself with the rhythm of my steps, thinking eventually I'll hit a tube station.

As I walk, my eyes start to smart and I tell myself it's the cold air. It's the wind. I shove my hands in my pockets and tighten my chin and start to walk faster, trying to keep my mind empty. But there's a blank dread inside me; a hollow panic that is getting worse and worse. I haven't got my job back. I haven't even got the prospect of a job. What am I going to say to Suze? What am I going to say to Mum?

What am I going to do with my life?

"Oy! Watch out!" yells someone behind me—and to my horror I realize I've stepped off the pavement in front of a cyclist.

"Sorry," I say in a husky voice as the cyclist swerves off, shooting me the finger. This is ridiculous. I've got to pull myself together. I mean, where am I, for a start? I start to walk more slowly along the pavement, peering up at the glass doors of offices, looking for the name of the road I'm on. And I'm just about to ask a traffic warden—when suddenly I see a sign. King Street.

For a moment I stare at it blankly, wondering why it's chiming a bell inside my head. Then, with a jolt, I remember: 17 King Street. Alicia.

I peer at the number embossed on the glass doors nearest me—and it's 23. Which means . . . I must have just walked past number 17.

Now I'm completely consumed by curiosity. What on earth goes on at 17 King Street? Is it some secret cult, or something? God, it wouldn't surprise me if she was a witch in her spare time.

My whole body is prickling with intrigue as I retrace my steps until I'm standing outside a modest set of double doors marked 17. It's obviously a building with lots of different little companies inside, but as I run my eye down the list, none sounds familiar.

"Hi!" says a bloke in a denim jacket, holding a cup of coffee. He comes up to the doors, presses a code into the keypad, and pushes the door open. "You look lost. Who are you after?"

"Erm . . . I'm not sure actually," I say hesitantly. "I thought I knew somebody who worked here, but I can't remember the name of the company."

"What's her name?"

"It's . . . it's Alicia," I say—then immediately wish I hadn't. What if this guy knows Alicia? What if she's in there somewhere and he goes and fetches her?

But he's frowning puzzledly. "I don't know an Alicia . . . Mind you, there's a few new faces around at the moment . . . What sort of business is she in?"

"PR," I say after a pause.

"PR? We're mostly graphic design, here . . ." Suddenly his face clears. "Hey, but maybe she's with the new company. B and B? BBB? Something like that. They haven't started trading yet, so we haven't met them." He takes a sip of cappuccino and I stare at him. My mind is starting to twitch.

"A new PR company? Based here?"

"As far as I know, yes. They've taken a big space on the second floor."

Thoughts are sparking round my head like fireworks.

B and B. Bridges and Billington. Billington and Bridges.

"Do you . . ." I try to keep calm. "Do you know what sort of PR?"

"Ah! Now, this I *do* know. It's financial. Apparently one of their biggest clients is Bank of London. Or will be. Which must be a nice little earner . . . But as I say, we haven't met them yet, so . . ." He looks at me and his face changes expression. "Hey. Are you OK?"

"I'm fine," I manage. "I think. I just have to . . . I have to make a phone call."

I dial the number of the Four Seasons three times— and each time hang up before I can bring myself to ask for Luke Brandon. At last I take a deep breath, dial the number again, and ask to speak to Michael Ellis.

"Michael, it's Becky Bloomwood here," I say when I'm put through.

"Becky!" he says, sounding genuinely pleased to hear from me. "How are you doing?"

I close my eyes, trying to keep calm. But just the sound of his voice has taken me back to the Four Seasons with a whoosh. Back to that dim, expensive lobby. Back to that New York dreamworld.

"I . . ." I take a deep breath. "I'm fine. You know . . . back to normal life . . . busy, busy!"

I'm not going to admit I've lost my job. I'm not going to have everyone feeling sorry for me.

"I'm just on my way to the studio," I say, crossing my fingers. "But I wanted a quick word. I think I know why there's a rumor going around that Luke's going to lose Bank of London."

I tell him exactly what I overheard in the office, how I went to King Street, and what I've discovered.

"I see," says Michael at intervals, sounding grim. "I see. You know, there's a clause in their contracts forbidding employees to do this? If they poach a client, Luke could sue them."

"They talked about that. They seem to think he won't sue because he'd lose too much face."

There's silence—and I can almost hear Michael thinking down the line.

"They have a point," he says at last. "Becky, I have to talk to Luke. You did a great job finding out what you did . . ."

"That's not the only thing." I take a deep breath. "Michael, someone's got to talk to Luke. I went into the Brandon Communications office, and it was completely dead. No one's making any effort, everyone's going home early . . . it's a whole different atmosphere. It's not good." I bite my lip. "He needs to come home."

"Why don't you tell him this yourself?" says Michael gently. "I'm sure he'd like to hear from you."

He sounds so kind and concerned, I feel a sudden prickle in my nose.

"I can't. If I ring him up, he'll just think . . . he'll think I'm trying to prove some point, or it's just some more stupid gossip . . ." I break off, and swallow hard. "To be honest, Michael, I'd rather you just kept me out of it. Pretend someone else spoke to you. But someone's got to tell him."

"I'm seeing him in half an hour," Michael says. "I'll talk to him then. And, Becky . . . well done."

Miss Rebecca Bloomwood
c/o Four Seasons Hotel
57 East 57th Street
New York 10022

October 3, 2000

Dear Miss Bloomwood:

I was delighted to meet you at Nina Heywood's lunch-
eon the other day. It was a great pleasure to meet
such a cultured and well-connected young lady as
yourself.

I write because I am coming to England in two weeks'
time and I was very much hoping that you might be
able to introduce me to Prince William and, if
possible, the queen? I would be honored to take the
three of you to dinner, whenever is convenient.

I look forward to hearing from you.

With kind regards,

Marion Jefferson (Mrs.)

P.S. If not the queen, then maybe Prince Philip?

Fifteen

AFTER A WEEK, I give up on hearing anything from Michael. Whatever he's said to Luke, I'm never going to hear about it. I feel as though that whole part of my life is over. Luke, America, television, everything. Time to start again.

I'm trying to keep positive, and tell myself I've lots of avenues open to me. But what *is* the next career move for an ex–television financial expert? I rang up a television agent, and to my dismay, she sounded exactly like all those TV people in America. She said she was thrilled to hear from me, she'd have absolutely no problem finding me work—if not my own series—and that she'd ring back that day with lots of exciting news. I haven't heard from her since.

So now I'm reduced to looking through the *Media Guardian,* looking for jobs I might just have half a chance of getting. So far, I've ringed a staff writer job on *Investor's Chronicle,* an assistant editorship of *Personal Investment Periodical,* and editor of *Annuities Today.* I don't know much about annuities, but I can always quickly read a book about it.

"How are you doing?" says Suze, coming into the room with a bowl of crunchy nut cornflakes.

"Fine," I say, trying to raise a smile. "I'll get there." Suze takes a mouthful of cereal and eyes me thoughtfully.

"What have you got planned for today?"

"Nothing much," I say morosely. "You know—just trying to get a job. Sort out my mess of a life. That kind of thing."

"Oh right." Suze pulls a sympathetic face. "Have you found anything interesting yet?"

I flick my fingers toward a ringed advertisement.

"I thought I'd go for editor of *Annuities Today*. The right candidate may also be considered for editorship of the annual *Tax Rebate* supplement!"

"Really?" She involuntarily pulls a face—then hastily adds, "I mean . . . that sounds good! Really interesting!"

"Tax rebates? Suze, please."

"Well—you know. Relatively speaking."

I rest my head on my knees and stare at the sitting-room carpet. The sound on the television has been turned down, and there's silence in the room apart from Suze munching. I close my eyes and slump down farther on the floor, until my head's resting on the sofa seat. I feel as though I could stay here for the rest of my life.

"Bex, I'm worried about you," says Suze. "You haven't been out for days. What else are you planning to do today?"

I open my eyes briefly and see her peering anxiously down at me.

"Dunno. Watch *Morning Coffee*."

"You are *not* watching *Morning Coffee*!" says Suze

firmly. "Come on." She closes the *Media Guardian*. "I've had a really good idea."

"What?" I say suspiciously as she drags me to my room. She swings open the door, leads me inside, and spreads her arms around, gesturing to the mess everywhere.

"I think you should spend the morning decluttering."

"What?" I stare at her in horror. "I don't want to declutter."

"Yes, you do! Honestly, you'll feel so great, like I did. It was brilliant! I felt so good afterward."

"Yes, and you had no clothes! You had to borrow knickers from me for three weeks!"

"Well, OK," she concedes. "Maybe I went a bit too far. But the point is, it completely transforms your life."

"No, it doesn't."

"It does! It's feng shui! You have to let things *out* of your life to allow the new good things *in*."

"Yeah, right."

"It's true! The moment I decluttered, I got Hadleys phoning me up with an offer. Come on, Bex . . . Just a little bit of decluttering would do you a world of good."

She throws open my wardrobe and begins to leaf through my clothes.

"I mean, look at this," she says, pulling out a blue fringed suede skirt. "When did you last wear that?"

"Erm . . . quite recently," I say, crossing my fingers behind my back. I bought that skirt off a stall in the Portobello Road without trying it on—and when I got it home it was too small. But you never know, I might lose loads of weight one day.

"And these . . . and these . . ." She gives an incredulous frown. "Blimey, Bex, how many pairs of black trousers have you got?"

"Only one! Two, maybe."

"Four . . . five . . . six . . ." She's leafing through the hangers, sternly plucking out pairs of trousers.

"Those ones are just for when I feel fat," I say defensively as she pulls out my comfy old Benetton boot-cuts. "And those are jeans!" I exclaim as she starts rooting around at the bottom. "Jeans don't count as trousers!"

"Says who?"

"Says everybody! It's common knowledge!"

"Ten . . . eleven . . ."

"Yeah . . . and those are for skiing! They're a completely different thing! They're *sportswear.*" Suze turns to look at me.

"Bex, you've never been skiing."

"I know," I say after a short silence. "But . . . you know. Just in case I ever get asked. And they were on sale."

"And what's this?" She picks up my fencing mask gingerly. "This could go straight in the bin."

"I'm taking up fencing!" I say indignantly. "I'm going to be Catherine Zeta-Jones's stunt double!"

"I don't even understand how you can fit all this stuff in here. Don't you *ever* chuck things out?" She picks up a pair of shoes decorated with shells. "I mean, these. Do you ever wear these anymore?"

"Well . . . no." I see her expression. "But that's not the point. If I did chuck them out, then shells would come back in the next day—and I'd have to buy a new pair. So this is like . . . insurance."

"Shells are *never* going to come back in."

"They might! It's like the weather. You just can't tell."

Suze shakes her head, and picks her way over the piles of stuff on the floor toward the door. "I'm giving you two hours and when I come back I want to see a transformed room. Transformed room—transformed life. Now start!"

She disappears out of the room and I sit on my bed, staring disconsolately around at my room.

Well, OK, maybe she does have a point. Maybe I should have a little tidy-up. But I don't even know where to start. I mean, if I start throwing things out just because I never wear them—where will I stop? I'll end up with nothing.

And it's all so hard. It's all so much *effort*.

I pick up a jumper, look at it for a few seconds, then put it down again. Just the thought of trying to decide whether to keep it or not exhausts me.

"How are you doing?" comes Suze's voice from outside the door.

"Fine!" I call back brightly. "Really good!"

Come on, I've got to do something. OK, maybe I should start in one corner, and work my way round. I pick my way to the corner of my room, where a heap of stuff is teetering on my dressing table, and try to work out what everything is. There's all that office equipment I ordered off the Internet . . . There's that wooden bowl I bought ages ago because it was in *Elle Decoration* (and then saw exactly the same one in Woolworth's) . . . a tie-dye kit . . . some sea salt for doing body rubs . . . What *is* all this stuff, anyway? What's this box which I haven't even opened?

I open up the package and stare at a fifty-meter roll of turkey foil. Turkey foil? Why would I buy that? Was I once planning to cook a turkey? Puzzledly I reach for the letter on top, and see the words, "Welcome to the world of Country Ways. We're so pleased your good friend, Mrs. Jane Bloomwood, recommended our catalogue to you . . ."

Oh God, of course. It's just that stuff Mum ordered to get her free gift. A casserole dish, some turkey foil . . . some of those plastic bags she was stuffing patio cushions into . . . some weird gadget for putting in the . . .

Hang on.

Just hang on a minute. I drop the gadget and slowly reach for the plastic bags again. A woman with a dodgy blond haircut is staring proudly at me over a shrink-wrapped duvet, and a bubble from her mouth reads, "With up to 75 percent reduction, I have so much more room in my closet now!"

Cautiously I open my door, and tiptoe along to the broom cupboard. As I pass the sitting room I look in—and to my astonishment Suze is sitting on the sofa with Tarquin, talking earnestly.

"Tarquin!" I say, and both their heads jerk up guiltily. "I didn't hear you arrive."

"Hello, Becky," he says, not meeting my eye.

"We just had to . . . talk about something," says Suze, giving me an embarrassed look. "Have you finished?"

"Erm . . . nearly," I say. "I just thought I'd hoover my room. To make it look really good!"

I shut my door behind me, and pull the bags out of their packaging. Right. This should be nice and easy. Just stuff them full, and suck out the air. Ten sweaters per bag, it says—but frankly, who's going to count?

I start to stuff clothes into the first bag, until it's as tightly packed as I can get it. Panting with effort, I close the plastic zip—then attach the hoover nozzle to the hole. And I don't believe this. It works. It works! Before my eyes, my clothes are shrinking away into nothing!

Oh, this is fantastic. This is going to revolutionize

my life! Why on earth declutter when you can just shrink-wrap?

There are eight bags in all—and when they're all full, I cram them all into my wardrobe and close the door. It's a bit of a tight squash—and I can hear a bit of a hissing sound as I force the door shut—but the point is, they're in. They're contained.

And just look at my room now! It's incredible! OK, it's not exactly immaculate—but it's so much better than it was before. I quickly shove a few stray items under my duvet, arrange some cushions on top, and stand back. As I look around, I feel all warm and proud of myself. I've never seen my room look so good before. And Suze is right—I do feel different, somehow.

You know, maybe feng shui's got something to it after all. Maybe this is the turning point. My life will be transformed from now on.

I take one final admiring look at it, then call out the door, "I'm done!"

As Suze comes to the door I perch smugly on the bed and beam at her astounded expression.

"Bex, this is fantastic!" she says, peering disbelievingly around the cleared space. "And you're so quick! It took me ages to sort all my stuff out!"

"Well, you know." I shrug nonchalantly. "Once I decide to do something, I do it."

She takes a few steps in, and looks in astonishment at my dressing table.

"I never knew that dressing table had a marble top!"

"I know!" I say proudly. "It's quite nice, isn't it?"

"But where's all the rubbish? Where are the bin bags?"

"They're . . . I've already got rid of them."

"So did you chuck loads out?" she says, wandering

over to the almost-empty mantelpiece. "You must have done!"

"A . . . a fair amount," I say evasively. "You know. I was quite ruthless in the end."

"I'm so impressed!" She pauses in front of the wardrobe, and I stare at her, suddenly nervous.

Don't open it, I pray silently. Just *don't* open it.

"Have you got anything left?" she says, with a grin, and pulls open the door of the wardrobe. And we both scream.

It's like a nail-bomb explosion.

Except, instead of nails, it's clothes.

I don't know what happened. I don't know *what* I did wrong. But one of the bags bursts open, showering jumpers everywhere, and pushing all the other bags out. Then another one bursts open, and another one. It's a clothes storm. Suze is completely covered in stretchy tops. A sequined skirt lands on the light shade. A bra shoots across the room and hits the window. Suze is half-shrieking and half-laughing, and I'm flapping my arms madly and yelling, "Stop! Stop!"

And oh no.

Oh no. Please stop. Please.

But it's too late. Now a cascade of gift-shop carrier bags is tumbling down from their hiding place on the top shelf. One after another, out into the daylight. They're hitting Suze on the head, landing on the floor, and spilling open—and revealing the same contents in each. Gray sparkly boxes with a silver S C-S scrawled on the front.

About forty of them.

"What . . ." Suze pulls a T-shirt off her head and stares at them, openmouthed. "Where on earth did you . . ." She scrabbles among the clothes littering the floor, picks up one of the boxes, and pulls it open and stares in silence. There, wrapped in turquoise tissue paper, is a photo frame made out of tan leather.

Oh God. Oh God.

Without saying anything, Suze bends down and picks up a Gifts and Goodies carrier bag. As she pulls it open, a receipt flutters to the floor. Silently she takes out the two boxes inside—and opens each to reveal a frame made of purple tweed.

I open my mouth to speak—but nothing comes out. For a moment we just stare at each other.

"Bex . . . how many of these have you got?" says Suze at last, in a slightly strangled voice.

"Um . . . not many!" I say, feeling my face grow hot. "Just . . . you know. A few."

"There must be about . . . fifty here!"

"No!"

"Yes!" She looks around, cheeks growing pink with distress. "Bex, these are really expensive."

"I haven't bought that many!" I give a distracting laugh. "And I didn't buy them all at once . . ."

"You shouldn't have bought *any*! I told you, I'd make you one!"

"I know," I say a little awkwardly. "I know you did. But I wanted to buy one. I just wanted to . . . to support you."

There's silence as Suze reaches for another Gifts and Goodies bag, and looks at the two boxes inside.

"It's you, isn't it?" she says suddenly. "You're the reason I've sold so well."

"It's not! Honestly, Suze—"

"You've spent all your money on buying my frames." Her voice starts to wobble. "All your money. And now you're in debt."

"I haven't!"

"If it weren't for you, I wouldn't have my deal!"

"You would!" I say in dismay. "Of course you would! Suze, you make the best frames in the world! I mean . . . look at this one!" I grab for the nearest box and pull out a frame made out of distressed denim. "I would have bought this even if I hadn't known you. I would have bought all of them!"

"You wouldn't have bought this many," she gulps. "You would have bought maybe . . . three."

"I would have bought them all! They're the best frames in the world! They'd make a perfect present, or a . . . an ornament for the house . . ."

"You're just saying that," she says tearfully.

"No, I'm not!" I say, feeling tears coming to my own eyes. "Suze, everybody loves your frames. I've seen people in shops saying how brilliant they are!"

"No, you haven't."

"I have! There was this woman admiring one in Gifts and Goodies, just the other day, and everyone in the shop was agreeing!"

"Really?" says Suze in a small voice.

"Yes. You're so talented, and successful . . ." I look around my bomb-site room, and feel a sudden wave of despair. "And I'm such a mess. John Gavin's right, I should have assets by now. I should be all sorted out. I'm just . . . worthless." Tears start to trickle down my face.

"You're not!" says Suze in horror. "You're not worthless!"

"I am!" Miserably, I sink to the carpet of clothes on the floor. "Suze, just look at me. I'm unemployed, I haven't got any prospects, I'm being taken to court, I owe thousands and thousands of pounds, and I don't know how I'm even going to start paying it all off . . ."

There's an awkward cough at the door. I look up, and Tarquin is standing at the door, holding three mugs of coffee.

"Refreshments?" he says, picking his way across the floor.

"Thanks, Tarquin," I say, sniffing, and take a mug from him. "Sorry about all this. It's just . . . not a great time."

He sits down on the bed and exchanges looks with Suze.

"Bit short of cash?" he says.

"Yes," I gulp, and wipe my eyes. "Yes, I am." Tarquin gives Suze another glance.

"Becky, I'd be only too happy to—"

"No. No, thanks." I smile at him. "Really."

There's silence as we all sip our coffee. A shaft of winter sunlight is coming through the window, and I close my eyes, feeling the soothing warmth on my face.

"Happens to the best of us," says Tarquin sympathetically. "Mad Uncle Monty was always going bust, wasn't he, Suze?"

"God, that's right! All the time!" says Suze. "But he always bounced back, didn't he?"

"Absolutely!" says Tarquin. "Over and over again."

"What did he do?" I say, looking up with a spark of interest.

"Usually sold off a Rembrandt," says Tarquin. "Or a Stubbs. Something like that."

Great. What is it about these millionaires? I mean, even Suze, who I love. They just don't get it. They *don't know what it's like to have no money.*

"Right," I say, trying to smile. "Well . . . unfortunately, I don't have any spare Rembrandts lying around. All I've got is . . . a zillion pairs of black trousers. And some T-shirts."

"And a fencing outfit," puts in Suze.

Next door, the phone starts ringing, but none of us moves.

"And a wooden bowl which I hate." I give a half-giggle, half-sob. "And forty photograph frames."

"And fifty million pots of lavender honey."

"And a Vera Wang cocktail dress." I look around my room, suddenly alert. "And a brand-new Kate Spade bag . . . and . . . and a whole wardrobe full of stuff which I've never even worn . . . Suze . . ." I'm almost too agitated to speak. "Suze . . ."

"What?"

"Just . . . just think about it. I haven't got nothing. I *have* got assets! I mean, they might have depreciated a little bit . . ."

"What do you mean?" says Suze puzzledly—then her face lights up. "Ooh, have you got an ISA that you forgot about?"

"No! Not an ISA!"

"I don't understand!" wails Suze. "Bex, what are you talking about?"

And I'm just opening my mouth to answer, when the answer machine clicks on next door, and a gravelly American voice starts speaking, which makes me stiffen and turn my head.

"Hello, Becky? It's Michael Ellis here. I've just arrived in London for a conference, and I was wondering— could we perhaps meet up for a chat?"

It's so weird to see Michael here in London. In my mind he belongs firmly in New York, in the Four Seasons. Back in that other world. But here he is, large as life, in the River Room at the Savoy, his face creased in a beam. As I sit down at the table he lifts a hand to a waiter.

"A gin and tonic for the lady, please." He raises his eyebrows at me. "Am I right?"

"Yes, please." I smile at him gratefully, and shake out my napkin to cover my awkwardness. Even though we talked so much in New York, I'm feeling a bit shy at seeing him again.

"So," he says, as the waiter brings me my drink. "Quite a lot has been going on since we last spoke." He lifts his glass. "Cheers."

"Cheers." I take a sip. "Like what?"

"Like Alicia Billington and four others have been fired from Brandon Communications."

"*Four* others?" I gape at him. "Were they all planning together?"

"Apparently so. It turns out Alicia has been working on this little project for some time. This wasn't just some tiny little pie-in-the-sky scheme. This was well organized and thought out. Well backed, too. You know Alicia's future husband is very wealthy?"

"I didn't," I say, and remember her Chanel shoes. "But it makes sense."

"He put together the finance. As you suspected, they were planning to poach Bank of London."

I take a sip of gin and tonic, relishing the sharp flavor.

"So what happened?"

"Luke swooped in, took them all by surprise, herded them into a meeting room, and searched their desks. And he found plenty."

"Luke did?" I feel a deep thud in my stomach. "You mean—Luke's in London?"

"Uh-huh."

"How long has he been back?"

"Three days now." Michael gives me a quick glance. "I guess he hasn't called you, then."

"No," I say, trying to hide my disappointment. "No, he hasn't." I reach for my glass and take a deep swig. Somehow while he was still in New York, I could tell myself that Luke and I weren't speaking because of geography as much as anything else. But now he's in London—and he hasn't even called—it feels different. It feels kind of . . . final.

"So . . . what's he doing now?"

"Damage limitation," says Michael wryly. "Upping morale. It turns out as soon as he left for New York, Alicia got busy spreading rumors he was going to close the U.K. branch down completely. That's why the atmosphere plummeted. Clients have been neglected, the staff has all been on the phone to headhunters . . . Meanwhile Alicia was spinning a completely different story to Luke." He shakes his head. "That girl is trouble."

"I know."

"Now, that's something I've been wondering. *How* do you know?" He leans forward interestedly. "You picked up on Alicia in a way neither Luke nor I did. Was that based on anything?"

"Not really," I say honestly. "Just the fact that she's a complete cow."

Michael throws his head back and roars with laughter.

"Feminine intuition. Why should there be any other reason?"

He chuckles for a few moments more—then puts his glass down and gives me a twinkling smile. "Speaking of which—I heard the gist of what you said to Luke about his mom."

"Really?" I look at him in horror. "He told you?"

"He spoke to me about it, asked if you'd said anything to me."

"Oh!" I feel a flush creeping across my face. "Well, I was . . . angry. I didn't *mean* to say she was a . . ." I clear my throat. "I just spoke without thinking."

"He took it to heart, though." Michael raises his eyebrows. "He called his mom up, said he was damned if he was going to go home without seeing her, and arranged a meeting."

"Really?" I stare at him, feeling prickles of intrigue. "And what happened?"

"She never showed up. Sent some message about having to go out of town. Luke was pretty disappointed." Michael shakes his head. "Between you and me—I think you were right about her."

"Oh. Well."

I give an awkward shrug and reach for the menu to hide my embarrassment. I can't *believe* Luke told Michael what I said about his mother. What else did he tell him? My bra size?

For a while I stare at the list of dishes without taking any of them in—then look up, to see Michael gazing seriously at me.

"Becky, I haven't told Luke it was you who tipped me off. The story I've given him is I got an anonymous message and decided to look into it."

"That sounds fair enough," I say, gazing at the tablecloth.

"You're basically responsible for saving his company," says Michael gently. "He should be very grateful to you. Don't you think he should know?"

"No." I hunch my shoulders. "He'd just think . . . he'd think I was . . ." I break off, feeling my eyes grow hot.

I can't believe Luke's been back for three days and hasn't called. I mean—I knew it was over. Of course I did. But secretly, a tiny part of me thought . . .

Anyway. Obviously not.

"What would he think?" probes Michael.

"I dunno," I mutter gruffly. "The point is, it's all over between us. So I'd rather just . . . not be involved."

"Well, I guess I can understand that." Michael gives me a kind look. "Shall we order?"

While we eat, we talk about other things. Michael tells me about his advertising agency in Washington, and makes me laugh with stories of all the politicians he knows and all the trouble they get themselves into. I tell him in turn about my family, and Suze, and the way I got my job on *Morning Coffee*.

"It's all going really well, actually," I say boldly as I dig into a chocolate mousse. "I've got great prospects, and the producers really like me . . . they're thinking of expanding my slot . . ."

"Becky," interrupts Michael gently. "I heard. I know about your job."

I stare at him dumbly, feeling my whole face prickle in shame.

"I felt really bad for you," continues Michael. "That shouldn't have happened."

"Does . . . does Luke know?" I say huskily.

"Yes. I believe he does."

I take a deep swig of my drink. I can't bear the idea of Luke pitying me.

"Well, I've got lots of options open," I say desperately. "I mean, maybe not on television . . . but I'm applying for a number of financial journalism posts . . ."

"On the *FT*?"

"On . . . well . . . on *Personal Investment Periodical* . . . and *Annuities Today* . . ."

"*Annuities Today*," echoes Michael disbelievingly. At his expression I can't help giving a snort of shaky laughter. "Becky, do any of these jobs really excite you?"

I'm about to trot out my stock answer—"Personal finance is more interesting than you'd think, actually!" But suddenly I realize I can't be bothered to pretend anymore. Personal finance *isn't* more interesting than you'd think. It's just as boring as you'd think. Even on *Morning Coffee,* it was only really when callers started talking about their relationships and family lives that I used to enjoy it.

"What do you think?" I say instead, and take another swig of gin and tonic.

Michael sits back in his chair and dabs his mouth with a napkin. "So why are you going for them?"

"I don't know what else to do." I give a hopeless shrug. "Personal finance is the only thing I've ever done. I'm kind of . . . pigeonholed."

"How old are you, Becky? If you don't mind my asking?"

"Twenty-six."

"Pigeonholed at twenty-six." Michael shakes his head. "I don't think so." He takes a sip of coffee and gives me an appraising look.

"If some opportunity came up for you in America," he says, "would you take it?"

"I'd take anything," I say frankly. "But what's going to come up for me in America now?"

There's silence. Thoughtfully, Michael reaches for a chocolate mint, unwraps it, and puts it in his mouth.

"Becky, I have a proposition for you," he says, looking up. "We have an opening at the advertising agency for a head of corporate communications."

I stare at him, glass halfway to my lips. Not daring to hope he's saying what I think he is.

"We want someone with editorial skills, who can co-ordinate a monthly newsletter. You'd be ideal on those counts. But we also want someone who's good with people. Someone who can pick up on the buzz, make sure people are happy, report to the board on any problems . . ." He shrugs. "Frankly, I can't think of anyone better suited to it."

"You're . . . you're offering me a job," I say disbelievingly, trying to ignore the little leaps of hope inside my chest, the little stabs of excitement. "But . . . but what about *The Daily World*? The . . . shopping?"

"So what?" Michael shrugs. "So you like to shop. I like to eat. Nobody's perfect. As long as you're not on some international 'most wanted' blacklist . . ."

"No. No," I say hurriedly. "In fact, I'm about to sort all that out."

"And immigration?"

"I've got a lawyer." I bite my lip. "I'm not sure he exactly likes me very much . . ."

"I have contacts in immigration," says Michael reassuringly. "I'm sure we can sort something out." He leans back and takes a sip of coffee. "Washington isn't New York. But it's a fun place to be, too. Politics is a fascinating arena. I have a feeling you'd take to it. And the salary . . . Well. It won't be what CNN might have offered you. But as a ballpark . . ." He scribbles a figure on a piece of paper and pushes it across the table.

And I don't believe it. It's about twice what I'd get for any of those crappy journalism jobs.

Washington. An advertising agency. A whole new career.

America. Without Luke. On my own terms.

I can't quite get my head round all of this.

"Why are you offering this to me?" I manage at last.

"I've been very impressed by you, Becky," says Michael seriously. "You're smart. You're intuitive. I took your advice about my friend, by the way," he adds with a twinkle. "He paid up the next day."

"Really?" I say in delight.

"You have a good head on your shoulders—and you're someone who gets things done." I stare at him, feeling an embarrassed color come to my cheeks. "And maybe I figured you deserve a break," he adds kindly. "Now, you don't have to decide at once. I'm over here for a few more days, so if you want to, we can talk again about it. But, Becky—"

"Yes?"

"I'm serious now. Whether you decide to take up my offer or not, don't fall into anything else." He shakes his head. "You're too young to settle. Look into your heart—and go after what you really want."

Sixteen

I DON'T DECIDE straight away. It takes me about two weeks of pacing around the flat, drinking endless cups of coffee, talking to my parents, Suze, Michael, my old boss Philip, this new television agent Cassandra . . . basically everyone I can think of. But in the end I know. I know in my heart what I really want to do.

Luke hasn't called—and to be honest, I shouldn't think I'll ever speak to him again. Michael says he's working about seventeen hours a day—trying simultaneously to salvage Brandon Communications and keep interest open in the States—and is very stressed indeed. Apparently he still hasn't got over the shock of discovering that Alicia was plotting against him—and that Bank of London was still considering moving with her. The shock of discovering he wasn't "immune to shit," as Michael so poetically put it. "That's the trouble with having the whole world love you," he said to me the other day. "One day, you wake up and it's flirting with your best friend instead. And you don't know what to do. You're thrown."

"So—has Luke been thrown by all this?" I asked, twisting my fingers into a knot.

"Thrown?" exclaimed Michael. "He's been hurled across the paddock and trampled on by a herd of wild boar."

Several times I've picked up the phone with a sudden longing to speak to him. But then I've always taken a deep breath and put it down again. That's his life now. I've got to get on with mine. My whole new life.

There's a sound at the door, and I look round. Suze is standing in the doorway, staring into my empty room.

"Oh, Bex," she says miserably. "I don't like it. Put it all back. Make it messy again."

"At least it's all feng shui now," I say, attempting a smile. "It'll probably bring you loads of luck."

She comes in and walks across the empty carpet to the window, then turns round.

"It seems smaller," she says slowly. "It should look bigger without all your clutter, shouldn't it? But somehow . . . it doesn't work like that. It looks like a nasty bare little box."

There's silence for a while as I watch a tiny spider climbing up the windowpane.

"Have you decided what you're going to do with it?" I say at last. "Are you going to get a new flatmate?"

"I don't think so," says Suze. "I mean, there's no rush, is there. Tarkie said why not just have it as my office for a while."

"Did he?" I turn to look at her with raised eyebrows. "That reminds me. Did I hear Tarquin here again last night? And creeping out this morning?"

"No," says Suze, looking flustered. "I mean—yes." She catches my eye and blushes. "But it was completely the last ever time. Ever."

"You make such a lovely couple," I say, grinning at her.

"Don't *say* that!" she exclaims in horror. "We're not a couple."

"OK," I say, relenting. "Whatever." I look at my watch. "You know, we ought to be going."

"Yes. I suppose so. Oh, Bex—"

I look at Suze—and her eyes are suddenly full of tears.

"I know." I squeeze her hand tightly and for a moment neither of us says anything. Then I reach for my coat. "Come on."

We walk along to the King George pub at the end of the road. We make our way through the bar and up a flight of wooden stairs to a large private room furnished with red velvet curtains, a bar, and lots of trestle tables set up on both sides. A makeshift platform has been set up at one end, and there are rows of plastic chairs in the middle.

"Hello!" says Tarquin, spotting us as we enter. "Come and have a drink." He lifts his glass. "The red's not at all bad."

"Is the tab all set up behind the bar?" says Suze.

"Absolutely," says Tarquin. "All organized."

"Bex—that's on us," says Suze, putting her hand on me as I reach for my purse. "A good-bye present."

"Suze, you don't have to—"

"I wanted to," she says firmly. "So did Tarkie."

"Let me get you some drinks," says Tarquin—then adds, lowering his voice, "It's a pretty good turnout, don't you think?"

As he walks off, Suze and I turn to survey the room. There are tables set out round the room, and people are milling around, looking at neatly folded piles of clothes, shoes, CDs, and assorted bits of bric-a-brac. On one table is a pile of typed, photocopied catalogues, and people are marking them as they wander round.

I can hear a girl in leather jeans saying, "Look at this coat! Ooh, and these Hobbs boots! I'm definitely going to bid for those!" On the other side of the room, two girls are trying pairs of trousers up against themselves while their boyfriends patiently hold their drinks.

"Who *are* all these people?" I say disbelievingly. "Did you invite them all?"

"Well, I went down my address book," says Suze. "And Tarquin's address book. And Fenny's . . ."

"Oh well," I say with a laugh. "That explains it."

"Hi, Becky!" says a bright voice behind me—and I swivel round to see Fenella's friend Milla, with a pair of girls I half-recognize. "I'm going to bid for your purple cardigan! And Tory's going to go for that dress with the fur, and Annabel's seen about six thousand things she wants! We were just wondering, is there an accessories section?"

"Over there," says Suze, pointing to the corner of the room.

"Thanks!" says Milla. "See you later!" The three girls trip off into the melee, and I hear one of them saying, "I *really* need a good belt . . ."

"Becky!" says Tarquin, suddenly coming up behind me. "Here's some wine. And let me introduce Caspar, my chum from Christie's."

"Oh hello!" I say, turning round to see a guy with floppy blond hair, a blue shirt, and an enormous gold signet ring. "Thank you so much for doing this! I'm really grateful."

"Not at all, not at all," says Caspar. "Now, I've been

through the catalogue and it all seems fairly straightforward. Do you have a list of reserve prices?"

"No," I say without pausing. "No reserves. Everything must go."

"Fine." He smiles at me. "Well, I'll go and get set up."

As he walks off I take a sip of my wine. Suze has gone off to look round some of the tables, so I stand alone for a while, watching as the crowd grows. Fenella arrives at the door, and I give her a wave—but she's immediately swallowed up in a group of shrieking friends.

"Hi, Becky," comes a hesitant voice behind me. I wheel round in shock, and find myself staring up at Tom Webster.

"Tom!" I exclaim in shock. "What are you doing here? How do you know about this?" He takes a sip from his glass and gives a little grin.

"Suze called your mum, and she told me all about it. She and my mum have put in some orders, actually." He pulls a list out of his pocket. "Your mum wants your cappuccino maker. If it's for sale."

"Oh, it's for sale," I say. "I'll tell the auctioneer to make sure you get it."

"And my mum wants that pink hat you wore to our wedding."

"Right. No problem." At the reminder of his wedding, I feel myself growing slightly warm.

"So—how's married life?" I say, examining one of my nails.

"Oh . . . it's all right," he says after a pause.

"Is it as blissful as you expected?" I say, trying to sound lighthearted.

"Well, you know . . ." He stares into his glass, a slightly hunted look in his eye. "It would be unrealistic to expect everything to be perfect straight off. Wouldn't it?"

"I suppose so."

There's an awkward silence between us. In the distance I can hear someone saying, "Kate Spade! Look, brand-new!"

"Becky, I'm really sorry," says Tom in a rush. "The way we behaved toward you at the wedding."

"That's all right!" I say, a little too brightly.

"It's not all right." He shakes his head. "Your mum was bang on. You're one of my oldest friends. I've been feeling really bad, ever since."

"Honestly, Tom. It was my fault, too. I mean, I should have just admitted Luke wasn't there!" I smile ruefully. "It would have been a lot simpler."

"But if Lucy was giving you a hard time, I can really understand why you felt you just had to . . . to . . ." He breaks off, and takes a deep swig of his drink. "Anyway. Luke seemed like a nice guy. Is he coming tonight?"

"No," I say after a pause, and force a smile. "No, he isn't."

After half an hour or so, people begin to take their seats on the rows of plastic chairs. At the back of the room are five or six friends of Tarquin's holding mobile phones, and Caspar explains to me that they're on the line to telephone bidders.

"They're people who heard about it but couldn't come, for whatever reason. We've been circulating the catalogues fairly widely, and a lot of people are interested. The Vera Wang dress alone attracted a great deal of attention."

"Yes," I say, feeling a sudden lurch of emotion, "I expect it did." I look around the room, at the bright, expectant faces, at the people still taking a last look at the tables. A girl is leafing through a pile of jeans; someone else is trying out the clasp on my dinky little white case. I can't quite believe that after tonight, none of these things will be mine anymore. They'll be in other people's wardrobes. Other people's rooms.

"Are you all right?" says Caspar, following my gaze.

"Yes!" I say brightly. "Why shouldn't I be all right?"

"I've done a lot of house sales," he says kindly. "I know what it's like. One gets very attached to one's possessions. Whether it's an eighteenth-century chiffonier, or . . ." He glances at the catalogue. "A pink leopard-print coat."

"Actually—I never much liked that coat." I gave him a resolute smile. "And anyway, that's not the point. I want to start again and I think—I *know*—this is the best way." I smile at him. "Come on. Let's get going, shall we?"

"Absolutely." He raps on his lectern and raises his voice. "Ladies and gentlemen! First, on behalf of Becky Bloomwood, I'd like to welcome you all here this evening. We've got quite a lot to get through, so I won't delay you—except to remind you that 25 percent of everything raised tonight is going to a range of charities—plus any remainder of the proceeds after Becky has paid off all her outstanding accounts."

"I hope they're not holding their breath," says a dry voice from the back, and everyone laughs. I peer through the crowd to see who it is—and I don't believe it. It's Derek Smeath, standing there with a pint in one hand, a catalogue in the other. He gives me a little smile, and I give a shy wave back.

"How did he know about this?" I hiss to Suze, who has come to join me on the platform.

"I told him, of course!" she says. "He said he thought it was a marvelous idea. He said when you use your brain, no one comes near you for ingenuity."

"Really?" I glance at Derek Smeath again and flush slightly.

"So," says Caspar. "I present Lot One. A pair of clementine sandals, very good condition, hardly worn." He lifts them onto the table and Suze squeezes my hand sympathetically. "Do I have any bids?"

"I bid £15,000," says Tarquin, sticking up his hand at once.

"Fifteen thousand pounds," says Caspar, sounding a bit taken aback. "I have a bid of £15,000—"

"No, you don't!" I interrupt. "Tarquin, you can't bid £15,000!"

"Why not?"

"You have to bid *realistic* prices." I give him a stern look. "Otherwise you'll be banned from the bidding."

"OK . . . £1,000."

"No! You can bid . . . £10," I say firmly.

"All right, then. Ten pounds." He puts his hand down meekly.

"Fifteen pounds," comes a voice from the back.

"Twenty!" cries a girl near the front.

"Twenty-five," says Tarquin.

"Thirty!"

"Thirt—" Tarquin catches my eye, blushes, and stops.

"Thirty pounds. Any further bids on 30 . . ." Caspar looks around the room, his eyes suddenly like a hawk's. "Going . . . going . . . gone! To the girl in the green velvet coat." He grins at me, scribbles something on a piece of paper, and hands the shoes to Fenella, who is in charge of distributing sold items.

"Your first £30!" whispers Suze in my ear.

"Lot Two!" says Caspar. "Three embroidered cardigans from Jigsaw, unworn, with price tags still attached. Can I start the bidding at . . ."

"Twenty pounds!" says a girl in pink.

"Twenty-five!" cries another girl.

"I have a telephone bid of 30," says a guy raising his hand at the back.

"Thirty pounds from one of our telephone bidders . . . Any advance on 30? Remember, ladies and gentlemen, this *will* be raising funds for charity . . ."

"Thirty-five!" cries the girl in pink, and turns to her neighbor. "I mean, they'd be more than that each in the shop, wouldn't they? And they've never even been worn!"

God, she's right. I mean, thirty-five quid for three cardigans is nothing. Nothing!

"Forty!" I hear myself crying, before I can stop myself. The whole room turns to look at me, and I feel myself furiously blushing. "I mean . . . does anyone want to bid 40?"

The bidding goes on and on, and I can't believe how much money is being raised. My shoe collection raises at least £1,000, a set of Dinny Hall jewelry goes for £200—and Tom Webster bids £600 for my computer.

"Tom," I say anxiously, as he comes up to the platform to fill in his slip. "Tom, you shouldn't have bid all that money."

"For a brand-new Apple Mac?" says Tom. "It's worth it. Besides, Lucy's been saying she wants her own computer for a while." He gives a half-smile. "I'm kind of looking forward to telling her she's got your castoff."

"Lot Seventy-three," says Caspar beside me. "And one which I know is going to attract a great deal of interest. A Vera Wang cocktail dress." He slowly holds up the inky purple dress, and there's an appreciative gasp from the crowd.

But actually—I don't think I can watch this go. This is too painful, too recent. My beautiful glittering movie-star dress. I can't even look at it without remembering it all, like a slow-motion cine-film. Dancing with Luke in New York; drinking cocktails; that heady, happy excitement. And then waking up and seeing everything crash around me.

"Excuse me," I murmur, and get to my feet. I head quickly out of the room, down the stairs, and into the fresh evening air. I lean against the side of the pub, listening to the laughter and chatter inside, and take a few deep breaths, trying to focus on all the good reasons why I'm doing this.

A few moments later, Suze appears beside me.

"Are you OK?" she says, and hands me a glass of wine. "Here. Have some of this."

"Thanks," I say gratefully, and take a deep gulp. "I'm fine, really. It's just . . . I suppose it's just hitting me. What I'm doing."

"Bex . . ." She pauses and rubs her face awkwardly. "Bex, you could always change your mind. You could always stay. I mean—after tonight, with any luck, all your debts will be paid off! You could get a job, stay in the flat with me . . ."

I look at her for a few silent moments, feeling a temptation so strong, it almost hurts. It would be so easy to agree. Go home with her, have a cup of tea, and fall back into my old life.

But then I shake my head.

"No. I'm not going to fall into anything again. I've found something I really want to do, Suze, and I'm going to do it."

"Rebecca." A voice interrupts us, and we both look up to see Derek Smeath coming out of the door of the pub. He's holding the wooden bowl, one of Suze's photograph frames, and a big hard-backed atlas which I remember buying once when I thought I might give up my Western life and go traveling.

"Hi!" I say, and nod at his haul. "You did well."

"Very well." He holds the bowl up. "This is a very handsome piece."

"It was in *Elle Decoration* once," I tell him. "Very cool."

"Really? I'll tell my daughter." He puts it slightly awkwardly under his arm. "So you're off to America tomorrow."

"Yes. Tomorrow afternoon. After I've paid a small trip to your friend John Gavin."

A wry smile passes over Derek Smeath's face.

"I'm sure he'll be pleased to see you." He extends his hand as best he can to shake mine. "Well, good luck, Becky. Do let me know how you get on."

"I will," I say, smiling warmly. "And thanks for . . . You know. Everything."

He nods, and then walks off into the night.

I stay outside with Suze for quite a time. People are leaving now, carrying their loot, and telling each other how much they got it all for. A guy walks by clutching the mini paper shredder, a girl drags a bin liner full of clothes, someone else has got the invitations with the twinkly pizza slices. Just as I'm starting to get cold, a voice hails us from the stairs.

"Hey," calls Tarquin. "It's the last lot. D'you want to come and see?"

"Come on," says Suze, stubbing out her cigarette. "You've got to see the last thing go. What is it?"

"I don't know," I say as we mount the stairs. "The fencing mask, perhaps?"

But as we walk back into the room, I feel a jolt of shock. Caspar's holding up my Denny and George scarf. My precious Denny and George scarf. Shimmering blue, silky velvet, overprinted in a paler blue, and dotted with iridescent beading.

I stand staring at it, with a growing tightness in my throat, remembering with a painful vividness the day I bought it. How desperately I wanted it. How Luke lent me the twenty quid I needed. The way I told him I was buying it for my aunt.

The way he used to look at me whenever I wore it.

My eyes are going blurry, and I blink hard, trying to keep control of myself.

"Bex . . . don't sell your scarf," says Suze, looking at it in distress. "Keep one thing, at least."

"Lot 126," says Caspar. "A very attractive silk and velvet scarf."

"Bex, tell them you've changed your mind!"

"I haven't changed my mind," I say, staring fixedly ahead. "There's no point hanging on to it now."

"What am I bid for this fine designer accessory by Denny and George?"

"Denny and George!" says the girl in pink, looking up. She's got the hugest pile of clothes around her, and I've no idea how she's going to get them all home. "I collect Denny and George! Thirty pounds!"

"I have a bid at £30," says Caspar. He looks around

the room—but it's swiftly emptying. People are queuing up to collect their items, or buy drinks at the bar, and the very few left sitting on the chairs are mostly chatting.

"Any further bids for this Denny and George scarf?"

"Yes!" says a voice at the back, and I see a girl in black raising a hand. "I have a telephone bid of £35."

"Forty pounds," says the girl in pink promptly.

"Fifty," says the girl in black.

"Fifty?" says the pink girl, swiveling on her chair. "Who is it bidding? Is it Miggy Sloane?"

"The bidder wishes to remain anonymous," says the girl in black after a pause. She catches my eye and for an instant my heart stops still.

"I bet it's Miggy," says the girl, turning back. "Well, she's not going to beat me. Sixty pounds."

"Sixty pounds?" says the chap next to her, who's been eyeing her pile of stuff with slight alarm. "For a scarf?"

"A *Denny and George* scarf, stupid!" says the pink girl, and takes a swig of wine. "It would be at least two hundred in a shop. Seventy! Ooh, silly. It's not my turn, is it?"

The girl in black has been murmuring quietly into the phone. Now she looks up at Caspar. "A hundred."

"A hundred?" The pink girl swivels on her chair again. "Really?"

"The bidding stands at one hundred," says Caspar calmly. "I am bid £100 for this Denny and George scarf. Any further bids?"

"A hundred and twenty," says the pink girl. There are a few moments' silence, and the girl in black talks quietly into the phone again. Then she looks up and says, "A hundred and fifty."

There's an interested murmuring around the room, and people who had been chatting at the bar all turn toward the auction floor again.

"One hundred and fifty pounds," says Caspar. "I am bid £150 for Lot 126, a Denny and George scarf."

"That's more than I *paid* for it!" I whisper to Suze.

"Bidding rests with the telephone buyer. At £150. One hundred and fifty pounds, ladies and gentlemen."

There's a tense silence—and suddenly I realize I'm digging my nails into the flesh of my hands.

"Two hundred," says the girl in pink defiantly, and there's a gasp around the room. "And tell your so-called anonymous bidder, Miss Miggy Sloane, that whatever *she* bids, *I* can bid."

Everyone turns to look at the girl in black, who mutters something into the receiver, then nods her head.

"My bidder withdraws," she says, looking up. I feel an inexplicable pang of disappointment, and quickly smile to cover it.

"Two hundred pounds!" I say to Suze. "That's pretty good!"

"Going . . . going . . . gone," says Caspar, and raps his gavel. "To the lady in pink."

There's a round of applause, and Caspar beams happily around. He picks up the scarf, and is about to hand it to Fenella, when I stop him.

"Wait," I say. "I'd like to give it to her. If that's all right."

I take the scarf from Caspar and hold it quite still for a few moments, feeling its familiar gossamer texture. I can still smell my scent on it. I can feel Luke tying it round my neck.

The Girl in the Denny and George Scarf.

Then I take a deep breath and walk down, off the

platform, toward the girl in pink. I smile at her and hand it over to her.

"Enjoy it," I say. "It's quite special."

"Oh, I know," she says quietly. "I know it is." And just for a moment, as we look at each other, I think she understands completely. Then she turns and lifts it high into the air in triumph, like a trophy. "Sucks to you, Miggy!"

I turn away and walk back to the platform, where Caspar is sitting down, looking exhausted.

"Well done," I say, sitting down next to him. "And thank you so much again. You did a fantastic job."

"Not at all!" says Caspar. "I enjoyed it, actually. Bit of a change from early German porcelain." He gestures to his notes. "I think we raised a fair bit, too."

"You did brilliantly!" says Suze, coming to sit down too, and handing Caspar a beer. "Honestly, Bex, you'll be completely out of the woods now." She gives an admiring sigh. "You know, it just shows, you were right all along. Shopping *is* an investment. I mean, like, how much did you make on your Denny and George scarf?"

"Erm . . ." I close my eyes, trying to work it out. "About . . . 60 percent?"

"Sixty percent return! In less than a year! You see? That's better than the crummy old stock market!" She takes out a cigarette and lights it. "You know, I think I might sell all my stuff, too."

"You haven't got any stuff," I point out. "You decluttered it all."

"Oh yeah." Suze's face falls. "God, why did I do that?"

I lean back on my elbow and close my eyes. Suddenly, for no real reason, I feel absolutely exhausted.

"So you're off tomorrow," says Caspar, taking a swig of beer.

"I'm off tomorrow," I echo, staring up at the ceiling. Tomorrow I'm leaving England and flying off to America to live. Leaving everything behind and starting again. Somehow, it just doesn't feel real.

"Not one of these crack-of-dawn flights, I hope?" he says, glancing at his watch.

"No, thank God. I'm not flying until about five."

"That's good," says Caspar, nodding. "Gives you plenty of time."

"Oh yes." I sit up and glance at Suze, who grins back. "Plenty of time for just a couple of little things I've got to do."

"Becky! We're so glad you changed your mind!" cries Zelda as soon as she sees me. I get up from the sofa where I've been sitting in reception, and give her a quick smile. "Everyone's so thrilled you're coming on! What made you decide?"

"Oh, I'm not sure," I say pleasantly. "Just . . . one of those things."

"Well, let me take you straight up to makeup . . . we're completely chaotic, as usual, so we've brought your slot forward slightly . . ."

"No problem," I say. "The sooner the better."

"I have to say, you look very well," says Zelda, surveying me with a slight air of disappointment. "Have you lost weight?"

"A little, I suppose."

"Ah . . . stress," she says wisely. "Stress, the silent killer. We're doing a feature on it next week. Now!" she exclaims, bustling me into the makeup room. "This is Becky . . ."

"Zelda, we know who Becky is," says Chloe, who's

been doing my makeup ever since I first appeared on *Morning Coffee*. She pulls a face at me in the mirror and I stifle a giggle.

"Yes, of course you do! Sorry, Becky, I've just got you down in my mind as a guest! Now, Chloe. Don't do too good a job on Becky today. We don't want her looking too glowing and happy, do we?" She lowers her voice. "And use waterproof mascara. In fact, everything waterproof. See you later!"

Zelda sweeps out of the room, and Chloe shoots her a scornful glance.

"OK," she says. "I'm going to make you look as good as you've ever looked in your life. Extra happy and extra glowing."

"Thanks, Chloe," I say, grinning at her, and sit down on a chair.

"Oh, and please don't tell me you're really going to need waterproof mascara," she adds, tying a cape around me.

"No way," I say firmly. "They'll have to shoot me first."

"Then they probably will," says a girl from across the room, and we all start giggling helplessly.

"All I can say is, I hope they're paying you well to do this," says Chloe, as she starts to smooth foundation onto my skin.

"Yes," I say. "They are, as it happens. But that's not why I'm doing it."

Half an hour later, I'm sitting in the Green Room when Clare Edwards comes walking in. She's wearing a dark green suit that really doesn't do much for her—and is it my imagination, or has someone made her up far too pale? She's going to look really pasty under the lights.

"Oh," says Clare, looking discomfited as she sees me. "Hello, Becky."

"Hi, Clare," I say. "Long time no see."

"Yes. Well." She twists her hands into a knot. "I was very sorry to read of your troubles."

"Thanks," I say lightly. "Still—it's an ill wind, eh, Clare?"

Clare immediately blushes bright red and looks away—and I feel a bit ashamed of myself. It's not her fault I got sacked.

"Honestly, I'm really pleased you got the job," I say more kindly. "And I think you're doing it really well."

"Right!" says Zelda, hurrying in. "We're ready for you. Now, Becky." She puts a hand on my arm as we walk out. "I know this is going to be very traumatic for you. We're quite prepared for you to take your time . . . again, if you break down completely, start sobbing, whatever . . . don't worry."

"Thanks, Zelda," I say, and nod seriously. "I'll bear that in mind."

We get to the set, and there are Rory and Emma, sitting on the sofas. I glance at a monitor as I walk past, and see that they've blown up that awful picture of me in New York, tinted it red, and headlined it "Becky's Tragic Secret."

"Hi, Becky," says Emma, as I sit down, and pats me sympathetically on the hand. "Are you all right? Would you like a tissue?"

"Erm . . . no, thanks." I lower my voice. "But, you know. Perhaps later."

"Terrifically brave of you to come and do this," says

Rory, and squints at his notes. "Is it true your parents have disowned you?"

"Ready in five," calls Zelda from the floor. "Four . . . three . . ."

"Welcome back," says Emma somberly to camera. "Now, we've got a very special guest with us today. Thousands of you will have followed the story of Becky Bloomwood, our former financial expert. Becky was, of course, revealed by *The Daily World* to be far from financially secure herself."

The picture of me shopping appears on the monitor, followed by a series of tabloid headlines, accompanied by the song "Hey, Big Spender."

"So, Becky," says Emma, as the music dies away. "Let me begin by saying how *extremely* sorry and sympathetic we are for you in your plight. In a minute, we'll be asking our new financial expert, Clare Edwards, just what you should have done to prevent this catastrophe. But now—just to put our viewers straight . . . could you tell us exactly how much in debt you are?"

"I'd be glad to, Emma," I say, and take a deep breath. "At the present moment, my debt amounts to . . ." I pause, and I can feel the whole studio bracing itself for a shock. "Nothing."

"Nothing?" Emma looks at Rory as though to check she's heard correctly. *"Nothing?"*

"My overdraft facilities director, John Gavin, will be glad to confirm that this morning, at nine thirty, I paid off my overdraft completely. I've paid off every single debt I had."

I allow myself a tiny smile as I remember John Gavin's face this morning, as I handed over wads and wads of cash. I so wanted him to wriggle and squirm and look pissed off. But to give him his due, after the first couple of thousand he started smiling, and beckoning people round to watch. And at the end, he shook my hand really quite warmly—and said now he understood what Derek Smeath meant about me.

I wonder what old Smeathie can have said?

"So you see, I'm not really in a plight at all," I add. "In fact, I've never been better."

"Right . . ." says Emma. "I see." There's a distracted look in her eye—and I know Barry must be yelling something in her earpiece.

"But even if your money situation is temporarily sorted out, your life must still be in ruins." She leans forward sympathetically again. "You're unemployed . . . shunned by your friends . . ."

"On the contrary, I'm not unemployed. This afternoon I'm flying to the States, where I have a new career waiting for me. It's a bit of a gamble . . . and it'll certainly be a challenge. But I genuinely think I'll be happy there. And my friends . . ." My voice wobbles a little, and I take a deep breath. "It was my friends who helped me out. It was my friends who stood by me."

Oh God, I don't believe it. After all that, I've got bloody tears in my eyes. I blink them back as hard as I can, and smile brightly at Emma.

"So really, my story isn't one of failure. Yes, I got myself into debt; yes, I was fired. But I did something about it." I turn to the camera. "And I'd like to say to anyone out there who's got themselves in a mess like I did . . . you can get out of it, too. Take action. Sell all your clothes. Apply for a new job. You can start again, like I'm going to."

There's silence around the studio. Then suddenly, from behind one of the cameras, there's the sound of clapping. I look over in shock—and it's Dave, the cameraman. He grins at me and mouths "Well done." Suddenly Gareth the floor manager joins in . . . and someone else . . . and now the whole studio is applauding, apart from Emma and Rory, who are looking rather nonplussed—and Zelda, who's talking frantically into her mouthpiece.

"Well!" says Emma, over the sound of the applause. "Um . . . We're taking a short break now—but join us in a few moments to hear more on our lead story today: Becky's . . . Tragic . . . umm . . ." She hesitates, listening to her earpiece. ". . . or rather, Becky's . . . um, *Triumphant* . . . um . . ."

The signature tune blares out of a loudspeaker and she glances at the producer's box in irritation. "I wish he'd make up his bloody mind!"

"See you," I say, and get up. "I'm off now."

"Off?" says Emma. "You can't go yet!"

"Yes, I can." I reach toward my microphone, and Eddie the sound guy rushes forward to unclip it.

"Well said," he mutters as he unthreads it from my jacket. "Don't take their shit." He grins at me. "Barry's going ballistic up there."

"Hey, Becky!" Zelda's head jerks up in horror. "Where are you going?"

"I've said what I came to say. Now I've got a plane to catch."

"You can't leave now! We haven't finished!"

"I've finished," I say, and reach for my bag.

"But the phone lines are all red!" says Zelda, hurrying toward me. "The switchboard's jammed! The callers are all saying . . ." She stares at me as though she's never seen me before. "I mean, we had no idea. Who would ever have thought . . ."

"I've got to go, Zelda."

"Wait! Becky!" says Zelda as I reach the door of the studio. "We . . . Barry and I . . . we were having a quick little chat just now. And we were wondering whether . . ."

"Zelda," I interrupt gently. "It's too late. I'm going."

It's nearly three by the time I arrive at Heathrow Airport. I'm still a little flushed from the farewell lunch I had in the pub with Suze, Tarquin, and my parents. To be honest, there's a small part of me that feels like bursting into tears and running back to them all. But at the same time, I've never felt so confident in my life. I've never been so sure I'm doing the right thing.

There's a promotional stand in the center of the terminus, giving away free newspapers, and as I pass it, I reach for a *Financial Times*. Just for old times' sake. Plus, if I'm carrying the *FT*, I might get upgraded. I'm just folding it up to place it neatly under my arm, when I notice a name which makes me stop dead.

Brandon in bid to save company. Page 27.

With slightly shaky fingers, I unfold the paper, find the page, and read the story.

Financial PR entrepreneur Luke Brandon is fighting to keep his investors on board after severe loss of confidence following the recent defection of several senior employees. Morale is said to be low at the formerly groundbreaking PR agency, with rumors of an uncertain future for the company causing staff to break ranks. In crisis meetings to be held to-

*day, Brandon will be seeking to persuade backers to approve
his radical restructuring plans, which are said to involve* . . .

I read to the end of the piece, and gaze for a few seconds at Luke's picture. He looks as confident as ever—
but I remember Michael's remark about him being
hurled across the paddock. His world's crashed around
him, just like mine did. And chances are, his mum
won't be on the phone telling him not to worry.

For a moment I feel a twinge of pity for him. I almost
want to call him up and tell him things'll get better. But
there's no point. He's busy with his life—and I'm busy
with mine. So I fold the paper up again, and resolutely
walk forward to the check-in desk.

"Anything to check?" says the check-in girl, smiling
at me.

"No," I say. "I'm traveling light. Just me and my bag."
I casually lift my *FT* to a more prominent position. "I
don't suppose there's any chance of an upgrade?"

"Not today, sorry." She pulls a sympathetic face. "But
I can put you by the emergency exit. Plenty of legroom
there. If I could just weigh your bag, please?"

"Sure."

And I'm just bending down to put my little case on
the belt, when a familiar voice behind me exclaims,
"Wait!"

I feel a lurch inside as though I've just dropped
twenty feet. I turn disbelievingly—and it's him.

It's Luke, striding across the concourse toward the
check-in desk. He's dressed as smartly as ever, but his
face is pale and haggard. From the shadows under his
eyes he looks as though he's been existing on a diet of
late nights and coffee.

"Where the fuck are you going?" he demands as he gets nearer. "Are you moving to Washington?"

"What are you doing here?" I retort shakily. "Aren't you at some crisis meeting with your investors?"

"I was. Until Mel came in to hand round tea, and told me she'd seen you on the television this morning. So I called Suze and got the flight number out of her—"

"You just *left* your meeting?" I stare at him. "What, right in the middle?"

"She told me you're leaving the country." His dark eyes search my face. "Is that right?"

"Yes," I say, and clutch my little suitcase more tightly. "Yes, I am."

"Just like that? Without even telling me?"

"Yes, just like that," I say, plonking my case on the belt. "Just like you came back to Britain without even telling me." There's an edge to my voice, and Luke flinches.

"Becky—"

"Window or aisle seat?" interrupts the check-in girl.

"Window, please."

"Becky—"

His mobile phone gives a shrill ring, and he switches it off irritably. "Becky . . . I want to talk."

"*Now* you want to talk?" I echo disbelievingly. "Great. Perfect timing. Just as I'm checking in." I hit the *FT* with the back of my hand. "And what about this crisis meeting?"

"It can wait."

"The future of your company can *wait*?" I raise my eyebrows. "Isn't that a little . . . irresponsible, Luke?"

"My company wouldn't *have* a fucking future if it weren't for you," he exclaims, almost angrily, and in spite of myself I feel a tingling all over my body. "I've just been on the phone to Michael. He told me what you did. How you cottoned on to Alicia. How you warned him, how you sussed the whole thing." He shakes his head. "I had no idea. Jesus, if it hadn't been for you, Becky . . ."

"He shouldn't have told you," I mutter furiously. "I told him not to. He promised."

"Well, he did tell me! And now . . ." Luke breaks off. "And now I don't know what to say," he says more quietly. " 'Thank you' doesn't even come close."

We stare at each other in silence for a few moments.

"You don't have to say anything," I say at last, looking away. "I only did it because I can't stand Alicia. No other reason."

"So . . . I've put you on row thirty-two," says the check-in girl brightly. "Boarding should be at four thirty . . ." She takes one further look at my passport and her expression changes. "Hey! You're the one off *Morning Coffee,* aren't you?"

"I used to be," I say with a polite smile.

"Oh right," she says puzzledly. As she hands over my passport and boarding card, her eye runs over my *FT,* and stops at Luke's photograph. She looks up at Luke, and down again.

"Hang on. Are you him?" she says, jabbing at the picture.

"I used to be," says Luke after a pause. "Come on, Becky. Let me buy you a drink, at least."

We sit down at a little table with glasses of Pernod. I can see the light on Luke's phone lighting up every five seconds, indicating that someone's trying to call him. But he doesn't even seem to notice.

"I wanted to ring you," he says, staring into his drink. "Every single day, I wanted to ring. But . . . it's been so crazy since I got back. And what you said about me not having time for a real relationship? That really stuck with me. Plus . . ." He breaks off into silence.

"Plus what?" I say at last.

"I wasn't sure," he says, and looks up with frank brown eyes. "The truth is, I didn't know whether we could make it work. It seemed in New York that we suddenly split apart, and started going in different directions. It was as though we didn't understand each other anymore."

I should be able to hear this without reacting. But for some reason the back of my throat feels tight all over again.

"So—what happened?" I say, forcing myself to sound matter-of-fact. "Why are you here? The day when all your investors have flown in to see you."

"Not ideal. I'll give you that." A flicker of amusement passes briefly across his face. "But how was I to know you were planning to skip the country? Michael's been a secretive bastard. And when I heard you were leaving . . ." He meets my eyes. "I suddenly realized."

"Realized . . . what?" I manage.

"That I'd been a fucking . . . stupid . . ."

He pushes his glass around the table abstractly, as though searching for something, and I stare at him apprehensively. "You were right," he says suddenly. "I was obsessed with making it in New York. It was a kind of madness. I couldn't see anything else. Jesus, I've fucked everything up, haven't I? You . . . us . . . the business . . ."

"Come on, Luke," I say awkwardly. "You can't take credit for everything. I fucked up a good few things for you . . ." I stop as Luke shakes his head. He drains his glass and gives me a frank look.

"There's something you need to know. Becky—how do you think *The Daily World* got hold of your financial details?"

I look at him in surprise.

"It . . . it was the council tax girl. The girl who came to the flat and snooped around while Suze was . . ." I tail away as he shakes his head again.

"It was Alicia."

For a moment I'm too taken aback to speak.

"Alicia?" I manage at last. "How do you . . . why would she . . ."

"When we searched her office we found some bank statements of yours in her desk. Some letters, too. Christ alone knows how she got hold of them." He exhales sharply. "This morning, I finally got a guy at *The Daily World* to admit she was the source. They just followed up what she gave them."

I stare at him, feeling rather cold. Remembering that day I visited his office. The Conran bag with all my letters in it. Alicia standing by Mel's desk, looking like a cat with a mouse.

I *knew* I'd left something behind. Oh God, how could I have been so *stupid*?

"You weren't her real target," Luke's saying. "She did it to discredit me and the company—and distract my attention from what she was up to. They won't confirm it, but I'm sure she was also the 'inside source' giving all those quotes about me." He takes a deep breath. "The point is, Becky—I got it all wrong. My deal wasn't ruined because of you." He looks at me matter-of-factly. "Yours was ruined because of me."

I sit still for a few moments, unable to speak. It's as

though something heavy is slowly lifting from me. I'm not sure what to think or feel.

"I'm just so sorry," Luke's saying. "For everything you've been through . . ."

"No." I take a deep, shaky breath. "Luke, it wasn't your fault. It wasn't even Alicia's fault. Maybe she fed them the details. But I mean, if I hadn't got myself into debt in the first place, and if I hadn't gone crazy shopping in New York—they wouldn't have had anything to write about, would they?" I rub my dry face. "It was horrible and humiliating. But in a funny way, seeing that article was a good thing for me. It made me realize a few things about myself, at least."

I pick up my glass, see that it's empty, and put it down again.

"Do you want another one?" says Luke.

"No. No, thanks."

There's silence between us. In the distance, a voice is telling passengers on flight BA 2340 for San Francisco to please proceed to Gate 29.

"I know Michael offered you a job," said Luke. He gestures to my case. "I assume this means you accepted it." He pauses, and I stare at him, trembling slightly, saying nothing. "Becky—don't go to Washington. Come and work for me."

"Work for *you*?" I say, startled.

"Come and work for Brandon Communications."

"Are you mad?"

He pushes his hair back off his face—and suddenly he looks young and vulnerable. Like someone who needs a break.

"I'm not mad. My staff's been decimated. I need someone like you at a senior level. You know about finance. You've been a journalist. You're good with people, you already know the company . . ."

"Luke, you'll easily find someone else like me," I chip in. "You'll find someone better! Someone with PR experience, someone who's worked in—"

"OK, I'm lying," Luke interrupts. "I'm lying." He takes a deep breath. "I don't just need someone like you. I need you."

He meets my eyes candidly—and with a jolt I realize he's not just talking about Brandon Communications.

"I need you, Becky. I rely on you. I didn't realize it until you weren't there anymore. Ever since you left, your words have been going round and round in my head. About my ambitions. About our relationship. About my mother, even."

"Your mother?" I stare at him apprehensively. "I heard you tried to arrange a meeting with her . . ."

"It wasn't her fault." He takes a swig of Pernod. "Something came up, so she couldn't make it. But you're right, I *should* spend more time with her. Really get to know her better, and forge a closer relationship, just like you have with your mother." He looks up and frowns at my dumbfounded expression. "That is what you meant, isn't it?"

I try for a moment to imagine Luke and his mother chatting away in the kitchen like me and Mum—and fail completely.

"Erm . . . yes!" I say hastily. "Yes, that's exactly what I meant. Absolutely."

"That's what I mean. You're the only person who'll tell me the stuff I need to hear, even when I don't want to hear it. I should have confided in you right from the start. I was . . . I don't know. Arrogant. Stupid."

He sounds so bleak and hard on himself, I feel a twinge of dismay.

"Luke—"

"Becky, I know you've got your own career—and I completely respect that. I wouldn't even ask if I didn't think this could be a good step for you too. But . . . please." He reaches across the table and puts a warm hand on mine. "Come back. Let's start again."

I stare helplessly at him, feeling emotion swelling in me like a balloon.

"Luke, I can't work for you." I swallow, trying to keep control of my voice. "I have to go to the States. I have to take this chance."

"I know it seems like a great opportunity. But what I'm offering could be a great opportunity, too."

"It's not the same," I say, clenching my hand tightly round my glass.

"It can be the same. Whatever Michael's offered you, I'll match it." He leans forward. "I'll more than match it. I'll—"

"Luke," I interrupt. "Luke, I didn't take Michael's job."

Luke's face jerks in shock.

"You didn't? Then what—"

He looks at my suitcase and back up to my face—and I stare back in resolute silence.

"I understand," he says at last. "It's none of my business."

He looks so defeated, I feel a sudden stab of pain in my chest. I want to tell him—but I just can't. I can't risk talking about it, listening to my own arguments waver, wondering whether I've made the right choice. I can't risk changing my mind.

"Luke, I've got to go," I say, my throat tight. "And . . . and you've got to get back to your meeting."

"Yes," says Luke after a long pause. "Yes. You're right. I'll go. I'll go now." He stands up and reaches into his pocket. "Just . . . one last thing. You don't want to forget this."

Very slowly, he pulls out a long, pale blue, silk and velvet scarf, scattered with iridescent beads.

My scarf. My Denny and George scarf.

I feel the blood drain from my face.

"How did you—" I swallow. "The bidder on the phone was you? But . . . but you withdrew. The other bidder got the—" I tail off and stare at him in confusion.

"Both the bidders were me."

He ties the scarf gently round my neck, looks at me for a few seconds, then kisses me on the forehead. Then he turns round and walks away, into the airport crowds.

Seventeen

TWO MONTHS LATER

OK. SO IT'S TWO PRESENTATIONS, one to
Saatchis, one to Global Bank. One awards lunch with
McKinseys, and dinner with Merrill Lynch."

"That's it. It's a lot. I know."

"It'll be fine," I say reassuringly. "It'll be fine."

I scribble something in my notebook and stare at it
thinking hard. This is the moment of my new job I love
the most. The initial challenge. Here's the puzzle—find
the solution. For a few moments I sit without saying anything, doodling endless small five-pointed stars and letting my mind work it out, while Lalla watches me
anxiously.

"OK," I say at last. "I have it. Your Helmut Lang
pantsuit for the meetings, your Jil Sander dress for the
lunch—and we'll find you something new for the dinner." I squint at her. "Maybe something in a deep green."

"I can't wear green," says Lalla.

"You can wear green," I say firmly. "You look great in
green."

"Becky," says Erin, putting her head round my door.
"Sorry to bother you, but Mrs. Farlow is on the phone.

She loves the jackets you sent over—but is there something lighter she can wear for this evening?"

"OK," I say. "I'll call her back." I look at Lalla. "So, let's find you an evening dress."

"What am I going to wear with my pantsuit?"

"A shirt," I say. "Or a cashmere tee. The gray one."

"The gray one," repeats Lalla carefully, as though I'm speaking in Arabic.

"You bought it three weeks ago? Armani? Remember?"

"Oh yes! Yes. I think."

"Or else your blue shell top."

"Right," says Lalla, nodding earnestly. "Right."

Lalla is high up in some top computer consultancy, with offices all over the world. She has two doctorates and an IQ of about a zillion—and claims she has severe clothes dyslexia. At first I thought she was joking.

"Write it down," she says, thrusting a leather-bound organizer at me. "Write down all the combinations."

"Well, OK . . . but, Lalla, I thought we were going to try to let you start putting a few outfits together yourself."

"I know. I will. One day I will, I promise. Just . . . not this week. I can't deal with that extra pressure."

"Fine," I say, hiding a smile, and begin to write in her organizer, screwing up my face as I try to remember all the clothes she's got. I haven't got much time if I'm going to find her an evening dress for tonight, call Mrs. Farlow back, and locate that knitwear I promised for Janey van Hassalt.

Every day here is completely frenetic; everyone is always in a hurry. But somehow the busier I get, and the more challenges are thrown at me—the more I love it.

"By the way," says Lalla. "My sister—the one you said should wear burnt orange . . ."

"Oh yes! She was nice."

"She said she saw you on the television. In England! Talking about clothes!"

"Oh yes," I say, feeling a faint flush come to my face. "I've been doing a little slot for a daytime lifestyle show. 'Becky from Barneys.' It's a kind of New York, fashiony thing . . ."

"Well done!" says Lalla warmly. "A slot on television! That must be very exciting for you!"

I pause, a beaded jacket in my hand, thinking, a few months ago I was going to have my own show on American network television. And now I have a little slot on a daytime show with half the audience of *Morning Coffee*. But the point is, I'm on the path I want to be.

"Yes, it is," I say, and smile at her. "It's very exciting."

It doesn't take too long to sort Lalla out with an outfit for her dinner. As she leaves, clutching a list of possible shoes, Christina, the head of the department, comes in and smiles at me.

"How're you doing?"

"Fine," I say. "Really good."

Which is the truth. But even if it weren't—even if I were having the worst day in the world—I'd never say anything negative to Christina. I'm so grateful to her for remembering who I was. For giving me a chance.

I still can't quite believe how nice she was to me when I hesitantly phoned her up, out of the blue. I reminded her that we'd met, and asked if there was any chance I could come and work at Barneys—and she said she remembered exactly who I was, and how was the Vera Wang dress? So I ended up telling her the whole story, and how I had to sell the dress, and how my TV career was in tatters, and how I'd so love to come and work for her . . . and she was quiet for a bit—and then she said she thought I'd be quite an asset to Barneys. Quite an asset! It was her idea about the TV slot, too.

"Hidden any clothes today?" she says, with a slight twinkle, and I feel myself flush. I'm *never* going to live this down, am I?

It was during that first phone call that Christina also asked me if I had any retail experience. And like a complete moron, I told her all about the time I went to work in Ally Smith—and got the sack when I hid a pair of zebra-print jeans from a customer because I really wanted them myself. I came to the end of the story, and there was silence on the phone, and I thought I'd completely scuppered my chances. But then came this bellow of laughter, so loud I almost dropped the phone in fright. She told me last week that was the moment she decided to hire me.

She's also told the story to all our regular clients, which is a bit embarrassing.

"So." Christina gives me a long, appraising look. "Are you ready for your ten o'clock?"

"Yes." I flush slightly under her gaze. "Yes, I think so."

"D'you want to brush your hair?"

"Oh." My hand flies to my neck. "Is it untidy?"

"Not really." There's a slight sparkle to her eye, which I don't understand. "But you want to look your best for your customer, don't you?"

She goes out of the room, and I quickly pull out a comb. God, I keep forgetting how tidy you have to be in Manhattan. Like, I have my nails done twice a week at a nail bar round the corner from where I live—but sometimes I think I should increase it to every other day. I mean, it's only nine dollars.

Which in real money, is . . . Well. It's nine dollars.

I'm kind of getting used to thinking in dollars. I'm kind of getting used to a lot of things. Jodie was a real star when I called her, and helped me find a studio apartment. It's tiny and pretty grotty and in a place called Hell's Kitchen (which I haven't told Mum. To her it's "Clinton," which she thinks sounds very nice and respectable.). For the first few nights I couldn't sleep for the traffic noise. But the point is, I'm here. I'm here in New York, standing on my own two feet, doing something I can honestly say I adore.

Michael's job in Washington sounded wonderful. In many ways it would have been much more sensible to take it—and I know Mum and Dad wanted me to. But what Michael said at that lunch—about not falling into anything else, about going after what I truly wanted—made me think. About my career, about my life, about what I really wanted to do for a living.

And to give my mum her due, as soon as I explained what this job at Barneys would involve, she stared at me, and said, "But, love, why on earth didn't you think of this before?"

"Hi, Becky?" I give a small start, and look up to see Erin at my door. I've got to be quite good friends with Erin, ever since she invited me home to look at her collection of lipsticks and we ended up watching James Bond videos all night. "I have your ten o'clock here."

"Who is my ten o'clock?" I say, frowning puzzledly as

I reach for a Richard Tyler sheath. "I couldn't see anything in the book."

"Well . . . uh . . ." Her face is all shiny and excited, for some reason. "Uh . . . here he is."

"Thank you very much," comes a deep male voice.

A deep male British voice.

Oh my God.

I freeze like a rabbit, still holding the Richard Tyler dress, as Luke walks into the room.

"Hello," he says with a small smile. "Miss Bloomwood. I've heard you're the best shopper in town."

I open my mouth and close it again. Thoughts are whizzing round my mind like fireworks. I'm trying to feel surprised, trying to feel as shocked as I know I should. Two months of absolutely nothing—and now here he is. I should be completely thrown.

But somehow—I don't feel thrown at all.

Subconsciously, I realize, I've been expecting him.

"What are you doing here?" I say, trying to sound as composed as I can.

"As I said, I've heard you're the best shopper in town." He gives me a quizzical look. "I thought perhaps you could help me buy a suit. This one is looking rather tired."

He gestures to his immaculate Jermyn Street suit, which I happen to know he's only had for three months, and I hide a smile.

"You want a suit."

"I want a suit."

"Right."

Playing for time, I put the dress back on a hanger, turn away, and place it carefully on the rail. Luke's here.

He's here. I want to laugh, or dance, or cry, or something. But instead I reach for my notepad and, without rushing, turn round.

"What I normally do before anything else is ask my clients to tell me a little about themselves." My voice is a little jumpy and I take a deep breath. "Perhaps you could . . . do the same?"

"Right. That sounds like a good idea." Luke thinks for a moment. "I'm a British businessman. I'm based in London." He meets my eyes. "But I've recently opened an office in New York. So I'm going to be spending quite a bit of time over here."

"Really?" I feel a jolt of surprise, which I try to conceal. "You've opened in New York? That's . . . that's very interesting. Because I had the impression that certain British businessmen were finding it tough to do deals with New York investors. Just . . . something I heard."

"They were." Luke nods. "They were finding it tough. But then they downscaled their plans. They decided to open on a much smaller scale."

"A smaller scale?" I stare at him. "And they didn't mind that?"

"Perhaps," says Luke after a pause, "they realized that they'd been overambitious the first time round. Perhaps they realized that they'd become obsessed to the point where they'd let everything else suffer. Perhaps they realized they needed to swallow their pride and put away their grand plans—and slow down a little."

"That . . . that makes a lot of sense," I say.

"So they put together a new proposal, found a backer who agreed with them, and this time nothing stood in the way. They're already up and running."

His face is gleaming with a suppressed delight, and I find myself beaming back.

"That's great!" I say. "I mean . . ." I clear my throat.

"Right. I see." I scribble some nonsense in my notepad. "So—how much time are you going to be spending in New York, exactly?" I add in a businesslike manner. "For my notes, you understand."

"Absolutely," says Luke, matching my tone. "Well, I'll be wanting to keep a significant presence in Britain. So I'll be here for two weeks a month. At least, that's the idea at the moment. It may be more, it may be less." There's a long pause and his dark eyes meet mine. "It all depends."

"On . . . on what?" I say, scarcely able to breathe.

"On . . . various things."

There's a still silence between us.

"You seem very settled, Becky," says Luke quietly. "Very . . . together."

"I'm enjoying it, yes."

"You look as though you're flourishing." He looks around with a little smile. "This environment suits you. Which I suppose comes as no great surprise . . ."

"Do you think I took this job just because I like shopping?" I say, raising my eyebrows. "Do you think this is just about . . . shoes and nice clothes? Because if that's really what you think, then I'm afraid you're sadly misguided."

"That's not what I—"

"It's far more than that. *Far* more." I spread my arms in an emphatic gesture. "It's about helping people. It's about being creative. It's about—"

A knock at the door interrupts me, and Erin pops her head in.

"Sorry to bother you, Becky. Just to let you know, I've put aside those Donna Karan mules you wanted. In the taupe *and* the black, right?"

"Erm . . . yes," I say hurriedly. "Yes, that's fine."

"Oh, and Accounts called, to say that takes you up to your discount limit for this month."

"Right," I say, avoiding Luke's amused gaze. "Right. Thanks. I'll . . . I'll deal with that later." And I wait for Erin to leave, but she's gazing with frank curiosity at Luke.

"So, how are you doing?" she says to him brightly. "Have you had a chance to look around the store?"

"I don't need to look," says Luke in a deadpan voice. "I know what I want."

My stomach gives a little flip, and I stare straight down at my notebook, pretending to make more notes. Scribbling any old rubbish.

"Oh right!" says Erin. "And what's that?"

There's a long silence, and eventually I can't bear it anymore, I have to look up. As I see Luke's expression, my heart starts to thud.

"I've been reading your literature," he says, reaching into his pocket and pulling out a leaflet entitled *The Personal Shopping Service: For busy people who need some help and can't afford to make mistakes.*

He pauses, and my hand tightens around my pen.

"I've made mistakes," he says, frowning slightly. "I want to right those mistakes and not make them again. I want to listen to someone who knows me."

"Why come to Barneys?" I say in a trembling voice.

"There's only one person whose advice I trust." His gaze meets mine and I feel a small tremor. "If she doesn't want to give it, I don't know what I'm going to do."

"We have Frank Walsh over in menswear," says Erin helpfully. "I'm sure he'd—"

"Shut up, Erin," I say, without moving my head.

"What do you think, Becky?" he says, moving toward me. "Would you be interested?"

For a few moments I don't answer. I'm trying to gather all the thoughts I've had over the last couple of months. To organize my words into exactly what I want to say.

"I think . . ." I say at last, "I think the relationship between a shopper and a client is a very close one."

"That's what I was hoping," says Luke.

"There has to be respect." I swallow. "There can't be canceled appointments. There can't be sudden business meetings that take priority."

"I understand," says Luke. "If you were to take me on, I can assure you that you would always come first."

"The client has to realize that sometimes the shopper knows best. And . . . and never just dismiss her opinion. Even when he thinks it's just gossip, or . . . or mindless tittle-tattle."

I catch a glimpse of Erin's confused face, and suddenly want to giggle.

"The client has already realized that," says Luke. "The client is humbly prepared to listen and be put right. On most matters."

"*All* matters," I retort at once.

"Don't push your luck," says Luke, his eyes flashing with amusement, and I feel an unwilling grin spread across my face. I catch Erin's eye and with a sudden blush of comprehension, she hurries out, leaving us alone.

As the door closes, Luke and I stare at each other. My throat is suddenly tight with emotion.

"Well, Mr. Brandon . . ." I say at last. I clear my throat and doodle consideringly on my notepad. "I suppose 'most' would be acceptable. In the circumstances."

"So." His eyes are warm and tender. "Is that a yes, Becky? Will you be my . . . personal shopper?"

He takes a step forward, and I'm almost touching him. I can smell his familiar scent. Oh God, I've missed him.

"Yes," I say happily. "Yes, I will."

FROM: Gildenstein, Lalla
[L.Gildenstein@anagram.com]
TO: Bloomwood, Becky [B.Bloomwood@barneys.com]
DATE: Wednesday, January 28, 2001, 8:22 a.m.
SUBJECT: HELP! URGENT!

Becky:

Help! Help! I lost your list. I have a big formal dinner tonight with some new Japanese
clients. My Armani is at the cleaners. What
should I wear? Please e-mail back soonest.

Thanks, you are an angel.

Lalla.

P.S.: I heard your news—congratulations!

SECOND UNION BANK
53 WALL STREET
NEW YORK

Ms. Rebecca Bloomwood
Apt. 4D
418 W. 46th Street
New York

January 30, 2001

Dear Ms. Bloomwood:

New Account No.: 4567 2346 7689

Welcome to Second Union Bank! We are sure you will be happy with the wide range of banking services we can provide.

We at Second Union Bank pride ourselves on our highly individual approach to clients. May I invite you now to contact me personally at any time if there is anything I can help you with. No matter is too small for my attention.

Thank you for choosing Second Union Bank, and I am sure this is the beginning of a long and fruitful relationship.

With kind regards.

Yours sincerely,

Walt Pitman
Head of Customer Services

Acknowledgments

HUGEST THANKS to Susan Kamil and Zoë Rice for their help and encouragement, to Nita Taublib and everyone at The Dial Press, who made me so incredibly welcome in New York, and again to Zoë for a wonderful afternoon of research (shopping and eating chocolate). Special thanks as always to Araminta Whitley, Celia Hayley, Mark Lucas, Kim Witherspoon and David Forrer, and all at Transworld. Also to David Stefanou for the gimlets and Sharyn Soleimani at Barneys who was so kind, and to all the people who have given me ideas, advice, and inspiration along the way, in particular Athena Malpas, Lola Bubbosh, Mark Malley, Ana-Maria Mosley, and all my family. And of course, Henry, who has the best ideas.

And don't miss the novel that introduced the fabulous Becky Bloomwood!

CONFESSIONS OF A SHOPAHOLIC

Becky Bloomwood has everything: a fabulous flat in London's trendiest neighborhood, a troupe of glamorous socialite friends, and a closet brimming with the season's must-haves. The only problem is that she can't actually afford any of it. Her job as a financial journalist not only bores her to tears, it doesn't pay much at all. And lately, Becky's been chased by dismal letters from Visa and the Endwich Bank—and they're getting ever harder to ignore. She tries cutting back; she even tries making more money. But none of her efforts succeeds. Becky's only consolation is to buy herself something . . . just a little something . . .

Finally a story arises that Becky actually cares about, and her front-page article catalyzes a chain of events that will transform her life—and the lives of those around her—forever.

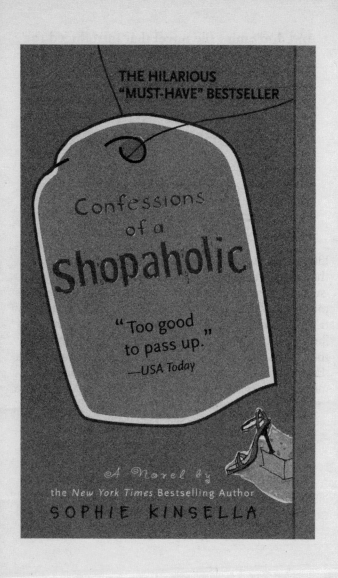

THE HILARIOUS
"MUST-HAVE" BESTSELLER

Confessions
of a
Shopaholic

" Too good
to pass up. "
—USA Today

A Novel by
the *New York Times* Bestselling Author
SOPHIE KINSELLA

There's never been a better excuse to buy a new dress (or two) as Becky Bloomwood walks down a whole new aisle in . . .

SHOPAHOLIC
TIES THE
KNOT

Life has been good for Becky Bloomwood: She's become the best personal shopper at Barneys, she and her successful entrepreneurial boyfriend, Luke, are living happily in Manhattan's West Village, and her new next-door neighbor is a fashion designer! But with her best friend, Suze, engaged, how can Becky fail to notice that her own ring finger is bare? Not that she's been thinking of marriage (or diamonds) or anything . . .

Then Luke proposes! Bridal registries dance in Becky's head. Problem is, two other people are planning her wedding: Becky's overjoyed mother has been waiting forever to host a backyard wedding, with the bride resplendent in Mum's frilly old gown, while Luke's high-society mother is insisting on a glamorous, all-expenses-paid affair at the Plaza. Both weddings for the same day. And Becky can't seem to turn down either one. Can everyone's favorite shopaholic tie the knot before everything unravels?

on sale in mass market . . . fall 2004

SOPHIE KINSELLA

New York Times Bestselling Author of
Confessions of a Shopaholic

Shopaholic
Ties the Knot

Can You Keep a Secret?

a novel

SOPHIE KINSELLA

The New York Times Bestselling Author of *Confessions of a Shopaholic*

OF COURSE I have secrets.

Of course I do. Everyone has a few secrets. It's completely normal.

I'm not talking about big, earth-shattering secrets. Not the-president-is-planning-to-bomb-Japan-and-only-Will-Smith-can-save-the-world–type secrets. Just normal, everyday little ones.

Like, for example, here are a few random secrets of mine, off the top of my head:

1. My Kate Spade bag is a fake.
2. I love sweet sherry, the least cool drink in the universe.
3. I have no idea what NATO stands for. Or even exactly what it is.
4. I weigh 128. Not 118, like my boyfriend, Connor, thinks. (Although in my defense, I was planning to go on a diet when I told him that. And, to be fair, it is only one number different.)
5. I've always thought Connor looks a bit like Ken. As in Barbie and Ken.

6. Sometimes, when we're right in the middle of passionate sex, I suddenly want to laugh.

7. I lost my virginity in the spare bedroom with Danny Nussbaum, while Mum and Dad were downstairs watching *Ben-Hur*.

8. I've already drunk the wine that Dad told me to lay down for twenty years.

9. Sammy the goldfish at home isn't the same goldfish that Mum and Dad gave me to look after when they went to Egypt.

10. When my colleague Artemis really annoys me, I feed her plant orange juice. (Which is pretty much every day.)

11. I once had this weird lesbian dream about my flatmate Lissy.

12. My G-string is hurting me.

13. I've always had this deep-down conviction that I'm not like everybody else, and there's an amazingly exciting new life waiting for me just around the corner.

14. I have no idea what this guy in the gray suit is going on about.

15. Plus, I've already forgotten his name.

And I only met him ten minutes ago.

"We believe in multi-logistical formative alliances," he's saying in a nasal, droning voice, "both above and below the line."

"Absolutely!" I reply brightly, as though to say "Doesn't everybody?"

Multi-logistical. What does that mean, again?

Oh, God. What if they ask me?

Don't be stupid, Emma. They won't suddenly demand, What does "multi-logistical" mean? I'm a fellow marketing professional, aren't I? Obviously I know these things.

And anyway, if they mention it again, I'll change the subject. Or I'll say I'm post-logistical or something.

The important thing is to keep confident and businesslike. I can do this. This is my big chance, and I'm not going to screw it up.

I'm sitting in the offices of Glen Oil's headquarters in Glasgow, and as I glance at my reflection in the window, I look just like a top businesswoman. My shoulder-length hair is straightened, after half an hour with the hair dryer and a bottle of serum this morning. I'm wearing discreet gold swirl earrings like they tell you to in how-to-win-that-job articles. And I've got on my smart new Jigsaw suit. (At least, it's practically new. I got it from the Cancer Research shop and sewed on a button to replace the missing one, and you can hardly tell.)

I'm here representing the Panther Corporation, which is where I work. The meeting is to finalize a promotional arrangement between the new cranberry-flavored Panther Prime sports drink and Glen Oil, and I flew up this morning from London, especially.

When I arrived, the two Glen Oil marketing guys started on this long, show-offy "who's traveled the most?" conversation about air miles and the red-eye to Washington—and I think I bluffed pretty convincingly. But the truth is, this is the first time I've ever had to travel for work.

OK. The *real* truth is, this is the first business meeting I've attended on my own. I've been at the Panther Corporation for eleven months as a marketing assistant, which is the bottom level in our department. I started off just doing menial tasks like typing letters, getting the sandwiches, and collecting my boss Paul's dry cleaning. But after a couple of months, I was allowed to start checking copy. Then a few months ago, I got to write my very own promotional leaflet, for a tie-in with washing powder! God, I was excited. I bought a creative-writing book especially to help me, and I spent all weekend working on it. And I was really pleased with the result, even if it didn't have a misunderstood villain like the book suggested. And even if Paul did just glance at the copy and say "Fine" and kind of forget to tell anyone that I wrote it.

Since then I've done a fair bit of writing promotional literature, and I've even sat in on a few meetings with Paul. So I really think I'm moving up the ladder. In lots of ways I'm practically a marketing executive already!

Except for the tiny point that I still seem to do just as much typing as before. And getting sandwiches and collecting dry cleaning. I just do it *as well as* the other jobs. Especially so since our departmental secretary, Gloria, left a few weeks ago and still hasn't been replaced.

But it's all going to change; I know it is. This meeting is my big break. It's my first chance to show Paul what I'm really capable of. I had to beg him to let me go—after all, Glen Oil and Panther have done loads of deals together in the past; it's not like there'll be any surprises. But deep down I know I'm here only because I was in his office when he realized he'd double-booked with an awards lunch that most of the department were attending. So here I am, representing the company.

And my secret hope is that if I do well today, I'll get promoted. The job ad said "possibility of promotion after a year"—and it's nearly been a year. And on Monday I'm having my appraisal meeting. I looked up "Appraisals" in the staff induction book, and it said they are "an ideal opportunity to discuss possibilities for career advancement."

Career advancement! At the thought, I feel a familiar stab of longing. It would just show Dad I'm not a complete loser. And Mum. And Kerry. If I could just go home and say, "By the way, I've been promoted to marketing executive."

Emma Corrigan, marketing executive.

Emma Corrigan, senior vice-president (marketing).

As long as everything goes well today. Paul said the deal was pretty much done and dusted, and all I had to do was raise one point about timing, and even I should be able to manage that. And so far, I reckon it's going really well!

OK, so I don't understand some of the terms they're using. But then I didn't understand most of my GCSE French Oral either, and I still got a B.

"Rebranding . . . analysis . . . cost-effective . . ."

The man in the gray suit is still droning on. As casually as possible I extend my hand and inch his business card toward me so I can read it.

Doug Hamilton. That's right. I can remember this. Doug. Dug. Easy—I'll picture a shovel. Together with *ham*. Which . . . which looks *ill* . . . and . . .

OK, forget this. I'll just write it down.

I write down "rebranding" and "Doug Hamilton" on my notepad and give an uncomfortable little wriggle. God, my knickers are really uncomfortable. I mean, G-strings are never that comfortable at the best of times, but these are particularly bad. Which could be because they're two sizes too small.

Which could possibly be because when Connor bought them for me, he told the lingerie assistant I weighed 118 pounds. Whereupon she told him I must be size 4. Size 4!

So it got to Christmas Eve, and we were exchanging presents, and I unwrapped this pair of gorgeous pale pink silk knickers. Size 4. And I basically had two options.

A: Confess the truth: "Actually these are too small. I'm more of an eight, and by the way, I don't really weigh one hundred eighteen pounds."
B: Shoehorn myself into them.

Actually, it was fine. You could hardly see the red lines on my skin afterward. And all it meant was that I had to quickly cut the labels out of my clothes so Connor would never realize.

Since then, I've hardly ever worn this particular set of underwear, needless to say. But every so often I see them, looking all nice and expensive in the drawer, and I think, Oh, come on, they can't be *that* tight, and somehow squeeze into them. Which is what I did this morning. I even decided I must have lost weight, because they didn't feel too bad.

I am such a deluded moron.

". . . unfortunately, since rebranding . . . major rethink . . . feel we need to be considering alternative synergies . . ."

Up to now I've just been sitting and nodding, thinking this business meeting is really easy. But now Doug Hamilton's voice starts to impinge on my conciousness. What's he saying?

" . . . two products diverging . . . becoming incompatible . . ."

What was that about incompatible? What was that about a major rethink? I felt a jolt of alarm.

"We appreciate the functional and synergetic partnership that Panther and Glen Oil have enjoyed in the past," Doug Hamilton is saying, "but you'll agree that clearly we're going in different directions."

Different directions?

My stomach gives an anxious lurch.

He can't be—

Is he trying to pull out of the deal?

"Excuse me, Doug," I say in my most relaxed voice. "Obviously I was closely following what you were saying earlier." I give a friendly, we're-all-professionals-together smile. "But if you could just . . . um, recap the situation for all our benefits . . ."

In plain English, I beg silently.

Doug Hamilton and the other guy exchange glances.

"We're a little unhappy about your brand values," says Doug Hamilton.

"My brand values?" I echo in panic.

"The brand values of the *product*," he says, giving me an odd look. "As I've been explaining, we here at Glen Oil are going through a rebranding process at the moment, and we see our image very much as a *caring* petrol, as our new daffodil logo demonstrates. And we feel Panther Prime, with its emphasis on sport and competition, is simply too aggressive."

"Aggressive?" I stare at him in bewilderment. "But . . . it's a fruit drink."

This makes no sense. Glen Oil is fume-making, world-ruining petrol. Panther Prime is an innocent cranberry-flavored drink. How can it be too aggressive?

"The values it espouses." He gestures to the marketing brochures on the table. "Drive. Elitism. Masculinity. The very slogan 'Don't Pause.' Frankly, it seems a little dated." He shrugs. "We just don't think a joint initiative will be possible."

No. No. This can't be happening. He can't be pulling out.

Everyone at the office will think it was my fault. They'll think I cocked it up and I'm completely crap.

My heart is thumping. My face is hot. I can't let this happen. But what do I say? I haven't prepared anything. Paul said the promotion was all set up, and all I had to do was tell them we wanted to bring it forward in June.

"We'll certainly discuss it again before we make a decision," Doug's saying. He gives me a brief smile. "And as I say, we would like to continue links with the Panther Corporation, so this has been a useful meeting, in any case. . . ."

He's pushing back his chair.

I can't let this slip away! I have to try to win them around.

"Wait!" I hear myself say. "Just . . . wait a moment! I have a few points to make."

There's a can of Panther Prime sitting on the desk, and I grab it for inspiration. Playing for time, I stand up, walk to the center of the room, and raise the can high in the air where we can all see it. "Panther Prime is . . . a sports drink."

I stop, and there's a polite silence. My face is prickling. "It, um, is very . . ."

Oh, God. What am I doing?

Come *on*, Emma. *Think.* Think Panther Prime. . . . Think Panther Cola. . . . Think. . . .

Yes! Of course!

"Since the launch of Panther Cola in the late 1980s, Panther drinks have been a byword for energy, excitement, and excellence," I say fluently.

Thank God. This is the standard marketing blurb for Panther Cola. I've typed it out so many times, I could recite it in my sleep.

"Panther drinks are a marketing phenomenon," I continue. "The Panther character is one of the most widely recognized in the world, while the classic slogan 'Don't Pause' has made it into dictionaries. We are offering Glen Oil an exclusive opportunity to strengthen its association with this premium, world-famous brand."

My confidence growing, I start to stride around the room, gesturing with the can. "By buying Panther health drink, the consumer is signaling that he will settle for nothing but the best." I hit the can sharply with my other hand. "He expects the best from his energy drink, he expects the best from his petrol, he expects the best from himself."

I'm flying! I'm fantastic! If Paul could see me now, he'd give me a promotion on the spot!

I come over the desk and look Doug Hamilton right in the eye. "When the Panther consumer opens that can, he is making a choice that tells the world who he is. I'm asking Glen Oil to make the same choice."

As I finish speaking, I plant the can firmly in the middle of the desk, reach for the ring pull, and, with a cool smile, snap it back.

And a volcano erupts.

Fizzy cranberry-flavored drink explodes in a whoosh out of the can, drenching the papers and blotters in lurid red liquid . . . and—oh, no, please no—splattering all over Doug Hamilton's shirt.

"Fuck!" I gasp. "I mean, I'm really sorry—"

"Jesus Christ," says Doug Hamilton irritably, standing up and getting a handkerchief out of his pocket. "Does this stuff stain?"

"Er . . ." I grab the can helplessly. "I don't know."

"I'll get a cloth," says the other guy, and leaps to his feet.

The door closes behind him and there's silence, apart from the sound of cranberry drink dripping slowly onto the floor.

I stare at Doug Hamilton, my face hot and blood throbbing through my ears.

"Please . . ." My voice is husky. "Don't tell my boss."

Carnival Elation

7 Day Exotic Western Caribbean Itinerary

DAY	PORT	ARRIVE	DEPART
Sun	Galveston		4:00 P.M.
Mon	"Fun Day" at Sea		
Tue	Progreso/Merida	8:00 A.M.	4:00 P.M.
Wed	Cozumel	9:00 A.M.	5:00 P.M.
Thu	Belize	8:00 A.M.	6:00 P.M.
Fri	"Fun Day" at Sea		
Sat	"Fun Day" at Sea		
Sun	Galveston	8:00 A.M.	

TERMS AND CONDITIONS

PAYMENT SCHEDULE:
50% due upon booking
Full and final payment due by July 26, 2004

Acceptable forms of payment are Visa, MasterCard, American Express, Discover and checks. The cardholder must be one of the passengers traveling. A fee of $25 will apply for all returned checks. Check payments must be made payable to **Advantage International, LLC and sent to: Advantage International, LLC, 195 North Harbor Drive, Suite 4206, Chicago, IL 60601**

CHANGE/CANCELLATION:
Notice of change/cancellation must be made in writing to Advantage International, LLC.

Change:
Changes in cabin category may be requested and can result in increased rate and penalties. A name change is permitted 60 days or more prior to departure and will incur a penalty of $50 per name change. Deviation from the group schedule and package is a cancellation.

Cancellation:

181 days or more prior to departure	$250 per person
121 - 180 days or more prior to departure	50% of the package price
120 - 61 days prior to departure	75% of the package price
60 days or less prior to departure	100% of the package price (nonrefundable)

US and Canadian citizens are required to present a valid passport or the original birth certificate and state issued photo ID (drivers license). All other nationalities must contact the consulate of the various ports that are visited for verification of documentation.

We strongly recommend trip cancellation insurance!

For further details call 1-877-ADV-NTGE or visit www.GetCaughtReadingatSea.com

- -

For booking form and complete information
go to **www.getcaughtreadingatsea.com** or call **1-877-ADV-NTGE**

Complete coupon and booking form and mail both to:
Advantage International, LLC,
195 North Harbor Drive, Suite 4206, Chicago, IL 60601